Praise for Riley & Ben

"A fascinating exploration of how a singular family tragedy can affect generations to come, Riley and Ben is a beautiful novel about good people in impossible situations, and a poignant reminder of the power of self-determination. We always knew J.T. White was a great dad; now we know he's a great writer, too!"

—*Mary Ellen Evangelista,* Former adjunct professor at Georgia State University-Perimeter College

—*Lauren Myracle,* NYT bestselling author of *Victor and Nora: A Gotham Love Story, ttyl,* and the *Winnie Series.* Her latest book is *This Boy.*

—*Susan Rebecca White,* critically-acclaimed author of *We Are All Good People Here, Bound South, A Place at the Table,* and *A Soft Place to Land.*

"With *Riley & Ben,* J.T. White gives readers multi-generations of hopeful, flawed, and struggling characters who grapple with hard emotional realities. This is a heartfelt story about the messiness of love, both familial and romantic, amid seminal social changes in America."

—*John W. Holman,* PhD, Professor of English and Co-director of the Creative Writing Program at Georgia State University; author of *Luminous Mysteries,* chosen as one of the "25 Books All Georgians Should Read," and his Whiting Award Winner, *Triangle Ray*; 1991

"Emerging author J.T. White delivers a real and readable story with characters that you will feel you might know somewhere in your own life. Weaving through childhood, into historical scenes of WWII, and on to the slower-paced days in a small southern town, readers will revel in the resilience and intelligence of the main character and root for Ben. It is a wonderful novel that I could not put down. I would recommend this to every book club!"

— *Clea Calloway,* Author of *Burning Gold*

Riley & Ben

To Annie
the task master
Jim

Riley & Ben

Life Offers Second Chances

a novel

J.T. White

Deeds Publishing | Athens

Published by Deeds Publishing in Athens, GA
www.deedspublishing.com

Printed in The United States of America

Cover design by Mark Babcock.

ISBN 978-1-950794-47-8

Books are available in quantity for promotional or premium use. For information, email info@deedspublishing.com.

First Edition, 2021

10 9 8 7 6 5 4 3 2 1

To Ruth, Marilyn, and Jerry

Part I

I

August 21, 1941

Riley McHaney adjusted the visor to block the blinding rays of the setting sun. His wife, Claire, nursed their infant son in the seat behind him. Her father snored rhythmically, his mouth ajar. Sikeston was only a few miles away. They would be home from their day trip to Halls in time for supper, and baby Ben would have a normal bedtime. Trying to make out the numbers on the highway sign at the intersection ahead, Riley rubbed his eyes with his sleeve.

He heard the crunch of steel against steel and felt the wheel spin out of his hand. A kaleidoscope of reds, browns and blues whirled before his eyes. Then nothing. For several heartbeats Riley lay in a pile of loose dirt gasping for breath. The smell of gasoline seared his nostrils. His whole body ached. The sound of metal shearing and glass breaking rang in his ears, masking the screams that seemed to come from far away. He stumbled toward the crumpled steel lying thirty feet away that had been his father-in-law's Chevrolet. Nearby, two of its hubcaps mirrored the sun. A barely damaged Kenworth tractor-trailer sat in the middle of the intersection, its motor still running, its driver scrambling to get out of the cab. When he reached what was left of the car, Riley saw Arthur Clinton still in his seat with a jagged sheet of glass piercing his chest and his shirt drenched in blood. He spotted Claire lying on the ground, clutching her stomach.

"Sweetheart," he said as he dropped to her side.

Blood gushed from a gash across Claire's midsection. She whispered, "Where's Ben?"

Riley frantically scanned the road. "It's okay, sweet. I see him."

As if those words gave permission, the light went out of Claire's eyes. Riley gathered her to him and wept.

"Tell Cox Funeral Home we have two for them," the investigating officer who arrived eight minutes later barked into his two-way radio. "And alert Sikeston General. We're sending over a baby with hardly any pulse."

Two medics pulled Riley away from Claire and strapped him onto a gurney in the ambulance with his son. Then, siren screaming, they sped toward the small privately owned hospital that served the southeast Missouri town of four thousand.

"This man doesn't have any visible injury," the medic told the attending physician at the hand-off. "But this baby is probably a goner. His skull is fractured, and glass shards are sticking out all over his head. He went through the window. We found him on the pavement, 40 feet away."

As he was rolled into an examining room, Riley could see one nurse dressing the back of Ben's skull and another removing glass from his scalp, gently dabbing each cut with alcohol. Riley immediately recognized Dr. Allen Buckley walking up with a stethoscope hanging from his neck and a penlight in his hand.

"Hello, Riley. The medics say you have no broken bones, and your blood pressure is normal. So, I only need to check a few things while the nurses clean up your baby. Look at my light, please. Up, down, right—don't blink—left."

Dr. Buckley returned the penlight to his pocket.

"Looks good," he said. "Now, sit up, unbutton your shirt and breathe deeply."

Dr. Buckley moved the head of the scope from place to place on Riley's chest and back. "That's good. Does this hurt? Good. How about this? Good. Now let's check your reflexes. Very good. You can button your shirt now."

The doctor tore off the top sheet of the pad he had scribbled on and handed it to Riley. "You don't have any broken or displaced bones, and I can't detect any signs of internal bleeding. You'll be sore for a couple of days. This prescription will help with that. You don't need to be admitted. Just get some rest. Let us know if you develop a severe headache or start throwing up."

Dr. Buckley's voice cracked as he continued, "I'm

heartbroken about Claire. I delivered her twenty years ago, and I was at your wedding."

He took a moment to try to conceal his grief. Riley's own grief overcame him. He grabbed Dr. Buckley's arm for support.

"Your son is two doors down the hall," the doctor said. "Give me a few more minutes with him, then you can come in."

Ten minutes later a nurse directed Riley to the tiny room that the hospital had designated for infant emergency care. Riley hesitated before entering. All he could see of his son was bandages, tubes, and a baby blanket. If his legs had co-operated, he would have fled. Instead, he collapsed on a chair by the door, buried his head in his hands and moaned. He tried to recall the accident but couldn't. He felt a hand on his shoulder and recognized a voice.

"I can't tell you how sorry I am," Claire's uncle Jim said. "I've just come from Millie. She's in a bad way and had to be sedated. Alan told me he didn't think you needed to be admitted, so I can take you home. Or to Millie's if you prefer."

"I'll stay here with Ben for a while, then I'll come to Millie's. Without Claire, I don't want to go home. Don't wait for me, though. I'll walk over when I'm ready."

"Take your time, son," Jim Clinton said. "Dr. Buckley and his staff are doing all they can for Ben. I'll tell everyone you'll be over later."

Five more minutes in that bleak room, watching his little boy's labored breathing and seeing the bandages that covered his head and the tubes which protruded from his mouth was all Riley could take. The pain of knowing his son was dying, that he was responsible and that he could do nothing to help, was too intense. He had to get out of there. He took one last look at his son, placed his hand momentarily on Ben's swaddled head, then tearfully walked to the front of the hospital, ignoring the sympathetic faces he passed. Through the window he could see the Citizens Bank building where he had first met Claire less than two years before.

"May I help you?" she'd said in the gentlest, kindest voice he had ever heard.

"I'd like to cash my paycheck," he'd replied. His voice came out gruffer than he'd intended, and without exactly knowing why, he was nervous. Was it simply this young woman's charm, or was it more? Did she feel the same spark he did? Was she the woman he had been searching for since he, freshly certified as a linotype operator arrived in Sikeston two months earlier, ready to show the world he could stand on his own two feet, and eager to start a new life in a new town?

"You don't have an account with us, do you?" Claire had said. "Why not open one?" Her eyes, which looked hazel in the indoor light, had locked on his while her slender hand pushed a pen toward him. Her nails were perfect ovals.

Riley leaned over the counter to get closer to the slight scent of gardenias coming from her reddish-brown hair and to try to guess her height, which couldn't be over five foot one.

"I only have a few minutes," he said. "My lunch break is over at one."

"It'll only take a moment. Aren't you Riley McHaney, the new man at Uncle Jim's newspaper? I'm Alice Claire Clinton. My friends call me Claire."

Riley turned crimson. Claire smiled, handed him the form he needed to sign, took $45 out of the drawer, watched Riley sign the signature card and handed him the cash.

"Hope to see you again," Claire had said as he turned away.

Riley was smitten and struggled to muster the courage to ask Claire out. Three Mondays later as he walked toward her window, Claire came out to meet him.

"Would you like to see *Mr. Smith Goes to Washington* Saturday night?" he stammered.

Claire picked an imaginary thread from his shirt and said, "Let's not wait till Saturday."

Within six weeks they were engaged. Three months later they were married. Their trip to Halls that day was to introduce him and Ben to Claire's Aunt Ann.

Staring out the hospital window, Riley remembered details of their first year together: How beautiful Claire had been on their wedding day, carrying a small bouquet of calla lilies, wearing the delicate wedding gown her mother had made and her petite white shoes. How happy she had appeared when Reverend Morgan pronounced them man and wife before two dozen well-wishers at the First Presbyterian Church of Sikeston. Why had he not joined that church, even though he had been taught that the Church of Christ was the one true church? It would have made Claire so happy.

"I'm Maureen Connelly," a nurse said, snapping Riley back into the present. "I've been looking after your son. I'm so sorry for him and for you. His injuries are severe. We're doing everything we can. I was in school with Claire from the first grade on. She was so sweet and kind. Everybody loved her. My shift ends at midnight, but someone will be with your son all night. Go home and get some rest. We'll let you know if anything changes."

Riley left the nurse certain that he had seen Ben alive for the last time. He walked past the Bank, past Rexall Drugs and Beard Chevrolet and turned down White Oak Street to Millie Clinton's small Craftsman style house at the end of the block. He pulled himself up the steps and sat down on the swing where he had proposed to Claire less than two years before. It still creaked as it swung. He thought about their last meal together and how happy Claire was for her aunt to finally meet him and their baby. He thought about the hordes of Aunt Ann's friends who had come to see baby Ben and him for the first time, who would never see the baby or Claire again. He wondered why Arthur, who seldom drank, had taken the nip of Four Roses after dinner that required him to turn over the driving to Riley. He wondered why the sun had blinded him at the instant he reached that damn intersection.

A man with a gold cross on his lapel opened the front door. Riley recognized him as the minister who had married them. *What was his name*? He hesitated, then took the cleric's extended hand.

"I'm Reverend Morgan, Millie's pastor. Chief Kelly gave us a full report." The minister beckoned Riley to follow him inside.

"Mildred's in her bedroom sleeping off her sedative. She blames herself. She thinks that if she had gone to Halls with you, Arthur and Claire would still be alive. The family and some friends are in the living room. Would you like to join them?"

Riley shook his head.

"Is there anything you want to discuss with me?"

Again, Riley shook his head.

"Then I'll leave you to your thoughts. Let me know if you get hungry or want to talk."

Riley wasn't hungry and he wasn't up to talking with anyone. He wanted to be alone with his grief, his guilt, and his thoughts of Claire.

"How many stars can we see in the sky tonight?" Claire had asked as they walked hand in hand home from their third movie date. He loved her inquisitive mind, which matched her quick wit.

"Well, it's not cloudy tonight but there's a full moon, so we won't see as many. Still too many to count-that's for sure. Why?"

"I want to know how many wishes I can make."

"Do you need a different star for each wish?"

"Of course, silly," she'd said. "You can't wish on the

same star twice. Everybody knows that. I want to wish us happiness every day for the rest of our lives."

Claire stood on tiptoes when they reached her house and kissed him. That kiss told Riley she was as ready for him as he was for her.

They had married in February, and Claire was soon pregnant. Benjamin Riley McHaney was born the following December. Three months before Ben arrived, Riley was promoted to shop manager at the *Standard-Democrat* and received a raise that had given him the confidence to borrow $3000 from the bank to go with the five hundred he had saved and buy a bungalow near the elementary school. With his fifty dollar per week salary and regular monthly payments, in five years the house would be paid for. Claire had made his life perfect.

Some twenty minutes had passed when Riley, still lost in his thoughts, saw a woman wearing a tattered robe approach. She was slightly built and a bit taller than Claire, with almost identical facial features. Riley stood to embrace her.

"I'm so sorry, Mother Millie," he said. "I wish it had been me. Please forgive me."

"There's nothing to forgive," Millie Clinton said. "It was an accident. The Lord will get us through this."

"Why didn't the Lord get me through that intersection?" Riley said.

"Let's not question His ways, Riley. When I first learned Arthur and Claire were dead, I wanted to die. Fortunately, the nurse who came with Jim gave me some drug that knocked me out quickly. An hour later I was still groggy, barely able to listen to Reverend Morgan assuring me that Arthur and Claire are with God, and that He will give me the strength to bear this loss. With God's help, I will be strong for Ben, Riley. You must be strong also. Ben needs us."

"Why?" Riley said. "There's nothing we can do for him."

"We can be with him," Millie said. "I'd like to see him tonight. I'll get dressed and see if Jim can take us now."

"I' m sorry I can't be more hopeful," Dr. Buckley explained when they arrived at Sikeston General, shortly after 6 p.m. "Ben was comatose when he arrived and would not respond to any stimuli. The trauma his brain suffered was so severe it will be a miracle if he survives. If he does, he will never fully recover. We have no way of knowing the extent of his injuries, or how the damage to his brain will affect his behavior. We'll keep him here as long as necessary, watch him closely, give him nourishment, and try to ease his pain. That's all I can tell you now."

A frown crossed Millie's face and she asked the question Riley most wanted answered. "What do you mean, he'll never fully recover?"

"I don't like to speculate, Millie, but with trauma this severe, if he survives much could go wrong. He may not be able to create or store memories. He could be deaf, blind or . . . "

"So, all you can tell us is he's alive right now," Riley

interrupted, "will probably die, and if he lives, you won't know how much of his brain has been injured or the extent of the injury; and you won't know what his condition will be. You have no plan for treatment other than to feed him and try to ease his pain. Right?"

"Yes," Dr. Buckley said. "As much as I'd like to tell you otherwise, your son will probably not survive. We'll do everything we can to save him. I wish I could be more positive. I just can't."

Riley awoke the next morning to the sound of perking coffee. Millie placed a tray of toast, butter, and jam before him. Riley chewed mechanically. Would he ever be able to taste food again, or only the salt from his tears? Millie's hand shook ever so slightly as she sipped her coffee with him. Her face showed her grief.

"I talked to the hospital a few minutes ago," she said. "Ben's condition has not improved. Dr. Buckley ordered more X-rays and wants to send them for evaluation to an infant trauma specialist at St. Louis Children's Hospital. Alan says Dr. Marcus Fedderman is the best in this field, and he wants his opinion. Also, he says we should engage private duty nurses to be with Ben all the time."

"Stop right there," Riley said. "I can't afford that."

"Don't think about the cost," Millie said. "We must do it and worry about the cost later."

Riley felt for the Lucky Strikes in his pocket, shook one out of the pack, lit it, took a long draw, then slowly exhaled. Smoke coiled slowly upward, then dispersed as it reached the ceiling fan twirling slowly above.

"All right." Riley said. "Tell Dr. Buckley to send the X-rays to St. Louis. How I'll pay for it, I have no idea."

"I've already talked to Alan," Millie said. "He'll have Fedderman's report this afternoon and will see us at four."

Riley was too emotionally drained to answer or to challenge Millie's peremptory actions. He knew Ben's survival was as important to her as it was to him, and she was trying to help. He just didn't want her calling the shots. He had to decide what was best for Ben, not her. Right now, however, that was to swallow his pride, accept whatever help Millie could give and, as she had said, worry about how to pay for Ben's care later. Maybe he could moonlight with the paper at Cape Girardeau, thirty miles away. But he had no car. Maybe he could sell concessions at the movie theater nights and Saturdays, as he had at Halls in high school. Maybe his brother Eugene would lend him some money.

"I'm cautiously optimistic," Doctor Buckley said that afternoon. "Ben has come out of the coma and his vital signs have improved. He sleeps a lot from the drugs we administer. He whimpers when he is waking up, which is a good sign. Make no mistake about it, however, he still has a long way to go."

"Thank you, Lord," Millie exclaimed. "And thank you, Alan."

"X-ray is a fairly new technology," Dr. Buckley told them. "We've only had it here since January. We took pictures of Ben's brain, which show swelling has gone down in the last few hours, and there are no foreign particles in the brain cavity. The skull was fractured, but the skull of any nine-month-old infant has not completely formed, so Dr. Fedderman and I believe the fracture will heal in time …"

Riley broke in. "So, what's the bad news?"

Alan Buckley leaned back in his chair and looked sadly at Millie. Claire had told Riley that if Dr. Buckley had not gone on to medical school immediately after graduating first in his class from the University of Missouri, her mother would have married him. The couple had been Prom King and Queen his senior year at Sikeston High and in May 1915, Millie had accepted his fraternity pin. Three years later, however, Arthur had returned home from the Army and with Alan miles away, a lonely Millie accepted Arthur's proposal.

"Let's not call it bad news," Dr. Buckley said. "Just unknowns. Dr. Fedderman confirmed the damage to his brain is extensive. A I told you, we have no way of knowing how extensive. Over time you will be able to observe any effect on his motor skills or his learning ability. Most likely, however, you will never be able to correct them."

Deep in his contemplation of this grim assessment, Riley could not speak.

"How long will you keep him here?" Millie asked. "One week? Two?"

"Until he is stable and has no infection," Dr. Buckley replied. "It is too soon to think about discharging him."

In a daze, Riley left the hospital alone and walked to the house he and Claire had shared for such a short time. Inside he was a ghost wandering through the past. He could open the Frigidaire and see the vegetable soup Claire had prepared for the supper they never got to eat. He could lie on the bed she had carefully made the morning of their departure. He could spin the mobile Claire had placed above Ben's crib and watch the bird chase the pony and the pony chase the puppy in an endless circle. He could even turn on the Philco in the small living room and listen to Cardinal baseball on KMOX, while reclining on the sofa and staring at the ceiling he and Claire had repaired and repainted when they moved in. He could imagine Claire cradling his head in her lap and stroking his hair. He could not imagine his life without her. Like the spinning mobile, the cycle of despair Riley had entered was endless. He had called his widowed mother collect from the hospital to tell her of the tragedy. He must remember to give her fifty cents to cover the cost of the call.

At sixty-five, living on the pittance she received from social security, rent from another widow who rented her upstairs apartment and occasional checks from Eugene and William, Riley's older brothers, she had neither the means nor the strength to take care of Ben. Riley knew he could not live in Newbern, a dying town half the size of Sikeston. His skill as a linotype operator and his experience running a print shop made him invaluable to a newspaper or book publisher—practically worthless to anyone else.

"You can take as much time off as you need," Uncle

Jim had told him at the hospital. "Your job will be waiting when you are ready."

This kindness was comforting. Still despair and uncertainty paralyzed him. He didn't know what he wanted—except for Claire to be with him. He lay there, lost in the familiar voice of Dizzy Dean calling the play by play of the Cardinal-Dodger game, hoping the fantastic rookie Stan Musial would lead the Birds to victory over the Bums again. Soon he was asleep. An hour later he woke with a start.

"Claire, can you answer the phone?" he mumbled.

He dragged himself off the couch after the next ring and found the phone in its nook in the hall. He tried to think what time it was - what day it was. Then reality struck. It was early Friday evening and Claire was gone. He picked up the receiver.

"Collect call for Mr. Riley McHaney from Lorene McHaney. Will you accept the charges?"

"Yes," Riley said.

"Hold the line, please. I'll connect you."

"Riley?"

"Mother? Why didn't you call station to station? It's so much cheaper."

"I wanted to be sure to get you."

"Who else would answer?"

"Your in-laws, friends—my goodness, Riley. Don't tell me you're alone."

"Yes, everyone's over at the Clintons. This is the first time I've been home since the morning of the accident. I came here to be alone."

"Someone should be with you," Mrs. McHaney said.

"Don't worry, Mother. I'm okay."

"What's Ben's condition?" Mrs. McHaney asked. "Things sounded awful when you called from the hospital."

Riley sighed. "His head took a severe blow. He has come out of the coma, but they won't tell us anything specific. The specialist in St. Louis looked at his X-rays."

"Don't let 'experts' talk you into sending him off somewhere for treatment. They don't know that much. It's up to God."

"God doesn't give a damn about me or my family, Mother," Riley said. Anger saturated his words. He braced for his Mother's lecture against swearing and her spirited defense of the Almighty, the power and majesty of whom had been drilled into her every Sunday since childhood and at weeklong revivals every summer.

"Have funeral arrangements been made?" she said instead.

"Millie is planning a joint funeral for Claire and Arthur Tuesday at eleven at the First Presbyterian Church. She considered delaying the service a day because of Ben. I'm glad she didn't."

Riley's voice broke and he paused for a moment. "Losing Claire is so painful, Mother. I can't talk about it, even with you. I let Millie select Claire's casket. I wouldn't have spent so much—certainly wouldn't have bought a vault for it. Dust to dust. That's the way it should be."

"You'll get through this, Riley. Put your trust in the Lord. He'll give you strength."

"I haven't been on good terms with the Lord for a long time," Riley replied.

"Don't say that," his mother snapped. "You grew up in God's church. Trust Him."

"Let's not get into that again, Mother," Riley said. "You dragged me to church till I was sixteen and could get a Sunday job. If the Lord wanted to save my soul, he had plenty of time to do it. Now let's change the subject. You'll come to the funeral, won't you?"

"Certainly. I'll get Mrs. Van Cleave to take me to the bus in Dyersburg. I'll be there tomorrow. I've written everyone about Claire's death. Eugene's always on the road and Nora has a two-year-old, so they won't be able to come. Of course, William can't come."

"I understand," Riley said. "It's enough that you will be here."

"I'd better hang up now," Mrs. McHaney said. "No telling how much this call is costing. Get some rest, son. I'll pray for you."

"Thank God I'm off that bus," Riley's mother said the next afternoon as she hung her hat on the coat rack by his front door. "After three and a half hours in this heat, I need a bath and some lunch. I've been up since 5:30 and haven't eaten since breakfast. I couldn't bring myself to buy anything along the way. Too expensive."

Riley put his mother's things in his bedroom and placed the spare set of sheets on the arm of the sofa, which was not quite long enough to accommodate his five-foot eleven-inch frame but would work for a night or two. While his mother freshened up, he lit the front burner of the Magic Chef to warm the rest of the soup, and set saltines, sweet gherkins, and butter on the table for lunch.

"Doesn't visitation begin at four this afternoon?" Mrs. McHaney said as she emerged from the bedroom, dressed in black. "We need to be there by three forty-five."

"Uncle Jim is letting his son Bill run a shuttle service for us," Riley said. "But as you noticed at the bus station, it's hard to squeeze into the back seat of Bill's coupe. We could walk. Cox's is only five minutes away."

"In this heat? It's ninety-five outside. I'd keel over. Let's eat lunch. Then call Bill."

For a few moments, except for the occasional slurp of soup and the crunch of crackers, Riley and his mother ate in silence. Then she spoke.

"If Ben dies, will you stay in Sikeston?"

"If that happens, I'd like to get as far away from here as I can."

"If he lives, what will you do?"

"Honestly, Mother, I haven't worked that out for certain. At first, everyone said he would die. Now, with no reason other than that he hasn't died yet they say he could live. I don't know how long he'll be in the hospital, or how much care he'll need if he survives, so it's hard to make plans. I won't be able to stay home and take care of him 'cause I need to get back to work, and I can't afford a housekeeper. I don't like it. I just don't believe I have any choice other than to stay in Sikeston and let Millie help me raise him."

"Has she offered to keep Ben?"

"Yes," Riley said. "Although I'll have to pay her something and she'll have to go to work herself—at least part time. Arthur had to mortgage their house to get the money to buy the paper with Jim. I don't know all the details. I do know there isn't enough money to go around."

"How do you feel about your mother-in-law raising your son?" Mrs. McHaney asked. Riley's jaw twitched.

"Absolutely rotten," he said. "Of course, I want what's best for Ben. I certainly want him to recover and have as full a life as possible. He's my responsibility and I love him, but I'm limited in how much time I can give him and in how much medical treatment I can afford. Whatever Millie could do for Ben would help. I just don't want her to take over his life. I don't want him to grow up thinking I abandoned him."

"I know it's painful, Riley," Mrs. McHaney said as she rose and put her arms around Riley, "but you'll get through this. You'll never abandon Ben. Keep in mind—a more financially secure life is not necessarily a better life. A father can give his son a lot more than money. You've only lived in Sikeston a couple of years and none of your family is here. You don't have to stay."

"You're right. I don't. However, I have a job here, and anywhere I go I'll have the same problem of finding someone to keep Ben while I work. Millie has arranged for the woman who lives next door to her to keep Ben weekdays for a dollar a day and Millie would keep him at night and on weekends. I could walk to Millie's to see him as often as possible and when he's old enough, he could live with me."

Riley's mother stepped back and fixed her eyes on his. "You can't leave Ben with Mrs. Clinton. He's your son. Someday you'll remarry and when you do, you'll want him with you, whatever his age."

"Remarry? Never!" Riley said. "I could never love another woman."

The First Presbyterian Church in Sikeston nearly reached its 300-seat capacity on that hot Tuesday morning in late August when funeral services for Claire and her father were held. Senior Minister Morgan delivered the eulogy and Ralph Biggs, the chancel choir soloist, had everyone's attention with his booming baritone rendition of *How Great Thou Art.* Photographs of Claire and Arthur were placed on easels near the pulpit. Arthur Clinton's mutilation prohibited an open casket service. Garlands of red roses draped each casket, and flower arrangements spilled from the altar into the aisles. Riley and his mother sat on the front row with Millie and Arthur's two brothers, Jim and Carl, and his sister, Ann.

Mrs. McHaney wore the same simple black cotton dress and black hat she had worn to the funeral home the Saturday before. She was unadorned except for a single, narrow band of gold on her left hand. Millie was also modestly dressed and wore no jewelry except her wedding rings. Riley sat by his mother in silence. He was not comforted by the minister's assurance that God had taken Claire to be with him for eternity. As much as he didn't want to listen to platitudes, he didn't want the service to end, for then would come the solemn procession to the cemetery where he would say good-bye to Claire forever.

"I assume you're not returning home this afternoon," Millie said, leaning across Riley to address his mother at the luncheon the Women's Auxiliary had prepared for the family after the interment. "Why don't you and Riley come over this evening and share some of the food our friends have brought?"

"Unless Riley has other plans," Mrs. McHaney said, "I'd be glad to come."

Riley knew his mother had brought nothing other than what she had on and the dress she had traveled in, and he presumed she would prefer to spend the time alone with him, which would have been his choice. He was surprised she accepted the invitation.

"Bill's waiting to take you home when you are ready. Tell him to pick you up shortly before six," Millie said as she rose. "Please excuse me. I must thank Reverend Morgan before he leaves."

Back at Riley's, Mrs. McHaney poured Riley a cup of the tea she had brewed.

"If you stay in Sikeston," she said, "Ben will end up living with Mrs. Clinton and you'll only see him occasionally."

"At least he'll be taken care of and I won't have to worry about what to do with him during the day. I have to work, you know."

"Think about it, Riley. Do you want your son raised by Mrs. Clinton? Do you want him to be cut off from your family?"

Riley walked over to his mother, took both her hands into his and said, "Don't worry, Mother. I'd never let that happen."

At the hospital an hour later, Mrs. McHaney and Riley both cried at the sight of Ben, whose condition had hardly changed. Drug-induced sleep kept him as still as death and head bandages encapsulated all but his eyes and nose.

"Can I hold him?" Riley asked the attending nurse, an older lady with a kindly face, who had taken over for Nurse Connelly at the shift change.

"I'm so sorry," she said. "Not now. Maybe in a few days. He needs to remain as still as possible. Please don't worry. The IV keeps him nourished and drugged, and all the nurses talk to him every time we check him or change his bandages." She rubbed a spot between her eyebrows, and Riley saw how weary she was.

"We're waiting for him to be able to take a bottle," she said, smiling gently at her tiny charge. "This little man still has a long way to go."

For over an hour, Riley and his mother stood vigil over Ben.

"God is smiling down on you, my sweet boy," Mrs. McHaney whispered as she and Riley prepared to leave. "He has you in his arms."

They rode home in silence. Mrs. McHaney rested while Riley washed the few dishes left from breakfast, showered, and shaved. As they waited to be picked up for dinner, Mrs. McHaney puttered around the living room wiping smudges off windows and watering the geraniums and begonias Claire had placed on windowsills and on the table in the small nook off the kitchen where Riley and Claire had usually eaten. She fiddled with the arrangement of lilies from Nora that City Florist had delivered that morning. On the mantel was a picture of Claire and Riley taken at their wedding. She picked up the picture, turned toward Riley and said, "She was beautiful. I know you loved her very much. Tell me about the accident."

"There isn't anything to tell, Mother. I ran into a tractor-trailer. The road was dusty, and the sun was glaring in my eyes, but that's no excuse for not seeing the stop sign—or the truck."

"Has Mrs. Clinton blamed you for the wreck?"

"She doesn't have to. I blame myself. I have killed my wife and probably my child."

"Don't say that, Riley. You have not killed your son. If God wanted Ben to die, He'd have taken him with Claire."

"I wish I had the faith in God you and Millie have," Riley said. "I just don't. I can't accept that some unknowable being in some unknown place decides whether to let cars crash or pass safely every time they approach intersections. And if they crash, who dies and who lives."

"You think too much, Riley. God is unfathomable, and He is in control."

"No, Mother. No one's in control."

The squeal of approaching brakes preempted Mrs. McHaney's response. Riley helped his mother into Bill's car and held her hand during the short ride to Millie's—all the while reflecting on their conversation and wondering how he could carry on without Claire, and probably without Ben, with no God to help.

"Everything was absolutely delicious,"Mrs. McHaney said to Millie at the conclusion of a modest supper of lady peas and corn from some friend's garden and ham from the cold storage locker some other family friend rented in town. "Thank you so much for having us."

"Coffee, anyone?" Millie asked.

"We can only stay a little longer," Mrs. McHaney said, "My bus leaves shortly before nine in the morning."

"Then I'll have Bill pick you up at 8:30."

Riley sat on the couch and balanced his coffee cup and saucer on his lap. His mother sat to his left and placed her coffee on the small table separating her from Millie. He felt very small, almost invisible. He looked at the waning moon through the wooden blinds covering the window which was cracked open to let in some of the night air. A few specks of dust could be seen reflecting light as they lazily floated by.

"Has Riley talked to you about the hospital and doctor bills?" Millie asked Mrs. McHaney.

"Only that he has no savings and no insurance and doesn't know how to pay them."

"I'm worried sick about it," Millie said. "Arthur's liability insurance is only $20,000. Our agent has assured Jim that because Arthur had asked Riley to drive, State Farm will pay out the full amount of the policy for Claire's death and Ben's injuries..."

Millie burst into tears.

"That leaves nothing for me," she said. "Unless I sue Riley for Arthur's death, which I would never do. He needs everything for Ben."

"What about life insurance?" Mrs. McHaney asked.

Arthur was covered for $25,000," Millie said, "but all the cash value had been borrowed to put into the newspaper, so there's little left."

As Ben's guardian and Claire's spouse, Riley would receive all the insurance proceeds. Millie, as Arthur's widow, would receive nothing. He had to help her. She had solved his immediate childcare problem, and she intended to use her friendship with Dr. Buckley to get a reduction in the hospital and doctor bills. What could he do for her?

"Did Arthur receive income from the paper?" he asked.

"Only the $100 per month necessary to pay our house note," Millie answered, "which has five more years to go."

"Here's a suggestion," Riley said. "Let's pay the funeral and other final expenses for Arthur and Claire and ask the hospital to cut their bill in half, then you and I split what's left."

"Come here and let me hug you," Millie said. "That's more than fair. I'm sure Allen will take whatever you can pay. He owns the hospital and he and I were sweethearts long ago."

"When can we bring Ben home and stop those awful bills?" Mrs. McHaney asked.

"Allen says he won't know for at least another week," Millie answered. "which gives me time to turn Claire's room into a nursery. Her baby bed was passed around to her uncles after she outgrew it, but Jim tells me it's still in good condition. I'll repaint the room in light blue with little white clouds on the ceiling and hang some pictures of bunnies and baby chicks on the walls. Everything will be ready for him."

"How nice," Riley's mother said. "You have it all worked out."

Taking a final sip of coffee, she rose from her chair and said, "It was a lovely evening. Thank you for having us, but we really must go."

Minutes later they were at Riley's house.

"I can't believe that woman!" Mrs. McHaney exclaimed as soon as she walked in the door. "She acts like Ben belongs to her."

"Don't get upset, Mother. Millie means well."

"I am upset and I'm angry. If Ben goes home from the hospital with her, you'll never get him back. She'll take over his life."

"What other choice do I have?" Ben said.

"I'll talk to Nora," Mrs. McHaney replied. "We'll think of something."

Ten days later, Riley's sister arrived in Sikeston.

"That was the longest one hundred seventy miles I've ever driven," Nora Campbell exclaimed as she drained the rest of her Budweiser and plopped down on Riley's sofa. "There are ten towns between Memphis and Sikeston, and I must have hit every red light in every one of them. To top it off, I had to wait thirty minutes for the ferry."

Nora pulled a pack of Camels from her purse and offered Riley one. "Want a smoke?"

"Not now," he said. "I took a few too many puffs while I was waiting for you." Riley flipped open his Zippo and extended her a light. "I'll get you an ash tray."

"I wish I could have come to the funeral," Nora said, "but Frank was traveling and there was no one to stay with Annie. I'm sorry I couldn't be there for you. Did my flowers arrive in time?"

"They did and they stayed beautiful for over a week," Riley said "Thanks for your thoughtfulness. I'm really glad you're here. Why didn't you bring Annie?"

"I could never have made this trip with her. She's 'helping' Frank wash the windows in our new apartment. I must get back tomorrow. Two days of solo child-care are all Frank Campbell can handle. Plus, he has a big territory to cover and needs to get back on the road."

Nora left her half-smoked Camel in the ash tray, opened the Frigidaire, and took out another Bud. "I see you are well supplied with beer. Want anything?"

Riley shook his head.

"I'm okay."

"Are you really okay? It's only been three weeks since the accident. When we talked after the funeral, I got really concerned about your state of mind."

"If you mean am I over Claire's death, of course not. I can't get her off my mind. I miss her terribly."

"I'm sure you do, and you always will. I promise you, as time goes on, missing her won't hurt so much."

"How do you know?" Riley scoffed.

Nora shrugged her shoulders. "That's what everybody tells me." She took her nearly empty bottle to the kitchen, quickly washed and put away the few dishes, spoons, and forks in the sink, dried her hands, lit another Camel, and walked back into the living room.

"Is everything set for us to get Ben tomorrow as we discussed?" she asked.

Riley rose from his seat, walked slowly to the window, lit a fresh cigarette, and took a long puff before he answered.

"Millie is picking up Ben."

"And bringing him here?"

Riley took two more quick puffs.

"No, she's taking Ben home with her. She's turned Claire's old room into a nursery and has hired a woman to keep him during the day. I wanted to wait till you got here to tell you. I was afraid you wouldn't come if you knew, and Nora, I need you with me tomorrow."

Nora walked to the window, stood next to Riley, and stared into the dark. Riley watched the reflection of the tip of her cigarette in the glass brighten briefly, dim, then brighten again.

"I thought we had this all worked out. Have you told Mother about your change of plans?"

"No. I've been avoiding that conversation. I know Mother convinced you to take Ben because she was afraid of losing him. I've thought things over carefully, Nora. I can't impose on you and Frank. You just got to Memphis and your apartment only has one bedroom."

"Mother didn't have to convince us," Nora said. "Frank and I want to take care of Ben while you decide what you are going to do. Annie turns three in a few days and is eager to 'help' me with her baby cousin. We'll manage."

"I don't see how in a one-bedroom apartment, with all the extra medical expense. I won't have Millie's help if I take Ben away from her, and I won't have much money to send you."

"Don't worry about the money. L. B. Price is expanding into Mississippi and the company wants Frank to take over a route there. We'll be in Memphis less than a year. Then he'll get his pick of towns along the Gulf coast and a two-hundred-dollar relocation allowance. With Keesler Air Base expanding, he thinks Biloxi will be a great area for door-to-door sales. He wants to get established before Jewel Tea moves in."

"I can't help worrying about the money," Riley said. "I have no insurance and Ben's care has cost over $3000 already. That's more than I make in a year."

"You won't have all that expense after he leaves the hospital. Frank and I will help. As I said before, we'll manage. The important decision for you to make while

Ben is recovering is whether to stay here or look around and find some other paper that needs a linotype operator. Either way, you need time to settle into your new life. When he's fully recovered, we'll bring your little boy to you."

Riley stared at the wall. "I'm pretty sure I could find work in Nashville," he said. "There are several printing companies and two newspapers in Nashville. It's just so far away."

Riley stubbed out his cigarette. A smile curled his lips. He didn't have to find work somewhere else, and he didn't have to leave Ben with Millie. Staying in Sikeston and sending Ben with Nora to recuperate was the answer. In six months or so when Ben recovered, he could come home, and Riley would hire someone to look after him during the day.

"And if I stay in Sikeston," Riley said, "I could take the *City of New Orleans* to Memphis any day of the week."

Riley and Nora arrived at Sikeston General on Saturday morning with a blanket and a bottle for Ben.

"Maureen, I'd like you to meet my sister, Nora Campbell," Riley said to the nurse whose temperament and disposition had given him so much comfort. "Maureen has taken such good care of Ben almost three weeks."

Maureen nodded at Nora and said, "You're early. We weren't expecting Mrs. Clinton until nine, but Ben is ready. The good Lord had to be watching over this little boy. We didn't think he would make it through the first week. Then miraculously he started getting stronger and stronger. He takes his bottle eagerly and loves pablum and Gerber's apple sauce. You have to be careful with the back of his head. The bandages need to be changed every morning and every night. If you see any bleeding or if he starts running a fever, let Dr. Buckley know. Also, tiny pieces of glass are still working out of his scalp. You need to dab a little alcohol on the spot where you remove the glass. Dr. Buckley would like you to bring him in for a checkup in a week."

"What do I need to do to get Ben released?" Riley inquired.

"The paperwork is ready for you at the front desk. Go sign him out, and Mrs. Campbell, if you will take this package of medicines and supplies we have for you, I'll get Ben and carry him to your car. Everyone here has become very attached to him. We're glad he's going to make it."

Riley signed the discharge papers, noted no money was due and walked toward the door where Nora, holding the medical supplies, and Maureen, holding Ben, were waiting. Behind them he saw Millie hurrying up the steps.

"Why, hello, Maureen," Millie said. "So nice of you to bring Ben to the door to meet me. And hello, Riley. Is this your sister you spoke so highly of?"

"Yes, I'm Nora," Nora said. "And you must be Millie Clinton."

"Glad to meet you, Nora," Millie said. "Would you please take that package to the driver in the coupe parked across the street, Nora, and if you don't mind, take my purse too, so I can carry the baby."

Nora thrust the medical supplies into Riley's hands and grabbed Ben out of Nurse Connelly's arms. "Come on, Riley," she said. "Let's go."

For a long moment Riley did not move. He saw Millie's eyes show bewilderment, then anger. He saw his sister clutching Ben as if to protect him from a marauding bear. He saw a puzzled Maureen.

Then he said, "Good morning, Millie," as if he had just come down to breakfast, put his free hand on Nora's waist and hustled her and the baby to her car, leaving a stunned Millie standing on the hospital steps. During the seven-minute drive home, Riley constantly checked his rear-view mirror for flashing red lights. As soon as they got in the house, he locked all the doors and windows, then lit the cigarette he so desperately needed.

"What do we do?" Riley asked. "She may have the police arrest you for baby snatching."

"I didn't steal a baby," Nora scoffed. "You're the baby's father and I went with you to check him out of the hospital. You have every right to bring your son home, and you don't have to explain to anyone that I have agreed to take care of him until he recovers."

"I should have told Millie I had changed my mind and had decided to pick him up myself," Riley said.

Nora sighed.

"Quit waffling," she said. "We went over everything last night and agreed it would be better to get Ben out of the hospital before we let Millie know, so she wouldn't grab him first. We couldn't let Millie take Ben home. Like Mother said, once Millie got Ben, she would never let him go."

"Do you think we should pack the car and leave now?"

"Stop acting like a criminal, Riley. What can Mrs. Clinton do now? If she calls the police, what will she tell them? That her son in law, the baby's father, took her grandson home from the hospital with him? We'll leave this afternoon, as we planned, and you will come back on the train tomorrow, go to work on Monday and act normal. If anyone asks, your son is home from the hospital and is staying with his aunt until he fully recovers."

"Let us in, Riley! We know you're in there!"

Uncle Jim was pounding on the door and Millie was bristling at his side. Nora took Ben into Riley's bedroom and locked the door. Riley braced himself, then opened the door. Millie rushed past him.

"Where's Ben?" she demanded, her eyes searching the room.

"In the bedroom asleep," Riley said.

"Well, bring him to me. Right this minute."

"Thank you for all you've done, Millie, but now that Ben is strong enough to recover at home, I want to be responsible for him."

"Of course, you're responsible for him, but you can't take care of him," Millie sounded as if she were addressing a recalcitrant child. "He needs constant attention, and you need to work. I can give him that attention. You can't. Enough of this nonsense. Go get him."

Riley met her eyes and in his most authoritative voice said, "My sister will be looking after Ben."

"Your sister!" Millie roared. "That girl whose husband is a peddler? What kind of life can she give him?"

"She can give him love and personal attention, which is what Ben really needs now," Riley huffed. "If he needs a doctor, Memphis has plenty of good ones."

"You're taking him to Memphis!" Millie exploded. "You can't! He's in no condition to travel. He might not survive the trip. Besides, he has everything he needs here—a nursery in a good home, a personal caretaker, and doctors and nurses who have gotten him, with God's help, through the valley of the shadow of death."

Millie's words reminded Riley of all she had to offer his son. Her withering look made him turn away. To Claire's uncle he said, "We're driving to Memphis today. I'll be at work Monday morning."

"You bastard!" Millie shouted. "You killed my husband and my only child and now you're trying to take my grandson away from me. I won't let you. You better give Ben to me now or, so help me, I'll have your sister arrested for baby snatching. She jerked him away from his nurse on the hospital steps. I was standing right there. I saw it all. And as for you, I'll sue you for everything you have for killing Arthur and Claire. Do you hear me!"

"Riley," Nora said as she emerged from the bedroom, "if your guests cannot be civil, they should leave, or is it going to be necessary to call the police?"

"Let's go, Millie," Uncle Jim said as he took her arm. "I'll call our lawyer and let him take care of this."

A sobbing Millie left with her brother-in-law. Twenty minutes later Riley, with Nora in the backseat carefully holding Ben, left for Memphis, having crammed clothing, bedding, bottles, and food into her Chevy's small trunk alongside Nora's overnight bag and Riley's shaving kit. In the rearview mirror, Riley saw a police car following them as they drove through Sikeston, finally dropping back as they turned onto Highway 62 south of town. Riley broke the silence about a mile down the road.

"That scared the shit out of me." Riley said, "I thought that red light would come on any second. Do you know the ferry schedule?"

"I checked when I came up. There's a crossing from the Missouri side at 3:30, which we should make. We're only thirty miles away."

"I sure hope the ferry's on time. I don't want to be waiting at the river and have the cops show up."

Nora laughed and cracked her window an inch or two to let in some fresh air. "Lighten up, Riley. You are simply taking your child on a trip."

The Dorena-Hickman ferry was docking when they arrived at the river. Nora had purchased a dollar round trip fare Friday evening, so they did not have to get out of the car before boarding along with the two other vehicles making the half hour crossing. As they approached the landing on the Kentucky side, the pilot shot tobacco juice into the spittoon four feet away, grinned at Riley and tilted his head back to avoid dribbling out of the side of his mouth, then brought the ferry to a shuttering stop against the tires lashed to posts at the dock to absorb the force of landing. Riley waited his turn to exit, then headed south toward Union City where he would pick up US 51 to Memphis.

"You can relax," Nora said. "The Missouri cops can't get you now."

"Is this my little nephew?" Frank Campbell said two hours later as he reached into the car to get Ben. Nora cut him off.

"Better let me carry him, Frank. He's still pretty fragile."

"His eyes come straight from Claire," Frank said, "I just don't see much of you in him, Riley. Are you sure he's yours?"

"Cut it out," Nora said. "Help Riley unload the car. I'll change Ben's diaper and introduce him to Annie."

"Want a beer?" Frank said as he and Riley headed for the house, arms loaded.

"Yeah, if you're having one."

"I can't thank you enough for letting Nora and me have Ben for a while. I've always wanted a little boy, but Nora said she wasn't having any more kids. I'll be such a good daddy to Ben, maybe she'll change her mind."

Frank Campbell, a gruff red-faced, dark haired, big man Riley had liked from the beginning handed Riley a Pabst. Frank had lots of stories and loved telling them.

"As a boy I dreamed of being a doctor. My second year at the University of Texas ended when Dad went broke in 1929 and couldn't pay my tuition. I took temporary jobs in South Texas and Arkansas until I got on with the WPA in July 1935 and was assigned to a project in the Ozarks. That assignment ended in early 1937, so I thumbed a ride to Memphis and got a job selling cars at Honest Abe's Wheels and Deals."

Frank always paused when he got to that part of this story. Riley took it from there.

"And you met Nora at the South Perkins Diner where you and she ate breakfast every morning. She made as much money as a stenographer as you did selling cars, so you could afford to get married."

"Exactly!" Frank beamed. "And when Annie was born in August 1938, I knew what I really wanted was a wife and a family, not a medical career."

As he sipped his Pabst and followed Frank into the living room to join Nora, Riley felt good about his decision. Memphis was only 140 miles from Sikeston and the Illinois Central ran trains both ways every day.

"Tell me about your apartment," he asked. "It looked large from the outside."

"That's because this is a shotgun duplex," Nora said. "Our living room, bedroom and kitchen are all in a row and the bath is tucked into a corner of the kitchen. The other side of the house is a mirror image. Two apartments and two families in one house, with a wall down the middle. Big enough for us now, just no room to expand. Ben can sleep in a crib until we get a baby bed for him. Our dresser is big enough for his clothes and there's a chest on the sleeping porch where we can store blankets and pillows. We'll be fine."

Riley looked for a place to put his empty bottle. Nora took it and said, "Why don't you lie down and rest a while, Riley. Frank, had you rather fix supper or watch Ben and Annie?"

As he lay sweating in his trousers and undershirt on the sleeping porch, Riley closed his eyes and tried to remember Claire's instructions on how to take care of Ben. "Don't let him sleep on his back. Turn him over after you change him and be sure to put a cloth on your shoulder when you burp him. Watch out when you take his diaper off, he may not be finished."

Everything sounded easy, but Riley never felt comfortable taking care of Ben. He constantly feared he would drop the child or scald him in the bath or let him choke on a bite too big to swallow. Claire had been so good at mothering and enjoyed it so much Riley gladly stood back and watched. As a result, childcare for Riley, with Claire's benign acquiescence, had been a task un-mastered. His responsibility was to earn a living—"bring home the bacon" his father would say—and make Claire's life pleasant by making her coffee in the morning and rubbing her back and feet at night. He believed a man's share of household duties was to mow the yard, take out the garbage, clean the oven and the commode, and occasionally help with the dishes. It seemed like a fair bargain to him. Except now Claire was gone; Nora had Ben, and practically nothing was expected of him.

Tomorrow he would return to Sikeston unattached—just as he was when he answered the *Standard-Democrat's* ad in the *Publisher's Auxiliary* for a linotype operator. Only this time the girl he had quickly fallen in love with was gone, and no one could take her place. He intended to lose himself in his job and come to Memphis as often as possible.

Riley heard a whimper. He wiped the sweat off his face and neck, put his shirt on and went to the bedroom where Ben had been sleeping under Nora's watchful eye.

"He's about to wake up," she said. "You want to give him his bottle? I'll warm it up and get a towel you can hold under him."

Riley gently lifted Ben out of his crib and sat down on the bed to position the baby in the crook of his arm so the bottle could be held in the correct position, the cloth Nora had provided would stay in place and the bandages would not be disturbed. Sitting ramrod on the bed, careful not to touch the back of Ben's head, Riley watched his son eagerly suck the bottle. As he watched, he tried to picture his son as an adult. Would Ben's hair stay brown, like his, or turn auburn, like Claire's? Would his eyes stay greenish brown like his mother's or turn light blue like his father's? Would he be slight in build like his mother, or a little above average in height like his father? Would the scars on the back of his head go away?

And what about his intellect, his spirit? How much damage had his brain suffered?

"That's right. Keep your arm at the base of his skull and protect the bandages," he heard Nora say. "Frank, come here. You've got to see this. Bring the camera."

2

"The boss wants to see you," Rose, the counter girl, who rationed out fifteen copies of the hot-off-the-press papers to each of the dozen or so boys who fanned out through the city every Thursday afternoon to hawk the news from street corners they had claimed and fought over, said to Riley as he walked in the door at the *Standard-Democrat* Monday morning. The back shop was quiet. The presses that would print the paper would not roll until Wednesday and Riley was the only operator of the linotype machine that noisily created the type, which when properly inked and pressed, transformed unreadable letters written backwards on lead into news. Riley made his way past the sales counter to the small office with a big desk cluttered with prior editions of the paper, samples of print stock, a ledger, and a phone. Franklin Roosevelt beamed from the wall behind Uncle Jim, who motioned Riley to sit while he wrote checks. A couple of minutes passed. Rose brought in another handful of bills. Riley smiled at her and cleared a spot on the desk for the bills. Uncle Jim kept writing. Another two minutes passed before Jim Clinton spoke.

"You're an excellent typesetter, Riley," he said, "and you have the best knowledge of how to put a paper together of anyone in the shop. I expected you to be running the place one day. Unfortunately, I'm going to have to let you go."

"But..." Riley began.

Jim Clinton dropped his pen, looked at Riley and let out a sigh Riley thought signaled defeat rather than relief.

"Please let me finish. It's not my choice, but I'd rather find a new linotype operator than hurt Millie further. You have betrayed her by taking Ben, who was her only connection to her daughter, away from her. If you'll stay till we get the paper out this week, I'll give you two week's severance and a good recommendation. I'm sorry, Riley. I really am."

Uncle Jim stood up and offered his hand. Riley remained seated in shocked disbelief. The relief he had felt when his mother, his sister, and he had worked out a plan for Ben's care had blinded him to the obvious downside, that his employer, Claire's uncle, and his mother-in-law, might not agree with that plan. He felt like a fool.

Riley finally rose and limply shook his boss's hand. The rest of the morning passed in slow motion. Riley could not concentrate. Too many thoughts competed for his attention. Why had he naively assumed nothing would change at work, when Uncle Jim had stood by

Millie every step of the way? What other consequences would he suffer from his actions? What should he do now? Riley re-cast the three error-filled galleys of type he had produced that morning which had been rejected by the proofreader, then punched his timecard and left.

"Boss is waiting for you in his office," a tearful Rose told Riley when he arrived at work his last day. "I'm going to miss you. Come here and let me give you a hug."

"I promised you a good reference if you worked out the week," Uncle Jim said as he motioned Riley to sit. "Would you take a job in Nashville? An old friend of mine who manages production at Vincent Publishing is hiring. It's not a newspaper, but it is a job setting type. The pay is good, and the work is steady."

Riley sat straight up in his chair.

"Is it day or night shift?" he asked.

"I can find out. Do you want me to call and ask?"

"No, now that I'm single, it really doesn't matter," Riley said. "What's more important is would I get to work weekends."

"Well, that's a twist," Uncle Jim said. "Most folks, including the two guys I interviewed for your old position, want Saturdays off."

"I'd work as many hours as I could," Riley said. "Beats sitting home alone in a big city."

Uncle Jim made the call and Riley got the job. One week later he was working the four p.m. to midnight shift at Vincent's Publishing, Nashville, Tennessee.

2222 White Oak Street
Sikeston, Missouri

December 2, 1941

Dear Riley,

Thank you for the box of Claire's things you left at the Standard office for me. I especially treasure the hairbrush, comb, and mirror that I had given to Claire when she turned thirteen. I was still angry with you when Jim brought the box to me, so I didn't open it until my anger had waned, which took almost two months. My delight in regaining a part of Claire dampened my ever-present sorrow over my loss of her. How thoughtful of you to save those personal items for me.

Claire's death has been tragic for both of us. I should never have said those cruel things the day you left for Memphis. Please forgive me. I don't blame you for letting your sister keep your son, and I don't blame you for the accident. With the sun in your eyes and the dust in the air you can't be faulted for not seeing the stop sign. We'll never know why God wanted Claire and Arthur with Him. We must put this tragedy behind us, focus on the future and be thankful that in His mercy, He let Ben and you survive.

After paying all funeral expenses and the lawyer's fee, about $10,000 was left of the insurance *money, and as we hoped, Allen agreed to take $5,000 for all the medical expenses. He's such a dear. With the newspaper money taking care of my house note, I'll get by, so I want you to have the $5,000 remaining for future medical expenses and, hopefully, for Ben's education. The money is still in the bank, in your name. Arthur and I couldn't afford to send Claire to college. Perhaps her death will make her son's college education possible.*

Jim greatly appreciates your staying the rest of the week until the new man—I can't remember his name—arrived. Jim says he is good at setting type, just not as good as you, and doesn't know anything about running a print shop. It was fortunate he wanted to rent your house. Since he is moving his family here, I'm sure he'll buy it if you don't ask too much for it.

Enclosed is a photo of Arthur and me. I hope you'll save it for Ben and let him know he has another grandmother who loves him and would like to remain in his life. Please forgive my terrible behavior and let me stay in touch with him wherever he is. And tell my little grandson Happy Birthday from his Grandmother Millie.

Affectionately,
Millie

Riley re-read the letter, folded it, and put it in his breast pocket. He knew he should write Millie back to thank her for all she had done for him, for the strong presence she had been in his and Ben's lives, to apologize for keeping her in the dark on his decision to let Nora take Ben, and to assure her he would not cut Ben off from her. That letter, however, would require much effort which he wasn't yet up to.

On December 7, 1941, Japan bombed Pearl Harbor and in the shock that followed, Millie's letter receded from Riley's thoughts. On April 1, 1942, he received notice that his draft status had been re-classified He was now 1-A. Frank and Nora urged him as a widower with a child, to appeal. He had thirty days to file.

"Riley, Riley McHaney! Over here! Under the exit sign!" Frank's booming voice rang above the din. Riley turned sharply to his right and saw Annie, straddling Frank's shoulders. After elbowing his way to them, Riley dropped his duffel bag and helped his niece down from her perch.

"Uncle Riley, why don't you have on a uniform like everyone else?"

"Because I'm not a soldier—yet."

"Did you have to stand all the way?" Frank asked. "The train looked packed. I counted twenty cars when it rolled into the station."

"Only for the first two hours. I grabbed a seat at Jackson when a lot of guys got off. Soldiers were everywhere—even in the toilets. Good thing I didn't have to pee. Thanks for picking me up. I could have taken a local from Jackson to Newbern, but I wanted to come on to Memphis to have as much time with Ben as possible."

"Glad to do it. Seems like the Army has taken over the rails. Central Station has been like this since early January. Where and when is your appeal to the Draft Board being heard?"

"In Dyersburg at 11:30 tomorrow morning, right after William's memorial service, which, unfortunately, Mother had already scheduled. I'll barely have time to drive over. By the way, thanks for lending me your car."

"Think nothing of it," Frank said. "I still like your chances. The Selective Service Commission announced in January they weren't drafting married men with children. Tomorrow is May 1st and they've said nothing different, so I'm hoping Ben will keep you out."

"The troubling point of the announcement," Riley said, "is the phrase 'married men with children.' As a married man, you are protected—not me.

"Yeah," Frank laughed, handing Riley a copy of the *Commercial Appeal*. "I don't think they'd take a flat footed, overweight guy like me anyway. Did you see the *Commercial's* headline?"

"The surrender in Bataan was the *Tennessean's* headline this morning, also," Riley said. "Damn those Japs. If they hadn't bombed Pearl Harbor, we wouldn't be going to William's memorial service, and the US wouldn't be in this war. What's going on in Europe doesn't involve us."

"I think you're wrong," Frank said. "France has already fallen, and the Krauts are kicking the crap out of the Brits. The US couldn't stand by and watch Hitler invade England. We'd have been in the war by now even without Pearl Harbor."

Frank pointed across the street to the line of parked black Fords and Chevrolets.

"My car is the second from the corner. There are so many black Chevrolets in Memphis I had to put a dent in the front fender, so I'd recognize it. Throw your stuff into the trunk, and we'll pick up Nora and Ben."

"Hold Ben," Nora said to Riley to as she climbed into the Chevy's back seat with Annie and Raggedy Ann to begin the two-hour drive to Newbern for Staff Sergeant William McHaney's memorial service. Ben showed his unhappiness with the seating arrangements by standing up in Riley's lap, turning toward the back seat and shrieking "Mama! Mama! Mama!"

"Annie," Nora said, "take Raggedy Ann and climb into the front seat with Uncle Riley so I can calm Ben down."

"Thanks," Riley said. "I'll spend some time with Ben when we get to Mother's. I'm sorry I haven't been able to visit these last few months, with my sixty hours a week work schedule and only Sunday's off."

"We understand," Nora said. "Your new job and your draft status have been weighing on you, but when you get this awful draft situation resolved, you can make time to visit Ben more often."

Ben snuggled into Nora's lap and Annie settled into the middle seat between her daddy and her Uncle Riley and began quietly combing her doll's hair. Riley cracked his window, lit a Lucky, stared at the passing scenery, and turned his thoughts to his brother. William had joined the Army Air Corps in 1938, three months out of high school, when there were no regular jobs for musicians in West Tennessee, and no money for college. Riley had driven William to the station to leave for basic training.

"Got it straight, now?" William had said as they sat in his 1931 Plymouth Coupe waiting for the train, "change the oil regularly, and keep 36 pounds of pressure in the tires. Take care of this baby like it's yours. Just don't do anything with it or in it I wouldn't do."

"That gives me lots of latitude," Riley laughed, bursting with excitement at his good fortune. "Don't worry, your wheels will be waiting for you when you get back."

"Remember Mother's shriek when she saw me drive up in this last fall, not knowing I had used money I saved from our band's gigs to pay our drummer five dollars for his fifteen dollar pawn ticket to get the car out of hock?"

"Yeah, Mom quieted down after she learned you hadn't gone into debt for it. She was scared to death of debt."

"Can you blame her?" William said. "Dad lost his print shop in '32, and we almost lost our house."

"Mom still believes worrying over debt was what killed him," Riley said, "not the pneumonia. Lucky

Dad's insurance was enough to bury him and pay off the house mortgage. Too bad there wasn't more."

During the first year after his death, Riley often thought about his father, and wished he had known John Lee McHaney better. This much he knew. His dad was fiercely independent, proud of him, and aloof. Riley remembered a challenge from his father to 'get a college education and make something of yourself.' Good advice, but that did not make up for not spending more time with his youngest son. As the years passed, thoughts about his father were less frequent and less vivid, finally blurring into an image of an elderly man who had once been important in his life.

William made it home for two weeks after basic training, then for another few days before being posted to Honolulu in the fall of 1939 and assigned to the Quartermaster Corps.

"Give me fifty bucks and she's all yours," William told Riley before leaving for California to join his unit headed for Hawaii.

"You know I don't have that kind of money. Will you take a twenty and let me send you the rest when I get it?"

"No, little brother," William said. "Mom wouldn't like for you to go into debt to anybody—not even me. I'm sure I can get a fifty for it in San Diego—probably more. I can pick up hitch hikers along the way to pay for gas."

The telegram arrived from the Army Air Corps on December 13, 1941. Riley and Nora were in Newbern with their mother. William survived the first wave of the Japanese air attack on Pearl Harbor, made his way to his duty station, but did not survive the second. The war was going so badly that the Air Corps would not say whether or when they would ship him home for a funeral, so before another son was sent to war, Mrs. McHaney scheduled a memorial service for William without his body.

Riley turned his thoughts back to his situation when they arrived at Newbern. Although he had tried to remain upbeat, he had lurched from extreme hope to bottomless despair as he waited out the few weeks until his appeal was heard. A clap of thunder had awakened him that morning, which he took as an ominous sign. He was not going to convince three men his motherless son needed him more than the Army.

"We'll consider your request and let you know our decision soon," Jeremiah Bishop, owner of Bishop's Auto Parts and Chairman of the Dyer County, Tennessee, Selective Service Board said at the conclusion of the Board's fifteen-minute meeting with Riley, a large part of which had been spent expressing condolences for William's death and sympathy for Mrs. McHaney.

"I assure you, the members of this Board don't enjoy sending young men to war, however, we have our duty, and so do you. Everyone has to make sacrifices."

Hands in his pockets, shoulders drooping, and spirits sagging, Riley walked to Frank's car and drove the ten miles back to Newbern. The radio was full of news of Japanese victories in the Philippines and Southeast Asia, and of German submarines spotted off the North Carolina coast. Riley parked in front of his Mother's house and listened to the last of the dismal report on the war. The itch on his ring finger that began at Claire's death had become unbearable. He took off his wedding ring, intending to put it in the packet of Claire's things he was saving for Ben, and opened the car door. The morning shower had refreshed the day. He could see hydrangeas everywhere. Riley gazed at the pink and blue blossoms in the front yard of Henry Hall, who had given Riley his first job—if you didn't count selling popcorn and other concessions on Sunday afternoons at the Bijou—at the print shop Riley's father had formerly owned, which Hall had bought from the Dyer County Bank at the foreclosure sale. He thought again of his father, a proud man who never made enough to support his family, but was always striving, and even during the depression refused to put his family on the dole.

"We can grow our own vegetables and keep chickens," his father declared when he lost his business to the bank. "I started out carving tombstones for a living. I can go back to that."

Riley admired his father's ambition and forgave his failures. He refused to dwell on how little attention his father had paid him as a boy. After all, he was the youngest of six children spanning twenty years from first birth to last, two of whom had died in childhood. By the time Riley came along, his father was too old and too busy keeping his family clothed, sheltered, and fed to spend time with him.

"Sweet or unsweetened?" his mother asked when Riley finally went inside to join his family for lunch. "I can't keep everybody's preferences straight. Weren't sure when you'd get back, so we started without you."

"Unsweetened," Riley said. All eyes were on him when he took the chair across from his mother and started spreading pimento cheese onto a slice of Wonder bread. She handed him a tall glass of tea. Riley tasted it, grimaced, and said, "Got any lemon?"

"How'd it go?" Frank asked.

"They said they'd let me know, but from the looks on their faces, I'm a dead duck. Plus, the chairman hectored me on my duty to my country."

"Isn't the chairman Jeremiah Bishop?" Nora snorted. "He may be the only Republican left in Dyer County. Thinks Herbert Hoover was a great President and Roosevelt would never have won if it hadn't been for the Jews and the Commies. I was in high school with his son Jimmy, who, to his credit, was totally different from his dad. Jimmy used to joke about the "evidence" his dad claimed to have on people in Washington who were Communists. He couldn't wait to get away from home and join the Navy when Jeremiah wouldn't let him go to college unless he went to Freed-Hardeman or David Lipscomb. UT was too far away and far too liberal . . . Mom, why are you crying?"

Mrs. McHaney had left her seat and was standing behind Riley. She put her hands on his shoulders and said, "I don't want you to go, son. William didn't join the air corps to fight. He wanted to save his money and go to college when he got out. He didn't expect to get shot at. There was no war going on. He only joined because there was no work here, except playing trumpet at smoky honky-tonks and school parties and dance halls for three or four dollars a night and getting home at two in the morning. He wanted to be a serious musician. He had talent, and now he's gone."

Riley stood up and embraced his mother. Over his shoulder he saw the picture she kept on the mantel of William in his band uniform, holding his trumpet. He felt his mother's warm breath on his cheek as she spoke.

"You may not be as musically talented as William," she said, "but you're brighter. Principal Higgins begged me to send you to Knoxville when you graduated. But with our savings gone and your Father in the ground, college wasn't possible. I've lost enough already, son. I can't lose you. I'm praying you won't have to go."

On June 1, 1942, Riley received the official Notice of Denial of his appeal. The Draft Board's decision to change his selective service classification from 3-A to 1-A stood. Two weeks later, the dreaded "Greetings from the President" letter arrived, ordering him to report on July 8, 1942, to Camp Forrest, Tennessee for induction into the Armed Forces of the United States for the duration of the war. That night he caught the last train to Memphis for a final visit with Ben, Nora, and Frank.

"Ben is such a sweet little boy," Nora told him at

breakfast the next morning. "He's learning new words every day. You and I can take him for a walk later. There's a park with swings about two blocks away. Frank can look after Annie. We can talk easier if we leave her here."

"Ben, hold your Daddy's hand," Nora said as the three of them got to the sidewalk.

Ben shook his head. He would not hold Riley's hand, but would toddle a few yards ahead, look back at Nora, grin and start toddling again till Riley caught him and the game started over. When Ben saw the bench swing in the park, he rushed toward it as fast as his little legs would carry him, shouting "Swing, Mama, swing."

Riley and Nora, with Ben between them, swung gently back and forth. A young pregnant woman was in the adjacent swing, watching a toddler play in the sandbox. It wasn't long until Ben crawled into Nora's lap, stuck his thumb in his mouth and fell asleep. Riley looked at his sleeping child, swallowed the lump in his throat and said, "He loves you, Nora. Do you love him?"

"That's a silly question. Of course I do. Frank does too, and so does Annie, even if she thinks he gets attention she deserves. Frank wants his mother to come from San Antonio to see Ben."

"Claire's mother wrote me that she was coming to see Ben," Riley said. "Did Millie make it?"

"A couple of weeks after William's memorial service," Nora said. "Ben wasn't shy around her at all. In fact, he takes to everybody. He is going to be a politician. Millie could make him cackle by burrowing her face in his tummy and blowing. She stepped right in, changed Ben, washed his dirty diapers, and boiled his baby bottles, as if it was her job. She treated that child like he was her own. She and I both cried when she left."

"Did she tell you anything about how she is getting along?" Ben asked.

"She didn't talk much about herself. It was all about Ben."

They swung in silence for a few moments. Then Riley spoke.

"You and I need to talk about Ben. I don't know whether I'll be sent to Europe or North Africa. Wherever I go, I won't come back."

"Don't say that, Riley. Of course, you'll come back. This war will eventually end, just like all wars before."

Continuing to gently rock the swing with his foot on the ground, Riley gazed at the sky and saw a formation of Corsairs heading for the naval air base at Millington. Then he looked across at the mother and child playing a few yards away. Finally, he turned back to Nora.

"Two guys who were with me at print school are MIA in the Pacific. Johnny Darling, who was a year behind me in high school was killed in North Africa, and William's dead. Something will get me. I just don't know what or when."

Nora touched her brother's hand. "Nobody knows what will happen in a war. You may not be sent to the front. You may even get to stay stateside. Think positive. Be an optimist."

"The difference between a pessimist and an optimist," Riley scowled, "is a pessimist has more facts."

Nora secured her hold on Ben, put her foot firmly on the ground to stop the swing and said, "I don't like the way this conversation is headed. Let's go home."

"I'm trying to be realistic," Riley said. "Trying to get my life in order."

"Planning to die when you have no idea what the future holds? How morbid is that?"

Riley took her arm and said, "will you and Frank take care of Ben?"

"Till you get back? Of course."

"Until he's grown. In case I don't get back."

"And when you come back?"

"Even then," Riley said. "I would like for you and Frank to raise Ben as your own child, whatever happens to me. I think it would be better all around. It would put my mind at ease and make it easier for you and Frank to treat Ben like Annie and not like a ward. Frank won't be drafted, so Ben will have a home with a mama and a daddy—during the war and after. If I do get back, I can be Uncle Riley to him. He thinks of Frank as his daddy now. It would confuse him to change things, so I'd like for him to be yours—even if I survive."

Nora looked incredulous. "You want to give your son away!"

Riley's eyes watered under the weight of that statement. His voice breaking, he said, "I want to provide for my son, whatever happens."

Nora's tone softened.

"Let me talk it over with Frank," she said.

With Ben asleep on his shoulder and tears running down his cheeks, Riley trudged the few blocks back to Nora's, renewing his resolve with each passing step to give his son to Nora while he was still alive and able to do so.

3

No seats were available on any train the day of Riley's departure, so Frank took Riley to the Greyhound Bus terminal early Sunday morning for the seven-hour ride to Nashville, where he would continue to work until his induction. He, Nora, and Frank had stayed up past midnight discussing the arrangement for Ben, finally agreeing that rather than have Nora and Frank adopt Ben right away, which Nora preferred, Riley would register Ben with the Army as his dependent and Nora as Ben's temporary guardian, thereby allowing Nora to receive an allotment of one fourth of Riley's military pay. Riley was to make Ben beneficiary of his GI life insurance. Nora and Frank's part of the unwritten bargain was to raise Ben as their own and adopt him at the appropriate time.

"Are you sure this is what you want?" Nora asked as she walked Riley to the car.

Riley did not tell her his aching heart had kept him

awake the rest of the night and even now, the only way he could go through with the arrangement was to concentrate on the certainty that he would never return.

"Yes, I'm sure," Riley said. "Ben needs a family, and I don't believe I'll be able to provide one for him."

Frank and Riley rode to the Greyhound terminal in silence. Riley thought of the day he had taken William to the train to begin military service. Life was different then. No war was raging. Unlike me, Riley thought, William did not know he was doomed.

"Try to get some sleep on the bus," Frank said when he left Riley at the station. "You look pretty ragged. Let's hope this war is over soon."

"Mind if I take that seat?"

Riley looked up from his *Time* magazine to see a blue-eyed petite young woman standing in the aisle beside him, her shoulder length brown hair held off her unsmiling face by a tortoise shell barrette. Her unblemished complexion gave only a small hint of make-up. She was wearing a white cotton sweater over a pale-yellow dress, and black patent pumps. She carried a small black purse and an overnight case.

Riley stepped into the aisle, put the case on the overhead rack and motioned her to slide over to the window seat. As she brushed by him, he caught a faint whiff of Chanel Number 5, the much too expensive perfume he had asked Nora to send him from Memphis to give Claire as a birthday gift, which had quickly become her favorite.

"When he invited me, he asked if I could stay over till Monday. He was a cute guy, and I knew he had a good job, so of course I said yes. I was so excited I used most of my paycheck on an outfit I couldn't afford, hoping for a thrilling weekend during which I could get to know this guy better, and something might develop. As I was dressing for our Saturday night date, his sister informed me she was going with us. I was appalled but decided to let it slide, but when he suggested we go to the Pink Palace Museum today and then pick up his sister for dinner, I lost it—right there on the doorstep. I was so mad I brushed off his attempt to kiss me, said I had a headache and ran upstairs, leaving him standing at the door. I immediately called to change my ticket, learned the trains were full, and had to use most of the money I had left to catch a cab to the bus station and take a Greyhound home."

Riley listened closely to her voice. The pitch was not unpleasant, just slightly higher than Claire's, and the texture did not quite match Claire's sexy softness.

"I assume this was your first date," he said.

"I met him at a wedding reception, and we chatted for—oh, I don't know—ten or fifteen minutes. We hit it off, so I let him know I was interested in seeing him again if he were ever back in Nashville. Two days later he called and told me if I could come to Memphis for a weekend, I could stay with his sister and he would wire me the money for the train ticket. I thought he wanted to see me—not entertain his sister. That creep! I wouldn't go out with him again if he sent a limousine for me. And now I don't have enough left for cab fare home."

"Where do you live?" Riley asked as he searched for his bag among those that had been unloaded from the belly of the bus.

"In a studio apartment on 21st Avenue, near Belmont Methodist Church."

"I live two blocks from the church," Riley said. "Why don't we take a cab to your apartment and I'll pay the fare? I can walk home from there."

"Would you?" the girl said. "I would be so grateful."

Riley hailed a cab and extended his hand to help her in.

"Where to?" the driver asked. Riley looked at the girl.

"1601 21st Avenue," she said. "Directly across from the church."

"Your hands are so soft," Riley said when they both settled into their seats, their arms and legs touching. "You must not scrub floors or wash many dishes."

"You're right," the girl laughed. "I live alone, and my landlady takes care of the cleaning. And I swear by Jergens lotion. What do you do?"

"Oh, I use Lava soap," Riley said. "It gets the ink off."

The girl laughed again. "I meant for a living."

"I'm a typesetter for a book publishing company," Riley said. "I operate a huge typewriter that prints on lead rather than paper."

"Oh," she said, "I'm a parts clerk at Vultee Aircraft."

Riley was disturbed by the rising sexual tension

within him. *Is nine months in mourning long enough?* The cab slowed to a stop.

"Is this the address?" the cabby asked.

"Yes," she said, "and thank you for the ride Mr. . . ."

"McHaney," he said. "Riley McHaney. And you are?"

"Eileen," she said. "Give me your pen and your magazine. Lots of people misspell my name."

On his copy of *Time,* she wrote, Eileen Crosley MU8-6400.

The lingering scent of Chanel stayed with Riley all night. He awoke at seven and stared at Eileen Crosley's phone number on the magazine he had left on the nightstand on top of his draft notice beside the Olan Mills shot of Claire in the frame that formerly held his graduation photo.

He was still in love with Claire and always would be. She was his wife and the mother of his child. He could never have feelings for any woman as complete or as deep as his were for her. He thought of Claire strolling Ben up the street to meet him walking home from work in Sikeston and the tenderness of her kiss when she greeted him. He felt her presence as if she had fallen asleep on his arm after an hour of love making. He ached to hold her, to caress her, to make love to her again. As vivid as they were, these memories were his past. His future was war. In three weeks he would report for duty. Basic training meant eight weeks of strenuous calisthenics, hand-to-hand bayonet-fighting drills, "dirty fighting" classes, machine gun and barbed wire infiltration courses, runs over combat style obstacle courses, and speed marches. Training designed to turn peaceful civilians into hardened warriors who hated Japs and Germans and who were ready to die for their country.

After basic came a month of specialized training, then, certainly by year's end, Riley would be in battle. And inevitably a bullet, grenade, or bomb would find him. He knew the sleep of death would be permanent and peaceful. He chose not to consider that the act of dying might be agonizingly painful, or that the instrument intended to kill him might blow off an arm or a leg and leave his mutilated body functioning for years in agony. The only bad side to dying he considered was that he and Ben would never know each other. His consolation was that Nora and Frank would be loving parents and even though Claire and he would be gone, Ben would have a home.

So, Riley's loyalty to Claire's memory struggled with his desire for the company of a woman in the short time remaining until his going into combat to meet his doom. *Claire would not want me to be alone during these last few weeks, and Eileen would welcome my company—if I don't burden her with my past.* Hands shaking, he lit a Lucky and dialed MU8-6400.

"It's chicken soup and salad for us tonight," Eileen, barefooted, wearing white shorts and a blue sleeveless blouse, her hair pulled back in a ponytail, said when she kissed Riley at the door. "We can't eat out three nights in a row. Make yourself comfortable for a few minutes while I put everything together."

Riley returned the kiss with a breezy "Hope the soup is as good as the omelet you fixed Monday night," walked past the hot kitchen to the couch, kicked off his shoes and loosened the top button of his shirt, grateful for what little fresh air came through the open window.

"Omelets are my specialty," Eileen said, "and eggs are free — at least mine are."

"So, it took a week after you met me to prepare supper for me," Riley said. "And after one meal we went back to eating out."

"Stop complaining!" Eileen laughed. "I didn't want you to learn the limits of my cooking skills too soon."

Frank Sinatra's *This Love of Mine* was playing softly and the stack of records near the phonograph promised an evening of romantic music.

Riley had showered at his apartment after his last day at Vincent Publishing, and had splashed Old Spice on his freshly shaved face. The small scar on his chin from an encounter with a table edge as a four-year-old had caught his eye in the bathroom mirror and reminded him that Claire had told him that scar and his heavy eyebrows made him look rugged, and that his blue-green eyes were the kindest she had ever seen. As he listened to Sinatra, visions of Claire once again flashed in his head.

"Soup's on," Eileen said as she placed two steaming bowls on the coffee table in front of the couch and motioned for Riley to sit beside her.

"Let's eat our soup while it's hot and have our salad later."

"Delicious!" Riley said after the first spoonful. "Reminds me of my Mother's."

"This soup is my mother's," Eileen confessed. "I brought back a quart when I visited her last Saturday. I worked until five, so I needed something I could prepare in a hurry."

"Hmm," Riley said. "You can make omelets but not soup. Looks like I reached the end of your cooking skills Monday."

"Shut up," Eileen laughed. "I may surprise you with something else I prepare in a week or two."

When they finished the soup, Eileen picked up the spoons and bowls and said, "Why don't you put on the next record while I toss the salad."

"Anything you want to hear?"

"I like everything Sinatra sings. Play the one on top."

The One I Love Belongs to Somebody Else was on top of the stack. *I'll Never Smile Again* was next. After rejecting those two and one more, Riley chose *I Could Make You Care*. As soon as the music started, Eileen abandoned salad preparation, glided over to Riley, put her hands on his shoulders and started to sing along.

In a space much too small for dancing, the couple swayed in place to the music. As the song ended, Eileen stood on tiptoes, kissed Riley, and said, "Let's skip the salad and dance."

Riley pushed the couch hard against the window,

inverted the coffee table and placed it and the magazine rack on the couch.

"Here it is," he said, "our own private dance floor."

Riley and Eileen held each other close as they carefully circled the tiny area he had created. The space between them disappeared as Eileen drew him closer and closer to her. Their kisses became more intense. At the end of *Be Careful My Heart*, Eileen whispered, "I love you."

Riley slid his hands under her blouse and felt her shiver when he ran the tips of his fingernails over her back. As his hands approached her hips, Eileen took them in hers, pulled them down to his side and said, "Do you love me?"

Riley pressed his hips against hers. "We've been together practically every night for the past two weeks. I quit my job today so I could spend my last week with you. Let me show you how much I love you."

"Oh, Riley, I fell in love with you our first date. You are smart, handsome, thoughtful, and sweet—the man I've always dreamed of. I want us to make love, just not until our wedding night. I want to make you happy, and I will—when we are married."

Riley released her, stepped back and said, "Married? Honey, we've only known each other two weeks. I haven't met your folks. You haven't met mine. There are lots of things we don't know about each other."

"But if you love me and I love you, does anything else matter?"

Riley lit a cigarette and inhaled deeply. Eileen

wrapped her arms around him from behind and leaned against his shoulder.

"We don't need a church wedding. A justice of the peace could marry us."

"Slow down, honey. Do you think it's wise to get married right now? What if I don't come back from the war?"

"Don't even think about that!"

"We must!" Riley said. "Lots of men won't come back."

Eileen tightened her embrace and began to kiss the back of Riley's neck.

"Let's get married now," she purred.

"Shouldn't we at least wait till I get back from basic training to give you time to prepare?"

"I don't need to prepare, and I don't want to wait eight weeks to show you how much I love you." Eileen was gently stroking his cheek as she nibbled on his ear. "The courthouse is open till one Saturday. We could take the bus to Tullahoma, get the license, spend the rest of the day with Mother and get married on Sunday. Oh, Riley, that would make me so happy. I already have a wedding ring—Mother Grace left me hers. When we're married, we can make love every day until you leave. After you're gone, I'll pray every night for you to return, so we can start all over again."

Riley put out his cigarette, turned around and put his arms around her waist. "And if I say yes, can we make love now?"

"You silly goose. We'll make love on Sunday, and it will be wonderful."

Eileen put her right hand on the bulge in Riley's pants. "If we are engaged," Eileen purred, "I can let you go almost all the way."

Riley pressed his penis hard against her hand and began moving his hips up and down. The rational compass in his brain spun out of control. "Damn, it, Eileen. I need you now!"

"Oh, my darling," Eileen said as she pulled him to the couch on top of her and pressed her body harder against his. "You can have me now—just outside."

Riley's moans became louder as he felt his orgasm building with each thrust against Eileen's leg until his ejaculation exploded in waves of pleasure. He took the cigarette Eileen had lit for him, then felt the warm semen spreading over him. After the explosive release of his sexual tension, his emotions subsided, and his reason partially returned. He had gone to Eileen's apartment hoping for sex and learned that marriage was the price. He had not been certain he wanted to pay that price. In the afterglow of a scintillating sexual experience, however, his first with a partner in over nine months, he began to justify his lust-driven action and chart a course. Eileen was a beautiful woman to whom he was physically attracted, and in superficial ways she reminded him of Claire. All he knew about her, however, was that she, along with an older sister, had been raised on a farm in one of the poorer counties in Tennessee, by a widowed mother who taught school to supplement the meager income she scratched out of the soil. When she was ten years old, her father had been given Sulfa, a "miracle drug" to cure a worsening pneumonia. An hour later he was dead.

A month after graduating from high school, her older sister had eloped to California with a former classmate who had not stuck around to finish. Eileen, restless and bored, had come to Nashville to find a job after a year of college. Riley knew nothing of her beliefs, her hopes or her fears. Her intoxicating scent and her assistance in releasing his pent-up sexual tension, however, had whetted his desire for more, and convinced him that if the price of intercourse were marriage, he would pay it. If Eileen wanted to marry him knowing practically nothing about him except that he was a recent draftee on his way to war and certain death, that was her decision. If they were to marry, however, he could not keep his dead wife and injured child a secret.

Riley's small apartment on the back side of an elderly couple's house, away from the light and noise of 21st Avenue, was dark and quiet at six a.m. when he awoke in a haze and stumbled into the adjoining bathroom containing a commode and a sink, but no tub or shower. A window, blackened with soot from the trains that made Nashville a rail hub, gave him a smudged view of a large oak tree five feet away, and nothing else except a sliver of light, barely enough to allow him to check the time. He couldn't remember walking home from Eileen's. He did remember he was due back at her apartment at seven for their trip to Tullahoma. That left him little time to dress, have a cup of coffee, and check the mail.

When he and Eileen took their seats on the

Greyhound for the two-hour ride, she wove her fingers through his, snuggled up to him and immediately fell asleep. Still drowsy himself, Riley leaned back against his headrest and closed his eyes.

"Honey, can you lotion my feet?" Claire, wrapped in a bath towel large enough to cover her breasts, leaving her slender shoulders exposed, asked.

"That's part of the deal, isn't it?" Riley laughed. "I lotion your feet and you scratch my back."

Claire began brushing her auburn hair at the small dressing table where she sat waiting for Riley. "Does that mean if I want you to scratch my back, I have to lotion your feet?"

"Oh, No," Riley grinned. "I'd scratch your back for free."

Claire leaned up and kissed Riley. "My sweet, sweet husband," she said. "I love you so much."

Jolted out of his dream by a sudden stop, Riley realized he was still full of guilt about marrying Eileen. He still loved Claire and he had no idea how to tell Eileen about Claire. An easy out would be to reveal his unremitting love for Claire and his grief over the loss of his son, which would surely stamp out whatever feelings Eileen had for him. Best to end it now. But Eileen did love him, and in the few months left before he was shipped to Europe, he might come to love her. Certainly not as deeply as he loved Claire—deep enough, however, for them to enjoy their slice of time together. She was intelligent enough, determined, and resourceful and he had to admire her for having stood by her principles and converted his request for sex into a marriage proposal. And she was very pretty.

So, now the task was to delicately disclose his previous marriage, downplaying the intensity of his feelings for Claire, emphasizing that Ben's care had been permanently assumed by Nora, and assuring Eileen that Ben would remain with Nora forever, even if he miraculously returned from the war. He kissed her cheek gently and said, "Wake up, honey. We need to talk."

Eileen smiled at him through half-closed eyes and said, "Let me sleep a little longer. I was so excited thinking about us I couldn't get to sleep until after two, and I had to be up at six so I could call Mother to tell her of our engagement and ask her to arrange for Cousin Ted to pick us up in Tullahoma. Wake me when we get there."

While Eileen slept, Riley reached in his jacket pocket for a cigarette but instead pulled out the letter he had taken out of his mailbox that morning.

June 20, 1942

Dear Riley,

Frank and I wanted to let you know Ben is happy, healthy, and loved. It's such a pleasure to watch him grow—to hear him laugh at anything remotely funny, and to hear his speech progress from single words to simple sentences. He eats well and lets me know by pushing my hand or swatting the cup away when he's had enough. He is completely off the bottle, and only a few weeks away from being potty trained. I hope to accomplish that by the time you visit. Will you be able to come before you report to basic training? If not, please plan to come as soon as you can. Frank and I are eager to see you and I know Ben would like to see his Uncle Riley. You will be amazed at how much he has grown and how independent he wants to be.

We are so grateful for the opportunity to raise this delightful little boy. So far, he has shown no signs of problems from the accident. Frank and I still occasionally pull glass slivers out of his scalp, but not nearly as often as when we first got him. Mrs. Clinton visited him again last week and gave me five dollars to spend on him. Hope to hear from you soon.

Love,
Nora

Re-assured that he had done the right thing, Riley tucked the letter back into its envelope and slid the envelope back into his jacket pocket. He grasped the sleeping Eileen's hand and held it the rest of the way to Tullahoma where Cousin Ted met them for the final leg of their trip to introduce him to his future mother-in-law.

"Eileen tells me you've only known each other a couple of weeks," Mrs. Marjorie Crossley said to Riley after being introduced to him on the front porch of her country home on a dirt road six miles outside the Tullahoma city limits.

"Exactly two weeks," Riley responded.

"Fourteen days and four hours," corrected Eileen, "and we've seen each other almost every one of those fourteen days."

"And you want to get married? Aren't you being a little hasty?"

"No, Mother, we're not," Eileen exclaimed. "We've spent hours and hours together in the last two weeks and have fallen deeply in love. Riley has to report for active-duty next Monday. We don't have time to wait."

"Well, Riley, you have certainly won my daughter's heart. She was so excited when she called me this morning, I could hardly understand her. Now, tell me about yourself. What makes you as wonderful as Eileen claims?"

"Oh, Mother, you can grill Riley at lunch. I want to show him the farm."

"Perhaps your mother needs help in the kitchen," Riley said.

"No, but thanks for offering," Mrs. Crosley said. "I made some deviled eggs this morning. All I have to do is peel a few tomatoes, bake the biscuits, and slice some ham. The table is already set. Why don't you show Riley the barn now, and save the rest of the farm till after we eat? Can you be back in forty-five minutes when the biscuits are ready?"

Eileen led Riley across the road through the gate and

down a narrow path created over the years by thousands of steps going in the same direction, past a small pond to her mother's barn that stood in the middle of a five-acre pasture about a hundred yards from the road. Its age was evident from its listing roof, and the unpainted weathered boards that didn't quite fit together and let the sun stream through. What was left of the winter's supply of hay was stored in the loft. A huge bin of corn with a hand-cranked sheller to strip the kernels from the cobs was visible near the entrance to the barn.

"My admiration for your mother grows by the minute," Riley said. "How does she manage a one hundred sixty-acre farm with all those chickens, cows, and pigs while she teaches school?"

"Mother has an arrangement with Mr. Parks who lives up the road. He supplies the labor and equipment for forty-five percent of the profits. She supplies the land, fertilizer, and seed, gathers, and sells the eggs and milks the two cows, morning and night, every day of the year. She can't take a trip unless one of Mr. Parks' sons agrees to do the daily milking. It is a hard life, and not one for me. That's why I wouldn't consider marrying any boy I knew in school."

A ten-foot wooden ladder hung from a hook a third of the way to the back of the barn. Eileen pulled it down, propped it against the loft floor with sufficient angle to ensure a safe ascent and said, "Let's climb up to the loft so I can show you my favorite hiding place. This ladder looks rickety but it's safe. I've climbed it hundreds of times."

Riley carefully followed Eileen up, accepting her hand to help him onto the bare dusty floor made of ten-inch-wide oak boards showing the marks from the crosscut saw that had produced them. Beginning about ten feet from the front edge of the loft, a dozen or so rows of baled hay stacked four high extended to the back of the loft. The front ten feet contained loose hay to be tossed to the cattle below. The back side of the mound of loose hay provided an invisible, comfortable spot to read, sleep, or just contemplate.

"Here we are in my own private place," Eileen said. "Don't you love it?"

Riley reached for his cigarettes. Eileen stayed his hand.

"Not here," she said. "This hay is dry as dust and would catch fire from any spark. Would you like a stick of Juicy Fruit?"

She unwrapped the gum and pushed the entire stick into his mouth. Then Riley stretched out on the hay and listened to the clucking of the chickens in the distance and the soft mooing of the cows that had wandered into the barn, expecting a feeding at an unusual hour. Eileen lay down beside him with her head on his shoulder and began to stroke his cheek. Several minutes passed before Riley spoke.

"What I tried to tell you on the bus is I've been married before."

"What!!!"

Eileen bolted upright and glared at him.

"Don't tell me you're divorced!"

Riley sat up, faced her, and pulled his knees tightly to his chest.

"No, I'm not divorced. I'm a widower."

Eileen pulled away from him. "I can't believe this! What was her name? How long were you married? How did she die?"

"Claire and I were married a little over a year," Riley said, bracing himself for a further reaction. "She and her father were killed instantly when a truck ran into us at an intersection near Sikeston, Missouri. I was driving."

"You were driving, they were killed. Were you hurt?"

"Miraculously, I was not—only a few scratches and bruises. I wasn't even admitted to the hospital."

"This is shocking! How old was she? What did she look like? Why have you not told me about her before?"

"Because it's painful to talk about," Riley said, "and until last night, I didn't think there was any reason to tell you. What difference does it make what she looked like or how old she was? She's dead and gone. You will never see her."

Eileen's voice was trembling. "Because you are my first love," she sobbed, "and I wanted to be your first. I can't stand to know there was someone before me who may have been prettier or smarter than me. And I need to know whether you're over her."

After her sobs subsided, Eileen continued in a weak voice. "Do you still love her?"

Riley got to his knees, wiped Eileen's eyes, and said, "I loved Claire, and it has taken me a long time to get over losing her. Please believe me, I am over her. You are beautiful, Eileen, and the woman I am going to marry. Nothing else matters."

Eileen searched for his lips, kissed them, then buried her head in his chest. The couple lay silent for a moment or two before Eileen raised her head and said, "I love you so much, Riley. If I can't be your first wife, I'll be your best wife. As you said, she's gone, so let's not talk about her or your life with her anymore."

Riley was relieved Eileen had commanded him not to drop the other shoe. Silently they climbed down the ladder and walked back to the house hand in hand.

"Did Riley meet Elsie and Bossie?" Mrs. Crosley asked without looking up from the tomato she was peeling. "They always show up looking for an ear of corn when anyone comes to the barn, even if it's not milking time."

"They are such a nuisance," Eileen said. "We went up into the loft to avoid them. I see lunch is ready. Did you save some tomatoes for me to take back?"

"I put as many as I could in that sack for you. And a dozen eggs as well." Mrs. Crosley had put down her knife and wiped her hands on her apron. As she turned toward the table with the plate of tomatoes in hand, she noticed Eileen's puffy eyes.

"Have you been crying?"

"No, I just got some dust in my eyes. Let's eat."

Iced tea, a plate loaded with ham and a basket of hot biscuits were already on the table. Mrs. Crosley said a quick Grace and passed the tomatoes and pickles. The trio ate silently a yard away from the wood-burning stove Mrs. Crosley used every day to cook food and to heat the flat irons she used to press clothes, and that helped warm the house in the winter. Riley looked at the Farmer's Almanac turned to the month of June 1942, which shared a nail on the wall behind the stove with a fly swatter bearing the logo of Wayne Feeds. Directly across from him, above and behind Mrs. Crosley's diminutive head hung a reproduction of a painting of the head of Christ. Mrs. Crosley was barely five feet tall and could not have weighed over one hundred pounds. Her graying hair was pulled up in a bun, and rimless spectacles sat on the bridge of her nose. She was a quiet person and had a serenity Riley found appealing. She seemed at peace with herself and accepting of the hard life fate had dealt her. He wanted to learn more about her. He did not, however, want to start the conversation.

"I told Judge Stanton we'd be at his house at 1:30 tomorrow," Eileen finally said, "to give everybody time to have lunch after church. I'm sorry Gail won't be able to make it. Do you think Aunt Espa and Uncle Sammy would like to come?"

"I think your wedding is so sudden, you'd better keep the ceremony private," Mrs. Crosley said. Catching Eileen's eye, she continued, "You would tell me if you were expecting, wouldn't you?"

"Mother!!" Eileen gasped. "Of course, I would. You don't think I am, do you?"

"You are in such a rush to get married; most people will think you are."

Eileen swallowed hard. "Well," she said, "I do have to get married quickly, but not for that reason. It's because if I don't get married now, I won't be able to for at least two months, and maybe not till after the war. Riley might not be able to leave camp to come home to marry me before he's shipped out. Can't people understand that?"

Mrs. Crosley got up from the table to put her hands on her daughter's trembling shoulders. She kissed Eileen's cheek and said, "Don't cry, sweetheart. I believe you, and people will know soon enough you didn't have to get married. When they get to know Riley, they'll understand why you rushed to the altar. Riley, Eileen told me you have a mother and a sister you are close to. Do they know you're getting married tomorrow?"

"I haven't told them. They wouldn't be able to come. Mother is too frail to travel this far and my sister has a family she can't leave. I'll write and tell them about it."

"Does your mother have a phone?" Mrs. Crosley asked. "Why don't you call her right after lunch, while Eileen and I have a talk? Every mother has a right to know when her child is getting married. Remember, this is a party line, so don't say anything you wouldn't want four neighbors to hear."

Riley knew he should call his mother, but he hadn't decided on his story. Should he be breezy, "Hi, Mother, I'm getting married tomorrow. Sorry you can't come." Or should he be matter of fact, "Mother, I met this wonderful woman and we decided to get married before I report for duty." He knew his mother would not be happy he had made such an important decision without talking with her or giving her an opportunity to approve Eileen.

"That's a great idea," he said, "I'll call her tomorrow. She always goes to see her cousin Charlotte on Saturday afternoons."

"Better do it tonight," Mrs. Crosley said. "Tomorrow is going to be a busy day."

Caving to the pressure, Riley called his mother after supper while Eileen and Mrs. Crosley were upstairs seeing what clothes Eileen could take back with her.

"Yes, Mother," Riley said in response to her castigation about his tardiness in calling, "I know it's been a few weeks since I called. I've been busy. I visited Nora and Ben a couple of weeks ago. Didn't Nora tell you?"

"Yes, I know I should have called sooner, but I'm calling now. I have some news."

"No, Good news. I'm getting married."

"Tomorrow."

"Her name is Eileen Crosley. She's from Tullahoma. I met her on the bus coming home from Memphis."

"I can't bring her to see you, Mother. I have to report for duty a week from Monday."

"No, Mother, it can't wait till I get back from basic training. I might not get leave."

"MOTHER!!! How could you say such a thing?"

"Well, it's not that. Besides, we wouldn't know in two weeks anyway."

"I'm sorry I've disappointed you and I'm sorry you feel that way, Mother, but marrying Eileen now is important to me. I'll send you a picture of her and bring her to see you as soon as the Army lets me."

"Bye, Mother, I love you, too."

"Your mother seems so down to earth," Riley said as he and Eileen sat on the porch steps under the stars after Mrs. Crosley had retired at her customary 8:45 p.m. Far from the city, except for a thousand twinkling points of light overhead and the soft glow of the Milky Way, the sky was black.

"She is practical and kind—and generous. She wouldn't let me pay the long-distance charges when I called my mother."

"Your offer to gather the eggs and fetch a bucket of water from the well charmed her, and she was speechless when you got up and started clearing the table after supper. All the men around here go to the living room to smoke and talk after meals and leave cleaning up to the women. The only reservation she had about you disappeared when I assured her, we haven't slept together. I didn't tell her you tempted me."

"So, my previous marriage doesn't bother her?"

"Not at all. Uncle Earl lost his first wife in childbirth and has remarried."

Eileen snuggled closer to him.

"It's not as if you have a brood of children I'd have to put up with."

Riley found the Big Dipper overhead. Eileen's eyes followed his.

"Do you ever think about what's out there?" he asked.

"Besides God? Just the stars He made. And, of course, Heaven."

"And where is Heaven?"

"Out there with God, where all good people, like my daddy go when they die."

"And you expect to see your dad in Heaven when you die?"

"I most certainly do. And my Mother, too. Don't you expect to see your loved ones in Heaven when you die?"

"There went a shooting star," Riley said. "And there's another."

"God must be glad we're getting married," Eileen said. "Oh, Riley, I'm so happy."

Riley continued counting the stars visible around the Big Dipper while Eileen leaned against his shoulder with her arm around him and her scent performing its magic. He thought about the fifty stars he and Claire, only a few months before, had counted in the same spot in the sky. Of course, they had the benefit of Claire's father's high-powered binoculars. He fleetingly wished he could believe in Heaven with Claire waiting there for him, but he shook that thought away and inhaled deeply before speaking. His breath came out in a long sigh.

"There's one other thing I need to tell you, Eileen. I don't have a brood of children, but I do have a son."

Eileen jerked up. Even in the dim light Riley could see the dismay in her eyes. Then she pushed away from him as if he were a leper and burst into tears. "You have a son!" she shouted. "What else have you not told me?"

Without waiting for an answer, she ran into the house, slamming the door behind her. Riley remained glued to the steps, processing Eileen's reaction. He had expected surprise, perhaps even shock, but not instant, complete rejection. *That's it. She's gone. Maybe I can hitch a ride into town if I wait till dawn. Wonder if I can get a little sleep on the swing.*

"What happened?" Mrs. Crosley asked when she stuck her head out of the door a minute or two later. "Eileen's histrionics woke me up. She has locked herself in her room."

"Something I said upset her. I probably should leave. I would like to leave her a note."

"Don't be silly," Mrs. Crosley said as she walked toward Riley, tightening the sash on her robe. "I'm not driving you to town at this time of night. You wouldn't have any place to stay. You probably haven't experienced an Eileen tantrum before. I have. She often storms off to sulk when things haven't gone her way."

Mrs. Crosley hung the kerosene lantern she had brought with her on an empty hook that had once held a bird feeder and said, "She loves you very much, Riley. When we talked after lunch, she was gushing about how good you made her feel, and how happy she has been since she met you. And how glad she was that you like me. You probably hurt her feelings. Give her a few minutes. She'll be back. I'll leave the lantern with you. I'm going back to bed."

Riley smoked two Lucky's while he waited, flicking his ashes off the side of the porch, and stubbing the butts into the cracked cup Mrs. Crosley had given him when he first arrived. He desperately needed a drink of water, but didn't want to risk missing Eileen, should she return. Half an hour after she stormed away, she did return, having re-applied her makeup and brushed her hair. The moon had risen and bathed the porch in a luminescence that made her look ethereal. Riley stood up to greet her. She brushed past him, keeping her head turned away, took a seat on the swing, and began studying her nails. Finally, she turned toward Riley and said, "Did you marry Claire because you had to?"

"No."

"Were you ever engaged to anyone other than Claire?"

"No."

"Did you ever sleep with another girl?"

"No."

"So, you don't have any other children to support."

"No, and I haven't robbed any banks either. Ben is my only child and when you're through giving me the third degree, I'll tell you about him, if you want to listen."

"I'm not sure whether I do or not. I don't know if I can trust you, Riley. I want to trust you. I just can't understand why you didn't tell me all this the night we decided to get married, or at least when you told me about your wife."

"As I said earlier, until we decided to get married, I

didn't think it important to tell you about either Claire or Ben. I tried to tell you about them on the bus this morning, but you wanted to sleep. I was going to tell you about Ben when we were in the loft before lunch, but you said you didn't want to talk about my life with Claire anymore. At least you've learned about my son in time to call off the wedding—if you want to."

"But not before I fell in love with you," Eileen sniffled. "I wouldn't have let myself fall in love if I'd known you had a child. Plus, now that I know you have a constant reminder of your first wife, I'll never know if you have really gotten over her, and I'll always wonder if there are other things you haven't told me."

Riley sat down on the steps, shaking his head, trying to decide whether to patch things up with Eileen, or go to bed, hitch hike to Tullahoma in the morning and catch the bus back to Nashville. He walked over to the swing and sat down beside her.

"The accident that killed Claire fractured Ben's skull and no one thought he would live. While he was recuperating, he needed constant attention, which I could not give him. My sister, who is married and has a little girl, offered to take him. When the war started in December, I knew if I were drafted, I couldn't care for him, so I asked Nora and her husband to take him."

"Take him till you got back from the war?"

"No, take him permanently and raise him as their child. It broke my heart to do that, I just couldn't think of any other way to provide for him."

The beginning of a smile began to form around

Eileen's lips. She leaned her head against Riley's shoulder. "Are you telling me that if we get married, he won't be living with us when you get home from the war?"

"That's right."

"You are sure?"

"Yes," Riley said. "It's set in stone. Even if I make it through the war, Ben will continue to live with Nora and Frank, and I'll be an uncle to him."

"Cross your heart and hope to die?" Eileen said.

"I haven't heard anyone say that in a long time," Riley said. "But if it will make you happy, yes."

Eileen put her arms around him and tilted her head back to kiss him.

"And when you get back," she said, "we'll have a baby of our own."

Ethel Eileen Crosley and Whitcomb Riley McHaney were married on June 14, 1942 at 1:40 p.m. at the home of the Honorable Elmer Stanton in Tullahoma, Tennessee. Eileen wore the cream-colored dress she had bought for her aborted Memphis weekend. Riley wore the only suit he owned, a dark blue one Claire had picked out for him to wear for Ben's christening. Marjorie Crosley and the Judge's wife were the only attendees. Eileen's cousin Ted drove the couple back to Nashville early that evening with a picnic basket Mrs. Crosley had prepared for their first meal alone as husband and wife.

Eileen spread the cotton cloth she found inside the basket over her kitchen table and lit candles on either side of the small bouquet of roses Judge Stanton's wife had given her at the wedding. Their flickering light reflected in the small mirror by the door, emphasizing the closeness of their quarters.

"Would you rather put on a record or listen to *Sunday Serenade* on WSM?" Riley asked.

"Whatever you want, darling. I have you and that's all I want."

Eileen disappeared into the bedroom as Riley turned on the radio. She returned wearing a sheer black baby-doll nightie edged with lace.

"I went straight to Cain-Sloan when I saw the picture of Rita Hayworth wearing this in *Life* magazine," she said, twirling to expose her black lace panties. I had to have one for my wedding night. I wish I could have afforded the negligee that went with it. Do you like it?"

"I love it!" Riley said. "You look better in it than Rita Hayworth did."

"Oh, Riley," Eileen said, reaching up to kiss him for the hundredth time that day, "I love you so much. I want tonight to be perfect."

Taking Riley's hand, she led him to the bedroom where, to the music of Sammy Kaye and the light scent of Chanel, they made love. Riley's climax came with the same intensity as if Claire's legs were wrapped around him and her hips were moving in rhythm with his. The feeling of intimacy was just as it had been with Claire. Riley lay there with his eyes closed, deeply satisfied, until *It Had to Be You* ended. Then he sat up, lit a Lucky and in vain tried to peer through the wall of war that blocked his view of the future. Frustrated by his inability to do so, he stubbed out his cigarette and said, "I'm starved. Let's eat."

With Eileen constantly reaching across the table to touch Riley's arm or stroke the back of his hand, the couple ate a candlelight supper of deviled eggs, sliced tomatoes, sweet pickles, ham, and Mrs. Crosley's biscuits. Then leaving the table un-cleared, they put on a record and swayed back and forth to the music until the song ended and Eileen, removing the needle from the record as she passed by, guided them back into her bedroom.

One week later Riley reported to Camp Forrest for induction.

"You look great." Nora said as she hugged Riley when he met her at the Visitor Center at Camp Shelby, Mississippi on the Saturday after he completed his eight weeks of basic training. "You must have gained ten pounds. I thought basic training was supposed to make you lean and mean."

"The army trains you hard and feeds you well," Riley laughed. "I'm so glad you and Frank could come up."

"It's fortunate Biloxi is only an hour's drive away," Nora said. "Otherwise, we could not have brought Ben and Annie."

Riley knelt on one knee to be face to face with Ben, took off his garrison cap and handed it to his son. Ben shook his head sharply and backed away. Riley took a piece of bubble gum from his pocket and held it in his hand in front of Ben. Ben took a step toward the gum, looked up at Nora, then back at Riley and said, "Mama, won't let me take gum from strangers."

Nora stepped in. "Ben, honey, this is your Uncle Riley. He's not a stranger. He is your friend."

Ben flashed a smile, revealing two rows of small white teeth and one large dimple. He took the gum and darted to the safety of Nora's leg before he carefully unwrapped it, handed the paper to Riley, and put the gum in his mouth before saying, "Thank you for the gum, Mr. Soldier, can I wear your army hat?"

Riley handed Ben his cap again and said, "He has such chubby little legs. How much does he weigh?"

"About 25 pounds," Nora replied. "Which is about right for a 2½ year old boy who stands 26 inches tall. He drinks most of our milk ration, and he loves oatmeal. By the way, where's Eileen?"

"She's on her way. It's a ten-hour ride from Nashville, which means her bus won't get here till after you leave. She can't stay on the base overnight. Fortunately, I found a room in town. I have a 24-hour pass beginning at 1700 hours, so I'll catch a ride into Hattiesburg and meet her at the station. We'll only have one night together. I have to be back on base early Sunday night."

"That's a long trip for a short visit," Nora said. "Too bad we won't get to meet her. I'm sorry you weren't able to bring her to Memphis before we moved to Biloxi."

Riley stood up and brushed himself off.

"Everything happened so quickly, I didn't even get a chance to tell Mother about her until the day before we married. A week later, I was in the Army."

"Your wedding certainly caught Mother and me by surprise. She was disappointed you didn't give her enough notice so she could attend. I know the war is causing couples who have decided to marry to rush things up, but you only knew this woman for two weeks. It wasn't like you'd been going together for months and suddenly got your draft notice. You can't know very much about her."

"I know she's beautiful," Riley said, "and I did get to meet her mother, whom I liked a lot. Aren't women supposed to become like their mothers as they grow older?"

Riley took a photo of Eileen out of his wallet and handed it to his sister.

"She's very pretty," Nora said. "I still can't understand why you married so quickly. If it's true love, she would have waited for you."

"Hah," Riley said. "I'll share Eileen's logic with you. She wanted us to marry before I reported, because there might not be another opportunity before I shipped out. And once I got overseas, who knows."

"Oh, well, what's done is done. What have you told her about Ben and Claire?"

"Everything. She knows Ben is yours now."

"To her immense relief, I suspect," Nora said.

Riley had been watching his son amuse himself by digging into the ground around Nora's feet with his fingers and wiping his dirty hands on his shirt, his light brown hair, much the color of Riley's, glistening in the sunlight. His eyes were brown with flecks of green and yellow. Much like Claire's. After a few minutes, Ben lost interest in the dirt and toddled toward Frank who was keeping half an eye on Annie while watching off-duty soldiers play touch football on that hot August day. Riley watched his son stop midway, squat down, pick up a shiny rock, then run toward Frank shouting "Rock, Daddy. See pretty rock."

His heart pierced, Riley stuffed Eileen's picture back into his wallet before turning toward his sister.

"Is there anything you'd like to see or do?" he asked.

"Can we drive into Hattiesburg and have lunch?"

"Unfortunately, no. I can give you a walking tour of the unrestricted portions of the camp and we can have lunch at the canteen, but I can't leave until 1700 hours. What time do you need to start for home?"

"Before then. The children will be worn out and cranky if we wait till five to start back to Biloxi."

The five of them walked around the camp for an hour before stopping at the canteen for a Coke and a hamburger. Riley tried to pick his son up twice, only to have Ben wriggle away. He felt a twinge of jealousy when Ben wrapped one arm around Frank's leg to steady himself while he tilted his head as far back as he could to get the last drop of juice from the bottle Nora had brought for him. Handing the bottle to Nora, Ben said, "More juice, mama."

"More juice, mama, PLEASE," Frank corrected.

"More later, Ben. Go with Daddy while I talk to Uncle Riley."

Then she turned to Riley and said, "Are you okay? You look pale."

"I'm fine," he said, trying to regain his composure. "I must have eaten lunch too fast."

Nora squeezed his arm. "You don't have to hide your feelings from me. I know it was hard for you to give Ben up. It is still hard for me to believe you could actually do it."

Riley signaled with his hand that he did not want to respond.

"Where will the Army send you next?" Nora asked.

"My unit is reporting to Fort Benning on Tuesday. We'll pack up Monday and they'll truck us to Benning the next day."

Riley wiped his face with his shirt sleeve and lit a Lucky, his first since lunch. He had been trying to stay under a pack a day, which was difficult when cigarettes were either cheap or free to soldiers, and he often needed the calming effect a good smoke gave.

"Have you heard of the *Stars and Stripes?*" Riley said. "It's the newspaper the Army publishes for the troops. The European edition is printed in London and my commanding officer told me I may get assigned to work on the paper once I get sent over. It's a special assignment—like playing in the Army Band. If I get it, I could stay out of the fighting indefinitely, which would be great. Otherwise, the next stop after Benning is either Italy or North Africa."

"What about Eileen? Will she be with you at Fort Benning?"

"Not at first. Maybe later if I can find her a place to stay. She would have to give up her great job. Benning is about three hundred fifty miles from Nashville and there is good train service, so we can visit often. And she writes every day."

After an hour of chasing squirrels and trying to catch butterflies and grasshoppers, a tired Ben did not resist when Riley picked him up to carry him back to the Visitor Center. He put his arms around Riley's neck and let Riley hold him without complaint. The sound of his son's gentle breathing and the feel of Ben's warm body against his triggered a wave of memories which for the thousandth time, brought remorse over having caused the accident that had changed their lives so dramatically. And for the thousandth time Riley told himself that giving Ben to Nora was the right thing to do. By the time they reached Frank's car, Ben was asleep. Riley handed his son to his sister, kissed the top of the sleeping boy's head, wiped his own cheeks dry and waved a silent good-bye.

Riley arrived at Fort Benning the following Tuesday and began training to be a rifleman in the 109th Infantry Regiment of the 28th Division of the United States Army, all the while hoping to become part of the team that brought the news to servicemen throughout the United States and in the war zones in Europe and in the Pacific.

September of 1944 found everyone jubilant about the changing tide in the war in Europe and apprehensive about the upcoming invasion of Japan. Allied forces were pushing the Germans out of France. Paris had been liberated on August 25, and the Russian Army was hammering the Germans on the Eastern Front. Riley thought it ironic that he had missed two rotations overseas, only to be ordered into action in the final stages of the war in Europe. No matter, he shrugged. If he survived the Germans, the Japanese would get him. He felt like a condemned man who had received two last minute stays of execution, allowing him to live another year, yet knowing that unless a pardon came in the form of an assignment to the *Stars and Stripes*, the next execution date would not be passed. Receiving his orders to report to Camp Shelby again, which was for the sole purpose of refreshing his combat skills, was the same as the warden's telling him the Governor had denied his pardon. He hoped to make the most of the few weeks he had left.

"I let the landlady know we're leaving before the end of the month," Riley said as he put cornflakes and milk on the table while Eileen, still in her robe, hurriedly made up the bed and got out the dress and shoes she planned to wear to work that day. "My leave begins on the 26th and I don't have to report to Camp Shelby until the second of October..."

"That's almost a week," Eileen said. "Let's go somewhere romantic and exciting."

"I thought we'd spend two or three nights in New Orleans with Aunt T, then..."

"We're going to New Orleans and staying with your aunt? How awful!"

"You think it's 'awful' for us to visit my aunt before I go to war?"

Eileen grabbed his hand and said, "I didn't mean that honey. I just wanted us to have a romantic time alone before we are separated."

Riley was not mollified.

"You know how hard it is to find hotel rooms these days, and how expensive they are. Aunt T lives in a great neighborhood near Tulane and goes to work every day. We'll have plenty of time alone. It will be fun to take the trolley from her house to the French Quarter."

"I want to go to New Orleans, but I really want us to stay in a hotel at least part of the time. Oh, Riley, we can afford it. I've saved a lot of the money I've earned since we got married. We can make it the honeymoon we never had."

"How much do you have?"

"Two hundred and sixty-four dollars," Eileen beamed.

"Wow, that much?" he said. "Well, maybe we can spend the night we get to New Orleans in a hotel, then go to Aunt T's for two more days."

Eileen stood in the doorway frowning. Riley poured milk on his cereal and began to eat.

"Only three days in New Orleans? "she said. "Why not the whole time?"

Riley continued eating. "We need to go to Biloxi

for a couple of days," he said between bites, "so you can meet my sister and Ben."

"So that's what this is all about. You'd rather see Ben than spend a romantic week with me."

"Don't say that, Eileen. We've had a wonderful seven months together since this apartment became available. It's been like an extended honeymoon. Plus, you and I'll have ten days together after Camp Shelby before I ship out. I want to see Ben once more before I go. I probably won't come back, you know, and I want you to meet him."

Eileen walked over to Riley's chair and massaged his shoulders.

"Of course you'll come back," she said. "I'll be praying for you every day. God will answer my prayers."

Eileen sat down and very deliberately ate her cereal. Having no idea what was on her mind, Riley said nothing. Eileen finished, went to the sink, rinsed her empty bowl, turned to Riley and said, "Alright, I'll go to Biloxi with you. Just don't make any promises that I'll visit them while you're gone."

The train from New Orleans to Biloxi had more soldiers than seats and Riley had to stand at the end of the car by the toilet and luggage racks until they reached Slidell. Out the window, he could see Lake Pontchartrain. If he leaned forward and looked toward Eileen, through the haze of cigarette smoke, he could see her perfectly coiffed hair, her yellow sun dress, which stood out in the sea of khaki and green, and the disdainful look on her face when passing soldiers leered or whistled at her.

"They must think I'm a dance hall girl," Eileen said when Riley was able to join her at the Slidell stop. "I decided if you didn't get to sit with me soon, I would come stand with you."

"Relax, honey. What's wrong with being admired? No one pinched you or tried to kiss you."

"No," she said, "but they ogled me as if I were a call girl."

"These guys are headed overseas and won't have an opportunity to be with or even see a pretty woman for months. Why not cut them a little slack?"

"A little slack!" Eileen hissed. "If I give these guys an inch, they'll take a mile. Swap seats with me. I don't want to be on the aisle."

An hour and twenty-five minutes later, Frank hailed them at the station in Biloxi. After exchanging hellos, they got into Frank's car and listened to his spiel about the wonders of Biloxi until they pulled up to a small house, clad with asbestos shingles and wooden storm shutters, a block off the coast road.

"Here we are," Frank said. "Nora timed lunch for your arrival. I have to get right back on my route, so I'll eat and run."

With Ben and Annie running ahead of her, Nora came out to greet them as soon as Frank's car squealed to a stop. She ran her hands through her hair when she saw Eileen for the first time and quickly wiped them on her apron.

"Nora, meet Eileen," Riley said as he opened the car door. "Eileen this is my sister, Nora."

"Good to meet you," Nora said, glancing at Eileen before giving Riley a bear hug, "I'm so glad to see you, soldier boy. Y'all talk to Annie and Ben while I get lunch on the table."

Annie jumped into Frank's arms as soon as he held them out. As they started toward the house, she tried to pull his hat off his head. Running behind them, Ben said, "Wait for me, daddy."

Nora grabbed Ben and diverted him into the living room. "Ben, why don't you read to your Uncle Riley and your Aunt Eileen," she said, "while mommy gets lunch ready."

"I see Dick and Jane books on the table," Riley said. "Can you read them to me?"

Eileen was incredulous. "He's reading at four?"

"Yes, within two weeks after he started going to Miss Poole's kindergarten this fall, he was reading the books they have for the children. We weren't surprised. Annie did the same thing when she started kindergarten. Miss Poole encourages early reading."

Ben crawled into Riley's lap on the biscuit-colored easy chair that cradled the two of them. Feeling a surge of love for his son, Riley began stroking the top of his head. "Dick sees Jane," Ben began. "Jane sees Spot. See Spot run. See Spot catch the ball."

Eileen sat stiffly on the sofa. When Ben, bursting with pride, finished the first book, Riley said, "Very good! Now pick out another book and go read to your Aunt Eileen."

Ben slid off his father's lap, chose a second book and

cautiously approached Eileen, who had wrapped her arms tightly around her body as if to guard against a chill.

"That's all right," Eileen said. "I heard him read to you."

Before Riley could voice his displeasure, Nora called from the kitchen. "Lunch is ready. Anybody need to wash up?"

"Franks and sauerkraut make a tasty dish," Riley said as he finished his serving and swapped his plate for the barely-touched one in front of Eileen."

"We call it weenies and freedom cabbage now," Nora laughed—just like they did in the First War. "Eileen, can I get you something else to eat?"

"I'm not very hungry," Eileen said. "I ate cheese and crackers on the train. Must have spoiled my appetite. I will have another glass of tea."

Frank refilled her glass and grabbed his hat, "Gotta go. I'll try to get home in time for supper, but don't wait if I'm not here by six. Good to meet you, Eileen."

"Bye, honey," Nora said, walking him to the door. "We'll feed the children at five and wait for you before we eat. Get here when you can."

While Riley cleared the table, Nora put a recalcitrant Ben down for his nap.

"Big girls don't take naps," Annie proclaimed as she intently brushed her doll's hair while sitting in the small rocker that had been Nora's as a child. Eileen disappeared into the bathroom off the kitchen. Ten minutes later, Nora was back.

"While I was watching Ben fall asleep," Nora said, "I

decided Frank is right, his nose and eyes are like yours and his mouth and chin are like Claire's. He's such a handsome little boy. Frank and I feel blessed that we can raise him. Thank you again."

Riley didn't know what to say. "You're welcome," or "It was nothing," did not seem appropriate. He didn't want to display his sorrow to anyone—certainly not Nora. He simply nodded his head.

Nora reached for her purse and said, "I'll walk Annie down to the little grocery at the corner of First Street and see if they have coffee and sugar. It's only two blocks away. I'll be back in half an hour."

"Will Ben be cranky when he wakes up?"

"Oh, I should be back before he wakes up. If I'm not, get him to show you how he can tie his shoes. Or take him outside and let him ride Annie's old tricycle up and down the sidewalk and wave at soldiers. He loves to do that. Just don't let him go into the street."

"Yes, ma'am! Any other orders?"

"Just have a good time with him. He's a playful child. He laughs a lot and is interested in everything, but he's not very careful. Frank and I think he doesn't pay any attention to his surroundings. His injuries do not appear to have affected his learning and haven't made him timid. Just the opposite, he doesn't seem to have any sense of danger."

"I need to re-do my nails," Eileen called out from the bathroom, "but I can't find any polish remover."

"Don't use the stuff," Nora hollered back. "I'll get you some at the store, if they carry it."

Riley started to pull a dollar from his billfold, then stopped "Why don't I go to the store? Annie looks like she is having a good time with her dolls and I need some cigarettes. What else do you need?"

"Just coffee and sugar. Let me give you my ration book and some money—and thanks."

"The ration book is all I need," Riley said. "Be back soon."

"You'd better go talk to your wife," Nora said the moment Riley returned with coffee and nail polish remover, but no sugar. "She's in the bathroom fuming."

"How come?"

"Well, shortly after you left, she asked where you were. I told her you had gone to the grocery for me and would be right back. I offered her another glass of tea and suggested she and I have a talk while the children were quiet. She acted like she didn't hear me, sat down on the couch, and began flipping through an old Sears Roebuck catalogue. She was tapping her right foot so vigorously the floor shook. 'Is something bothering you?' I said. 'You bet something is,' she snapped. 'We're leaving as soon as Riley gets back.'

"Then she stormed out of the room and started banging her suitcase around. Ben woke up and asked if Aunt Eileen was having a bad dream."

"I'm sorry you had to suffer through an Eileen tantrum," Riley said. "Fortunately, she doesn't have them often."

Eileen cracked open the bathroom door when Riley knocked. She was furiously reapplying her makeup while looking into the tiny mirror over the sink.

"There's not enough light in here," she pouted. "I can't see what I'm doing."

"Why are you upset?"

"Why did you go off and leave me alone with your sister?" she said, catching his eye in the mirror. "She doesn't like me. All she wants to talk about is Ben."

"That's not true, honey. Nora likes you. She wants to get to know you better. To learn more about you."

"No, she doesn't. All she wants to do is talk about Ben, what he's done and how smart he is and how much he looks like Claire. I don't want to hear about that. When you asked me to marry you and finally got around to telling me about Ben, you said you were going to be his uncle, not his father."

"Yes, I did," Riley said. "Nothing's changed."

"Yes, it has," Eileen shouted. "You are acting like his father, not his uncle. You lied to me, Riley."

"Go to Hell!" Riley said as he slammed the bathroom door and went to the living room where Nora was playing Go Fish with Annie and Ben. He stared out the window at the huge water oak whose branches, laden with Spanish moss, scraped the ground as it shaded the front porch. He patted his pockets for his cigarettes and remembered he had forgotten to get any.

"Damn," he muttered under his breath.

"Careful with your language," Nora admonished. "Children."

"Let me have your nines," Annie demanded of Ben.

"Go Fish," Ben giggled. "Mama, let me have your threes."

"Come play with us, Uncle Riley," Annie said. "It's more fun with four."

Riley glared at the closed bathroom door, grabbed Nora's pack of wretched Camels and said, "Deal me in."

Eileen emerged from the bathroom about 2:30, having redone her nails and darkened her cheek color and lipstick to match. Go Fish had given way to Eights, a game which Ben had not yet mastered.

"Don't change it to hearts, Ben," Annie pleaded as Ben placed the eight of spades on the discard pile. "Mama will go out."

"But I have three of them," Ben said.

"Game over," Nora discarded her last card and headed for the kitchen. "I have work to do. Riley, do you and Eileen want to take these kids for a walk while I start supper?"

"How about it, Eileen," Riley said. "Are you up for a walk?"

"Not now," Eileen grumbled. "It's too hot outside. You take them. I'll lie down for a while."

When Riley returned from a thirty-minute walk with Annie and Ben, Eileen was still in the bedroom. At 5:30, when Frank came home, she was still there. Riley knocked on the door.

"Supper's ready, honey. Are you joining us?"

"Go on without me," Eileen said. "I'm not very hungry and I need to pack."

"Suit yourself," Riley said. "Frank and I are going out for a beer after supper. Be back about ten."

"Don't expect me to be awake," she yelled.

And she wasn't. At 7:30 the next morning, Eileen caught the train to Nashville to stay with her mother while Riley was at Camp Shelby. Riley hitchhiked the seventy miles to camp.

Camp Shelby was brutal. Since Riley had gone through basic training there a year and a half earlier, the excitement of a new experience was missing. There was nothing to lighten the drudgery or ameliorate the physical exhaustion from the six-week refresher course on becoming a combat ready killing machine. The sergeant's stripes on his shoulder meant nothing to the gunners who were firing live rounds eighteen inches over his head or to the drill instructor who was in his ear yelling, "Move It! Move It! Move It!" as Riley struggled with a forty-pound field pack and an M-1 rifle. The fading thoughts of being assigned to the *Stars and Stripes* and sitting the war out in London no longer mollified him.

On top of that, his emotions were in turmoil. As long as he was at Camp Shelby, he was not on a troop ship heading for Europe. But each day was as arduous, if not as deadly, as being on the battlefield. And he had unfinished business with Eileen. Her behavior at Nora's house, and his reaction, had hung over them like a black cloud their last night at Nora's and the next morning as they sullenly and silently prepared to leave. Neither was ready to talk, let alone, reconcile. The fiasco went unmentioned in their limited correspondence over the next few weeks.

Riley was to meet Eileen in Nashville at the start of his final leave before heading to New York to board a ship for England. He did not want to go off to war with bad feelings between them, and he dreaded spending his last days of freedom trying to thrash things out when he had no idea how. Just as distasteful was the idea of their having nothing to say to each other for ten days. Whatever his fate, he wanted his last leave to be remembered for frivolity and riotous sex—not his wife's stony silence.

On the morning his final leave began, Riley found a seat on the middle car of the Mississippi Central local to Birmingham where he would change to an L&N streamliner for the remainder of the trip. He was glad to have a few hours completely alone. As the train rumbled through the pine forests of eastern Mississippi and into Alabama, he ate the sandwich he had brought with him and the Moon Pie he bought onboard. He sipped a Pepsi while leafing through the issue of *Time* magazine with the picture of Lt. General Omar Bradley on the cover, which was largely about stories of the Allies advances in France, complete with accounts of German casualties. No mention was made of American losses. At Benning, Riley had learned an attacking army almost always suffers more casualties than a defending army, so he was not deceived by this imbalance of information. He knew Allied losses were at least as high as the Germans' which meant a lot of GI's were not coming back. If he didn't return, Eileen would never have to see Ben, or Nora, again, and Ben would probably have no memory of his Dad.

But if he did return? It seemed pointless to waste time thinking about that. He called Eileen from Birmingham to confirm she *was* meeting him. She answered on the second ring.

"You'll have to speak louder, Eileen. There are ten GI's outside this booth clamoring for me to get off the phone. Are you picking me up at the station?"

"Yes, I'll meet you. It's the 4:05 isn't it? I'll be wearing that red wool scarf you gave me. Mother is letting me borrow her car for the week since school is out for the Christmas break, and guess what, I've found a place for us to stay in Nashville for free."

"That's great. Got to go now. We're boarding. See you in a few hours. Bye."

"Goodbye, darling," Eileen said. "I love you."

As always since the start of the war, Nashville's Union Station was a madhouse. Nevertheless, Riley quickly spotted a red scarf moving toward him through the sea of uniforms and immediately realized how much he had loosened up since their brief telephone conversation in Birmingham, how much he had missed Eileen physically, and how relieved he was at her apparent change of attitude.

"Oh, darling, I have missed you so much," Eileen cooed through their kisses as they stood on the platform being jostled by soldiers in a hurry to reach wives and sweethearts of their own. "Have you thought about me?"

"More than you can imagine," Riley said.

Eileen wiped her lipstick off his mouth and cheek and said, "Let's get out of here."

Within minutes they were heading out West End Avenue toward White Bridge Road and the apartment Eileen had borrowed for the week from a former co-worker at Vultee. Riley drove as if he were being pursued by demons until Eileen touched his arm and said, "Slow down, honey, or you'll miss the turn-in. It's ahead on your right. Garden Oaks Apartments."

When he opened the door to the small space that would be his home for his final week in America, Riley smelled the roses Eileen had placed on the table by the couch. Eileen paused to light the pre-arranged candles in the bedroom before heading to the bathroom to strip down to her bra and panties. Riley took razor, Barbasol, toothpaste, and toothbrush from his duffel bag to the kitchen sink. Minutes later, the couple were under the covers. Supper and any discussion of the past could wait.

"Where will we live when you get out of the Army?" Eileen asked as they sipped coffee in bed after Riley had satisfied the most pressing of his needs.

"That's an easy question. Wherever I can get a job in the South—If I return."

"How many times do I have to tell you not to talk like that?" Eileen reproached him. "I'm going to pray you home."

"Wherever it is, it will be in the South," Riley said. "I wouldn't live anywhere else. All our relatives are here.

What I really want to do, if I survive, is someday publish a weekly newspaper in a small town like Tullahoma."

"You wish," Eileen snorted. "You couldn't possibly afford to buy a newspaper."

Riley brought his coffee cup to his lips with both hands and gently blew on it before taking a sip. He looked around the empty apartment as if to make sure no one else was listening.

"You're right, I couldn't—not for a long time, unless…"

Eileen cocked her head. "Unless what?"

"I shouldn't even think about this," Riley almost whispered. "much less tell you, but there is $5,000 in a savings account in my name in the Bank of Sikeston. When Millie Clinton and I got the insurance money, we deposited what was left after expenses in the bank to cover Ben's future medical needs and, hopefully, his college education."

"Five thousand dollars!!" Eileen exclaimed. "Why haven't you told me this before?"

Riley's eyes shifted their focus from Eileen's face to the floor.

"Because you have made it clear you don't want Ben in our lives after the war, I didn't want to let that money be a reminder to you I still have a connection with him. There's no legal restriction on my use of the money. Millie and I agreed, however, I would use any that was left to send Ben to college. I considered adding Nora to the account when you and I got married so that she could access the money if something happened to me, but I decided against that. I've left it to Ben in my will."

Eileen's eyes flashed. "You *CAN'T* leave that money in the bank," she said. "You know as well as anyone that banks can fail and if that happens, all the money will be gone. And you can't leave it to Ben. There's no telling what he would do with it."

"What would you do with it?" Ben asked.

Eileen stood up, put on her robe, and began to pace back and forth as if her steps were trying to keep pace with her mind. "You've obviously thought about investing it in a newspaper. Why not do that so we wouldn't have to borrow as much to buy one?"

"I have thought about it," Riley said, "But I can't. I'd feel awful if I bought a newspaper with the money and didn't make it. Ben's college fund would be lost. Putting money into a new business is far riskier than keeping it in a bank with an FDIC guarantee."

"I disagree," Eileen retorted. "With you working as hard as I know you would, the business wouldn't fail. Five thousand dollars would make a substantial down payment on a newspaper and make it easier to get a loan for the rest of the money. What better way to ensure Ben's college education than by building a business that made plenty of money?"

"For whom?" Riley said.

"For us!" Eileen exclaimed.

"I couldn't take that risk," Ben repeated. "That money is to ensure Ben's education, whatever happens to me. Maybe I should buy war bonds in Ben's name and hang onto them myself. If I don't return, the bonds will be his when he turns 21 and can be collateral for a loan when he is ready to go to college."

"That's a terrible idea!" Eileen scowled. "Who wants to trust $5,000 to a college kid and who wants to invest in a war?"

Riley let out a long sigh. "Let's change the subject. I should never have brought it up. I was thinking out loud. Now's the time to have fun, not speculate on the future."

He assumed from Eileen's silence that changing the subject suited her. For the rest of that week and part of the next they did have fun—going to movies and the Grand Ole Opry, visiting the Parthenon and the campus of Vanderbilt University, and spending lots of time in bed. On the appointed day, Eileen drove him to Union Station to catch the *Lookout* to Chattanooga, where he would switch to the *Birmingham Special*, made famous by Glenn Miller's *Chattanooga Choo-Choo*, for the remainder of the trip to New York's Penn Station. As they held each other on the platform in the few minutes left before departure, Eileen implored, "Why can't I go to New York with you? I can pay my way."

Riley hugged her, kissed her gently and spoke in a tender voice. "A troop train is no place for a woman. We've had our week together. Let's not spoil it now. Promise me you'll write, and I promise to think of you every day. I do love you, Eileen."

"And I love you, Riley, so very, very much. There is something I need to get off my chest before you leave.

My behavior at your sister's house was so terrible, I've been too embarrassed to talk about it. I don't know what came over me. I decided this morning I could not let you leave without asking you to forgive me."

"You're forgiven, darling," Riley said as he wrapped his arms around her. "Don't ever think about it again. Forget it ever happened."

"I'll try," Eileen said, trying to smile, "now get on the train before I bawl."

Full of soldiers heading to war, the train pulled out of the station. Eileen stood on the platform weeping, with her red scarf wrapped around her neck. Riley was sure he would never see her again. He focused on the scarf until the tail of the train blocked it from his vision. Then he settled back in his seat, took out his Zippo and shook out a Lucky. Now was not the time to cut back.

4

February 12, 1945

Dearest Eileen,

I received a packet containing all the letters you've sent me since I shipped out in December. They were just what I needed. I love you, too, sweetheart. Soldiers appreciate mail from home, except "Dear John," letters, which several guys have received, so we get mail deliveries at least once a week. I don't know why all yours came together. Maybe the Army didn't change my address when we broke camp in…Anyway, I was happy to get them.

Life in a foxhole is cramped, wet, and dirty. Getting any sleep at all is difficult. When I get a chance to sleep, I curl up and try to ignore all the noise and the conditions around me. Sometimes I can't sleep, even though I've been awake over twenty-four hours, and sometimes I can't stay awake and fall asleep out of sheer exhaustion, even though I'm on watch. Of course, there's no place to write in a foxhole. So, please don't expect letters from me often. I'll write you when I can and will cherish every letter, I get from you.

I have a chance to write today because I'm in a field hospital about 5 miles behind the lines being treated for a skin infection—don't worry, nothing serious—it's like an excused absence from the front for three days with a warm clean bed to sleep in.

I think about you all the time, darling, and hope to see you some day. The memories of our last few days together are still fresh in my mind. When I told my army buddies about our visit to the Ryman Auditorium to see the Grand Ole Opry, they thought I was kidding. Only the southern boys had ever heard of the Opry, and they couldn't believe Cowboy Copas and Minnie Pearl were real people.

I wish you could have come to New York to see me off, but among 15,000 troops being herded onto the Queen Mary at the same time, you would not have been able to see me, much less kiss me goodbye, so it was better that we said our goodbyes in Nashville. I thought going over on the Queen Mary would make the trip pleasant, but the North Atlantic was so rough in December it was impossible to go on deck, and three or four hours out of New York harbor I was so seasick I thought I was going to die. The next day I wished I had. When we landed . . . days later, they had to help me off the ship. My legs wobbled and my head spun for the next three days.

Enough about that ordeal. I'm beginning to feel queasy just thinking about it.

I'm glad your Mother's fuel ration was increased now that she has to drive further to teach. I'm sorry you are missing the great cakes and pies she can't make anymore because sugar is rationed. We get plenty to eat at the front, C-rations which taste like crap. I'd swap a week of rations for your Mother's fluffy biscuits or better yet, her coconut cake.

Hope your allotment checks are coming. For some reason when I started getting combat pay, the Army screwed up the calculations and when I questioned them about it, they stopped your payment and Nora's altogether till they figured out what was wrong, which they tell me they have, and everything is straightened out. Like they say about everything in the Army, "situation normal, all fucked up."

I'd better close for now. I need to write Mother and Nora. You may not hear from me again for weeks. Don't think I don't love you, or don't want to hear from you. Because I do.

Love,
Riley

February 12, 1945

Dear Nora,

Thank you for your letter of December 30th, which I just received. My division is right in the middle of the German counter offensive which began in mid-December. Fighting has been so intense I have been living in foxholes since the day I arrived. I can't tell you any more. I hope I haven't annoyed the censors already.

The reason I have time to write now is that I'm in the hospital recovering—not from enemy fire—from two boils on my hip which became infected and wouldn't heal in the foxhole. I'll be here two more days; then I'll be back in the thick of things. I'm enjoying clean sheets and hot water while I have them—and catching up on my mail. Fortunately, I'm not confined to a bed. I can walk around within the hospital compound and swap stories with other guys.

Nora, I can't begin to describe how terrible things are for the French, even away from the front. Starving children beg for food from every soldier they see. GI's break the bars of chocolate which are part of our C-rations into little pieces and hand them to the kids. Practically every farmhouse, barn and out-building has been blown up or burned down. There is no livestock anywhere. It's freezing cold all the time and civilians have no fuel for heat.

I've seen bodies lying around as if they were part of the landscape. I pray our country will never be invaded, and Americans will not have to live under these wretched conditions.

Yes, I am praying again. I don't remember how much I told you about my skepticism about God which evolved into complete disbelief when Claire died. I couldn't understand how a loving God could spare me in that accident and not Claire, or how He could allow an innocent little boy to lose his mother and be so badly injured. I have been re-thinking God the last few weeks, however. Like the chaplain says there are no atheists in foxholes.

The day I arrived I was sent straight to the front line to relieve guys who had been there since the German offensive began. The Jerries were shelling us constantly from less than three hundred yards away. My first foxhole buddy was a guy from Philadelphia named Robbie Shantz. He was only18, was being exposed to enemy fire for the first time, and just like me was terrified. Curled up in a ball, shaking and whimpering, Shantz barely made it through the first night. I tried to get him to talk to me, thinking we could help each other, but he completely ignored me. At daylight he begged me to move with him to a safer place. Our orders were to hold our position and there wasn't anywhere for us to go except into some other guy's foxhole or try to make it to the rear, which would have gotten us court-martialed.

I didn't want to be court-martialed, and I sure

wasn't going to make myself an open target for the Jerries. Apparently, Shantz did not feel the same way. About 0700 hours, he bolted. A split second after he left, I heard the whistle of a Nazi 88, which landed ten feet away and blew Shantz to kingdom come. The explosion created a crater three feet across and at least three feet deep. I got showered with dirt and my ears rang for an hour, but my foxhole saved me.

For the second time in my life I had escaped injury when people with me were killed and I easily could have been. Instinctively I thanked God for saving me. I kept on thanking Him and soon I began to think it was possible He was real and was looking out for me. I stopped trying to figure out why me and not Shantz.

Four more weeks of living in foxholes got me these boils and into this field hospital away from the fighting. Yesterday my company's position was overrun by Jerries attacking with Panzers. I heard we lost almost one hundred men. I likely would have been killed if I had been there, and not five miles behind the lines recuperating from skin infection. Were my boils providential?

That made me think back to Fort Benning and my missing two rotations overseas and kept me out of the fighting for over a year. Did God have a hand in that? Can dodging death four times be purely by chance? The best answer I can come up with is that God must be protecting me. But why? I'll leave that question to the theologians, and accept what the hymn says, "God moves in a mysterious way, His wonders to perform."

Don't worry. I'm not going to throw myself on a grenade or charge a machine gun nest trying to be a hero. I don't feel invincible. Since I'm not totally convinced God rather than blind luck is the answer, I certainly will not test Him to see how far He will go to protect me. From now on I plan to be a good, careful soldier and pray I get through this alive. And now, for the first time since I was drafted, I do not believe I am doomed to die in this war. I believe there is a chance I will get home, and now that I think there is a chance, I want desperately to make it back to my family.

Speaking of home, Eileen is sorry and embarrassed about the little tantrum she had in Biloxi. I do hope you two can get along. Please tell Ben his Uncle Riley loves him and doesn't want him to burn the house down trying to light a cigarette. You have to admit, if it weren't so dangerous it might be funny watching a four-year old smoke a Camel. I'm glad to hear he likes kindergarten so much and I am truly amazed at his reading skills. I'm sorry Eileen wouldn't let him read to her. She would love him if she would just get to know him. Please write often, even if I can't write back. And please send pictures.

Give my love to Frank and Annie, and much love to you.

Riley

Although Allied advances were steady during the late winter and early spring of 1945, from Riley's perspective as a foot soldier, every day was the same — more bitter cold, more fighting, more suffering, and more death. His objective was simply to obey orders and try to stay alive to fight the next day. As his division pushed through France, his closest brush with death was when his patrol came under fire as it approached a chapel near the village of Busing.

"Mothafucka, where'd that come from?" Lieutenant Miller exclaimed as he dropped to his knees when bullets tore through bushes around him. "Let's spread out and get closer."

"Has to be from that Goddam church," Corporal Lewis said. "That's five rounds in three seconds. Think there are five Krauts in there?"

"It's a semi-automatic," Riley, who had taken cover behind the stump of what used to be a large elm tree, said.

"Christ! My shoul…!" the Lieutenant cried out as more rounds zinged by. Riley saw him slump to the ground; his face contorted in pain. There was no cover between Riley and Miller. Nothing but open space.

"Corporal. Can you get to him?"

"If my butt doesn't stick up too high," Corporal Lewis replied.

Lewis crawled the few yards to where Miller had fallen, drug him to cover, tore open his shirt to examine the shoulder, gave the lieutenant a shot of morphine and said, "Hang in there, sir. Sarge and I'll get the bastards."

Riley motioned for Lewis to get close enough to the church to toss a grenade. With his binoculars Riley spotted movement, but he couldn't tell how many Germans were inside. He unstrapped his M-1 and fired at the open window, drawing withering fire. Lewis crawled through the brush to within thirty yards of the church, rose to his knees and tossed two grenades—one toward the crack in the doorway and the second toward the open window. The first explosion blew the door off its hinges. The second grenade sailed through the open window and detonated. When the debris cleared, the church was silent. Riley and Lewis cautiously approached the opening where the church door had been. The rest of the squad covered the rear.

"All I see is one dead bastard, Sarge," Lewis, who was prying a Karabiner 43 from the dead soldier's hands. "Damn those Jerries make good semi-automatics. This one's going to be mine."

Riley's eyes adjusted to the dim light in the small chapel. He knelt and with his fingertips permanently closed the eyes of the young soldier who lay covered in blood.

"Looks just like one of us, except for his uniform," the corporal said.

"Yes, he does," Riley responded, "and he probably has a mother at home who'll grieve at his death, just as yours would, and maybe a wife who is praying to the same God we pray to for his safe return."

Riley swallowed hard as he stared at the body. An image of Claire dying in his arms and thoughts of little

Ben back home who would never know his mother and might never have known his dad if the young German's aim had been true. Finally, he turned away and said, "We'd better go check on Lt. Miller."

"No hurry, Sarge. The lieutenant was on his way to heaven when I left him. He took one in the gut as well as the shoulder. Nothing I could do for him except ease his pain."

Riley grimaced. "Then let's retrieve our radio from him and get his body back to camp."

"The radio's gone, Sarge. I think we should get back ASAP. No telling who heard all this fire."

"You're right, of course, corporal. We don't want any more surprises. We can send a larger detail to recover Lewis's body. By the way, those were two strong throws you made."

"Double A ball. I was pitching for the Wilkes-Barre Barons when Uncle Sam called."

"I had to tell myself I couldn't feel sorry for that boy," Riley confided to the Chaplain that night. "He was a Kraut—one of Hitler's killers. He had fired at least fifty rounds at us and had killed one of our guys. He was the enemy, even if he was only a kid."

The next morning Riley was awakened by a message from Headquarters to report to HQ ASAP. Riley had slept in his fatigues and exchanged salutes with his Commanding Officer, Lt. Col. Harold Adams in less than ten minutes.

"Good work, soldier," the CO said. "You handled the situation yesterday well, just like an officer should. I understand you've been an exceptional NCO. It's time for you to take off that sergeant's chevron and attach a gold bar to your uniform. I'll have my aide fix you up right away. Now report to Major Dunleavy on the double. Dismissed."

"Yes, sir!" Riley said as he stepped back, pivoted, and tried to absorb what had just happened as he walked away. Battlefield promotions were not uncommon. Riley, however, never expected to receive one. What's more, he wasn't sure he wanted to be an officer. In his experience, a lieutenant was as likely to be killed as an enlisted man. He didn't want to make the military a career. He just wanted to get through this war alive. Nevertheless, he couldn't say no. He told himself the promotion was not going to change him. He knew it would change his relationship with the men in his squad. He was immediately joined by the CO's aide who handed him fresh fatigues bearing the insignia of his new rank and escorted him to Maj. Dunleavy's tent.

"Lieutenant," the major said, "I need you to take a squad and secure a group of deserted buildings about half a mile back which we bypassed in our push to reach Rouflach. One squad should be enough. Be thorough but be quick. Our orders are to join up with the Free French Army by 1800 hours Saturday."

The main road that went through Wuenheim was littered with burned-out German half-tracks and Schwimmwagens, but the side road, about the width of a half-track, which led to a hamlet of six houses and a few out-buildings was clear.

"Keep your eyes open and don't bunch up," Riley barked as his troops approached the first dwelling. "Don't let the quiet lull you into thinking nobody's around. Hanover, you and Smith check out the house ahead of us. Washington, you and Berger get the second house. The rest of you stay here and keep us covered."

"All clear," Corporal Hanover signaled as he headed toward the third house, which was barely the size of a tool shed and had no glass in its windows. Riley joined PFCs Washington and Berger at the second house which, like the others, showed no signs of life. Suddenly Berger dropped to one knee and put his rifle to his shoulder.

"Something moved," he whispered to Riley. "There, in the lower left corner of the window. It looks like a dirty curtain. It definitely moved."

His training told Riley to unleash a torrent of bullets through the window, but he paused. If the movement inside was the enemy, his troops should have been fired on already. They were well within range. No known friendlies were in the area. Was he leading his men into an ambush?

"Hold your fire," he ordered. "Either of you speak French?"

Washington shook his head, no.

"Negative, sarge, just a little Yiddish," said Berger, "with a Brooklyn accent."

"Well let's see if whoever is in there understands my high school French."

"*Parlez-vous Anglais*?" he called.

For a long moment, Riley waited. Corporal Hanover arrived with his weapon in firing position. No sound came from the house. The dirty curtain was no longer visible.

"Let's blast'em, Sir," Hanover said. "Can't take any chances. No one's around here except us and the Jerries."

"Do you see any guns, Corporal?" Riley replied. "Did you see that cloth in the window? This is still France. There may be civilians in there."

"Yeah, with Jerries using them as bait to lure us in. I don't like it."

Riley was torn. His military preparation said shoot to kill. His compassion said wait. He had to rely on instinct and judgment as well as training. Killing the young German in the church was the right thing to do, but whoever was in this house had not fired a shot, did not appear to be hostile and did not deserve summary execution. He called out again.

"*Est-ce que vous Francais? Nous sommes Americaines*"

"*Oui, Monsieur, nous sommes Francais. Je suis une femme avec mes trois enfants.*"

"Hold your fire!" Riley commanded. Then to the house he yelled, "*Attendez-vous, Nous vous aiderons.*"

Out through the door staggered a gaunt woman, carrying a child so emaciated Riley could not tell its sex or age, followed by two stick- thin children, with nothing on their feet and long straggly hair.

"Berger, get some blankets and food for these folks," Riley ordered. "Hanover, you and Washington join the rest of the guys. If you find any other civilians, let me know. Do not shoot unless you are fired upon. Understand!!"

After she had eaten and drunk as much as she could hold and helped each of her children drink from the canteens and devour the crackers and chocolate PFC Berger had produced, in broken English the woman spoke. "*Dieu te be'nissse, Monsieur,*"

"*Anglais, s'il vous plais,*" Riley said. "*Parlez vous Anglais?*"

"My English not good," the woman said. "I try."

She cleared her throat before she spoke again. "You have saved us from starving. *Je suis Helene Badoit. Ma mari* . . . husband, Jean and I are from Rouen. Jean joined *le Resistance* when Paris fell. *Tres ans* since I heard from him. I pray he still alive."

Madame Badoit crossed herself and continued. "*Mes enfants et moi* had no place to go but here with *mes parents*. Life with Germans always bad, but last few months *horrible*. When cattle were gone, they took chickens and ducks for themselves. *Ma mere* not eat after they shot *Papa*, so *les enfants* have more."

Madame Badoit's voice broke as she began to weep. Riley handed her a piece of cheese, which she broke in two and handed to her older children.

"Please, ma'am, eat some yourself. There's plenty of bread and cheese for you and your family," Riley said, motioning to PFC Berger to get more. "When did the Germans leave?"

"Two days ago. They shoot all men. Then they leave."

"How many Germans?"

"*Je ne sais pas,*" she sighed. "Not many—maybe *dix*—how do you say in English? Ten?

As a medic approached to treat her family and the few other women and children remaining in the hamlet, Madame Badoit grabbed Riley's hand and kissed it. "Please tell Army find my husband."

"If your husband is as strong as you are, madam," Riley said. "I'm sure we will."

In March 1945, U S forces crossed the Rhine. In late April, Mussolini was executed by Italian anti-fascists and two days later Hitler committed suicide. On May 7, 1945, Germany surrendered. The war in Europe was over. Riley had spent 111 days in combat. He vowed never to discuss those days with anyone, and throughout his life he mostly kept that vow.

"I was a soldier," he said when anyone asked what he did in the war, "and a damn good one."

May 17, 1945

Dearest Eileen,

I'M COMING HOME! I never thought I'd get to write this letter—but it's true. I'll be back in the States as soon as a ship is available and my number comes up—probably within six or seven weeks, including the time it takes to cross the Atlantic, which should put me in New York no later than August 14th. I'll have two weeks leave before deploying to Okinawa to be a part of the invasion of Japan. I wish the Army could get me home earlier, but there are too many men with a higher priority than I have, and too much material and equipment to move. I'll telegraph you the day I leave to let you know when to meet me in New York.

For the first few days after Germany surrendered, all we did was eat, sleep, drink booze and celebrate. And try not to think about Japan. Now they have me checking lists of MIAs against known dead. It's tedious work, but there are no mortar rounds exploding near me and no machine gunners trying to rip me apart. We knock off at five every afternoon and drink beer and play poker till midnight. Then I go to sleep on a cot with a pillow and dream about you and what we'll do during my leave. I want us to pick up right where we left off. I love you, Eileen, and can't wait to see you, which should not be much longer. For now, here are some hugs and kisses.

Love,
Riley

5

Riley looked over a sea of humanity at Penn Station, trying to spot Eileen's red scarf. Euphoria and his intense desire for her had propelled him straight from the boat to meet the 1:02 from Nashville. When the passengers dispersed with no Eileen, he ate lunch in the station and read the *New York Times* while waiting for the 2:58. If she were not on that train, he'd have to wait till the next day. She was not. By 3:30, euphoria had turned to anxiety, and Riley joined the line at the information booth to learn if any other train from Nashville arrived before morning.

"Goddam railroads," he muttered under his breath. "You'd think they'd put on extra cars to carry all this traffic."

"Young man," a sixty-ish woman dressed in a black silk dress and wearing a black hat with a feather in it said to him, "even though you are in uniform, you don't have the right to take the name of the Lord in vain."

Riley noticed the small gold cross hanging from her neck. *She's got to be kidding. What does she think I've been doing the last few months?* He wanted to say, "Get off my back, lady or I'll show you how GI's really talk." Instead, he smiled, said "beg your pardon," and walked away.

Since the moment he—thanks to massive doses of the test drug which was eventually known as Dramamine—got off the boat under his own power, he had been showered with thanks and good wishes by New Yorkers. Women—young, old, short, tall, thin, stout—grabbed him on the street and hugged and kissed him. Men twice his age stepped back to allow him to pass and practically everyone not in uniform opened doors for him. Three days earlier, a second atomic bomb had wiped out Nagasaki as completely as the first had destroyed Hiroshima. All New Yorkers expected Japan's imminent surrender, and all were ready to celebrate and honor their returning warriors.

Riley learned that another train from Nashville, by way of Cincinnati, was due at 6:07 that evening. Eileen had to be on it, and Riley had to find somewhere for them to spend the night. He had plenty of nickels, but the bank of pay phones in the Penn Station lobby was far too small to satisfy the demand, so Riley headed toward Times Square and the booth the USO had set up to assist returning service men.

"Any chance I can get a room for my wife and me tonight?" he asked a perky young woman with a boyish haircut wearing a volunteer band around her right arm.

"Your wife? Is that what you're calling her?" The girl

looked him over. "There are plenty of rooms available for soldiers but not so many for a soldier with a woman, unless you're willing to go to the Bowery."

"No, really. She's my wife. I'm picking her up at Penn Station this evening."

"Where's the ring?" the girl asked.

"She has it. We're already married."

"I mean on you, soldier boy."

Riley laughed.

"I can't wear a ring. Makes my finger itch."

"Must not be real gold then. Since you *say* she's your wife, try the Taft Hotel on 7th Avenue between 50th and 51st. They offer special rates to servicemen. Two to a room. Five dollars per person a night. You'd better get right on over. They've been booking up before five the last few nights. And she'd better have a ring. If she doesn't show up, I get off at seven. Call me."

The desk clerk at the Taft was less interested in Riley's marital status than his ten-dollar bill. Room paid for in advance, Riley decided to unpack his duffel bag and listen to the radio for news of the war. Ten minutes into the program he heard, "We interrupt this program to bring you this special announcement."

"The war is over!" H. V. Kaltenborn's voice rang out. "Japan unconditionally surrendered to Allied forces at approximately 3 p.m. Eastern Time. The Japanese Imperial Army has been crushed. General Douglas MacArthur will formally receive Japan's acceptance of the Potsdam Declaration as soon as possible. I repeat—the war is over!"

Thousands of people instantly spilled into Times Square. Riley quickly buttoned up his uniform, combed his hair and rushed to join them. Except for taxis and delivery trucks, which were going nowhere, there were no cars on the streets, just New Yorkers celebrating the end of a four-year nightmare, treating every other celebrant as a friend and Riley, along with every other man in uniform as a celebrity.

"Can I buy you a beer, soldier?"

"Need a place to stay tonight?"

"Hey, good lookin' want to spend some time with me?"

They acted as if he had won the war singlehandedly.

For almost two hours he inched toward Penn Station, arriving eight minutes after the 6:07. Among the few passengers remaining on platform 29 he spotted Eileen, looking away from him, standing by the same bag he had loaded onto the luggage rack of that bus from Memphis, wearing the same red scarf he had last seen in Nashville and tapping her foot to let the world know of her impatience. He sneaked up on her, grabbed her from behind, spun her around, kissed her and said, "Hi, gorgeous. Haven't you heard the war's over? Stop wasting your time in a train station. Come see the town with a soldier who loves you."

"Where did you learn to whistle so well?" Eileen asked as they lazed through the following day with no plans except to delight each other. Japan's surrender meant Riley's orders to report to Fort Mason on August 24th to be shipped to Okinawa would certainly be rescinded, and the sense of dread he had felt so strongly had been replaced with an immense sense of relief. He had been drafted "for the duration of the war," so the term of his conscription was over. All that was left was his formal discharge.

"I picked it up from my dad, who could whistle every Sousa march all the way through. Funny. It's been years since I felt like whistling. Now, I can't stop."

Eileen grabbed at his skivvies as he walked by the bed. "Can you do the one the radio plays all the time?"

"You mean the *Stars and Stripes, Forever*? That's easy."

Riley did a few bars of the well-known march, then sank into the chair closest to her and admired Eileen as she reclined on two pillows propped against the headboard, her Rita Hayworth nightie exposing her slender legs and the tops of her breasts. *Damn, she's beautiful. How fortunate I am to be here.*

"Aren't we lucky to live in a country that's not been bombed to smithereens and suffered millions of casualties like Europe, Russia, and Japan?" he said.

"Not lucky," Eileen said. "Blessed."

"I can't go that far," Riley said, "but I must admit, for me to have come through the war without a scratch seems almost miraculous. And instead of being penniless and homeless, like so many in Europe who survived the war, I have you to come back to and a little money waiting for me when I'm discharged."

Eileen stretched her arms and wiggled her toes at him.

"Why not admit it. God was on our side. How else could we have won?"

"Well, I do admit we weren't ready for war in 1941. Everyone I knew was glad the US was staying out of Europe. If Japan hadn't bombed Pearl Harbor, Germany would probably have swept the British off the continent, Churchill's government would have collapsed, and the Germans would have agreed to leave England alone if they would agree to let Germany keep its conquered territory. I'm sure Hitler and Stalin would have made a deal to carve up Eastern Europe and made peace."

Eileen yawned. "What happened and when it happened was up to God. Let's talk about us. Do you know I was able to use most of my allotment to buy savings bonds?"

Riley tickled the soles of her feet.

"They'll be worth over a thousand dollars in ten years, or we could buy a car if I cashed them in now."

"Or pay rent while I look for a job. Oh, Eileen, we've survived the worst ordeal imaginable and we have each other and a great future ahead. I want to get started on it now."

"I do too," Eileen said, "and I want us to have a baby. How long will it take for the Army to discharge you?"

"Maybe a couple of months. Maybe a year. Now that the war's over, they don't need me, but they don't need a lot of other soldiers either. I don't know how they'll carry out that process or how long it will take."

Riley continued rubbing Eileen's feet. His face was relaxed. His blue-green eyes sparkled. His voice was soft. "I want us to have a baby too, darling, and after last night and this morning…"

"Not likely," she laughed, grabbing his hand and pulling Riley toward her. "My period's about to start. Let's try again right now if you're up to it."

"Give me a couple of hours. Why don't I run across the street to Horn and Hardart and get lunch? What would you like?"

"I'd like a *Salade Nicoise* with iced tea and chocolate cake for dessert."

Having finished his club sandwich before Eileen got through the lettuce, tomatoes, tuna, boiled egg, and crouton salad which Riley presented to her as a *Salade Nicoise*, Riley sipped the Pabst he had brought back and let a thought that had been rolling around in his head slip out.

"I wonder what Ben is doing."

Eileen shot a disturbed look at him, "Don't think about him, dear, it'll just upset you."

"Wouldn't it be terrific if Ben could share our future with us and I could be his daddy?"

Eileen's face turned grim. "Are you thinking about breaking your promise to Nora and Frank, and even worse, your promise to me? They've had Ben four years now. I heard them tell you how much they love him and how delighted they are to have him. He is theirs now. You don't need Ben to be a father. We'll have a family."

"I know we'll have a family, honey, soon I hope, and I know Nora and Frank will be disappointed, but I think it would work. They know how much Ben means to me. And Eileen, if you would try, you would come to love Ben and make him a part of our family."

"You promised me Ben would never be part of... I mean, live with us."

"I know I said that darling..."

"Was it a lie?"

"No, it wasn't a lie. I meant it at the time, but so much has changed."

"Nothing's changed! You survived the war, just as I knew you would because I prayed every day for you. Ben has Nora and Frank, as you planned. He doesn't need you now. I do. Can't you understand what bringing a constant reminder of your first wife into our home would do to me? How can you even think about doing that?"

Riley went to the bathroom, dampened a washcloth, and walked back to Eileen, intending to wipe away the tears that had appeared, but she grabbed the cloth from his hand and flung it across the room. Riley retreated to the couch. Memories of the fit she had thrown in Tullahoma when he first told her about Ben three years earlier were quickly followed by those of her tiff with Nora in Biloxi. Obviously, Eileen deeply resented Claire. He could not comprehend how a woman who had been dead for four years, whom Eileen had never met, could evoke such strong emotions.

Then the truth grabbed him. It was not the memory of Claire that Eileen hated. It was the reality of Ben. The room was quiet except for Eileen's sniffling. The joy and exhilaration of their sexual reunion had drained away. The future, which had looked so bright and promising the last two days, had clouded over. One fact remained clear. However Eileen felt, he wanted his son.

After five minutes of silence, Riley spoke. "You don't want Ben to come live with us, right?"

Eileen nodded, yes.

"You want him to stay with Nora permanently."

"Now that he's settled there. That would be best for him."

"I guess you think I should let Nora and Frank adopt Ben—to make things legal."

"Yes. You could go see him, and maybe he could come visit us when he is older."

"And I shouldn't continue to send Nora money to help pay for Ben's care."

"Of course not, after they adopt Ben, his care should be their responsibility."

"And his education?"

"That too."

"Then I should send Nora the $5,000 Millie let me keep for his college."

Eileen jumped to her feet.

"I need to call Nora," Riley said, "to let her know I'll be sending the money."

"Wait," Eileen shouted as she scrambled to get into her slippers. Riley stopped halfway to the phone.

"You're right. It's too early to call now. I'd better wait till Frank gets home so we can discuss the adoption."

"You can't give them that money," Eileen said. "We are going to need it for a down payment on a newspaper."

"I have to send Nora the money, so she'll be able to send Ben to college. Mrs. Clinton did not agree I could use it to go into business."

Eileen grabbed his arm. "Have you already talked to Nora?"

Riley's eyes turned steel cold. "When could I have done that?"

"You had plenty of time to call her between when your ship docked and you met me at the train."

"I would never discuss this with Nora before I talked to you. Besides, I'd need to go to Biloxi for that conversation. I couldn't have it over the phone."

"I thought it was settled—Ben would live with Nora and you would keep the money to invest in a newspaper to make money to pay for his college. Now you're telling me either Ben comes to live with us, or you will send the money to Nora. Are you trying to make me choose?"

"I'm trying to understand what's upsetting you more—the thought of having Ben with us or losing $5,000."

Eileen glared at Riley for a full twenty seconds, then darted into the bathroom. Fifteen minutes later she reappeared, her make-up freshened, and her hair brushed. She began putting on her stockings.

"Let's walk over to Macy's and see if I can find a pair of nylons," she said. "We've been cooped up in this room too long."

After a day of celebration, most New Yorkers had gone back to work. The sidewalks, however, were still full of pedestrians, so the couple had to walk closely together to avoid getting separated. Riley liked Eileen's new hair style, which was teased on top, like Barbara Stanwyck, and he liked her new fragrance, Black Satin, which he had noticed instantly when he met her at Penn Station. He was in uniform, and passers-by still gave him nods of appreciation, but no offers for drinks or companionship. Eileen took Riley's hand and matched her stride to his. She pressed her mouth to his ear.

"You don't have time to go to Biloxi before your leave is up, honey. Can't this business with Ben wait till you're discharged?"

"It'll only take three days. One to get there, one to visit, and one to get back to Tennessee. If I leave tomorrow, I can make it."

"What about me. Do you plan to leave me here?"

"I need to make this trip alone, Eileen. I thought we would ride together to Chattanooga and your mother would pick you up there."

Eileen's eyes flared. She dropped his hand. "Okay. Go see your precious son—if that's what you want. Just don't bring him back with you."

Riley stopped and, ignoring the wave of pedestrians rushing by, put his hands-on Eileen's shoulders and said, "What I want is for you to love Ben and treat him like a son and not like a bastard. It's obvious you don't love him. It's almost obvious you don't even like him. What I don't want is to know you are unwilling to try, for my sake, to love and accept my son. Five thousand dollars, however, would persuade you to grit your teeth and put up with him."

"That's so unfair," she said. "Why are you making me the villain? You're the one breaking your promise."

Riley slept on the couch that night. Mercifully, the train from New York to Chattanooga allowed Riley and Eileen to move around and dissipate the unbearable tension between them. Riley spent the first third of the trip in the club car smoking, while Eileen stayed at their assigned seats, mostly staring out the window, sniffling. At the Baltimore stop she found him in the club car, with his Luckies and his coffee.

"May I have a sip?" she said.

"Would you like a cup of your own to take back to your seat?"

"Yes, if you'll sit with me so we can talk."

Handing her a fresh cup of coffee, Riley searched her face for a glimmer of something other than the unhappiness which had been so evident for the last twenty-four hours. She sat down, blew on her coffee, and said, "when Mother and I first talked about your having a child, she told me I was lucky to get to be a mother so soon without having to go through the pain of childbirth. She thinks Ben is a blessed child and a gift to me. She offered to keep him in the summer for as long as we liked. But Mother has children around her all the time and knows how to relate to them. I'm not like that. I don't have her way with children. I have a hard time imagining raising my own baby, let alone someone else's child. I'm scared, Riley. I'm afraid I won't be a good mother and you will always be comparing me with Claire, and I'll lose."

The train began to pull out of the Baltimore depot and a gaggle of noisy teen-agers wearing Kelly Green school uniforms rushed in with their chaperones, demanding service.

"Can we get out of here?" Eileen pleaded. "I feel faint."

Riley helped her up, set her coffee aside and gently put his arm around her. "Sure," he said. "Lean on me and I'll help you back to our seats."

As the train gathered speed, Riley steered them around passengers jostling for space in the aisles and through the shaking doors between cars, keeping a firm grip on Eileen. Settled in their seats, Eileen rested her head on his shoulder. She was soon asleep, but not Riley. He had to consider that being compared unfavorably to Claire as a mother was driving Eileen's hostility toward Ben. Was he responsible? Had he painted Claire as the perfect mother? Having acknowledged her fears, could Eileen overcome them? Could he trust her if she claimed she had? Riley wanted to trust Eileen. His fear that $5,000 sitting in the Sikeston Bank was Eileen's only reason for letting Ben share their lives made trust difficult.

The express to Mobile, with stops at Birmingham and Montgomery, left Chattanooga's Central Station at 4:04 p.m. With Eileen clinging to him as if he were going back into battle, Riley barely made it to the proper platform before the unsympathetic conductor blew his whistle.

"Promise me you'll come back alone," Eileen shouted from the platform.

"I promise," Riley said as the train pulled away. "I promise."

"Of course, you can stay with us," Nora said over a crackling line when Riley called her from Birmingham. "What time will you get here?"

"The train is scheduled to arrive in Mobile at 10:00 tonight and there is a 40-minute wait for the connecting train to Biloxi. With luck I should get to your house by 12:30 tomorrow morning. I'll get a cab from the station."

"You'll do nothing of the sort. Frank will pick you up in Mobile. How long can you stay?"

"Just what's left of tonight and tomorrow. I can't put Frank to the trou . ."

"Nonsense, that train is never on time. If Frank picks you up, you can be here before midnight."

"Okay, sis. If you say so. And thanks."

Riley awakened the next morning to the patter of little feet running up to his bed, stopping, then running away. He heard small voices whispering. "Is he awake?"

"Uh, Uh. Can we wake him now?"

"Mama said not till seven."

"How will we know when it's seven?"

"Mama will tell us."

He sat up on the side of the roll-away Frank had moved to the sleeping porch and looked for his pants. Two pairs of little eyes peered at him through the doorway. Two pairs of little feet padded toward him.

"Uncle Riley," Annie said. "Mama wants to know if you want your egg fried or scrambled."

"Tell her sunny side up," Riley said. "But ask her to wait a minute before she starts mine."

"Uncle Riley doesn't want his egg fried or scrambled," Ben shouted as he ran toward the kitchen. "He wants his sun side up."

Riley wanted to run after his son, scoop him up, hold him tight and rub Ben's soft cheek against his scratchy stubble. He put on his pants and joined Frank and Annie sitting at the breakfast table. Ben stood next to Nora at the stove.

"Coffee?" Frank offered.

"Sugar and cream, please. How long has everyone except me been up?"

"'Bout half an hour," Nora said. "I tried to keep the kids quiet. Did you get much sleep?"

"Enough, I dozed on the train, so getting to bed at one a.m. wasn't so bad. What time do you start on your route, Frank?"

"Depends on where I'm going. Today's Gulfport, so I need to leave as soon as I finish my coffee. Want to come with me?"

"Maybe next time. When will you get home tonight?"

"Five, five-fifteen. I'll try to knock off a little early."

"Sunny side up," Nora said as she set one egg, a piece of buttered toast, and two strips of crisp bacon before Riley. Ben's eyes widened at the sight of the plate turning yellow from the running yolk as Riley began to cut the egg with his fork.

"Would you like a bite?"

Ben backed away, shaking his head shyly. Nora laughed.

"This little boy demands that we scramble his egg in the skillet."

"I thought we would take the kids to the beach this morning," Nora said after breakfast dishes were cleaned and put away and the beds made. "You probably did not bring a swimsuit. I can pin up one of Frank's, so it won't fall off your bottom."

"I can't stay in the sun long. I burn easily."

"So do I and so does Ben. It must be a McHaney trait. Frank and Annie can stay out all day and just get brown."

Five minutes later Nora handed Riley a small hamper containing beach towels, a jug of ice water, some Ritz crackers and Oreo cookies, two packs of cigarettes, a book of matches and a jar of Vaseline.

"C'mon, kids," she said. "Time to go."

The concrete sidewalk radiated the blistering August sun through the soles of Riley's shoes during the four-block walk to the beach. Shielding his eyes with his free hand, he regretted he had not accepted Nora's offer of a cap from Frank's sweat-stained trove. Ben and Annie, each carrying a small bucket and shovel, pulled free from Nora's grasp and skipped a few yards ahead as they neared the traffic light where they could safely cross the coast highway.

"Wait for us at the light," Nora commanded. "Everyone needs to hold hands. Ben, let Uncle Riley help you climb down the seawall."

"I can do it all by meself," Ben insisted.

"All right," Riley laughed, "please let me go with you so you can show me how. Okay?"

The seawall, a concrete monolith built after the 1926 hurricane season to protect the inland from storm surges ran in one hundred-foot sections for miles along the Gulf Coast highway. Its stair-step structure placed each of the twenty steps two and one-half feet above the one below, and as Riley discovered, were difficult to traverse. Annie and Ben solved the problem by sitting on their bottoms on the sloped dividing wall between adjoining sections and using their hands and feet to inchworm their way down. Riley and Nora descended the traditional way.

"They play well together," Riley observed as he and Nora sat on the beach a few yards above the high tide line, watching the children run back and forth with the waves as they ebbed and flowed. "Unlike you and me at that age."

"We were never that age together," Nora laughed. "When you were Ben's age, I was nine and you were a pain in the you know what. I am delighted they enjoy each other's company. It makes parenting so much easier. Ben is a delightful little brother for Annie and a blessing for Frank and me. I can't tell you how much Frank and I love him and how much we appreciate your giving him to us."

Riley swallowed hard and shaded his eyes from the glare as he gazed at his sister's thickened mid-section, which caused a muffin-shaped bulge in her bathing suit.

The loss of ten pounds would give her a stunning figure again.

"You will have more children, won't you?"

"No, Frank and I agree we are through having children. Who could ask for a more perfect family than one little girl and one little boy? How many do you and Eileen plan to have?"

"One for sure, Eileen wants a baby right away, and probably more. We'll see."

"So, Annie and Ben should be looking for a new cousin in . . . let's see, May? I hope you settle close by so our children can grow up knowing each other."

For a quarter of an hour Riley silently nibbled on Ritz crackers and watched his son trying to catch the full force of the breaking wave directly against his body. When he was successful, the pounding surf tumbled him, cackling with glee, into the water, eager to get back up and catch the next wave. Deciding to defer his discussion about Ben till later, Riley jumped up and waded through the surf to join his son just as a large wave approached, crashed over them, and tossed them toward the shore.

"That was the biggest one ever!" Ben sputtered as he spit out a mouthful of salt water. "Bring me another one, Uncle Riley, an even bigger one."

After two hours in the sun, Nora shouted, "Lunch time!" loud enough to be heard over the surf, while motioning the children toward her.

"Not hungry," Ben shouted back, turning away from Nora and wading further into the Gulf.

"Please let us stay longer, mama," Annie pleaded, "please, please."

"We need to go now," Riley yelled. "Anybody want a piggy-back ride home and a nickel if you don't fall off?"

"I do!" yelled the children in unison, as they began to splash toward shore.

"Okay, but you'll have to take turns. Who wants to go first?"

"Me! Me!" both yelled.

"Annie," Nora said taking her daughter's hand as they began to ascend the seawall, "shouldn't we let Ben go first since he's younger than you?"

Annie tuned her lower lip to a pout but nodded assent. Ben gleefully climbed on when Riley squatted down at the top of the wall.

"Much lighter than a field pack," Riley said as he rose, using the picnic basket to balance himself. "Off we go."

After lunch came quiet time, during which the children sat on the porch and Annie read to Ben. Riley lit a Lucky and half listened to Annie read "Hansel and Gretel" from a child's edition of *Grimm's Fairy Tales* while he honed his approach to telling Nora he was taking Ben back.

"Mama," a little voice piped up from the doorway, "are there any witches in Mississippi?"

"Of course not, Ben."

"Are there any witches where Uncle Riley lives?"

"Witches live only in fairy tales, honey. You don't have to worry about them in Biloxi or anywhere else now days."

"Maybe the witches are hiding and only come out at night. If I hear one tonight, can I get in bed with you?"

"Of course, you can, darling."

"Or with Uncle Riley."

Nora smiled at Riley. "It looks like Ben considers you part of the family."

"How is Frank's business?" Riley asked as he and Nora sat on the porch after quiet time, while Annie and Ben played in the sand box Frank had constructed in the back yard.

"Growing every day. The military has such a big presence in Biloxi that a lot of people have money to spend. There's no problem finding people who can afford to buy. The problem is finding the things they want."

"Have you and Frank talked about how you'll manage when your allotment stops?"

"That won't be difficult. We didn't need $40 a month to take care of Ben, $25 would have been plenty. In fact, we've been able to save over $3,000 since the war began and are planning to buy Mrs. Atkins' house next door. She's moving to New Orleans in October to be with her daughter. It has two big bedrooms and a room which could be Frank's office. Practically nothing needs to be done to it."

"Would you buy the house if you didn't have Ben?"

"I suppose we would. It's a good deal for the $4,000 she wants and would keep us in this neighborhood. Why do you ask? We have Ben."

"I don't know," Riley said. "I was just thinking."

"About what?"

"About how much it costs to keep Ben. You haven't said anything about his medical expenses."

"Because he hasn't had any. Except for not seeing well out of his left eye, and needing glasses soon, Ben is a healthy little boy. His recovery was truly a miracle. We shouldn't have to worry about medical expenses. In fact, you don't have to worry about anything. Frank and I have it all worked out."

"Uncle Riley, Uncle Riley," Ben shouted as he ran up the steps nearly out of breath. "Come see the castle I built for you."

Ben tugged Riley toward the sand box. Riley admired the mound of wet sand shaped with a small shovel and patted into place by hand. The miniature American flag which Riley had brought from New York flew atop his creation. With his finger, Ben carefully carved a large door in the sand beneath the flag, then turned toward his father and beamed.

"I love it," Riley said. "It's the finest castle I've ever seen."

Nora had plucked clean and cut up the pullet Frank had taken as a down payment on a pair of shoes he had sold on his Gulfport route that day and was mashing potatoes and cleaning collard greens while the chicken fried.

"I usually make a chicken last two days," Nora said. "Tonight I'm serving it all to celebrate Uncle Riley's safe return from the war. Frank, did you pick up any Budweiser today?"

"No, but there are a couple of bottles of Pabst in the pantry and plenty of Schlitz."

"Fine for you and Riley, what about me?"

"Hell, Nora, you drink beer so infrequently, I never think about whether there's any Bud at home. Why don't you drink Pabst and Schlitz like us guys?

"Because I don't like the taste. Annie, take Ben to the bathroom and make sure both of you get the sand out from under your fingernails. Riley, will you hand me that platter to put the chicken on?"

The drumsticks went to the children and the thighs went to Riley, who preferred dark meat. Frank took the larger breast and Nora took the wish bone, which the children would later pull apart, each hoping for the long end to ensure a wish came true. The back, wings, and neck were left for seconds. Nora poured a little gravy on top of the mashed potatoes she had dished onto Ben's plate, scooped out a spoonful of potatoes for Riley, then paused.

"I almost forgot. You told me you don't eat mashed potatoes." she said.

"I peeled so many potatoes in the army I vowed I would never eat another one. But I had a taste of your gravy and I don't think I can resist."

"Stick around," Frank laughed, "and Nora'll teach you a dozen ways to make potatoes irresistible. What time do I need to get you to the station in the morning?"

"If I take the 6:25, I'll get to Mobile in time to catch the 8:10 express to Birmingham. But you don't need to bother. I'll say my good-byes tonight and get a cab in the morning. I won't disturb a soul."

"Nonsense," Nora said. "You can say goodbye to the children when we put them to bed, I'll have coffee with you in the morning, and it'll only take Frank fifteen minutes to run you to the station. No need to call a cab."

Riley said little during supper as he mentally went over the dreaded discussion coming up. He watched Nora constantly move food away from the edge of Ben's plate toward the center, clean his face with her napkin and remind him to sit up straight and be still. When asked, she poured a little more milk into the small jelly jars Annie and Ben used for glasses. Twice she retrieved a fork which Ben had knocked off the table. The battle playing out in his head made it difficult for Riley to keep up with Frank's rambling narrative about his expansion plans, but an "I see," or "uh huh" whenever Frank paused kept the story going. After supper he read an abridged version of *Puss in Boots* to Annie and Ben while Nora tidied the kitchen and Frank finished the day's paper-work. Ben fell asleep near the end of the tale about the talented cat, who with cunning and wile, enhanced his poor master's fortune. Annie stayed alert to the end and required a visit from Mama before she would consider saying good night.

"Need another beer?" Frank asked as he headed for the Frigidaire before joining Riley in the living room. Riley shook his head and lit another Lucky.

"Lord help me if they aren't down for the night," sighed Nora, closing the bedroom door behind her. "Where does all his energy come from?"

Riley took a deep breath and watched the column

of smoke he created head for the ceiling as he exhaled. "Can we talk for a while?" he said.

"Sure," Frank chuckled. "It's still daylight. Too early to go to bed and too few of us to play poker. Nothing to do but talk. Want to sit on the porch?"

Nora demurred and joined Riley on the couch before lighting her own cigarette. Frank leaned against the screen door which led to the porch, took a swig of his Pabst, and said, "Nora didn't want me to tell you this, but it's too funny not to. Nora caught Ben red-handed in a theft."

"What!" Riley exclaimed.

"Yes, that little boy sneaked a nickel out of Nora's purse, went to the little store by himself without telling anyone, and bought a popsicle. He ate it all before he got home and thought he had gotten away with it, but he had to confess when Nora spotted a wet red stain on his shirt and made him stick out his tongue. She probably nipped a life of crime in the bud."

"I wouldn't take credit for that," Nora said, "but I needed to teach him not to do anything like that again."

"Yes," Frank laughed, "and your punishment was to make him go to bed at five that night, and I'm the one who had to keep him there." A smile crossed Riley's face, but quickly faded. He tried to calm his nerves.

"I know how attached you've become to Ben," he said, "and I am so grateful for all you've done for him and for me, but now that I'm home from the war, I want Ben back. I want him to live with me when I get a job."

Nora's eyes widened. Frank's bottle of Pabst crashed to the floor.

"That is not what we agreed to," Nora blurted. "You gave Ben to us to raise whether or not you returned from the war. He is ours now as much as Annie is."

"I admit that was our agreement," Riley said, "and when I made it, I meant it. I was certain I would be killed in the war, so I thought I had to make permanent arrangements for Ben while I could. But God brought me home, which must have been so that Ben would have a father."

"Listen here, Riley," Frank blustered, ignoring the broken glass at his feet. "Don't get all religious on us. A deal is a deal. We kept our end of the bargain and you must keep yours. Ben is ours now. I don't want to hear any more about you taking him away."

"You know I have the right to take him. He's still my child."

"No, he's not!" Frank shouted. "You gave him up. He belongs to us."

"I never let you adopt him," Riley shot back, stung by Frank's belligerence. "Ben is still legally mine."

"You said that was only so we could get the allotment for Ben," Nora retorted.

"Damn, I wish we had forgotten about that frigging allotment," Frank said. "We didn't need the money."

Now alone on the couch, Riley could not look at his sister's tear-streaked face. He could not ignore her words.

"I'm horrified, Riley, and very hurt that you are threatening to take Ben away from us," Nora said, "but let's not shout and scream at each other. Have you thought about how Ben would feel about leaving me? I'm the only mother he has known."

"And I'm the only living parent he has. Wouldn't a son want to be with his father if his real mother were dead?"

"Bullshit," Frank snapped. "I never wanted to be with my old man. I couldn't wait to get away from him. And Nora *is* a real mother to Ben."

"Please, Frank, go get a waste basket to put that broken glass in and calm down," Nora said. "Tell me, Riley. What does Eileen think about having Ben as a part of her family?"

Riley lit a fresh Lucky to give his quivering hands something to do and took a quick draw. He wished he could tell his sister that Eileen was all in favor of the idea.

"We've talked about it. Eileen is hesitant. She'll have to spend some time with Ben to get used to him. Eventually she will. Besides, the decision is mine to make—not hers."

"That bitch doesn't want to spend any time with Ben," Frank snorted. "She doesn't want another woman's kid in her nest. I saw enough of her in a day and a half to know she'll treat Ben like a red-headed stepchild, or worse."

"Frank!" Nora scolded. "Watch your language! You can't call Eileen a . . . a . . ."

"Bitch? Why not? That's what she is."

"But she's Riley's wife!"

"She may be, Nora, but you know as well as I do that

woman despises Ben. You could see it by the way she acted around him the one time she was here. Did she write him or come see him while Riley was overseas? Not once! Did she send him a birthday card? Or give him a gift for Christmas? Hell, no! She didn't even call him. She thought we had taken him off her hands, and she was damn glad to be shed of him."

Riley leaped from the couch. "Damn it, Frank! Don't talk about Eileen that way. You don't have to like her, but for Christ's sake be civil when you talk about her. Ben might hear you. Don't ruin his chance to develop a good relationship with Eileen."

Frank's eyes moistened. "I love that little guy as much as I do my own flesh and blood. I spent hours picking glass out of his scalp and I taught him how to tie his laces and shine his shoes. I wouldn't do anything to hurt him or make his life more difficult. You're the one who is hurting him by taking him away from a stable home with loving parents and a sister who adores him. For what? Life as the unloved stepson of a heartless bitch."

Riley retreated to the couch and looked to Nora for help. He got none.

"Do you really think Ben would be happier having Eileen as a mother than me?" Nora asked in a voice full of concern. "Forget about how much you would hurt Frank and me. Think about Ben. What kind of life will he have if you uproot him? Also, think about your wife. How old is she? 22? 23? You and Eileen want to have a child right away. She will have her hands full dealing with a newborn. Adding a five-year-old stepchild might overwhelm her, even if she wanted Ben."

"You don't know Eileen doesn't want Ben," Riley objected.

"Come on, Riley," Frank said. "Get real. It's obvious to everyone who has been around her that Eileen does not want Ben. I don't know what BS she's laying on you to make you think otherwise, but you know damn well she doesn't. I can't understand how a level-headed guy like you can't see through her."

"She ... she, needs time," Riley sputtered. "I've been back less than a week. Eileen and I have barely had time to reconnect. We have a lot of readjusting to do. When we find a place to live and I get settled in a job, she'll think differently about Ben. She'll see how much he means to me and accept him. I know she will."

"Is Eileen already expecting?" Nora asked.

"I don't know. She could be. I thought it best to wait till I got discharged and found a job before we tried to have a baby. She wanted us to start working on it right away."

Nora came over and sat on the couch with Riley.

"I need another beer," Frank said as he stomped off to the kitchen. Nora took both of Riley's hands into hers.

"Why don't you take a job in New Orleans or Mobile," she said, "or even Biloxi so you'd be close by and could visit Ben practically any time? That would let you have lots of contact with him and would relieve Eileen of the problem of having to take care of Ben and a new baby, and would allow Ben to see you often, without being uprooted. Makes sense, doesn't it?"

Yes, it made sense. It did not, however, satisfy Riley's desire to have his son, his flesh and blood, his living, breathing connection to his first wonderful love, with him all the time.

"I'll think about it," he said. Even though he had already considered and rejected every argument Nora and Frank had made.

Riding the rails the next day gave Riley the opportunity to smoke — too much stress to quit now — and contemplate. He found the clickety-clack of steel wheels passing rail joints soothing as they measured the increasing distance between him and his son. He ignored the passing landscape and thought about his overwhelming desire to have Ben.

Yes, he was breaking a promise he had made to Nora and Frank. Yes, it had taken a five-thousand-dollar financial carrot to get Eileen to consider accepting his son, and yes, he would be uprooting Ben. Nora and Frank's feelings notwithstanding, a father has the right to raise his son. Riley was certain Nora would not stand in his way, and he was confident, despite Nora's and Frank's concerns, Eileen would come to love Ben. She would soon be won over by his innocence and charm. As for uprooting Ben, everyone was being uprooted. The wives and children of all returning service men had to adjust to the reality of their husbands and fathers being back. He wanted his new reality to be a fresh start with Eileen and his little boy.

As the train approached Birmingham, Riley, having resolved to bring Ben home without delay, headed for the club car for some company and a late morning coffee. When the train reached the station, however, the club car emptied as quickly as if everyone else had been swept out the door by the hand of God, leaving Riley to drink alone. He quickly downed his coffee and returned to his seat, where he spent the rest of the trip drifting in and out of sleep.

"Oh, Riley, I've missed you so much," Eileen, scented with Chanel and wearing aqua pedal pushers and a white blouse tied at the waist, said when she finally pulled her lips away from his on the platform at Union Station.

"I've missed you, too," Riley said. "Is that a new blouse?"

"Yes, Mother made it for me. How were things with your sister?"

"Oh, everyone was fine. It was good to see Ben again. He knows me now, and I can tell he likes me. We spent Thursday morning at the beach together with Nora and Annie. He is a happy child."

Riley put his arm on Eileen's shoulder and began to nudge her toward the street. "I have a lot of things on my mind, honey, and I want to talk to you about them soon, just not now," he said. "You look gorgeous, and your perfume reminds me of the first time I saw you. Let's spend the night here and drive to your mother's in the morning."

"I'd love that!" Eileen said. "I do need to let Mother know we won't be in tonight."

"Tell me her number," Riley said as he got out change for the payphone. "I'll let her know where we are, then I'll call the Alamo Motor Lodge on Highway 41 and reserve a room."

Eileen laughed. "Don't you remember? She doesn't have a number. She's on a party line. Her ring is two shorts and a long. Tell the long-distance operator to connect you with the Tullahoma exchange. They'll ring her up for you."

"Hello, Mrs. Crosley," Riley said when Eileen's mother answered. "Eileen and I are pretty tired and it's so late we decided to spend the night here and drive home tomorrow. Is that okay?"

"Of course it is, and welcome home," Mrs. Crosley said. "A telegram arrived this morning. I think it's from the Army. Would you like for me to read it to you now or do you want to wait 'til you get here?"

"Read it now, please," Riley said. His face flushed with excitement.

The message from HDQ 2nd Army Command, Ft Benning, Georgia was brief. "Order to report to Ft Mason, Calif, cancelled. Leave continued until 1 November 1945. Then report to Camp Forrest, Tenn., at 0900 hours for receipt of WD AGO discharge papers and muster-out pay. Normal monthly allowance after allotments will be sent to you in care of this address through 31 October 1945."

"Hot Damn!" Riley shouted as he handed the phone

to Eileen. "My discharge came through. I was practically certain I'd get an early release because I have dependents and am already in the States, but I never thought it would be this quick. I can start looking for work immediately."

"That's wonderful, honey!" Eileen said. Then she put her finger to her mouth and whispered, "Mother's trying to tell me something."

Riley tried to put some order into the tornado of thoughts raging in his brain.

"Mother says we can stay with her as long as necessary," Eileen said as she hung up. "And there's more good news. Forget the Alamo, we're driving home tonight. Mother's going to get Cousin Ted to take her to Aunt Espa's for the weekend, so except for the chickens, the pigs and the cows, which you and I have to milk, we have the farm to ourselves to make love and talk about where we want to live."

"My best job opportunities are in Memphis, Jackson, and Nashville," Riley said as he, reclining on a pillow against the headboard, finished the cup of JFG coffee Eileen had perked for him Sunday morning. "All the newspapers and publishing houses need linotype operators. My experience will help, and lucky for me, I'll be getting the jump on a lot of guys who won't be discharged for months. I'll check out Nashville Monday and Tuesday, then take the night train and spend Wednesday and Thursday in Memphis and catch Jackson on the way back."

Eileen was counting the strokes aloud as she brushed her hair at the mirror. "88, 89, 90." Over her shoulder she called out, "Are you going to see your mother?"

"Don't see how that can happen. My schedule will be too tight. I will call her."

"Then can I go with you?"

"Honey, you'd slow me down, and what would you do while I'm going to interviews? Plus, think of the money we'll save if I go alone. It'll only be a few days. Stay here and keep your mom company."

"I've been doing that for a year," Eileen pouted. "Oh, Riley, please take me."

Riley reconsidered. Eileen would be great company on the long train rides and their nights would be available for mutual pleasure. The downside was at some point their conversation might turn to Ben, and he wanted to delay that discussion until he had a job offer in hand and knew where they would be living. Then again, they had been apart for a long time, and he had missed her.

"Okay, we'll go together and while I'm interviewing you can search the classifieds for an apartment. Maybe we'll have time to check a few of them out."

"Oh, darling, you've made me so happy," Eileen gushed. "I'll iron your shirt and pack my bag this afternoon. Do you think two outfits will be enough? Which nightie do you want me to bring?"

"Here's an apartment on West End that sounds good," Eileen said as she circled the fourth prospect she had found in the *Tennessean* they had brought back from their trip. "It's only $90 a month, including utilities and it's on a bus line."

"Why are you only looking in Nashville?" Riley laughed. "The *Commercial Appeal* position pays $6 a month more than my highest Nashville offer, and I'd have a better chance for overtime. Besides, Memphis is a bigger town and has a larger selection of apartments."

"Because I know Nashville, and I don't know anything about Memphis except that a man I don't like lives there."

Eileen put the paper down, put her hand on Riley's bare chest and began to gently pull his hairs with her thumb and forefinger.

"And because I'm going to need to be close to Mother."

"Oh?" Riley said. "Why?"

"Because, sweetheart, I'm a week late and I've never been late before. It looks like we're going to have a baby."

Riley lowered his paper, cocked an eyebrow, and looked at Eileen but did not speak. He saw the delight on her face fade as the seconds ticked off. He wanted another child, just not now. The news was more sobering than exhilarating. He had not expected her to conceive within a week of their first get together after the war. He thought he would have a few months to get comfortable in a job and to settle the Ben situation before having to deal with a pregnant wife and all the mood swings experience had taught him to expect. A little too late he said, "Honey, that's wonderful."

"Do you really mean that Riley? I'm sure I'm pregnant. My breasts are swollen and my nipples itch. Oh, sweetheart, I want this baby so much, and I want you to want it too."

"I do want this baby," Riley said. "Your getting pregnant, however, puts pressure on me to have a job waiting when I'm discharged and on us to decide where to live." After a long sigh he added, "and it means we have to talk about Ben."

Eileen ran her fingers up his arm to his cheek, turned it toward her and kissed it. "I've been talking to Mother about Ben," she said. "Mother tells me raising a five-year-old is not hard, if you keep him occupied. I'm sure I can find plenty of things for Ben to do, so I'm willing to give it a try. But please do this for me. It looks like our baby will come in May; could you wait until school starts in the fall before you get Ben?"

Riley knew being willing to "give it a try," was about the weakest commitment Eileen could make. It was, however, a commitment. If she tried, she would soon come to love Ben—just like everyone else. He heard Mrs. Crosley come in through the front door and begin stoking the fire in the kitchen stove. He must wire her house for electricity as soon as the power line was extended the last two miles from the highway to her property. He hoped the Rural Electric Authority would have completed the line before the end of the year.

"Thank you, sweetheart," he whispered, nuzzling Eileen's neck. "You've made me the happiest man in the world."

Eileen responded with a huge hug which banished all the tension Riley had felt since returning from Biloxi. He still had to break the news to Nora, which he decided to do Monday morning, when Frank would be at work.

"It's me, "Riley said when his sister answered his call. After a few seconds of dead silence, he said, "can you hear me?"

"Yes, I can hear you," Nora said. "And I know what you're going to say. I've been dreading this call all weekend."

"It's going to be okay, Nora. Eileen has come around. The only thing is, she *is* expecting, and like you predicted, the baby should come in May, so I thought..."

"I would keep Ben till then?"

"Actually, I was hoping you'd keep him till school starts next fall."

"Damn you, Riley!" Nora shouted. "How can you be so insensitive? I spent Saturday and Sunday weeping because I'm losing Ben, and now you ask me to keep him a few more months until it is convenient for you to take him. If I do, I'll be even more attached to him and it will cause me more heartache when he leaves. I hate you, Riley! I hate you!"

Shame spread over Riley like a shadow.

"I'm sorry, Nora," he said. "I'm really sorry. I thought you'd want to keep Ben as long as you could."

Nora's loud sobs rendered her voice almost

unintelligible. Riley thought he heard her say, "I can't talk to you any longer. I need to call Frank."

And then the line went dead. Struggling with his own emotions, Riley lit a cigarette, picked up the new ash tray Mrs. Crosley had acquired for him and headed for the swing on the front porch. Mrs. Crosley, who was watering her potted plants with a sprinkler which looked like a giant teapot with a long spout, smiled at him.

"It's been twenty years since I've heard the sounds of little children playing in this house," she said. "I can't wait to hear them again."

6

August 21, 1946

Black coffee, cigarettes, and anxiety were Riley's companions during the thirty minutes he waited at the Mobile depot for Ben to arrive. Ten minutes before the 8:02 scheduled departure of the *Hummingbird* back to Nashville, Frank appeared carrying a small cardboard box. Ben lagged behind, carrying a sack. Without speaking, Frank handed the box to Riley and knelt down to face Ben.

"Good-bye, son. Remember your Daddy Frank when you tie your shoes in the morning, and your Mama when you say your prayers at night. Your father will take you on from here. Be a good boy and mind him. Mama and I will always love you."

Frank rose, wiped his eyes, pressed a coin into the palm of Ben's hand, and strode to his car without speaking to Riley. Riley groped for words of thanks or reconciliation as he watched Frank leave, but he could not find them. Finally, he turned to his son.

"Give me a hug," he said. "Are you ready to go to Nashville?"

Ben was staring at the engine of the streamliner, his face filled with awe. He nodded "yes" to his father but did not hug him. Riley steered Ben by the shoulder to car number 10, where the conductor welcomed them aboard.

"Can I sit by the window?" Ben asked. "I want to see if Daddy Frank has stopped crying."

"Sure, you can sit by the window, but you won't be able to see anything except the train that is on the track next to us. Daddy Frank is already in his car by now, and I'm sure he's not crying anymore. He was just a little sad to see you go. What's in your sack?"

"Two apples Mama gave me in case I got hungry."

"Would you like something to drink?"

"Is there a bathroom on this train? Mama told me I'd have to go to the bathroom if I got anything to drink."

"The bathroom is at the end of the car," Riley said. "We passed it getting on."

Ben got out of his seat and peered in the direction his father had pointed. Riley restrained him from stepping into the aisle.

"I need to see it. Mama said I shouldn't go unless I could lock the door and the train was moving."

"We'll check it out on the way to get some chocolate milk and maybe a Moon Pie for breakfast. Will you share an apple with me later?"

Ben inspected his two apples carefully, handed the smaller one to Riley and put the larger one back in his sack.

"Mama fixed me breakfast before I left, but can I have a Moon Pie anyway? I can pay for it. Daddy Frank gave me some money."

"Sure. We'll go to the club car and get you one. I'll get a cup of coffee."

As soon as they got back to their seats, Ben tore open the wrapper and took a huge bite of the Moon Pie he had proudly paid for.

"Uncle … Oh, I mean Daddy Riley," Ben said as he chewed, "how much change did I get?"

"Let's see, a quarter, a dime, and a nickel. Do you want me to keep it for you?"

Ben shook his head, "No. I'll keep it. I may need to buy something else, especially if we have to spend the night on the train, like you did last night."

"Don't talk with your mouth full," Riley said as he reached over to brush crumbs from the stiffly starched white shirt Ben wore with his Sunday pants and brand-new L. B. Price shoes.

"Why?" Ben asked.

"It doesn't look nice and your food may fall out."

Ben wiped his mouth with the back of his hand and sheepishly checked his shirt for crumbs or chocolate stains.

"I know, Mama told me that. I just forget sometimes."

"Are you excited about going to Nashville?" Riley asked.

Ben stopped chewing, wiped his mouth again, and looked as if he were in deep thought. Riley wondered what was going on in Ben's mind. Is this just a big adventure, or does Ben realize he is leaving everything he has known behind?

"I like to ride on trains," Ben finally replied. "Mama took Annie and me on one to New Orleans to see Aunt T. But I've never been on a streamliner before. Can streamliners go really fast?"

"Fast enough to get us to Nashville before dark. Your mommy and baby brother are expecting us for supper. They can't wait to see you."

"I don't have a brother," Ben responded emphatically. "I have a sister and she's not a baby. She'll be in third grade when school starts."

Ben took a big sip of chocolate milk before continuing.

"And I do not have a mommy."

Another bite of Moon Pie later he said, "Mama told me I could call you Daddy Riley, because when I was born, you were already my daddy, and after my mommy went to heaven and you were in the Army, she became my Mama and Daddy Frank became my Daddy and Annie became my sister."

"Why don't you just call me Daddy? Then you'll have a Daddy and a Daddy Frank. And Eileen can be your new mommy."

Ben frowned. "Eileen is *not* my mommy. Mama told me Eileen was my stepmother. My mommy died when I was a little baby and is in heaven watching over me."

"I'm sure your mommy is in heaven, and I'm sure she will watch over you in your new home in Nashville, just like she watched over you in your old home in Biloxi."

Ben twisted in his seat before he leaned forward and jutted out his chin. "No, Biloxi is my home. Daddy Frank told me this morning that he and Mama would always love me, and when I got big enough to ride the train by myself, I could come back to Biloxi to see him and Mama whenever I wanted to."

"Maybe come back for a visit sometime, but you will be living with Eileen and me in Nashville and going to school there. You'll be our little boy."

Ben finished his chocolate milk with a slurp, shook his head vigorously and said, "Mama told me I would be staying with you in Nashville so I could go to first grade in a big school with lots of kids like me, and that I would be as good as they were. Mama said I would always be her little boy, and Mama always tells the truth."

After the final bite of Moon Pie, Ben sat straight up, crumpled the wrapper into a ball and said, "Can I have another Moon Pie for lunch?"

"Tickets, please," the conductor droned as he reached out with his left hand, holding a hole-puncher in his right. Riley handed him the tickets to be cancelled.

"Going to Nashville, young man," the conductor said. "Want to see if my cap fits your head?"

Ben jumped up and stood straight and tall, as if to be fitted for a crown. The conductor's cap swallowed his ears and the bill came down over his eyes.

"Looks like you'll have to grow a little more," the

conductor laughed as he retrieved his cap and moved on.

"I have grown," Ben called back. "Mama told me I grew two inches since my birthday."

Riley was astonished that Nora had prepared Ben for the minutiae of train travel, but apparently had not prepared him for the earth-shattering change taking place in his life. He regretted not having patched things up with her, but their two phone conversations in the six months since he had pronounced his final decision about Ben had ended in acrimonious accusations and slammed receivers, without resolving any issues. Even his mother, who strongly supported reuniting Ben with Riley, had failed in her efforts to ameliorate Nora's bitter feelings. Eileen had strongly objected to being left pregnant and alone, so making another trip to Biloxi to negotiate peace with Nora had been impossible.

Arrangements for picking Ben up weren't finalized until three weeks before school was to start in a tense, painful conversation between Frank and Riley. Now that Ben was sitting next to him on the train bound for Nashville and a new life with a new family, Riley realized that he was just as unprepared for his son as his son was for him. He reached for the copy of the Birmingham *News* he had bought on the way down. "Would you like for me to read you the funny papers?"

"Daddy Frank helps me read *Blondie* and *Nancy* every Sunday."

"Well, why don't you read them to me?"

"Okay," Ben said, scooting as close to his father as he could in order to see the paper. "Can I read *Dick Tracy* to you also?"

The Sunday comics, two shared Moon Pies, and long naps together strengthened the relationship between father and son on that eight-hour train ride from Mobile to Nashville.

"What a handsome little boy you are!" Mrs. Crosley exclaimed when she met them at Nashville's Union Station. "Would you hold my hand and help me across the street to my car? I'm your new mother's mother. I teach first graders, just like you."

Ben cautiously took Mrs. Crosley's hand and they started for the exit, leaving Riley to deal with Ben's meager belongings.

"Are you going to be my teacher?" Ben asked.

"Oh, no," Mrs. Crosley said, "I teach in a little country school about sixty miles away. You will be going to a big school here in Nashville."

Ben inspected her carefully. "What is your name?"

"Marjorie Crosley. Most folks call me Miss Margie."

"Miss Margie," he said. "Mama told me to call little girls Miss, not old ladies."

"Well, I am 45," Mrs. Crosley laughed, "but I don't think I'm old. How old are you?"

"Five and a half. My birthday is in December. When is your birthday?"

"In August. In fact, I had a birthday just two weeks

ago. Too bad you weren't here then. You and I could have had a party."

"Really? Can you come to my birthday party in December—if I have one?"

"Of course, you'll have a party," Mrs. Crosley said with a big smile. "And I'll bring you a present."

She handed Riley the keys and said, "Why don't you drive. Ben can sit up front between us and he and I can get to know each other."

Beaming at the opportunity to ride in the front seat with this interesting woman, Ben climbed in beside Mrs. Crosley. Oblivious to his father and to the knobs and buttons he always had played with during his previous infrequent rides in the front seat of an automobile, he examined her small face and tiny glasses closely. Mrs. Crosley peered back at him and said, "I had no idea you'd be so big and handsome. I am going to take a picture of you when we get home so I can show it to all your new relatives. And since I'm going to be your new grandmother, what do you want to call me?"

Ben snuggled up to her. Riley felt tremendous relief seeing Ben go to Margie like a kitty to a bowl of cream. If Margie took to Ben instantly, why hadn't her daughter?

"I like you," Ben said. "I think I'll call you Margie."

Mrs. Crosley put both arms around him and hugged him tightly. "I like you too, you darling creature. I think I'll call you Ben."

Ben was puzzled by Riley's worried look each time he glanced at his father on the ride to his new home, but no warning signs flashed. His acceptance of Margie had come so soon, he lost himself in her company. By the time his father pulled into the drive that served the five unit apartment building on Blakely Street where Eileen and baby Charles were waiting, Ben had told Margie he liked chocolate milk - not white, his favorite cowboy was Gene Autry, his favorite foods were ice cream and fried chicken, his Mama and Daddy Frank both smoked in bed and that once he got a swat on his bottom because he ran outside naked to play in the rain after his Saturday bath.

"My, my, you were a naughty boy," Margie exclaimed as she exited the car, "but you don't do that anymore, do you?"

"No, now I put my pants on like Mama told me to."

Margie gave him another squeeze. "Tell you what. I'll keep a bathing suit for you at my house and you can play outside in the rain any time you want to in the summer. Unless there is lightning, and it wouldn't be safe."

Ben quickly took the hand she extended as they started toward the building. He surveyed the strange surroundings. There was no swing on the small porch, no trees and little grass in the front yard, and no flowers anywhere. Three cars were parked in the drive ahead of where Riley had pulled in. The setting sun's rays were filtered through a maze of soot that permeated the Nashville air and settled on the cars. With the back of his hand, Ben tried to wipe away the grit that had found its way into his eyes.

Suddenly the front door opened and there stood Eileen wearing a paisley robe and house slippers, holding a crying baby. Ben tightened his grip on Margie's hand, moved as close to her as he could and peered around her waist. Margie gently squeezed his hand.

"You're late!" Eileen fumed as they went inside. "I delayed nursing Charles to wait for you and now he is upset because I had to stop when I saw you coming."

"Give me that precious little thing," Margie said. "He probably just needs to burp."

With Ben clinging to a pocket on her dress, she rested Charles' head on her shoulder and began to pat his back lightly, cooing all the time. By the time they got to the apartment, Charles had let out a burp and stopped fretting. Riley held the door open for everyone.

"Come with me, Ben," he said, "and let Margie ..."

"No, No," Margie interrupted, handing Charles back to Eileen, "I'll help Ben unpack."

Riley released Ben's box of belongings and followed Eileen into the larger bedroom, leaving the door slightly ajar. Eileen resumed nursing the baby.

A small shelf in the closet of the smaller bedroom and a single dresser drawer were more than adequate to store the change of underwear, one shirt, one pair of pants, his old shoes, and the book of *Grimm's Fairy Tales* Ben had brought with him. His remaining clothes were too small or too worn out to justify buying a case for. His tricycle, sand bucket, and shovel were too bulky to bring.

"I guess you and I will share this bed tonight," Margie said as she let down the roll-away and made it up with sheets and a pillowcase. "But you'll have it all to yourself after I go home tomorrow."

"You're leaving tomorrow?"

"Yes, I have school Monday morning, just like you do," Margie said.

"Can I go with you?" Ben pleaded.

"That would be lovely, wouldn't it?" Margie said, "but you must stay here and go to your school and I must go home and go to mine. We still have tomorrow to enjoy together, don't we?"

On Sunday morning Margie and Ben were up and dressed at 6:30. By the time the baby woke everyone else up whimpering to be fed, she had fried a few strips of bacon and baked Martha White biscuits for breakfast. "Shall I fix your eggs, now?" she asked a sleepy Ben when she bent over to kiss him. "Your dad said you like them scrambled in the skillet."

Riley, sipping a cup of strong coffee to combat the effects of a night with little sleep, joined them at the table.

"Can I have a bite of your egg, cowboy?" he said. Ben scrutinized Riley's unshaven face and blood-shot eyes, before nodding his assent. "This coffee and one of Margie's delicious biscuits—and maybe a little jelly—are all I want."

"I thought I would walk Ben over to his school this morning," Margie said, "to see how long it takes to get there and to check out the traffic light at 21st Avenue."

"Thanks for doing that," Riley said. "Registration was Friday, so Eileen will need to take Ben a little early tomorrow to sign him in. She'll have to take the baby with her. I hope she can manage."

"If Miss Bess had been available to substitute, I'd have stayed over Monday to take him myself. Unfortunately, she wasn't, so I have to get back to my students."

Margie smiled at Ben and wiped a crumb from his cheek.

"Everything will be alright," she said. "I know it will."

Ben and Margie set out just after breakfast. Even at a leisurely pace, the trip took less than a quarter of an hour. They followed the sidewalk around the building to the main entrance of the school. With Margie's help, Ben sounded out the letters, "Aiken Elementary School," on the sign above the door. They stood on the steps and looked out at the empty driveway, then hand in hand headed home to a fretful Charles and an unhappy Eileen.

"Can you help me with Charles?" Eileen pleaded. "He's been like this all night. I barely got any sleep. He must have colic."

Margie cuddled Charles close to her and began to sing softly to him as she gently rocked him back and forth in her arms. Almost immediately Charles stopped crying,

"Is it time to nurse him?" Margie asked.

"Not for another hour," Eileen said. "Please watch him so I can get some sleep."

Margie took Charles to the rocker and scooted over

to make room for Ben. "Come sit with me," she said. "Let me introduce you to your baby brother."

Ben climbed into the chair and leaned over Margie to peer at Charles.

"His hands are so little," Ben said, "and his face is all puffed up. What color are his eyes?

"You were probably just like that when you were three months old," Margie laughed, "and look how big and strong you have become. You'll have to wait a while to know the color of his eyes, but I'll bet they'll be blue green. Just like your daddy's. It won't be long till Charles will be big enough for you and him to play together."

"Just like Annie and me?" Ben said. "Annie and I built forts and went to the beach together. Can I take Charles to the beach?"

Margie laughed. "Not for a while," she said. "For now, you can build imaginary forts and play with blocks by yourself."

Ben grimaced.

"Even better," Margie said, "you can read your brother stories."

"I know!" Ben said, "I can read him *Blondie* and *Nancy* in the funny papers."

Supper was early that night so that Margie could start home before dark.

"Come sit by me, Ben," Margie said. "I have to leave while it's light enough for me to drive, but I'll be back for your birthday and I'll bet your Daddy will bring you to my house real soon."

Ben was warmed by Margie's closeness for the few

minutes they sat together. When it was time to go, she took his hand, led him to her car and kissed him goodbye. When the car disappeared from sight, for the first time in his life, Ben felt totally alone.

Monday morning, eager to see what the first grade was all about, Ben awoke before seven and had put on the shirt and pants Mama had bought him for the train trip to Nashville and tied the laces on his new shoes before Riley came to check on him.

"Charles kept us up again last night," Riley said, "so I'll have to call in late for work and walk to school with you to get you registered. How does toast and bacon sound for breakfast?"

Father and son quickly finished breakfast and walked to school, entering the principal's office together where Riley signed the registration papers.

"All set," Riley said when he finished. "I'm sure you are going to like your teacher. Bye now, I'm late for work already."

Bewildered by activities around him that he did not understand, Ben wished his father could go to the classroom with him so he would not have to brave this new world alone. He meekly followed the teacher's aide to the classroom, peaked through the open door and saw 25 small faces sitting at 25 small desks and a pretty woman standing behind a large desk writing on the blackboard. The woman turned toward him and smiled.

"Hello, Benjamin," she said. "I'm Miss Johnson, your teacher. I saw you and your father in the principal's office. Wait right there for me to finish and I'll show you to your seat."

Susan Johnson, five years out of the Peabody School for Teachers, was also new to Aiken Elementary. By the end of the day, Ben adored her. Although she was much younger, she reminded him of Margie when she greeted him so kindly, and again when she knelt down beside him to explain that because his last name started with "M," he could not sit on the front row as he desired, but on the fifth, between a freckle faced girl named Alice Miller, who lived in the apartment building next to his and Ronald Mashburn, who had a brother in the second grade.

Ben skipped home that afternoon, happy with his first day in a new school in a new place. Not once had he thought of Eileen, but he had often thought of Margie and Mama. Two women who treated him kindly evoked the same loving thoughts. He was glad that his daddy had brought him to school that first day since Margie could not. He obeyed the crossing guard's instructions at the 21st Avenue intersection and broke into a run when he got to Blakely Street. He wished he had someone to tell about his day as soon as he got home and didn't have to wait till evening for Daddy.

The front door to the apartment building was unlocked, as was the door to his unit. He found Eileen in the kitchen washing baby bottles and Charles lying on a quilt at her feet, trying to capture his toes with his fingers, and cackling with pleasure when he succeeded.

"What's that pinned to your shirt?" was Eileen's greeting.

"Something my teacher wanted you to see."

"Let me have it."

Ben handed the note to Eileen, who read it silently, stuck it in her pocket, then looked sternly at Ben.

"You didn't make up your bed this morning, so go take care of that right away. As soon as you finish, wash your hands, be sure to use soap, and come play with Charles while I start supper. Tomorrow, be sure your bed is made before you leave for school, and each day when you get home, clean the toilet, and empty all the waste-baskets into the trash can outside. And be quiet about it. I don't want Charles's afternoon nap disturbed."

The coldness in Eileen's voice frightened Ben. Mama had taught him to set the table, dry the dishes, and hang up his clothes, but Eileen had added more chores and did not appear ready to stop. He tried to figure out what he had done to upset her. It must have been the note. Eager to get away, he shrugged his shoulders and turned to go. Eileen grabbed him.

"Don't you dare leave before I'm finished!" she shouted. "And wipe that smirk off your face. If you think you don't have to do anything around here, you have another think coming. Just because Mother and your daddy treat you like royalty, doesn't mean you are. You're not perfect. You didn't hang the moon."

Eileen met Riley at the door that night with the note in her hand. "Listen to this," she commanded.

"Dear Mrs. McHaney, I'm Susan Johnson, Ben's teacher, and am so glad to have him in our class. He is a delight to talk to and I can tell already he is going to be an eager learner. Since you missed registration, I'm sending this note to remind you to send me a copy of his vaccination record. Also, Ben needs two number two pencils, a lined beginner's writing tablet, a ruler, a small jar of paste or glue, and a pair of safety scissors to leave at school. Please obtain those as soon as possible. I look forward to meeting you. Sincerely, Miss Johnson."

"The nerve of that woman," Eileen hissed.

"What's the problem?" Riley said. "Sounds to me like a great first day." He turned to Ben. "I'm proud of you, son. Do you like Miss Johnson as much as she must like you?"

"Yes! I like her a lot. She was nice to me and—"

"Well, *I* don't like her," Eileen interrupted. "She shouldn't be scolding me for missing registration, and she should have given you the note this morning, not sent it home pinned to Ben's shirt, as if I wouldn't find it in his pocket. Anyway, we should only have to buy pencils and paper for him. The county should provide rulers, paste, and scissors for all the students to share, like they do at Mother's school."

"Good grief, Eileen," Riley said. "How much are you talking about? A dollar?"

"A dollar here, a dollar there, if we aren't careful, we'll be in the poor house."

"Ben needs school supplies," Riley said. "While you finish putting supper together, I'll take him down to the dime store in the village before it closes. We'll be back in twenty minutes."

"But I need you to watch Charles while I'm in the kitchen."

Riley sighed, put Charles in his stroller and said, "I'll take Charles with us. Come on Ben. Would you like to push Charley?"

Of course Ben did. Anything to be with his Dad and away from Eileen.

"Daddy," Ben said on their walk to the Village. "Do you know who hung the moon?"

Riley laughed. "Oh, that's just an expression used to indicate someone is pretty wonderful. Why do you ask?"

"Eileen told me this afternoon that I didn't hang the moon, and I was wondering what she meant. I thought God hung the moon."

Riley tried to mask his frustration. Finally, he took a deep breath, looked straight at Ben and said, "You're a wonderful little fellow and I love you very much. Do you understand that taking care of baby Charles is hard work and tires Eileen out? When Eileen is tired, sometimes she says things she doesn't mean. Don't let those things bother you."

Ben walked along in silence for a few moments, then said, "Does that mean I don't have to pay attention to Eileen if she's mad?"

"No, son, pay attention to her," Riley sighed, "and mind her. She is your mother."

"She's not my mother," Ben corrected.

"All right, she's your step-mother, but you need to treat her more like a mother," Riley said, frantically trying to decide what to say next. "Ben. I need you to respect Eileen and do as she asks. If she…if she snaps at you, just don't let it upset you."

"But, daddy," Ben said. "I don't know how to do that."

After their purchase, father and son jointly pushed Charley's stroller home. Riley thought of the burden he was putting on his son to act like an adult, when the adult in charge of him acted like a child.

The next night, Eileen met Riley at the door again. "We need to talk."

"Is it so important it can't wait until after I've read the paper and had a little time to unwind?" Riley asked as he brushed past her into the living room.

"You need to tell your son to flush when he uses the commode."

"I do flush," Ben, who was setting the table for supper, said. "I flush when I do a number two."

"Don't dispute my word!" Eileen shouted. "I can smell your pee when I take my bath in the morning."

"Mama told me not to flush when I just do a number one. It wastes water."

"Well, I don't care what 'Mama' says. You are to flush every time you use the commode. Do you understand?"

Riley shook a Lucky from its pack, lit it, took a draw, patted the seat beside him for Ben to join him on the couch and smoothed the wisp of Ben's hair that stuck up like a rooster's tail.

"Since the war is over, we don't have to be so careful about saving water, I think Mama would tell you it's okay to flush every time now—and in this house, our house, not only is it okay to flush every time, but I'd like you to do that for me. Can you, Ben?"

"And tell him not to use so much toilet paper," Eileen added. "He went through the rest of the roll this afternoon when he got home from school."

"Mama told me to keep wiping until I couldn't see any brown," Ben said.

Riley laughed. Eileen glared.

"Let me tell you how we did it in the Army. We would take two squares and fold them together. Wipe once, then fold again and wipe again. That usually did the trick."

Ben smiled. "Next time I go to the bathroom, will you to show me how to wipe the Army way?"

"Gladly," Riley said.

Then, turning to Eileen he said, "Anything else?"

"I don't see what's so funny about this," she growled. "And yes, there is something else. I don't want him calling me Eileen."

Turning back to Ben, Riley said, "I understand you don't want to call Eileen 'Mommy' because you have a Mommy in Heaven, and you don't want to call her 'Mama' because you have a Mama in Biloxi, but you can't continue to call her Eileen. Little Charles will hear you and when he starts to talk, he might call her Eileen, and that would hurt her feelings. I call my mama, Mother. Could you call Eileen Mother?"

"Like Mother Goose?" Ben grinned. "I'll call her Mother Eileen."

"How about just Mother?"

"No, Mother Eileen. I might have another Mother someday."

"Just Mother would be better. Would you do that for me?"

Ben's forehead wrinkled. He locked eyes with Riley. There was no mistaking the inner struggle revealed on Ben's face. At last, he nodded yes.

"Then it's settled," Riley sighed. "Are you ready to read the funnies to me? I want to see what *Buzz Sawyer* and *Dick Tracy* are up to."

On the Saturday in December before Ben's sixth birthday, Margie arrived with a three-layered devil's-food cake topped with chocolate icing half an inch thick. Ben jumped on her like an excited puppy.

"Careful, now," Margie said. "Don't make me drop this cake. I didn't know how many kids you would invite to your party, so I made a big one."

"I can't have any friends at my party. Mother said she didn't want anyone who might have a cold coming over and making Charles sick."

Margie shot a withering look at Eileen. Ben wondered why Eileen turned away.

"That's alright, darling. There will be the four of us and we can all have bigger slices. After lunch will you walk with me to the grocery store to get some vanilla ice cream and some candles for the cake? And, oh, yes, I need some ribbon to wrap your present."

The next day Margie and Riley vigorously sang happy birthday to a beaming Ben. Eileen mouthed the words.

"This is from your mother and dad," Margie said as she handed Ben an envelope after everyone had finished super-sized helpings of cake and ice cream.

"And this is from me."

Ben barely got out a "Thank you," for the dollar in the envelope before he carefully untied the ribbon he had picked out the day before and began to rip the Sunday funny papers off a box that was almost too large for him to hold. When he saw the logo on the box he shouted, "A train set! That's just what I wanted. I have been hoping Santa Claus would bring me one. Thank you, Margie."

Margie returned Ben's hug and kissed him on the top of his head. "Let's take this into your room and I'll help you put the track into a figure eight, and set up the tunnels, road crossings, roundhouse and train station. First you have to wind up the engine. After a few minutes the train will stop, and you'll have to wind it up again. I wish I could have afforded an electric train."

Ben grabbed the box and headed for his bedroom. "Come play trains with us, Daddy. Margie will be the conductor and I'll be the engineer. You can be the station manager."

"No, he can't," Eileen said. "I need him to help me give Charles a bath."

"Sorry, old buddy, not this time," Riley said. "Have fun with Margie. You and I can play next time."

In bed that night, Ben thought about the fun he had that day with Margie and wondered how she knew he wanted a train set. He remembered his fifth birthday in Biloxi when Mama and Daddy Frank had given him a cowboy suit, a cap gun, and a roll of caps, which was exactly what he had wanted. A tiny pain came over him just thinking about Annie's continuing to drop dead when he shouted "BANG" after he ran out of caps. He went to sleep regretting that Mama and Daddy Frank had not been with him this birthday, but thankful that Margie had.

The Wednesday before school was out for Christmas break the phone rang just as Ben arrived home. "I'll get it," Eileen said. "Dry the dishes in the sink and put them up before you clean the toilet."

"Hello. Yes, Mrs. Miller. I am Ben's mother, and what is your daughter's name?"

"No, he hasn't mentioned Alice. Has he done something mean to her?"

"Thank heaven," Eileen said. "Yes, I do have a new baby, but how did you get the idea that I wasn't sending cookies to the class Christmas party?"

"You are mistaken. I am sending cookies to the party, but I don't have time to bake them and thank you, but I don't need your help!"

Eileen slammed the receiver with such force the

phone's bell tingled. She grabbed Ben by the arm and began shaking him.

"OW!" Ben yelped. He tried to pull away but could not break Eileen's grip.

"What do you mean telling your teacher I wasn't sending cookies? Why did you lie to her?"

"I didn't lie to her. You told me you didn't have time to bake cookies and that's what I told Miss Johnson when she asked me what kind of cookies you were making."

Anger blazed in Eileen's eyes. "Because I was too busy to bake cookies didn't mean I wouldn't send cookies. Are you too stupid to understand that?"

Ben wracked his brain, trying to make sense of Eileen's fury. Was he stupid? What did he not understand? "You . . . you didn't say anything about sending cookies," he said. "You said you didn't have time to bake any and that's what I told my teach . . ."

Ben did not see it coming. His cheek took the full impact of Eileen's slap, and his face burned as if it were on fire. He felt blood trickling from his nose. Tears swam in his eyes, but he refused to cry.

"Don't talk back to me!" Eileen screamed. "Go to your room this instant and stay there until I tell you to come out."

Ben stopped by the bathroom and stuffed tissue up his nose to stop the bleeding. His chest rose and fell, and he swallowed hard. Daddy Frank had smacked him on the bottom with his bare hand a time or two, and Mama had occasionally threatened to "take a paddle to him if he didn't behave," but had never done so.

She slapped me! Mothers weren't supposed to slap . . . were they? Were there different rules for stepmothers?

The bleeding quickly stopped. and the pain subsided. His bewilderment, however, did not. He had told the truth, both to his teacher and to his stepmother. What had he done wrong? He carefully folded the tissue he had taken out of his nose, which showed only a small smear of blood, and put it in his pocket. He hoped the fading red patch on his cheek would remain until his Daddy got home. As he sat in his room, sullen and hurt, a sense of triumph came over him. He had survived Eileen's attack without shedding a tear.

Dinner was ready when Riley arrived that night. Charles was asleep in his playpen and Ben was in his room with the door open, practicing making his capital letters more legible. Freshly made up and perfumed, Eileen kissed Riley at the door. "Will you be ready to eat soon, sweetheart? I fixed your favorite—roast beef and a baked potato."

"After I've had a beer. Do we have any cold?"

"There's a Bud in the ice-box. I'll bring it to you in the living room."

Ben gathered up his afternoon's work as soon as he heard his father arrive and stood by the couch. The redness had completely disappeared from his cheek. He decided the "smear" of blood might not be enough to bother about.

"What you got there, tiger? A little homework?"

Ben grinned and handed Riley the paper containing the 26 rows of capital letters he had produced.

"Looks perfect to me. What else did you do in school today?

Before Ben could answer, Eileen appeared, handed Riley a Budweiser, and said to Ben, "I left my empty glass on the counter. Re-fill it from the water pitcher in the refrigerator and bring it to me."

Ben obeyed, disappointed at not being allowed to answer his father's question. Eileen sat down on the couch next to Riley.

"Why were you so abrupt with Ben?" Riley asked. "You spoke to him like a hired hand."

Ben quickly stopped pouring so he could hear better. Eileen picked a piece of lint off Riley's shirt.

"Oh, darling, you don't need to worry about my silly troubles. Enjoy your beer."

When Ben started back with Eileen's water, he saw his father look at him and soften his expression. "I can't enjoy a beer if you're unhappy, Eileen. Tell me what's going on."

Eileen sighed. "I had a hard day today, that's all. Charles is teething and Ben was absolutely awful."

"In what way?"

"He told his teacher a lie about me."

"He what! Ben told a *lie*!"

All of Ben's muscles tightened. He wanted to shout *She*'s lying! I did not tell a lie. Not one!

"He told her I refused to send cookies for his class party tomorrow," Eileen said. "He made me look bad on purpose."

Riley's voice changed. To Ben, it sounded as if he

were trying to figure out a puzzle, only he never would be able to because Eileen wasn't giving him all the pieces.

"On Saturday, you asked me to pick up a box of ginger snaps," Riley said slowly.

"Yes, I did," Eileen sniffed. "And then today, one of the room mothers called and offered to bake cookies for me, as if I were too feeble or lazy to bake a batch myself. Oh, Riley, it was terrible! I felt so humiliated!"

"Those ginger snaps were for a party?" Riley said. "You should have told me. I wouldn't have sampled them."

"No, no, that's not the problem. I only have to send a dozen," Eileen said as she rubbed Riley's arm. "I want you to reprimand Ben."

"Sweetheart," Riley said. Now it sounded as if he were choosing his words carefully. "I'm sorry for what happened. But to say Ben *lied*…"

"Are you suggesting he didn't?" Eileen huffed. "He lied to me. All children lie. Riley! I am your wife. I need your support!"

"And you are getting it. I'm just saying that lying doesn't sound like something Ben would do. Maybe it was a simple mix-up. Let's hear what he has to say. Ben!!"

Ben slowly approached with Eileen's half-filled glass of water. He tried to hand the glass to her, but she ignored him. Riley took the glass and set it on the coffee table.

"Ben," he began. "Eileen said you told your teacher a

story about some cookies for a party at school. Tell me about it."

Ben put his hands in his pants pockets, clasped the tissue he had saved from the afternoon and rocked back and forth as the story spilled out.

"Our class is having a Christmas party Friday, and last week Miss Johnson told everyone on my row to bring a dozen cookies for treats. She said it would be nice if they were made at home by our mothers." Ben stole a glance at Eileen, but the mean look on her face made him quickly turn away.

"When I got home, I told Mother that Miss Johnson wanted her to bake a dozen cookies for our party," he continued. "She said she had a baby and didn't have time." He tucked his hands beneath his armpits. "So that's what I told Miss Johnson."

Eileen glared at Ben but said nothing.

Riley said, "I see. Well, Ben, do you think it would be all right if you took ginger snaps from the store?"

Ben considered the question for a moment before breaking into a grin.

"I could take them out of the box and put them on a plate then pretend I had a mother who made them!"

Eileen stormed into her bedroom, slamming the door behind her.

Riley turned on the radio. The Jack Benny show was on.

"All right, buddy. Listen to Jack Benny while I go talk to your mother," Riley said. "It's just started."

Later, as Ben was putting on his pajamas for bed,

Riley came into his room and let down his roll-away bed.

"Listen, son," he said. "I know you didn't lie to anyone about the cookies. It was just a misunderstanding."

"Does Mother know that too? That she misunderstood?"

Riley sat down on the bed. Ben crawled into his lap. "There are things that it's hard for a little boy to understand, even a smart boy like you," Riley said. His voice was heavy, and Ben knew in a flash that his father was really saying, no, Eileen still thought he was a liar.

"I need you to do me another favor," Riley went on. "Will you try to be nicer to your mother? She truly is overwhelmed with baby Charles right now."

Ben felt the warmth of his daddy's body. When he leaned closer, he heard his daddy's strong, steady heartbeat. "Is she going to try to be nicer, too?"

"Ben..." his daddy said, and Ben knew that even though he hadn't meant to, he'd made his daddy sad. "Eileen loves you. She's doing the best she can. She's just under a lot of stress right now."

"What is stress, Daddy?"

"Stress is what you feel when you don't know what to do or have too many things to do."

Ben lifted his head and looked deeply into his father's eyes. "Or when you stay mad at somebody?"

"Yes, that's a good example also. Now, how about I read you a story to help you go to sleep?"

Ben jumped up and pulled his copy of *Grimm's Fairy*

Tales from the shelf, then thumbed through the book until he came to *The Three Dwarfs*.

"This one Daddy. Please?"

Riley quickly flipped the pages. There were lots of them.

"This is a long one, son. How about *Little Red Riding Hood?*"

"Okaaay," Ben said, casting his eyes toward the floor, "but I already know *Little Red Riding Hood* by heart. Mama was reading me all the stories, and after *Little Red Riding Hood* comes *The Three Dwarfs*."

Riley sat on the bed and read *The Three Dwarfs* as Ben snuggled happily under the covers. He found a way to rest his head on his daddy's leg. Two pages from the end, Eileen appeared at the door in her night gown with her hands on her hips.

"Are you going to be in here all night?"

"We're almost through, honey. Give me another two or three minutes."

"If you're going to be that long, I'm going on to bed."

Riley finished the story, rubbed his son's back while he checked to see if the covers were pulled tightly around him, gently kissed his cheek and whispered, "Goodnight, little guy. I love you."

"Are you still awake?" Riley whispered as he crawled into bed next to Eileen.

"Yes, but I'm not in the mood, so don't get any ideas."

"I thought we might talk a little more about your problem with Ben."

"*My* problem with Ben? *Mine*? *You* always take Ben's side—that's the problem."

Riley propped himself up on one arm and began to massage Eileen's temples. Hearing the gentle breathing of his younger son asleep in a crib next to him, he decided not to switch on the bed lamp.

"Don't do that," Eileen hissed as she pushed his hand away. "I don't want to have to wash my hair in the morning."

Riley lay back and stared at the barely visible ceiling. "If it seems as if I'm always taking Ben's side, I'm sorry," he said. He knew that his only chance of getting Eileen to loosen up was to avoid putting her on the defensive. "But sweetheart, do you think there's a possibility that what happened was just a misunderstanding?"

Eileen snorted.

"Children take things literally," Riley said. "I understand that you didn't have time to bake cookies from scratch, and he does too. But when you didn't tell him you would buy some, he thought he wouldn't have any to take."

"So, it's my fault. Again. Honestly, Riley."

"He's a child, Eileen. Children need things spelled out."

"What do you know about children? You haven't raised one. You were in a war for four years and now you're away all day at work. I'm left alone and barely have enough time and energy to take care of our little baby, let alone entertain your son. You and Mother think he's so smart. Well, if he is, he shouldn't need things spelled out." She pursed her lips. "If you ask me, he's conniving. He spends time thinking of ways to annoy me. His goal in life is to irritate me."

Riley tried to suppress the sigh that came out anyway. "All right, Eileen. What does he do specifically to irritate you?"

"Lots of things."

"Well, give me an example."

She ticked off offenses on her fingers. "He spends too much time in the bathroom and leaves a ring around the tub when he bathes. His idea of making up his bed is to pull the sheet and blanket up and put the pillow at the head of the bed. I have to smooth and tuck in the bedding and tidy his room after he leaves for school. He doesn't get pots and pans completely dry when he dries the dishes. He helps himself to food without asking and he barges into our bedroom when you and I are reading or listening to music. He bumps into furniture. Yesterday he bumped into Charles's crib and woke him up!"

"Eileen. I understand it's a challenge. You take time and care to keep our house nice—and I appreciate that. But sweetheart, it sounds to me like he's simply being a six-year-old. I'm not sure it's fair to say he's doing all of these things to annoy you."

"Of course you don't. Why do I even bother trying to explain? The worst thing is the sullen look on his face whenever I talk to him—and don't try to tell me that's just a little boy being six. He's sullen and ungrateful. And clumsy to boot."

"His bumping into things may be because of his eyesight. We should go ahead and get him glasses now and not wait till his sight gets worse."

"The school nurse told me his vision is good enough to get by without glasses for another year or so. That's $30 we don't need to spend right now."

"Well," Riley said. That statement just didn't sit right with him; if a child needed glasses, he should get them. But was this the fight he should be engaging in now? "As for the other irritants you mentioned, I wasn't aware of them, except his coming into our room to join us when we are listening to the radio, which I have encouraged."

"Oh, he's perfect when he's around you or Mother. You two think he is an angel."

"Could you be a little bit jealous?"

"Me jealous of a six-year-old? Don't be ridiculous."

"What would you like for me to say to him?" Riley sighed.

"Just tell him to do what I say and don't talk back. I swear if he talks back to me one more time, I'm going to scream."

Riley started to speak, but at that moment Charles began to whimper.

"He must be ready for his feeding," Eileen said. "We'll have to continue this discussion another time. And you'll have to go to the Parent/Teacher conference in the morning without me. I can't take Charles out in this weather."

"Ben's a proficient reader," Miss Johnson told Riley at their 7:45 a.m. conference the next morning. "I just give him a book and he practically teaches himself. He figures out the meaning of most new words from the context. I've taught him how to use our children's dictionary, so he rarely consults me. He's reading early fourth grade level books now, which opens up a lot of children's literature for him. I'm sending our library copy of *Black Beauty* home for him to read over the Christmas break. I'm delighted to report that he is excelling in every aspect of his schoolwork except penmanship, which should improve as his motor skills progress. If I have any concern, it's his vision. He seems to have no trouble reading at his desk, but he has to walk up to the chalk board to be able to read what I've written on it.

"My wife talked with the school nurse about that," Riley said. "She told us glasses aren't absolutely necessary now."

"Oh?" For a brief moment, Miss Johnson looked surprised. "I was under the impression that..." She paused. "I believe glasses would really help. As I said, he struggles to see the chalkboard. I hope you'll get them for him soon."

Miss Johnson put down her pencil and sat back in her chair. She seemed to relax.

"I can't say enough about Ben's deportment. He is so

cooperative and good-natured. He gets along well with everyone."

"I'm glad to hear that," Riley said as he rose to go. Miss Johnson rose with him.

"He is a stellar student," she said, "and a special, special boy."

"That he is," Riley said.

"Honestly, I can't emphasize that enough. You should be extremely proud of what a fine son you and your wife have."

Riley's instinct was to downplay the compliment, but why? Ben was a fine and special boy. Riley was proud of him, and it was gratifying to hear that sentiment echoed by someone who surely knew what she was talking about.

"Thank you," he said, "I'm very glad to hear that."

"Daddy, Daddy, look at the snow!" Ben exclaimed as he pulled his father to the living room window the morning of December 21st, the first full day of Christmas vacation. Morning had not yet risen, but the huge fluffy snowflakes were visible through the streetlights.

"When you get home tonight can we make a snowman?"

Riley smiled and looked at the thin cover of snow on the ground.

"Don't think we'll get enough for a snowman, unless a lot more falls. Have you ever seen snow before?"

Ben tried to remember. "I don't think so, except for

pictures in a magazine. Can I go outside and try to catch a snowflake?"

"Get dressed and have breakfast first. Then you can walk down to the bus stop with me. That would be a good time to catch snowflakes."

"How many times have I told you not to run in the house?" Eileen scolded as Ben scurried past her on his way to his room. "You'll knock something over and wake up the baby."

Ben quickly dressed and made up his bed. In the kitchen Riley had made oatmeal.

"Mix a little butter and brown sugar with this and stir. Your Grandmother always served me oatmeal on real cold mornings. She said it would stick to my ribs and keep me going. I only have to work till one today, so I should be home in plenty of time to play in the snow with you for a little while. I'll be ready to leave in ten minutes, so eat up."

Ben and Riley walked together over the same route Ben took to school—sometimes alone, but often with Alice and her mother. As he and his father approached the bus stop, he saw a bundled custodian shoveling snow from the steps of the Church. When the bus pulled up, men in overcoats shook the snow off their hats before entering and women lowered their umbrellas and lifted their skirts as they boarded. Ben marveled at how everyone was bustling around, intent on getting their jobs done or getting where they were going, and not stopping to enjoy the beauty of the falling flakes.

"Gotta go, son," Riley said as Bus number 29 rolled up. "Run on home now and get out of this weather. I'll see you this afternoon."

Ben watched the bus, bellowing black fumes crunch through the sludge of ice and snow that filled the street, as it carried his father to work. When it disappeared, he carefully crossed Acklen Avenue and walked boldly up to the man scraping the ice off the church steps.

"Howdy," Ben said. "Are you from Mississippi?"

The custodian's huge grin revealed one missing tooth.

"Why boy I ain't never been outside-a Davi'son County 'cept when I went to Memphis fo- five years ago to bury my brother. You from Mississippi?"

"I used to be," Ben said.

"You live 'round here now?"

"Down there," Ben said, pointing in the direction of home. "I walked with my daddy to the bus stop this morning. He's coming home to play in the snow with me this afternoon."

The custodian leaned against his shovel and wiped his face with a ragged kerchief. "You don't say! My name's Buck. What's yours?"

"Ben."

"Glad to meet you Mr. Ben. You better get on home now. Your momma's probably worrying 'bout you."

"Bye, Buck," Ben sang as he started toward home. As he turned the corner onto Blakely Street he saw Alice Miller's red hair peeking out from her scarf.

"Mama and I are going to the drug store for hot chocolate," Alice said as she approached. "Wanna go?"

"After he asks his mother, honey." Mrs. Miller added. "Why don't we wait right here till he gets back?"

Ben raced home, bounded up the stairs and stuck his head inside the apartment door. "I'm going to the drug store with Alice and her mother," he shouted. "To get some hot chocolate."

"Not until you've emptied the waste baskets and dried the breakfast dishes," Eileen shouted back. But before her words had penetrated his consciousness, Ben had bolted down the stairs and out the door to join Alice and her mother at the corner.

"We're so glad you can go with us," Mrs. Miller said as Ben slid to a stop. "If the weather weren't so bad, your mother could bring the baby and come with us. What's the baby's name?

"Charles."

"And how old is Charles?"

Ben counted on his fingers from May to December. Uncertain whether to count May as one month he said, "He'll be a year old in May."

"Oh, he's very young. No wonder your mother has her hands full."

Ben stopped and looked at Mrs. Miller intently. "She's not my real mother," he said. "She's my step-mother. My real mother is in heaven and my Mama is in Mississippi."

"My goodness," Mrs. Miller said. "We'll have to sort all this out later. Now you two hold hands while we cross the street and stay together when we get in the drug store. We don't want to lose anyone."

Ben and Alice sat in a booth facing Mrs. Miller, whose benign face reminded Ben of Margie.

"I want to meet your mother and your baby brother," Mrs. Miller said. "When it warms up, we can spread a blanket in the yard between our buildings and get to know each other. But tell me, Ben, did you live with your mama after your real mother died?"

Ben nodded yes.

"And you moved to Nashville when you started the first grade?"

Ben nodded again.

"Your Dad and step-mother and baby Charles were already in Nashville when you joined them to start school?

"I guess so."

"So," Mrs. Miller continued. "You got a step-mom, a new baby brother, a new home, and a new school at the same time. I bet you have a lot to get used to and your step-mother does have her hands full."

Ben had been kicking his feet back and forth as little boys often do when their feet don't quite reach the floor. He took the last slurp of his hot chocolate, wiped his mouth with his sleeve and said, "I guess she does. My brother cries a lot. I think that's why she's so mean to me, or are stepmothers supposed to be mean? Like in *Cinderella*?"

"Mean to you?" Mrs. Miller said. "Surely not."

"Yes, she is," Ben said. "But if stepmothers are supposed to be mean, maybe she can't help it."

Mrs. Miller touched Ben's hand, then picked up her

purse and stood up. "It's time to go," she said. "Make sure your coats are buttoned and your gloves are on. We don't want to lose the warmth from the hot chocolate."

"Bye, Alice. Thanks for the hot chocolate, Mrs. Miller," Ben said as he reached the walkway to his apartment building.

"Bye," Alice called back. "Be sure to ask your mother if you can come over to my house tomorrow."

Mrs. Miller and Alice disappeared into their building while Ben stood outside looking for a reason not to go into his. He tried catching snowflakes on his tongue, but soon decided the effort wasn't worth the reward. He fashioned a snowball with his hands and stood on the sidewalk with his arm cocked, ready to blast a passing car. His only potential target, however, was a man walking toward him, wearing a cap with a broad brim just like the one on the train conductor, carrying a large bag on his shoulder and a stack of letters in his hand.

"Howdy young man," the postman said. "You weren't thinking about throwing that at me, were you?"

Ben grinned sheepishly and shook his head.

"I haven't seen you before. Do you live here?"

"Yes, sir," Ben said. "In apartment 4."

"In apartment 4, you say?"

Ben nodded.

"Well, I have a letter here for "Master Ben McHaney in apartment 4."

"That's me! That's me!" Ben shouted.

"I'm supposed to put the mail in the mailbox, but

since you've come out to greet me, I suppose it'd be okay if I gave your letter to you, wouldn't it?"

Handing the letter to Ben the mail man touched the tip of his cap and said, "Bye now. Got to keep going if I'm going to finish by five. Dodging snowballs is slowing me down."

Ben inspected the envelope carefully. He could easily read his name and "Nashville, Tennessee" printed on the address lines. He thought the handwriting looked familiar, but he couldn't quite place it. Then he made out "Biloxi, Miss" in the return address and his eyes widened.

"It's from Mama!" He shouted. "I got a letter from Mama."

Ben tore open the envelope. The five-dollar bill inside a card that said simply "Happy Birthday!" caught his eye first. Then he saw stationery with handwriting on both sides. He could make out "Dear Ben" and the date, December 18, 1946, on the front and "Love, Mama" on the back, but the rest of the writing was unintelligible. He put the letter, the card, and the bill back inside the envelope, slipped quietly through the front door into his room, and slid the envelope into his book of fairy tales to await his father's return. He quickly made his bed and picked up the waste basket from the bathroom. The door to the other bedroom was closed, so he tiptoed past on his way to the kitchen to check for more trash before making the trip to the refuse container outside.

"Ben! Come here!"

It wasn't a shout. It was a harshly whispered command. He hesitated at the bedroom door. "I need you to take this dirty diaper to the pail. Then I want to talk to you."

Ben peeked into the room. Eileen was pinning a fresh diaper on Charles, who was playfully kicking his legs as if he were trying to make Eileen's task more challenging. Ben could not see Eileen's face. The soiled diaper lay near the foot of the baby bed, barely visible through the slats in the partially lowered side. He retrieved the diaper pail from the bathroom and walked to the foot of the baby bed.

"I told you to come get the dirty diaper," Eileen barked. "Not bring me the smelly pail. If you disobey me again, I'll get your father's belt."

Ben stood still a moment trying to figure out how he could reach the soiled diaper and get it through the slats into the pail, since he couldn't reach over the rail.

"Get that filthy pail out of here!" she shouted. "It's full of germs. Are you trying to make Charles sick?"

Ben grabbed the diaper, pulled it through the railing, dropped it into the pail and ran to the bathroom. In the process, a small brown lump rolled out of the diaper onto the floor and landed near Eileen's feet. When Eileen moved to pick up the freshly diapered Charles, she stepped on the mess and smushed it into the floor.

"Ben!" she screamed when she realized what she had stepped into. After quickly taking off her slipper, she stormed into the bathroom where Ben was washing his hands.

"What?" Ben said, without turning his head.

Eileen grabbed him by the shoulders and spun him around. "Look at me when I'm talking to you, young man. You have disobeyed me twice this morning. You went to the village with Alice Miller and her mother when I told you not to until your work was done, then you brought that filthy pail into the baby's room. Just wait till your father gets home and hears about all this."

Ben looked at Eileen defiantly. Rather than fear his father's hearing "about all this," he took comfort in the certainty that his father would listen to his side of the story.

"I put the diaper in the diaper pail, like you told me," Ben said.

"That's NOT what I told you to do. You were to carry the dirty diaper into the bathroom, not bring a smelly pail into the baby's room, and certainly not drop poop on the floor. Furthermore, I told you NOT to go out again when you came back from walking your father to the bus stop, until you had finished your chores."

Ben's face turned blank.

"Don't act like you don't know what I'm talking about. I gave you explicit instructions, which you deliberately disobeyed. If I didn't have to watch after Charles, I'd have run you down. As punishment you are to sit in your room for an hour. You can't read and you can't play with your train. And leave the door open a crack so I can keep an eye on you. I'm going to leave the mess for you to take out when your punishment is over. And if you ever do that again, I'll paddle you raw!"

Ben thought about the morning as he sat on his bed. He had awakened to falling snow, and until now, had experienced nothing but pleasure, highlighted by the letter from Mama that his Daddy would soon read to him. He hoped Mama's letter would tell him what she, Daddy Frank, and Annie had been doing since he left, and if the Baker's momma dog had had more puppies. He hoped his father would help him write Mama and tell her about his cute little brother, who was fun to play "peek-a-boo" with, but who seemed to cry a lot. As these thoughts drifted through his head, his eyes grew heavy.

Once again Ben did not see it coming. He felt the sting in his cheek from the slap just as he heard Eileen shout, "Wake up, you little monster! I didn't send you in here to take a nap. Your punishment isn't over."

More persistent than the pain from the slap was an urgent need to pee. He stood up and started for the bathroom.

"Come back here," Eileen shouted. "I'm not through with you."

"But I have to go to the bathroom."

"That's too bad," Eileen sneered. "You'll just have to hold it until you've finished cleaning up that mess you made on the floor. Get some old newspaper and the scrub brush and put some water in the pail. Get every trace of that poop off the floor, then wipe the floor dry and take everything to the trash container outside. I'll teach you to obey me if it's the last thing I do!"

Shortly after one, Riley came whistling through the door and shook the weather off his jacket. "What's to eat?" he said. "Or did you forget I would be home for lunch?"

"I didn't forget. Your son has been so awful this morning, I haven't had time to think about cooking anything, and I'm so upset I don't feel like eating."

Riley sighed and sat down at the kitchen table. "What happened this time?"

For the next ten minutes, Eileen told Riley her version of the events, after which Riley said, "Do you want me to talk to him before lunch?"

"Yes, I do. I'll fix you a peanut butter and jelly sandwich while you deal with him."

Riley took his coat from the rack. "Peanut butter and jelly won't be enough for me. Since you're not hungry, I'll take Ben with me to the café in the village for some of their Brunswick stew. I can talk to him there."

"I can't believe you are going to reward his behavior by taking him out to lunch. For what he's done, he should be sent to his room without anything to eat."

"After what I saw during the War, I'm not going to withhold food from any child to discipline him," Riley said. "This will give me an opportunity to talk to him and for you to have some time away from him. You've told me your side of the story. I'd like to hear his, and I'd like to get a decent lunch."

Eileen grabbed the broom and began sweeping the kitchen floor much more vigorously than necessary. Riley called out, "Ben, get your coat and cap. We're going to Denny's for lunch. Oh, yes, and your gloves too."

Ben darted into his bedroom to retrieve Mama's

letter, checked to make sure the money was still there, crammed the envelope into his coat pocket, dashed back to the door and said, "Wait for me, Daddy! After lunch are, we still going to build a snowman?"

Riley was glad he had the afternoon off. His work schedule at Vincent Printing was not nearly as onerous as it had been before the war. Nevertheless, he worked late at least two nights a week and till noon on Saturday. He needed the overtime. Everything was so much more expensive now. A nickel cup of coffee cost a dime, and a pound of coffee cost a dollar. Two hours with his son was costing him about $15 of lost overtime, but he couldn't think about that—or that dessert for Ben would cost a quarter.

Denny's Diner was past the noon rush when Riley and Ben arrived. "Let's sit in a booth," Riley said as he slid into the first available one. Ben pulled his coat off and Mama's letter fell out of his pocket.

"What's that?" Riley said. "Looks like a letter. Have you read it?"

"No," Ben said. "I can read books, but I can't read this. Will you read it to me?"

Riley smiled. "That's because it's written in cursive and books are in print. You are learning print now, but you'll learn cursive later. Hand me the letter and let's see what it says."

"It's from Mama," Ben said, "and there's a five-dollar bill in it. I hope it's for me."

December 15, 1946

Dearest Ben,

The birthday card I sent you came back marked "Return to Sender." It must have been put in the wrong mailbox in your apartment building. I am enclosing a Christmas card, and your combined birthday and Christmas gift, with this note. I'm so sorry you will get it after your birthday, but at least you'll know we were thinking of you on your special day and you'll get it before Christmas. How are you? I hoped I would hear back from you when I wrote your daddy in October, but Frank reminded me that you probably hadn't learned to write yet. Please ask your Daddy to help you write to us. We want to hear how you like first grade and the names of your new friends.

Annie is still sad you had to leave Biloxi. She says building sandcastles isn't as much fun without you. And she misses reading stories to you. But she likes third grade very much and still has Bitsy, Katie, and Charlie to play with. Mollie had three little boy puppies and one little girl puppy in November. Remember, I told you in my October letter the puppies were coming soon. All of them have new homes now. We thought about taking one of them but decided against it because I had just learned some wonderful news. I am going to have a baby! Probably in June, although we don't know exactly when, and of course, we won't know whether it is a little girl or a little boy until it is born. Isn't that exciting? Daddy Frank and I hope it is a little boy—just like you.

We hope you can come see us after the new baby is born, maybe the summer after next when you'll be big enough to ride on the train alone and when I won't have to spend so much time with the baby. I'll write your Daddy about it when the time comes.

I guess I'd better go. Ask your Daddy to send us some pictures of you, and as soon as you learn how, write us a long letter, and tell us all about Nashville and your new school. We love you and miss you very much.

Love,
Mama

Riley glanced at Ben repeatedly while reading the letter to him. He saw Ben's eyes light up on hearing the news about the puppies, but not at the mention of the new baby. Now he saw an inquisitive look on his son's face.

"Mama said she wrote us in October," Ben said. "Did we get a letter in October?"

Riley shook his head. "I'll ask your mother about it. I wonder if Nora addressed it incorrectly. Well, at least you got this one and the Christmas card."

"And five dollars," Ben said.

"What will you do with all that money?"

Ben looked at the huge coconut cake, moist and fresh on its stand, waiting to be cut. "Do I have enough money to buy pieces of that cake for you and me and Alice?" he said.

"You could buy two whole cakes with five dollars. But what about your mother? You need a piece for her."

"No," Ben said without hesitation. "You can give her a bite of yours."

Riley helped his son tuck his napkin into the neck of his shirt as the waitress set bowls of stew and their drinks before them. "This stew is hot," he said. "Blow it gently so you won't burn your tongue and try not to drip any on you."

Ben ate slowly and carefully. He said, "No thank you" when the waitress asked if he wanted more milk and "Yes, ma'am" when she asked if she could take his plate.

"Why don't we share a piece of that cake right now," Riley said, "while I have another cup of coffee? Plus, it would give us a chance to talk."

He waved the waitress over. "Miss, would you divide a slice of that coconut cake between the two of us and refill me?"

"Talk about what, Daddy?"

"Oh, you know, things that are going on with you, your school, your friends. Whatever you would like to talk about."

"Can I go play with Alice tomorrow? She asked me to."

"I'm sure you can. Did she and her mother take you to get hot chocolate this morning?"

"Yes," Ben beamed, "and it was sooooo good. Alice's mommy paid for it."

Riley pulled out a cigarette, then put it back in the pack. The lunch rush was over, and he and Ben were the only diners remaining, other than those seated at the counter. Ben had only two bites of cake left.

"Your mother said she told you not to go. That you had chores to do."

Ben shook his head. "I told her I was going to get hot chocolate with Alice and her mother and then I left. I didn't hear her say anything."

"Well, it's good that you told your mother you were going somewhere with a grown-up, but you need to make sure she understands and says okay before you actually leave. She might not know the grown-up, or she might want to know how long you'll be gone. Will you be more careful next time and make sure your mother heard you and has said it's okay before you leave?"

Ben stopped chewing his last bite and looked at his father. Crumbs fell from his open mouth. Tears came to his eyes. Riley reached across the table and touched his son's hand.

"I'm not scolding you, Ben. I'm just trying to protect you and to smooth things out between you and Eileen. You need to listen to her and understand what she's saying. The two of you have to get used to each other."

"I'll try Daddy, but I don't want to have to get used to being slapped."

"Slapped?" Riley said. "You mean…spanked, on your bottom."

"No, slapped on my face—like this."

With his palm open, Ben swung his hand through the air, stopping at his father's cheek. The color drained from Riley's face. The fork he was holding shook. He pushed his plate away, lit the Lucky and took a long draw. Ben eyed the uneaten cake on his plate.

"Are you through eating, Daddy?"

"Would you like my last bite?" Riley said as he pushed his plate toward Ben. "When you finish, let's walk to the park and build that snowman."

The huge feathery snowflakes that had fallen in the morning had turned to icy pellets by mid-afternoon when Riley and Ben started home. Their creation in the park was easily recognizable as one of Frosty's siblings, and to Ben's delight was almost as tall as he was. Buck was sprinkling salt on the steps when they passed the church. Ben pulled his father over to meet his new acquaintance.

"Hi, Buck," he said.

"That you, Benji? I guess this is your Papa.

Ben nodded yes. "We made a snowman in the park. Just Daddy and me."

"Mighty fine boy you got here. Mighty fine boy. Met him this mornin' and took a likin' t' him right off."

"Yes, he is quite a young man," Riley said. "Thank you for telling me you think so too. I'm very proud of him."

"I can see that." Buck laughed, "Bet his mama is too."

"Bye, Buck," Ben shouted as he and his father headed home.

"I had a good time with you this afternoon, old buddy," Riley said as soon as they got to their apartment. "Time for your bath while I spend some time with your little brother."

Riley decided that as much as the idea of slapping a child infuriated him, it would be unfair to condemn Eileen until he had heard from her. But he should try to patch things up between them before having that conversation.

"I didn't expect you to be gone such a long time," Eileen said as she handed Charles to Riley. "I was beginning to worry."

"Nothing to worry about. I promised Ben I would help him build a snowman after lunch. It was fun. Charles smells fresh and clean. Did you give him a bath?"

"Yes, I had hoped we could do it together, but by three I thought I'd better go ahead without you. He'll probably go to sleep right after I feed him."

Eileen nursed Charles for a few minutes, handed him to Riley and nuzzled Riley's cheek. Riley responded with a kiss.

"You smell great, too," he said. "I hope we can get to bed early tonight. It looks like Charley has conked out. Shall I put him in the cradle or in his bed?"

"The bed, please. He'll sleep better there. While you're up, would you pour us some coffee? I perked a fresh pot."

When Riley returned with the coffee, Eileen was sitting on the couch with her feet curled beneath her and her polished toenails peeking out. Her hair was clean and silky and her breasts plump and enticing. She looked as beautiful and as sexy as he had ever seen her.

"I did my toes while you were gone. They should be dry by now. Do you like this new shade I chose, just for you?"

Riley put their coffee mugs on the table in front of the couch and joined her. After glancing at her toes, he bent over and kissed her again.

"Just for me?" he said. "Then I'd better like it—and I do. Did you have a restful afternoon?"

"Restful, but lonely. You were gone so long. I missed you."

"Giving you some time away from Ben was the idea, wasn't it?"

"Yes, but not away from you. I thought when you came back from lunch, you'd let him play outside and you'd spend the afternoon with me."

"The afternoon's not over," Riley said as he squeezed her toes. "This coffee is delicious. Don't let yours get cold. By the way, I didn't see any mail on the table. Did we get any today?"

"Not today. Were you expecting something?"

"Ben got a letter from Nora, which I read to him at Denny's. Didn't you see it?"

"No, he must have taken it out of the box himself."

"He isn't tall enough to open the box," Riley said. "I assumed you gave him the letter."

"Not me. The box was empty when I checked. How do you suppose he got it?

"Beats me," Riley said. "In the letter Nora said she wrote him in October. Do you remember seeing any mail from Nora in October?"

Eileen began to chew her lower lip. "No, but you know there are four other boxes here. It could have been put in the wrong box."

"You'd think any of our neighbors would just put our mail in our box if they got it by mistake. Nora also said the card she sent Ben for his birthday was returned, marked 'addressee unknown.' Who would have done that?"

"We'll never know, will we?" Eileen said as she picked up the mugs and headed for the kitchen.

Ben and Charles were in bed and asleep by eight, leaving the night free for Riley and Eileen. The amorous mood they had shared briefly earlier had not survived the discussion about the missing mail, however, and their guarded conversations since then guaranteed that lovemaking would not take place that night. Two bottles of Budweiser and soft music on WSM had loosened Riley sufficiently to continue their earlier discussion about the mail.

"I wonder why Ben didn't ask you to read Nora's letter to him when it came," Riley began.

"He and I weren't getting along this morning," Eileen said without looking up from her *McCall's*.

"And why weren't you?"

"I've told you," Eileen sighed. "He does things to irritate me, he disputes my word and he often disobeys me. Let's face it. He just doesn't like me."

"I think he wants to like you, but he's wary of you," Riley said, "and I can see why." Choosing his words carefully, Riley continued. "Even around me, you treat him harshly. Do you think if you let up a little and treated him like your son—like Margie treats him—that perhaps you'd get along better?"

"You're asking me to treat a little brat who constantly disobeys me better? What he needs is a firm hand."

"What do you mean by that?" Riley huffed.

"You know, discipline. Let him know who's boss. Make him do what you say."

"And how do you propose to do that?"

"The way all boys are disciplined, with a switch or a belt. Or…"

Eileen hesitated.

"A slap?" Riley said.

"Exactly," Eileen said. "A good hard slap puts a child in his place."

Riley glared at Eileen. "Don't you EVER slap my son."

Twin spots of color rose on Eileen's cheeks. "I need to discipline him, you know. He has to learn to mind me. Like the Bible says, spare the rod and spoil the child."

"Discipline, yes. Slapping? No. Slapping a child is not disciplining him—it's just taking out your frustration on him."

Eileen's eyes were focused on something only she could see.

Riley took a deep breath. "Eileen. Have you ever slapped Ben?"

Eileen looked straight at Riley. "No, but I've often felt like it. And don't bother asking him. He'd just lie about it."

Sleep eluded Riley that night as he mulled the events of the day. Ben *could* have lied, but the circumstances of his revelation of Eileen's slap and Riley's own experience with her short temper persuaded him that his son had told the truth. Which meant that Eileen had lied. Why? Why would she risk the consequences of being caught in a lie when the safer course would have been to admit the slap and defend her actions, then after he made his position clear, try to arrive at a mutually agreeable method of discipline?

Perhaps something deeper was at the heart of the problem. Eileen had told him in August that she would "try" to accept Ben and that after consultation with her mother, she knew that the key to getting along with him was to keep him busy. Riley had seen little evidence of her trying to accept Ben. Keeping him busy had become her euphemism for turning Ben into a maid in the morning and a janitor at night. Was harsh treatment part of her way of showing Ben who's boss? Or was she trying to make life so miserable for Ben that he would ask to be sent back to Biloxi? That thought had been gnawing at Riley all afternoon, as he tried to balance his responsibility to protect his son from mistreatment, his desire to support his wife, and his hope to raise his son in his own household. Riley had no doubt that the joy of leaving Eileen and being reunited with Mama, Daddy Frank, and Annie would offset any sadness Ben might feel at leaving him. But how could he live if he lost Ben again?

As he lay sleepless while the night crawled on, the plusses and minuses for keeping Ben recycled through his mind. The plusses were that Ben would grow up with his brother; that Margie would stay in his life; that his schooling would not be disrupted, and, most of all, that he would remain with his father.

The minuses were that staying in Nashville subjected Ben to Eileen's continued torment and subjected their marriage to enormous strain. In the end, Riley decided to assume that sooner or later Eileen would accept Ben, as she had promised, and the torment would end. Her ever loving Ben was probably too much to expect. Ben had been with them almost four months and seemed well-adjusted in spite of Eileen's mistreatment. He was a McHaney. He had a strong will. If Ben could bear the torment a little longer, Riley could bear the marital strain. Furthermore, Nora was expecting another baby.

She might not want Ben back. Waiting Eileen out was the only answer.

The next morning's mail contained the new issue of *Publisher's Auxiliary*. In it was a small, classified ad tucked in the middle of the third column on the sixth page.

> FOR SALE, weekly newspaper in thriving West Tennessee county, population 24,200, audited circulation 3,000 per week. $20,000 cash or owner will finance responsible buyer with $5,000 down. Owner retiring and requires quick sale. No brokers. Principals only. Contact owner direct at PO Box 687.

7

"I've found it!" Riley shouted and immediately penned a letter of inquiry. Four days later he received an invitation to meet the owner of the *Weakley County Press*, Martin, Tennessee.

A deal was quickly struck, and Riley left to take over the paper on June 1st, the deadline for closing imposed by the seller. Eileen, Ben, and Charles spent that summer on the farm with Margie. On Saturday August 16, 1947, Margie drove them to Martin, and met Riley at the two-bedroom duplex he had rented, less than a mile from the elementary school. Students had registered for the new school year the Friday before. On Monday Margie walked Ben the four blocks to the school, arriving as the school bell rang the start of the day.

"Hello," Margie said to a woman leading a group of children about Ben's age into the building. "I'm here to register my grandson Ben in the second grade. Can you tell me where to take him?"

"You're at the right place," the woman said, "I'm just not the right person. My name is Christine Battle, and my section of the second grade is full. You need to see the other second grade teacher, Mrs. Fulton, who is standing right over there. IRENE! Can you come here a minute?"

Irene Fulton, in her early fifties, her pence-nez spectacles sitting high on the bridge of her nose, dressed entirely in black, wearing shoes usually seen on grandmothers and a hair style that had not been fashionable for twenty years, came over.

"My goodness, Ben, I'm so glad you arrived," Mrs. Fulton said after introductions by Mrs. Battle. "We now have twelve girls and twelve boys, a perfect pairing. You can sit between Rex and Leon on the second row, unless you'd rather sit on the girls' side. Now come with me and we'll all go inside together."

Margie knelt down to kiss Ben goodbye. Ben reluctantly released her hand.

"I think you'll like Mrs. Fulton," Margie said. "She looks like she means business, but I bet she has a heart of gold."

"Just like yours, Margie?" Ben said.

Mrs. Fulton did have a heart of gold and patience that allowed her students to tell her what was wrong or explain why Johnny deserved to be punched. Likewise, she had no qualms about telling Eileen Ben needed glasses NOW! Ben quickly learned he could trust her and soon decided she was almost as wonderful as Margie. Every grade thereafter Ben was such a willing student that teachers were delighted to have him in their classes, and the more Ben achieved success at school, the better he dealt with Eileen's mistreatment at home. Eventually he concluded that putting up with Eileen was the price he had to pay for living with his dad and spending most of the week attending a school he loved, and often playing chess with Charles, who had shown a talent for the game at an early age.

On Saturday the Fourth of July 1953, the family sat down for supper.

"I couldn't tell you this till now," Riley announced, "because everything just came together. I have tickets to the All-Star game in Cincinnati Tuesday after next. We could drive up Monday and drive back Tuesday after the game. Take your glove, Ben, and maybe you'll catch one of Stan's home runs."

Stan Musial, Ben's idol, was playing left field for the National League. Although Ben knew Musial's statistics—batting average, runs-batted-in, doubles, home runs, number of years he had been named to the All-Star team, number of World Series appearances—by heart, he had never seen his hero in action. Ben bubbled over with excitement.

"I thought you only had three tickets," Eileen said.

"I do, one for you, one for Ben and one for me. Hattie can stay with Charles. I spoke to her mother about it when I took her home last night. She's happy to make an extra $15."

"She most certainly will not!" Eileen said. "That girl's only seventeen, she couldn't handle an emergency or get Charles to the doctor. Plus, I don't want to pay her five dollars a day to sit around the house eating ice cream."

"Eileen, the hospital is only four blocks away. Mrs. Ellis would take Charles if necessary. Nothing is going to happen that Hattie can't handle."

"You don't know that!" Eileen retorted.

"You're right, I don't know if a falling star is going to land on us or if a speeding car is going to plow into the house, but I do know in all probability, nothing will happen we can't trust Hattie to handle for two nights."

"Guess what!!" Ben told his best friend Jerry at Sunday School. "Dad is taking me to the All-Star game this year. We're sitting in the left field stands. If I catch a ball, I'll bring it home and show it to you."

"Aww!!" Jerry exclaimed, "Wish I could go."

By mid-afternoon all of Ben's school buddies were envious that he was going to see the All-Stars play in person. Sunday night Riley came into Ben's room.

"What are you reading, slugger?"

"Grantland Rice's column about the All-Star game. I'm almost through."

Riley sat down on the bed and waited till Ben finished.

"I'm sorry, Ben," Riley said, "I'm not going to be able to take you to the game."

Ben burst into tears.

"But you told me you were taking me. You have the ticket."

"I asked for four tickets," Riley said, "but I could only get three. Eileen refuses to leave Charles with Hattie. You're twelve and old enough to stay home by yourself. Charles is only seven and isn't. That means I have to take Charles."

"But you promised! You said I could go! Mother doesn't even like baseball! Leave her!"

Ben pulled away when Riley tried to put his arms around him.

"I'm so sorry, Ben. Go down to Harkey's Tuesday afternoon. They are going to set up a TV in their store window to let people see the game. I'll buy you a portable radio so you can listen to the play by play while you watch."

"I hate Mother," Ben wailed. "Why can't you make her leave Charles with Hattie? Why don't I ever get what I want?"

"It's complicated," Riley said. "I'll make it up to you somehow. Please try to go to sleep and let's talk in the morning about something special for you."

"There isn't anything as special as the All-Star game!" Ben sobbed.

Riley paced the floor. His face showed his pain.

"You'll get over it, son," he finally said. "Everybody has to learn to deal with disappointment."

Ben cried himself to sleep that night. The following

week he spent hours fruitlessly racking his brain for a way to get to the game. The Monday everyone else was leaving, he said nothing at breakfast, and bolted out of the house at the first opportunity. He had to get away. He didn't want to be commanded to help Charles get ready for the trip or ordered to load the bags into the trunk.

"Where're you going!" Eileen shouted as Ben walked out the back door. Ben did not answer. He saw his father loading the car.

"Feeling better?" Riley asked.

Ben didn't respond. He reached the end of the driveway, picked up the morning paper, scanned the headlines, tucked the paper under his arm and ambled down the sidewalk.

"I got the radio for you," Riley called out. "Mr. Harkey said you could sit in the show room if you'd like so you could hear the play by play on TV."

Ben kept walking.

"Come on, Ben," Riley said. "I told you I'm sorry. The radio's yours whether you watch the game or not. Just don't miss the opportunity to see your first All-Star game on television. I left some money by your bed for you, and there is plenty of food in the Frigidaire if you want to eat at home. Mrs. Ellis is right next door if you need her."

Ben was now halfway past Mrs. Ellis's house.

"Where are you going?" his father shouted.

"I need to run to the little store," Ben said. "I thought I'd have a hot dog for lunch, and we're out of buns."

"Make it snappy," Riley said. "We need to leave soon, and Eileen has some final instructions to give you."

Thirty minutes later, Ben returned with his package of buns and sauntered up the driveway toward the back door. Eileen jumped out of the car and cut him off.

"It doesn't take thirty minutes to go to a grocery two blocks away," she growled. "Unless you hopped on one foot."

"And how would you know?" Ben asked.

"Don't get smart with me, young man!" Eileen snapped. "I don't have time to deal with your shenanigans. You've made us late already." They glared at each other for a full five seconds, then Eileen held out a receipt.

"The Merry Lee Shoppe is delivering a dress for me. They should be here before 5:30. When you get the dress, hang it on the top rack in my closet so it won't drag on the floor. Understand? The top rack, not the bottom one."

Ben took the receipt, nodded that he understood and walked to the house. Once inside he stood by the kitchen door trying not to cry as the others left for Cincinnati on the trip meant for him. He soon lost the battle and dropped into a chair where he cried himself dry, then tried to think of a way to get back at Eileen for ruining his life. It wouldn't bother him if his father suffered a little also. He quickly rejected burning down the house—everyone would know he did it. Hitch hiking to Tullahoma or Biloxi was too dangerous—he had heard of hitch hikers being murdered. He opened every drawer in his parents' bedroom, looking for ideas. He even looked through the issues of *Time, McCall's,* and *Ladies Home Journal,* in the magazine rack they kept by their bed, and inspected the pack of Trojans tucked away in the back of Riley's sock drawer. Only a letter from Margie he found lying on Eileen's nightstand interested him.

June 20, 1953,

Dear Eileen,

I was disappointed you did not let Ben spend the summer with me. I thought it would be good for the two of you to have a break from each other. I can understand why Riley wouldn't want Ben away all summer, but I can't deny I'm disappointed. Here's a suggestion. Ben's school doesn't start until the middle of August and he's old enough to ride the bus alone. Why don't you send him to Nashville on the Greyhound? I would meet him there. Then he could spend three weeks or so with me. My school starts the first Monday in August. That shouldn't be a problem. I could take him to class with me, which I'm sure he would enjoy. Let me know if that will work out.

Love,
Mother

Ben wondered if his Dad had seen Margie's letter. No one had mentioned it to him. Pickings were too slim to justify continued rummaging. He considered and rejected the idea of walking to Jerry's house. He couldn't take the certain humiliation waiting for him there. He hoped Charles had tired of the car ride by now, and was demanding they stop for ice cream, so he could pee, or simply to relieve his boredom. Ben felt no animosity toward Charles—only a twinge of jealousy. His war was with Eileen. He wondered if Charles had any idea, he was a pawn in Eileen's scheme to deprive his brother of the opportunity of a lifetime. The game meant nothing to Charles except the opportunity to enjoy a succession of treats designed to keep him from ruining the game for his parents. The ride in the car was probably the highlight of the trip for him. Six hours, however, was way past Charles's limit on good behavior.

Alone in the crowd of mostly retired old men who filled the showroom of Harkey's Hardware and Appliances, Ben watched Stan the Man go 2 for 3 and lead the National League to a 5-1 victory. After the game he stopped at the Capital Grill and had country fried steak, mashed potatoes, and creamed corn for an early supper. Somewhat rejuvenated, he picked up an abandoned copy of the *Press-Scimitar*, scanned the front page and the weather report, then started the ten-minute walk home. As he turned up Todd Street, he saw someone walking away from his front door toward a car parked in his drive. Ben broke into a trot thinking it was the Merry Lee delivery and reached home just as Western

Union drove away. Taped to the front door was a telegram to Riley McHaney. The envelope was so lightly sealed it came open when he pulled it from the door. The message read:

Not able to reach you by telephone on Monday July 13th to inform you that Banquet in Huntington in honor of Governor Gordon Browning's birthday re-scheduled from 7 p.m. Saturday July 18, to 7 p.m. Friday July 17. If unable to attend call 901-555-5841 by 12 noon, Wednesday, July 15. Donna Carter, Assistant to Chief of Staff.

Ben's mind whirred. Opportunity had presented itself in the form of a telegram and the weather forecast. Eileen had talked with great excitement about this event since Riley and she were invited two months earlier. Riley had teased her about spending an entire morning at the Merry Lee Shoppe trying on the latest arrivals before deciding on the exact outfit, which with her new girdle would allow the Governor and his important friends to see she was still a 'looker.' When the dress arrived later that afternoon, Ben was careful to hang it exactly as Eileen had instructed.

According to the *Press-Scimitar,* rain was predicted that night and with rain came wind. Ben decided to leave the telegram as lightly taped to the front door as he had found it. He had difficulty getting to sleep. His conscience told him to retrieve the note and give it to his Dad as soon as he returned. His desire for revenge insisted he leave it on the door and pray for a storm. At eleven p.m. Ben was awakened by heavy rain, which he interpreted as cosmic justice ensuring that the message would not get to his father. When the rain ended twenty minutes later, however, he decided not to rely on the high probability the note would be blown away. Better to check the door, shred the note if it were still intact, put the shreds in Mrs. Ellis's trash can and rely on the even higher probability no one would go dumpster diving before the Friday garbage pick-up.

"Out of bed, sleepyhead," Riley said as he gently shook Ben's shoulder the next morning.

"What time is it?" a groggy Ben asked.

"A little after nine," his dad replied. "We drove most of the way last night. Would have come on home if it hadn't been raining so hard I couldn't see the road, so we stopped at a Holiday Inn and just now got home. Did you watch the game? It was almost a rout. Musial played six innings and looked great."

"I didn't hear it rain," Ben said.

"Then you must have passed out," his dad laughed. "Our yard is full of leaves and tree branches, and there are still puddles in the road. Do you like the radio?"

"It's nice," Ben said. "It needs batteries, so I have to keep it plugged in. Thanks for getting it for me."

Riley gave Ben a bear hug and said, "Sorry about the batteries. Don't worry, I'll get them for you, and I won't forget I still owe you big time for what you've done for me. Get dressed and come help me clean up this mess."

Ben battled with his conscience whether to let his little game play on while he and his dad cleared the yard.

"I still have over three dollars left from my food money," Ben said. "Can I get myself a hamburger and a milkshake at the Dew Drop Inn?"

Riley cocked his head. "You sure that's where you want to go?

"Yeah, Dad, for a quarter you get a Whopper Burger, and their milkshakes are the best in town."

"Okay," Riley said. "If that's what you want. Need a lift?"

"No thanks," Ben said. "It's not far. I'll walk."

"Suit yourself," his dad said. "If you want a ride home, call me."

Ben walked to town the usual way which took him by the Methodist Church parsonage where Reverend Whitehead, sitting on the porch with pen and notepad in hand, hailed him.

"Yo, Ben," the preacher called out. "Are you in a rush?"

"No," Ben said. "I'm on my way to lunch downtown."

Ben decided to keep his destination to himself. The Dew Drop Inn sold beer and wasn't careful about checking ID's. If a person looked 21, that was good enough for them. As a result of this less than vigorous enforcement of the law prohibiting sale of alcohol to minors, the Dew Drop had a shady reputation. Unlike many in the First Methodist Church of Martin, Reverend Whitehead did not condemn drinking, if done in moderation. Primarily because of his concerns about drunk teenage drivers, however, he was firmly against selling alcohol to minors. Ben knew this because he actually listened when Reverend Whitehead preached. His sermons were concise, insightful, usually non-judgmental, and never long.

"You arrived at just the right time," said the Reverend. "My sermon this week is on the Commandment not to bear false witness, which I am modernizing to mean tell the truth—don't lie."

"Unless absolutely necessary," Ben added. Reverend Whitehead cocked his head.

"Okay," the Reverend said. "Give me an example of when it's necessary to lie."

Ben looked serious for a moment, then the corners of his lips turned up.

"Suppose you are the Sheriff of Weakley County," he said, "and you want to keep the county dry because it's the law and you think drinking is a sin."

"Yes," the minister said.

"Then suppose my Dad keeps sherry in our house for medicinal purposes. Then suppose, you come banging on my door and say: This is the Sheriff. We have reliable information there's alcohol in this house. If there is, your father us going to jail. Tell me where it is."

"What would you do?" the Reverend asked.

"I would lie," Ben said without hesitation. "Wouldn't you?"

"I see you understand Situational Ethics," Reverend Whitehead laughed. Setting aside his sermon notes, he said, "But I was expecting you to use a stronger example—like a rape or a killing."

"Going to jail is pretty serious," Ben said. "If you don't deserve to go."

"I've gotten very hungry," the Reverend said. "I know where we can get a whopper of a hamburger and the best milkshake in town. Want to go? My treat. By the way, if that situation you described ever happens, tell the Sheriff to show you his warrant."

For the rest of Friday Ben struggled to keep from spilling the beans. He wasn't lying or giving false data, he was only withholding important information. Besides, if he had not come home after the All-Star game exactly when he did, he would never have seen the telegram and the bad weather would probably have blown the note away. Did the end justify the means? He didn't have to play that intellectual game. By taking the note to Mrs. Ellis's trash can, he had simply insured that the "probably inevitable" happened.

Friday evening came and went. Saturday morning Ben slept late. Saturday afternoon Riley and Eileen dressed for their soiree with the Governor. Riley did not own a tuxedo, so he wore a dark blue suit and a white shirt with cuff links. He put an army shine on his black shoes.

"You have to go to bed at 8:30 with Charles tonight," Eileen told Ben when Riley went to pick up Hattie. "He won't go to sleep if I'm not here and you are still up. We should be back by eleven. It's less than an hour's drive to Huntington. And don't forget to empty the waste baskets and take the trash to the garage today. I don't want to come home to a smelly house. Hattie's coming to baby-sit—not to clean house."

As Riley and Eileen stood at the door giving Hattie final instructions, Eileen handed Riley a string of pearls and turned around so he could fasten them from behind.

"You look absolutely fabulous," Riley said. "That $100 you dropped at Merry Lee's was well spent."

As soon as his father's Buick rounded the corner on its way to Huntington, Ben began the waste basket round-up. He deposited the trash into their garbage can then headed next door. He knew Mrs. Ellis was at her son's variety store helping him on their busiest day. Once more he walked to the far side of Mrs. Ellis's garage, lifted the lid to the garbage can and peered inside. The can was empty except for one soggy, illegible, non-incriminating strip of telegraph paper stuck to the bottom. Ben closed the lid and walked triumphantly home without a trace of guilt, certain his actions were justified, but he would not ask Reverend Whitehead whether he agreed.

In a little over two hours, Riley and Eileen returned, still arguing about who had misread the date on the invitation.

Martin High, the largest high school in segregated Weakley County, had three hundred fifty students in grades nine through twelve. Half of the girls were married within two months of graduation. A quarter of the boys dropped out as soon as they turned sixteen, and many of them joined the military. Less than ten percent of the graduates attended college. Half of those who did received degrees. Because of the university, Martin High had an abundant supply of qualified teachers eager to help any student who wanted to learn. As a result, many of the few Martin High graduates who got college degrees went on to highly productive careers.

As a freshman playing in the marching and concert bands, Ben decided he would become a professional musician. After attending Boys' State and watching the Democratic and Republican national conventions in 1956, however, he knew he wanted to be a politician and to be a politician, he had to be a lawyer.

"Getting into an excellent law school requires excellent grades," Margie told him when she came to see him receive the Latin award at the end of his Junior year, presented by Professor Jefferson Reynolds, head of the Liberal Arts Department at UT-M and a member of the Weakley County School Board. "Not only in high school but in college. In my experience what keeps a smart young man from getting those grades is a pretty girl."

"No need to worry," Ben laughed. "Girls are not on my list of priorities. They are too expensive."

"Ben, come here," Eileen called from the back porch when Ben got home from school on a football Friday afternoon two weeks into his senior year. "I need to talk to you."

"Does it have to be now," Ben said, "the band bus

leaves at 4:30 and I have to press the pants to my uniform."

"This won't take long. It involves that precious band of yours. Charles told me he did not get elevated to the Junior Varsity band this fall and he is very upset. I want you to tell Mr. Taylor Charles is your brother and he deserves another try out."

Hearing the word "precious" was particularly galling to Ben. He was proud he had been a member of the band since his freshman year and Mr. Taylor had promoted him to first chair in the trombone section as a sophomore. He took to heart the instruction to practice at least an hour every day except Sunday, even though it meant practicing in the garage when Eileen was at home.

"Take that caterwauling outside," Eileen had ordered the first time Ben brought his instrument home and began to play the scales in his bedroom. The next day Riley added an overhead light in a corner of their unheated, unfinished garage, and built a small closet in which Ben kept his horn and his music stand, so he could play his "precious" trombone without disturbing his stepmother.

"Another try out isn't going to do Charles any good," Ben said. "His embouchure is so poor, he can't hold his notes, and he doesn't practi…"

Eileen's hand smashed into his left cheek before he had completed the sentence. His glasses flew off his face and landed at his feet. Blood gushed from his nose. In addition to being stunned, Ben was livid. He picked up his glasses, wiped the lenses clean, and tried to straighten the frame. Eileen was fuming on the couch in the den. Fists clenched, Ben walked into the den and stood directly over her.

"I didn't ask you for criticism …" Eileen began.

"SHUT UP!" Ben said raging with anger.

"How dare you tell me to shut up …" Eileen shouted.

"I said SHUT UP! I've put up with you for 12 years because Margie asked me to try to get along with you and Dad told me not to pay any attention to your cruel words, which he said you really don't mean. The truth is you mean every cruel thing you say, and I've had it. If you ever slap me again, I'll call the cops."

Eileen stormed into her bedroom and slammed the door. Ben washed his face, got out the ironing board, pressed his pants, donned his band uniform, and walked the few blocks to the school to wait for the bus to take the band to the game. The walk reset his emotional equilibrium and the bus ride with his friends brought fun back into his life. He never mentioned the incident to anyone, not even his father or Margie. Eileen never slapped him again.

A week before Ben's graduation an emergency meeting of the Student Council was called to make a recommendation to Principal Miles over punishment for a violation of school rules. A group of Juniors in the Honors Program who were exempt from final exams had left school at noon to go across the street to eat at the Quick Shop.

"The School Handbook clearly states that the Quick Shop is off limits to students between eight a.m. and three p.m. on any school day," Principal Miles intoned. "This rule is necessary to keep our students from wasting their parents' hard-earned money on junk food. Normally I would suspend them from class for a day and give them an unexcused absence, but there are no class days left except for exams and they are exempt. My current thinking is to reduce each miscreant's semester grade in one non-core class by half a letter. I would like the Council's input before I make my decision. Mr. President, I yield the floor for discussion."

"Jill Harrison, the Junior Class Student Council Member is one of the offenders," Ben said. "So, she cannot participate in this discussion. The proposed penalty sounds a little harsh to me. Does any other council member want to speak?"

Ben looked around the room. No hand went up.

"Okay, we'll take it by classes then. You've heard my thoughts. Bob, what do you say as sophomore rep?"

Bob Fields was an All-Conference running back on the football team and had led the Panthers to the quarterfinals of the State Class B basketball tournament.

"I dunno," Bob said. "Coach Garnett would paddle us if we did that. Guess you can't spank a girl, though, can you? Make them scrub the gym floor."

"That's a thought," Ben said. "Katie you have an erudite look. Do you have a proposal?"

Katie Reynolds, daughter of Jeff Reynolds, the professor who had delivered the Latin Award to Ben the year before, was a Freshman and in a stage where most of her close friends had matured physically quicker than she and as a result, were catching boys like pop ups to the infield, while everyone knew Katie went to sleep-overs with her likewise less developed best friend, Suzy Andersen. Her mind was sharp, and her insight was uncanny. Ben had admired her judgment and sense of fairness at Student Council meetings all year.

"No one's ever accused me of looking erudite before," Katie said. "I'm not going to hold that remark against you until I get to the dictionary and find out if you insulted me."

Principal Miles laughed. Katie blushed.

"Let's not forget these are honor students who have demonstrated their commitment to good grades all through high school," Katie said. "And it is the end of the year, so we don't need to set an example for the rest of the school."

Katie paused. Ben looked at her, thinking she should be a politician. Katie took a deep breath.

"My recommendation is Amnesty for all, with a note placed in their school files that a second offense will result in a double penalty."

"A Daniel come to judgment," Principal Miles declared. "I presume Katie speaks for the Council."

"Absolutely!" Ben said.

"Then I shall pass your recommendation on to the faculty," the Principal said. "Thank you all. This meeting is adjourned."

"Katie, hold up," Ben said as she walked past him

toward the door. "That was a great suggestion. You should definitely be on the council next year."

Katie blushed again, "I would like that," she said. "I won't be able to, though. My father is going to the University of Illinois this fall to get his PhD. I won't be here for the next two years. Maybe I'll run again when I'm a senior."

Ben graduated first in his class. His father's gift was a very expensive transistor radio he could carry in his shirt pocket. Margie's gift was a leather-bound copy of Jonathon Swift's essays, with a note that said, "I'm so proud of you, Ben. I hope you'll follow most of Swift's advice in these essays, and that you won't let yourself fall under the spell of a pretty girl before you get your degree."

Part II

8

"How long's it been?" Suzy Anderson asked when Ben and she ran into each other at Willard's Grocery in early June 1962.

"About four years," Ben said. "I just finished my first year of law school. "I'm clerking for Harry Biggs this summer—running titles, filing court papers, that sort of thing. What are you doing?"

"Summer school. Four or five of us enrolled in the summer session at the college, getting an early start on our freshman year."

"You'd rather study than play this summer?" Ben laughed. "Who else is doing this?"

"All the smart ones," Suzy said. "You know, Joetta, Tina, Katie . . ."

"Katie Reynolds?" Ben said. "I thought her family moved to Illinois so her dad could get his PhD."

"They did," Suzy said, "and they're back. It's Dr.

Reynolds now. And you should see Katie! She's all grown up."

The only vision of Katie in Ben's head was of a very smart, flat-chested, pre-pubescent freshman in high school, wearing thick glasses. "Tell me more," he said.

"You do know Katie had a monstrous crush on you when you were a senior," Suzy said. "And you practically ignored her. She was really hurt when you raved about Joetta's shorter cut for the spring prom and all you said about her new hair style was 'that's nice.'"

Ben grimaced. "I said that! And you remembered all these years?"

"You sure did," Suzy snorted. "And yes, I do remember. You were a real prick."

"A prick??!"

"Well, let's say insensitive. You weren't discourteous or mean."

"Thank goodness," Ben said. "Maybe I can make it up to her by taking her out now."

"You'd better hurry," Suzy said. "Some guy in her Chemistry class is already putting the moves on her."

"Wow!" Ben said. "She must have really changed."

"I have an idea," Suzy said. "Katie is studying with me Sunday evening. Why don't you drop by after supper to see if she wants to go out for a Coke?"

"Wouldn't that be rude of me to ask her and not you?"

"Don't worry about me," Suzy said. "I'll come up with a good excuse."

As he sat in front of Suzy's house about seven Sunday night, Ben stared out the window of the 1961 Renault Dauphine his dad had purchased on his first trip to France since the war. He had known Katie had a crush on him in high school, and he'd been flattered, but not much more. Even with her sharp mind, he had no romantic interest in her then. To him, she was a kid, plain and simple. According to Suzy, Katie had blossomed. Well, he thought as he walked to the door, we'll see.

"What a surprise!" Suzy shouted when she opened the door. "Hey everybody. It's Ben!"

Six girls, all of whom Ben knew, but not Katie, were chattering among themselves. For a moment Ben felt Suzy had set him up for a big joke at his expense. Then out of the powder room came a radiant young woman wearing a short-sleeved white blouse tucked into a black knee length skirt, her brown hair as lustrous as a model's. Ben was speechless.

"Cat got your tongue?" Suzy said. "Or is she just too gorgeous for words? You'd better come up with something fast."

"Hello, Ben," Katie said when she joined Ben and Suzy at the door. "It's so nice of you to offer to take me home early. These girls aren't ready to stop gossiping and I have a project due tomorrow."

Suzy winked. Ben tried to think of something witty or funny to say, but his mind was not under his control. Katie was so...grown up, so developed. Even her voice had matured.

"Do you have time for coffee at the Gateway before

I take you home?" he asked, wishing it could be a movie at the Starlight Drive In.

"I would love to," Katie said. "But I really do have to finish my project tonight."

"Could we do something next weekend?" Ben said when they arrived at Katie's house. "If UT is playing, we could go to the game."

"I don't think they are," Katie said. "but there is a college mixer next Friday night, which I believe is limited to students."

"I'm a student," Ben laughed. "Shall I pick you up at seven?"

A faint smile played across her face. Was she summing him up? Scrutinizing him to decide if *he* was still worthy of her attention?

"Yes," Katie said. "I'd like that. And Ben—thanks for bringing me home. Good night."

Ben couldn't contain his jubilation on the short drive to his house. She *must* still like me, he thought. I wonder where we can go after the mixer. Too bad she still lives with her parents and not in the dorm. I don't want us to be confined to their front porch with them in earshot. Then it hit him. The Brown Road farm his father owned was out of the way and dark—the perfect place for a couple who wanted to be alone. Maybe next time.

Ben washed and waxed the Renault Friday afternoon, showered, and shaved, then shot over to the Reynolds' house. On arrival he could see Katie through the open window of a Morris Minor, a British import which Ben considered vastly inferior to a Renault, or even a Beetle.

"Sorry I can't go tonight. I have other plans." Katie said as she jumped out of the car and walked toward Ben, who was intensely studying what he could see of the driver, noting his thin face and grey eyes showing immense displeasure as he scowled at Ben before mustering all 30 horses in the Morris Minor's puny engine in a lame attempt to scratch off.

"Who's that guy?" Ben asked. "Have you been somewhere with him?"

"He's just a guy in my chemistry class," Katie said, color rising on her cheeks. "We went to Rocky's last Friday. We didn't have a date for tonight—or at least, I didn't think we did." Ben thought her laugh sounded uncomfortable.

"What's his name?" he asked.

Katie ran her fingers through her hair, then smiled at Ben. "Clark," she said. "Clark Cooper."

Ben's jealously exploded internally. He wanted to kiss Katie on the spot—to claim her—then track down this Clark fellow and punch him in the nose. His strong reaction to seeing Katie sitting in another guy's car unsettled him. He didn't want her to see how much. Her radiant vivacity had captured his heart, but he had to maintain control over his feelings. He had to keep his cool. He'd be returning to law school in a few days, so he had no time to squander—especially with this guy Clark in the picture. He just had to avoid acting like the love-struck kid he was.

"What have you been up to today?" she asked.

"Nothing really. Just wondering whether I should

worry about your getting into any entangling alliances while I'm gone."

"Entangling alliances?" Katie scoffed. "Really, Ben, are you getting your quips from George Washington?"

Ben was flabbergasted. In addition to being beautiful, she was...erudite, just as he had described her as a high school freshman. And to top it off, she felt confident enough to tease him. He had to follow up.

"Do you know why Washington warned the country to avoid entangling alliances?"

"Of course," Katie replied. "I took the same honors history course you did. Washington wanted the new country to stay out of European conflicts. Dr. Lantz said that advice was good today, and the US should not get involved in Vietnam. He was dead set against sending troops, even as advisors. Did he talk about staying out of foreign conflicts when you had him?"

Even though Ben had asked the question that had led to Katie's question, he was too captivated by the glow in her eyes, making them look almost feline, and too overcome by her boldness to follow up. All he could do was secretly thank heaven Katie was smart and beautiful, and at that moment, his. His mind wanted the discussion to continue and reveal more of Katie's understanding of politics and the use of force to carry out policy. His heart, however, wanted nothing to detract from the aura of her presence. Katie's quizzical look turned into a smile.

"Don't worry, Ben," she said, in that soft voice which made him shiver. "There's so much new in my life right now. I plan to stay un-entangled for quite a while."

"Speaking of new," Ben said. "Let's go to the Wesley Foundation Wednesday night. They've begun a new series on Theology, and the first book for discussion is Bishop John Robinson's *A Study in Pauline Theology*. A New Testament expert from Lambuth College will be speaking."

Katie's smile faded. "I'm sorry, I can't," she said. "I have other plans."

As Ben feared, those "other plans," involved Clark and were revealed when Katie and Clark quietly entered the Fellowship Hall and took seats on the opposite side of the room from Ben. Clark's presence stifled his impulse to stroll over and start a conversation with Katie. Better to sit back, observe and hope for an opportunity. Because the seats were arranged in a semi-circle, Ben had a clear view of Katie. He saw the lines on her face harden as the speaker discussed Paul's view of marriage. He saw her raise her hand, and he saw an almost imperceptible shift in her focus from the speaker to him, then back to the speaker.

"You have a question, Miss?" the speaker asked.

"Sounds like Paul was a misogynist," Katie said.

All eyes turned toward her. A nervous murmur went through the group. Clark had a look of utter disbelief. Martin was in the buckle of the bible belt. You didn't question the authority of scripture and you didn't accuse a saint of anything un-saintly. Ben's face flushed with pride. The speaker brushed aside the question by explaining that church historians had debated whether Paul was making a case that men should remain single, as he was, for the good of the movement, and pointing out that the leaders of the early church were all men, so women clearly played a secondary role but that did not mean Saint Paul was a misogynist.

After the meeting Ben headed toward the speaker who had left the podium and seemed to be searching for someone. Following the speaker led Ben straight to Katie.

"I'm sorry for giving short shrift to your perceptive observation," Dr. Theodore Simpson, New Testament Professor at Lambuth said to Katie. "I just didn't want the hour to be consumed by arguments over Paul's views on marriage within the church."

Ben jumped in, "From the shocked look on everyone's face, I don't think you would have gotten much argument from this group."

"You're probably right," the professor said. "The Pauline letters is a Senior level course at Lambuth and there is rarely any complaint by students about Paul's views toward women. I must admit I was surprised by your comment, Katie, since you look much too young to be a Senior and since this is not a school with a religious affiliation. I wish I had time to discuss the subject further with you, but it's a long drive back to Jackson."

Ben was eager to continue the discussion also, but while he was saying a quick goodbye to Dr. Simpson, Katie and Clark slipped away.

Fortunately, he would see Katie once more before he returned to law school. He had invited her to a fellowship supper that Saturday night at the Student Center. Since the Reynolds' house was five minutes away, they walked over.

"Why did you accuse Paul of being misogynist?" Ben asked as they started out.

"Isn't it obvious?" Katie answered. "The early church did not want men to be encumbered by women, yet they were willing to let women clean their clothes, prepare their meals and take care of their children. Women were never given serious roles in the church. How misogynist can you get?"

"Hmm," Ben said. "I hadn't thought of it that way. You could be right."

"Could be right!!" Katie scoffed. "I am right. Men and women see things differently. Haven't you noticed?"

The Student Center was packed when they arrived. Ben spotted two empty seats on one of the many tables set up for the event.

"There's Suzy," Katie said as Ben pulled one of the chairs out for her, "sitting at the same table with Clark. I can't tell who she's with. Let's go see."

"Must we?" Ben said. "I don't want this to turn into a 'pull up a chair and join us' thing."

"Oh, Ben," Katie said. "Suzanne is my best friend. I can't ignore her." Katie waved at Suzy, grabbed Ben's hand, and pulled him toward the other table.

"Look who's here," Suzy exclaimed. "Slide down a seat, Brad, so Katie can sit by me. We need to compare notes on sororities. Ben, pull up a seat by Clark over there and talk cars."

Ben felt trapped. He wanted to grab Katie and leave but Katie was already seated.

"This won't take long," she whispered. "I promise."

Although he knew it was not true, Ben felt rejected. In such a short time, he had become so possessive of Katie he didn't want to share her with anyone, not even her girlfriends. He certainly did NOT want to waste valuable time talking cars with Clark Cooper.

"Gotta make a pit stop," he said to delay having to take a seat. Clark mercifully disappeared while he was gone. Ben looked for an empty spot close enough to Suzy and Katie to allow him to overhear their conversation, but not too close. There was no such spot. He slowly walked toward Katie.

"That's good to know," Suzy said as Ben approached. "We have the same first choice." Turning to him she said, "When are you going back to school, Ben?"

"Tomorrow," he said. "Classes don't start for another week, but I'm tired of the graduate students' dorm and would like to find a room off campus or an apartment to share. A friend of mine has been looking and thinks he has found a good situation for me, so I'm going early to check it out."

Katie looped her arm through Ben's and said, "I'm sure we'll see Ben soon. He's promised to take me to see UT-M play football this fall."

"Football!!" Suzy guffawed. "You hate football."

Katie pulled Ben closer to her and said, "I hate the

game, boys hitting each other and running over each other and the fans acting as if it were the most important event in the world. What I enjoy is watching the crowd."

After the event, Ben walked Katie home in a mild funk. He had loved the time they had spent together, but he was leaving, and did not know when he would be back. In his two semi-serious college relationships, considerable time had passed between his meeting the girls and asking them out. Each girl had been far more interested in him than he was in her, and each had created the situation for Ben to ask her for a date. The serious necking which had ensued made it awkward not to ask them out again. Ben's motivation, however, had been strictly libidinous. When the girls finally gave up on him and began pursuing other guys, Ben was relieved.

He always justified his tepid approach to dating by recalling Margie's advice and telling himself it's not time for me to get serious with so much school ahead. This time was different. He had rediscovered Katie and learned that all her "old" good qualities had been reinforced and strengthened by "new" good qualities. In his mind she was flawless. He was drawn to her like a gambler to a high stakes poker game. He wanted to be with her all the time. He didn't want a make-out session. He wanted a serious, long-term relationship.

"You've been so quiet," Katie said as they approached

her house. "Does my not being a big football fan bother you?"

"No, no, not at all," he said. "I was just trying to think of another exciting thing we could do when I'm home again."

"Don't give up on a ball game," Katie laughed. "You could watch the game and I could watch the crowd."

Ben grinned and opened her door, expecting to walk her up the steps and kiss her goodnight, but their path was suddenly illuminated by the high beams of Dr. Reynolds' Chevy which had just pulled up. All hopes for a tender goodnight kiss vanished. Ben squeezed her hand and said, "Goodnight, Katie, I've enjoyed tonight. I'll let you know when I'll be back."

"I hope it's soon," Katie said in a voice so sincere Ben knew she meant it. Yet as he drove home, he obsessed over his situation. Katie's saying she was avoiding entangling alliances applied to him as well as to Clark, and Clark had the clear advantage of being in the same school with her every day and having a class with her three days a week, while Ben was 150 miles away. What's more, he and Katie had not even kissed, much less made it to Brown Road Farm. Since Katie was going to play the field, he had to get back to Martin soon and often to keep the field level so he could stay in the game.

Settling into the new school year and moving into a new sparsely furnished apartment kept Ben from thinking of Katie every moment of every day during the first two weeks he was back in Nashville. As the days went by, however, his missing her became more intense. He had to find a time when he could go back to Martin. The Law Review work retreat the last weekend of September was a must attend for him, but the first weekend in October was open. He called Katie to invite her to the UT-M vs Troy football game the first Saturday in October.

"Oh, Ben," she said. "That's so nice of you."

Nice of me? Ben thought. What kind of response is that?

"I would really like to see you," Katie continued. "I would! I know we'd have a fun time at the game. It's just that it would upset Clark too much."

Ben's heart sank. He struggled for a reply that would turn this conversation around.

"So?" was all he could come up with.

"I know that must sound silly to you," Katie said. "When I do something with anyone else, even meet a friend for a Coke, Clark gets upset, and if I told him I was going to a game with you he would probably throw up."

"Why would that matter?" Ben's voice had hardened.

"How can I say this?" Katie said. "Clark and I have been eating lunch together after chemistry, and you have been a constant issue between us. We were sitting by the window at the T-Room last Wednesday and I saw a Renault pass by. I said, 'There's Ben.' Clark's face turned ghostly white and his hands started shaking. Of course, it wasn't you, which I knew as soon as I saw the Kentucky license tag, but Clark couldn't finish his lunch. Last Saturday he got an upset stomach and threw up when I casually told him you had talked about taking me to the next UT home game. Clark is a great guy and I know he likes me. We've been together so much since classes started my friends already think we are a couple."

"Well, are you?" Ben asked, dreading the answer.

"Not in any formal way," Katie sounded troubled. "Yet, we do a lot of things together."

Katie sighed, "How can I express what I really mean?"

Then she sighed again, sending Ben's heart to the pits. "You see, Ben, you are half a state away. Clark is here and would be here after you and I went to the game together. If I want to maintain a relationship with Clark—he *is* a really nice guy—I can't make him sick by going out with you every month or so. I'm sorry it has to be that way..."

Katie paused for a moment, giving Ben a sliver of hope that something good could come out of this conversation. Then she continued. "Anyway, thanks for asking, Ben. I have to go now, goodbye."

Ben thought *he* was going to lose *his* lunch. His heart could sink no further, and the finality of her goodbye guaranteed it would not soon rise again. Just when he had allowed himself to look past law school and take a relationship seriously, the girl he had totally and completely fallen for had thrown him to the curb.

Two months later, two days after Christmas, Suzy called.

"Are you going to the New Year's Eve dance at the Club?" she asked. "A lot of kids you know will be there."

"No, Suzy. I'm certainly not going alone and there's no one I know to ask."

Suzy's voice took on the impish tone Ben knew so well. "I saw Katie yesterday. Why don't you ask her?"

"Katie!" Ben felt a momentary surge of excitement, then felt his shoulders slump. "You know she blew me off back in October."

"Oh, Ben. That's ancient history. Call her."

"Why? Nothing's changed, has it?"

"Pretend October never happened," Suzy said. "Call her."

Ben agonized for an hour over whether to risk rejection again. He thought about the constant rejection he received from Eileen, which had started so early in his life, he was now insulated against hurt from her. It wasn't the same. He was not in love with Eileen. With butterflies in his stomach, he dialed Katie's number.

"Hi, Katie, this is Ben. Ben McHaney. Is this a good time to talk?"

Katie laughed and those butterflies flapped harder. The couple exchanged the usual pleasantries—how was her family, did she like her courses—then with bated breath Ben asked the question.

"Would you like to go to the New Year's Eve dance at the Club with me?"

"I'd love to," Katie replied without hesitation.

Ben had to bite his tongue to keep from shouting "Praise the Lord" as Grandmother McHaney did whenever good things happened. Ben McHaney was still in the game! Ben had been so afraid she would say no, he had not thought through the logistics of starting a midnight date. His mind immediately went into hyper drive.

"The party doesn't start till 10, so I'll pick you up at 9:30. Unless we could make an evening of it and go to dinner."

"Sounds exciting," Katie said, "but my grandmother's expecting me for supper that night. I will, however, be back in plenty of time to be ready by 9:30."

New Year's Eve morning dawned crisp and cool. Ben had drifted off shortly before midnight dreaming of his newly revived romance. That morning he shined his shoes, picked up his navy sports coat from the cleaners, and visited both florists in town searching for a corsage made of flowers other than carnations. Finding none, he scoured Fulton, where he located a florist who grew hothouse roses, and for ten dollars, all of Margie's Christmas gift, made him a corsage that "would be the envy of every other girl at the party."

Riley and Eileen had taken Charles and Margie to Daytona Beach the day after Christmas and wouldn't be back till Tuesday night. Ben had passed on the trip. He had better things to do than spend a week in a cramped car with Eileen. A couple of minor bowl games were being played that afternoon, but they couldn't keep Ben's attention away from the clock slowly ticking the day away. Supper at six, consisted of backs and wings leftover from an earlier fried chicken dinner, augmented with a cold baked potato. Ben enjoyed eating alone. He could gnaw the chicken bones without reprimand, and he didn't have to share the thighs with anyone. Showering and shaving took thirty minutes and getting dressed less than twenty. By 7:45 Ben had brushed his teeth, combed his hair, splashed on Old Spice, whisked the imagined lint off his trousers and checked on the rose corsage in the refrigerator, leaving almost two hours to kill before he could see Katie. By 8:45, he could take the wait no longer and decided to leave for Katie's on the chance she had cut short her visit to grandmother, and they could start their evening early.

As he approached Dr. Reynolds' home, in the darkened driveway he recognized the shitty Morris Minor. On the dimly lit porch sat Katie with Clark. Another young man stood facing them. Ben could not hear their conversation and he could not see Katie's face, but he could see Clark's arm stretched behind Katie, resting on her right shoulder, and the other young man gesticulating like a performer in a one-man show. Suddenly Clark and Katie stood up almost as one, and Clark wrapped both arms around her. Katie's arms hung limp at her side. More than a few seconds later Clark released his grasp, took her face in his hands, and kissed her.

Ben's adrenaline surged. Memories of Katie's previous rejection smothered all reason, leaving his reptilian brain in control. Ben pounded up the steps to where the party of three stood, threw the corsage at Katie's feet and stormed away.

"Ben! Come back!" Katie cried out. "Let me explain."

But Ben had his own explanation—Clark was in, he

was out. He jumped into his car and gunned it past the Reynolds' house, past the Club at the corner of the Fulton Bypass, turned onto unlit Mt. Pelia Road, heading into rural Weakley County. RFD mailboxes flashed by every hundred yards or so until the paved road turned to gravel, where he skidded to a stop and released his seething anger with a ferocious scream. "FUCK!!!"

Ben stayed in Nashville most of the school year and clerked with a Nashville firm the summer of 1963. He did not go home, except for occasional weekend visits, primarily to be with his father, who had begun to complain of lack of energy, until after the Vanderbilt graduation ceremonies in early May,1964, where he was inducted into the Order of the Coif honorary society and received his law degree. He was to start his job as an associate with a large Atlanta law firm three weeks later.

On his first Monday back in Martin, Ben headed to the Donut Shop. Standing at the door trying to decide if he should buy a half-dozen to take home, or more sensibly have one or two there with coffee, he heard someone call.

"Ben, Ben McHaney. Yoo-hoo!"

It was Suzy, wearing a bright red sundress, oversized sunglasses, and a floppy hat to protect her fair complexion from the sun, and flashing a huge diamond engagement ring. "Are you trying to decide how many donuts to eat this morning?" Suzy said. "Let's go inside and I'll have one with you."

Ben was glad to have Suzy's company. Nobody knew

more about what was going on in Martin than she did. He ordered a half-dozen glazed and two coffees at the counter, brought them in a sack to the two top table Suzy had chosen, spread napkins on the table, opened the sack and said, "Two doughnuts or three?"

"Only one for me," Suzie said. "Have to watch myself. By the way, have you heard my big news?"

"Only what I read in the *Weakley County Press*," Ben replied.

"So, I guess you saw the announcement of my wedding?"

Ben had seen the Society Page headline which had made him think of that disastrous New Year's Eve, causing his insides to churn so badly he could not finish the article.

"I don't normally read the Society section," he said, "but I can see the rock on your finger. Congratulations! Who's the guy and when's the wedding?"

"Brad Steiner, a Montanan who came to UT-M on a football scholarship. I've known him over two years. Not sure of the date yet. It'll be a big event. Peggy will be Matron of Honor and I'm having five bridesmaids, including Katie, of course. Mom has hired a wedding planner—she had to go to Memphis to get one—who wants all the colors coordinated and wants to go with the "in" color for weddings this season, which apparently is mauve. I nixed that. It's going to be rose. Daddy thinks a wedding planner is a terrible waste of $250—especially if I'm not going to listen to her. He says only big city folks make weddings into big productions. Mom doesn't listen to him. She's determined I'll have a wedding as grand as Flo Harding's, who is spending over $5,000, so we hear."

"Five thousand dollars!" Ben gasped. "That's as much as I'll be making in a year."

"Oh, Ben, I shouldn't have told you that. Please forget the cost and be happy for me. The big wedding is Mom's idea. I just want to get married."

"I am happy for you, Suzy. What's the hold up?"

"Mother. I'm thinking early October. She insists on next spring. She wants more time to plan, but I can't keep Brad at bay that long. The wedding will be at the Church and the reception will be at the Club, so the older folks can have their Jack Daniels and Coke, and the fellows can have their beer. Have you heard the Stanfords are having a big engagement party for us at their home Saturday? It's not a shower, it's a party. You will come, won't you?"

"I haven't been invited," Ben said, "If I am, I'll certainly come. Probably won't be able to make an October wedding."

"Splendid. I'll get the word to Mrs. Stanford that you're in town and will be coming. I'm sure it'll be okay. You were always one of her favorites. It's so good to see you, Ben. Thanks for the donut. Got to run."

Suzy wiped a crumb from her lip, kissed Ben on the cheek and was gone. Ben *was* happy for his friend. Nevertheless, he envied Suzy for finding a guy she wanted to spend the rest of her life with and was disappointed she had said practically nothing about Katie.

The Stanford's home, a Tara-styled mansion built

between the world wars and just across the county line, easily accommodated their nearly one hundred guests. The off-duty sheriff's deputy in charge of parking stopped traffic to allow a van to shuttle guests up the winding drive to the front entrance, sparing the elderly and women in high heels a strenuous climb.

Ben, standing alone at the bar on the sun porch, spotted Katie the moment she entered the room in a flowing skirt that swished when she walked and reflected light from the luminous silver threads woven into the fabric. After a wistful stare at this statuesque, beautiful young woman he had been determined to avoid, Ben motioned the bar tender for a pour. He tensed as he felt Katie approaching.

"Hello, Ben. It's been a while. How are you?"

There was no mistaking that soft voice. Without raising his head Ben lifted his Cutty Sark in a dismissive salute and said, "Fine. Can I get you something, or is Clark taking care of you?"

"Ginger Ale, please."

Katie brushed against him and said, "I'm alone tonight. And Ben, I really am sorry about our last date."

"Date? What Date?" Ben snapped.

He ordered a Schweppes, handed it to her, took a long sip of his scotch, looked around as if trying to locate someone, then locked his eyes on hers and said, "If this is going to be New Year's Eve all over again, I'm not interested."

Katie held his stare. "Ben, it wasn't like it appeared. I was excited about going to that party with you, but

Clark and his brother showed up unexpectedly. I can understand if you never want to speak to me again, but please, let me explain."

Ben didn't want an explanation. He wanted to punish and humiliate her, like she had humiliated him. To stoke his ill will toward her, he thought about the abuses Eileen had inflicted upon him. But comparing Katie's actions to Eileen's was flawed. Eileen had no power to hurt him. Katie had the power to destroy him. The more he tried to villainize Katie, however, the more her face showed tenderness and caring, rendering him helpless once again. He pulled out a stool and gestured for her to take a seat. The harsh lines on his face softened as Katie related her version of New Year's Eve.

"I had one of my Sharon cousins drive me home a little after eight so I could freshen up and be ready for you," she said. "I was hoping you'd come early, and when I heard someone at the door about 8:30, I thought it was you, and ran to greet you, but it was Clark and Jerry, who had sneaked out of their family's New Year celebration to wish me a Happy New Year. I tried to get them to leave as politely as I could, but Jerry started to tell me about the deer they almost hit on the way over and the story kept going on and on. Even though it was cold sitting on the porch, I didn't invite them in. Clark must have noticed my shivering and put his arm around me. He pulled me up when he got up to go. That kiss you saw was a Happy New Year kiss, that's all."

"And if I had waited till 9 to arrive," Ben said, "they

would have been gone, and I would never have known about it."

"Or if you had come at 8:30 like I hoped..."

"Clark and I would have pulled up at the same time," Ben said. "That happened once before, you know."

"Yes, I remember," Katie said, "and I walked away from Clark then to go with you and I would have done the same again. You never gave me a chance."

Ben's ebbing anger was replaced by shame—shame on himself. Had his jealousy cost him the opportunity to dance away the old year with Katie, and to kiss her at the start of the new? What could he say to keep the conversation going, to get Katie to reveal how she felt about him now?

While Ben stewed in his uncertainty, Katie sipped her Schweppes until she suddenly looked up and said, "They are motioning me to the microphone. I'm supposed to offer a toast to Suzy and Brad. I'm sorry we didn't get to talk longer."

The last drops of Cutty Sark converted Ben's shame to melancholy. With his eyes he followed Katie through the crowd and saw her take the microphone.

"Hello, everybody, and welcome. Although most of you know me, for those who don't, I'm Katie Reynolds, and I've known Suzie since we started kindergarten as four-year olds, so I probably know more about her than any other person here, including her sister Peggy, who may have lived with Suzie but didn't have sleepovers with her and wasn't in the same class with her from first grade on. And in the last few months I've learned a lot about Brad, mostly from listening to Suzy carry on about him and observing him and Suzy together. And Brad, even though you are a six-foot two-inch 245-pound linebacker, let me warn you, you are marrying a woman who isn't afraid of anything or any man. So, don't cross her."

For almost five minutes Ben listened to Katie skillfully weave together anecdotes about the couple, entertaining the crowd and reminding him how clever she was and how captivating her voice could be. He declined the second pour the bartender offered, and for another ten minutes, swirled the ice in his glass and tried to dull the ache in his heart. Then, as if she had sensed his heartache, Katie was there. She touched his arm.

"I'm about to call Dad to come get me," she said, "and wanted to say goodbye."

"Not Clark?"

A shadow crossed Katie's face. Ben cursed himself for meeting Katie's openheartedness with attempted sarcasm.

"This is a co-op term for Clark," she said. "I haven't seen him in weeks. Anyway, it was good to see you."

Ben realized he had been staring at Katie's sleeveless top a bit too long and redirected his gaze to the floor and her silver sandals with their three-inch heels. The embers glowing in his heart burst into flame and emboldened him to say:

"May I take you home?"

"I'd like that," she said.

Ben put his hand on Katie's waist and guided her through the crowd, out the door and onto the shuttle waiting to take them to the street.

"The weather's lovely," Katie said as they walked the short distance from the shuttle to his car. "I could have walked home."

"Not in those heels," Ben said. "By the way, those sandals are seriously sexy."

"Thank you," she blushed.

She likes me. She hasn't seen Clark in weeks. I can't botch things up again. Too soon they were at the Reynolds' home and he was opening the car door for her. Trying to sound casual, he said, "The Lettermen are at the College Auditorium Tuesday night. Would you like to go?"

Katie's eyes sparkled. "I love the Lettermen. What time should I be ready?"

For an awful moment, the pain of New Year's Eve roared back into Ben's thoughts. He shook them away, took a deep breath and said, "How about seven?"

"Perfect," she said over her shoulder as she hurried to the porch where her mother waited with a grim face and folded arms. Ben was glad he had borrowed his dad's convertible.

"Isn't that Ben?" he heard her mother ask.

"You know it is, Mother. He is taking me to see the Lettermen Tuesday."

"What about Clark?"

"What about him, Mother? We're not engaged."

Ben's heart soared. He knew he should drive off, but he couldn't leave—not yet.

"Listen to me, Kathryn," Ben heard Mrs. Reynolds say. "When Clark left three weeks ago, he thought you were committed to him. As I've said before, if you aren't, you owe it to him to let him know."

"Yes, Mother," Katie sighed, "and I will tell Clark the next time I see him."

"That's not soon enough. Write and tell him now, or better yet call him tonight. If you are sure Clark is not the guy, get it over with. The longer you play with fire, the more likely you are to get burned."

Glancing over her shoulder at Ben's car, she took Katie by the arm and said, "Let's continue this inside."

Ben replayed that conversation in his head several times, wishing he had been closer, or his eyesight had been keener so he could read Katie's face. What he clearly understood was that Katie and Clark were not engaged. What he did not understand was exactly what their relationship was.

Monday morning he asked Suzy to meet him for coffee at the Donut Shop to get her take on his evening with Katie. He told Suzy everything in as much detail as he could remember, including Katie's conversation with her mother.

"One thing I'm sure of," Suzy told him. "Katie's not committed to Clark. She has talked about breaking up with him for weeks. She just hasn't been able to pull the trigger."

"Has she dated anyone but him since she blew me off that New Year's Eve?"

"Blew you off? Aren't you being a little harsh? That's not like Katie—she's too kind."

"Call it what you will," Ben said with a touch of irritation. "At the Stanfords' party, Katie tried to explain what happened New Year's Eve on her father's porch and I wanted desperately to believe her, but after I got home, the more I thought about what I saw, the more convinced I was it must have been what it looked like, a blow-off pure and simple. She wanted to show me she preferred Clark, and..."

"Slow down, Ben. Don't get back into those negative feelings. Katie's not a liar. You know that. She planned to go to the party with you. She told me so. She just couldn't get out of the situation she was in with Clark that New Year's Eve."

Ben pressed his fingertips to his temples and tried to massage away his demons. He had never seen Katie look as if she were in love with Clark. Was it possible she was in a trap and didn't know how to get out? Of course, she could get out—if she weren't so concerned about Clark's feelings.

"All right, say she isn't so taken by Clark," Ben said. "Which brings me back to my question. Why is he still around? What is the hold he has on her?"

Suzy shrugged her shoulders.

"Help me out here, Suzy. Women are impossible to understand."

Suzy smiled ruefully. "Maybe she enjoyed making-out

in the beginning of their relationship. Girls have hormones, too, you know. Maybe she let him get attached to her too soon."

Ben cringed at the thought of Katie making out with Clark...and possibly more.

"Maybe all the other guys considered them a couple and stayed clear because they were together so much. Maybe it's because Clark does anything she asks and takes her anywhere she wants to go. What girl wants to give up being pampered?"

"Good Lord," Ben said. "This guy seems more like a servant than a boyfriend. If that's what Katie really wants, I've misjudged her."

"Katie's not vain," Suzy scolded. "It's complicated. Clark is her first serious relationship. He adores her and tells her so all the time. He tells her he can't imagine life without her. That's flattering, sure...It's also a big burden to carry."

"So why carry it?"

Suzy's frustration showed. "You're not listening, Ben. Katie's a sensitive girl. A girl *brought up* to be nice, to put others first. It's different for men. You men don't realize how different. What she really wants is for him to fall for another girl during his co-op term and break up with her. But I don't see that happening."

Ben grappled with what Suzy was telling him. He could accept that women face different pressures from men. Still, how could she let her actions be governed so much by the desire to please others? He wouldn't, but why? Was it her parents? Dr. and Mrs. Reynolds clearly loved Katie and were concerned about her welfare. They watched over her so carefully—maybe too carefully. If Ben had grown up with a mother like Mrs. Reynolds, how different might his life be? He tried to remember a single time Eileen had been concerned about his happiness. He couldn't. He couldn't even recall her ever kissing him or hugging him, other than to put on a show for others. Suzy pushed a lock of hair behind her ear, bringing Ben back to the moment.

"Some of its guilt, okay?"

"What do you mean?"

"Before Clark left for his co-op job in Memphis, he told her he had spent so much time with her or thinking about her that his grades had suffered, and he would not be permitted to re-enroll this fall. And if he is not in school, he loses his deferment and is subject to the draft."

"He flunked out??" Ben exclaimed. "That's her answer! She can't date a drop-out."

"Most girls would agree," Suzy said, "but not Katie. She's too moral—thinks she's partially responsible. She had her chance when Clark stopped by her house on his way out of town and asked her to wait for him. She told me she put him off. I told her to give him an emphatic NO. To grab the opportunity to see what other guys are like by dating around. Then she could decide whether Clark was the guy for her permanently. Clark thinks they are an exclusive couple. If they aren't, Katie needs to tell him. Being honest with Clark is the right thing to do. Besides, she isn't helping Clark by stringing him along if she doesn't love him."

Ben shook his head. "Other guys? What did she say about dating other guys?"

"Nothing. Because there aren't any, except you."

Ben sat back in his chair, took a quick sip of his lukewarm coffee, and mumbled.

"Nobody else but me," he said. "That's a line in a jazz piece we played in the dance band."

"I think it is true," Suzy said.

"Well," Ben said, "she'll have to break up with Clark to prove it to me."

"In a perfect world," Suzy said. "In our world you have to take Katie as she is. She dreads the actual break-up because she knows Clark will be deeply hurt, which will make her feel guilty and Katie can't handle guilt."

Ben recalled situations in the Student Council where Katie tried to be scrupulously fair. She *really* didn't want to hurt anybody. But everyone hurts somebody sometime, and you can't go through life feeling guilty about decisions that were right when they were made, even if someone was hurt. Pain etched Ben's face.

"I don't know what to do," he moaned.

Suzy groped around in her purse and pulled out a tube of lipstick. "Ben, you are in love with her. Follow Sinatra's advice and tell her. Let her know Clark is not her only choice."

Ben twisted in his seat. "You're right. I *am* in love with her. I would tell her in a flash if she had not rejected me twice already. And Clark's still around. My pride couldn't take being shot down a third time."

"Well, there you have it," Suzy said as she stood up

and perfectly re-applied her lipstick without a mirror. "Katie's afraid to break up with Clark because of the guilt it would cause her, and you're afraid to tell Katie you love her because she hasn't broken up with Clark. Looks like Clark has a strangle hold on both of you."

Ben drove home, his conversation with Suzy having almost convinced him that it was only a matter of time before Katie ditched Clark, and the two of them could begin to make serious plans. He decided it was time to confront her directly about Clark. She just needed a nudge. Late Tuesday afternoon he called her to confirm their meeting time for that night.

"May I pick you up half an hour early?"

"Come on over now," Katie laughed. "I'll be ready by the time you get here."

The May weather was mild and the evening breeze refreshing. Ben had once again, over Eileen's strenuous objection, borrowed his dad's Buick Electra 225 convertible with its soft blue exterior and creamy off-white leather interior. The flowered silk scarf Katie pulled from her purse to keep her hair in place during top-down driving went well with her muted turquoise shirt-waisted dress. She looked as elegant as Grace Kelly in "To Catch a Thief." To keep from shouting over the wind, Katie scooted toward the middle of the car, her hip barely touching Ben's. Ben struggled to keep both hands on the wheel.

Calls for encores kept the show going till near midnight. When Katie jumped out of the car to meet her midnight deadline she said, "Let's go see *Breakfast at*

Tiffany's Sunday night. We know exactly when it ends and won't have to worry about encores."

"I saw that movie when it first came out," he said. "But I'll gladly see it again."

Ben would have gladly seen anything again with Katie. As he got ready for bed, he thought about how lucky he was to have another chance with Katie and how exciting a permanent relationship with her could be. He wondered how often he would be able to visit her. He hoped her feelings for him were as intense as his were for her. He wished he had kissed her. The next morning he called Floral Express and ordered a bouquet of fresh flowers with this message: *Katie, Thank you for a magical evening. I hope there are more to come. Ben.*

The credits for *Breakfast at Tiffany's* had barely begun when they took their seats on the center aisle of the Varsity theater, five rows from the front. Ben held a large bag of popcorn in one hand and a bag of M&M's in the other. He poured the M&M's into the bag and stirred the contents.

"I love M&M's with hot popcorn," Katie whispered, reaching for a handful of the mixture. "Don't you?"

"Are you kidding? I always smuggle M&M's into a movie. They're too expensive to buy in the theater, with a large bag of popcorn costing fifty cents."

The movie was half over before the M&M laced popcorn was gone and Ben could wipe his hands on the empty bag and drop it to the floor. Katie's hands were folded in her lap, as if waiting for his. Ben gently picked up her left hand and moved it onto his knee in a warm trap she could easily have escaped. Katie pulled his hand into her lap and claimed it for the rest of the show, causing Ben's heart to soar. They held hands until Katie slid into her side of the car for the ride home.

"Do you remember," Katie said as Ben helped her into the car, "telling me the main reason you wanted to become a lawyer was so you could go into politics?"

"Yes," Ben said, "I did want to go into politics, until I saw that the people in politics who were in law school were the worst students. I thought I'd better raise my sights."

"So, what are you aiming for now?"

Ben thought a moment. "I think I might want to become a judge eventually," he said. "Right now, I want to concentrate on becoming the best lawyer I can be and making a good living."

"Aren't judges politicians?" Katie asked. "Judge Parker is running for re-election this fall My father is on his finance committee."

Ben thought another moment. "That's an astute observation," he said. "Judges in the federal court system are appointed, but they have to be aligned with the party in power or they won't be considered, so you'd have to say some politics is involved. State court judges are required to run for re-election every few years even if they were appointed originally. According to my Constitutional Law Professor, however, the federal system tries to keep the judges out of politics and concentrates on appointing well-qualified attorneys. On the other hand, there is a lot of cronyism in state court appointments."

"And why aren't there any women judges?" Katie asked.

"Why aren't there many women lawyers?" Ben responded. "There are only four women enrolled in Vanderbilt Law School."

This time Katie thought for a moment. "I guess girls don't think of law as a career for women. We are conditioned to be teachers or nurses or secretaries, or wives. We need to do something about that! By the way, it's still ten minutes till curfew. Let's sit on the porch."

As they sat in the swing, listening to the chorus of crickets or tree frogs, he could never tell which, Ben felt intensely alive. His skin prickled with excitement. He and Katie had so much in common—same schools, same church, same friends. He valued her opinions, and she seemed to value his. Was this the time to tell her he loved her? *No, I have to be sure about Clark first.*

"Why are you staring at me?" Katie asked. "Did I not cover a pimple?"

Ben laughed nervously. "Not that, your face is so expressive, and . . . you're so pretty. I have a hard time looking away."

Katie blushed. "Tell me, what's JAG?" she said. "I'd never heard of it until you mentioned that if you were in the military, you would be in JAG."

"It's the Judge Advocate General's Corp. All military lawyers are part of JAG. You are commissioned as a Captain and can make a career of it. But that's not what I want."

"What do you want?"

"Like I told you earlier," Ben said, "I'd like to become a judge, eventually. right now, in addition to becoming a good lawyer, I'd like to learn more about the civil rights movement. Atlanta is Martin Luther King's home and is the movement's center. Also, I'd like to learn more about why we are in Vietnam and how we can get out."

"I'm so glad to hear that," Katie said. "I don't have to tell you most people in this part of the country are in favor of the war and oppose expansion of civil rights. I didn't think much about civil rights until we moved to Urbana when Dad got his PhD. There I had black kids in class with me and realized they were no different from me. Dad's first lab assistant was a black girl only a couple of years older than me. Dad invited her home for dinner two or three times, and I heard her say that as a black person from the south side of Chicago, her life was in danger every day. She signed up for every after-school activity she could. Staying in school kept her off the streets and safer. I was profoundly changed by that experience and made up my mind to get involved, which isn't easy in Weakley County."

"As for the war, we all need to know what's going on in Vietnam. The anti-war movement claims the government is not telling us the truth."

Katie paused. Ben sighed and stretched to relieve the tension in his shoulders. "I can't get heavily involved in either civil rights or the anti-war movement," he said. "Dad said it would ruin my career. The most I can do is give them money."

The sound of shuffling feet came from the other side

of the door. "Uh, oh," Katie said. "Looks like Dad's ready to shoo you away. I'd like to continue this discussion, but I'd better go in now, before he comes out with a broom."

"Not a shotgun?" Ben said. "OK, I'll be on my way. Can we have dinner next Friday night? That will be my last weekend in Martin."

"Will Saturday work?" Katie said. "Where shall we go?"

"Somewhere in Fulton, so I can have a beer."

That Saturday night Ben took Katie to the Brown Derby in Fulton for dinner. She wore a red silk blouse and a full skirt, and the prettiest sandals Ben could imagine. Her nails were glossy pearl. A half hour thunderstorm Saturday afternoon dropped the temperature a few degrees and painted a beautiful sunset. The restaurant was nearly full when Katie and Ben were shown to their table.

"I'll have a Michelob," Ben told the waitress, "and she'll have a near beer."

"Would you like a Miller," the waitress looked at Katie. "A lot of co-eds drink Miller."

"I'll stick to near beer," Katie replied. "I'm underage."

"I know, honey," the waitress said. "Most college girls in here are underage. You didn't have to confess."

Katie blushed. Ben laughed.

"Yes, she did," Ben said. "I doubt Katie Reynolds has ever broken a rule her entire life."

Katie and Ben dawdled over coffee after dinner,

talking and laughing, then spent another half-hour sitting in the swing on her parents' porch, often in silence, with Ben's arm around her as she leaned against his shoulder, listening to the sounds of the night. The street was empty, and the Reynolds' house was quiet. The mood was too romantic to talk of war or civil rights. Shortly before eleven Ben said, "I've had a fabulous time with you these last few weeks. I want to tell you something but first we need to talk about…"

"Clark?" Katie asked.

"Yes," he said. "I've been haunted by him for two years. After that New Year's Eve fiasco, in spite of my hurt, I really wanted to see you, but my friends told me you were with Clark all the time, so I was afraid to call you. To protect my ego, I convinced myself to have nothing to do with you at the Stanfords' party…"

"I'm breaking up with Clark," Katie said.

Ben could feel his tension draining away. His face softened. He looked deeply into Katie's eyes and said, "Do you mean that?"

"Yes," she said. "I really do."

Ben pulled her up from the swing, held her close and said, "I'm crazy about you, Katie. You're beautiful and smart, and I love being with you. I've been waiting for you to tell me you were over Clark."

Katie snuggled closer and lightly touched Ben's mouth with her finger, as if to stifle any further conversation about Clark. Ben stroked her face and for the first time, they kissed.

"I don't want to leave tomorrow," he whispered. "But

my job starts Monday morning. I'll be able to come back over Labor Day for sure. Probably not for the 4th of July, though. It falls on a Wednesday this year."

"Come, if it's possible," Katie said as they kissed goodbye. "I'd very much like to see you."

Ben stopped by to see Katie on his way back to Atlanta the next morning. For half an hour they broke Dr. Reynolds' rule that Katie could not have a boy at her house unless a parent was home, and sat together in the swing, their hands entwined, hidden from anyone who might have passed by. When Ben rose to leave he said, "I'd like to stay all day, but I have to go."

"Please drive carefully," Katie said as she softly kissed his cheek and squeezed his hand goodbye.

Ben wrote the next day. Katie responded immediately. Their correspondence fell into a pattern. His letters went out on Saturday, telling of his experiences as a new lawyer, the book he was reading, and the questions it raised—and of his eagerness to see her again. He never asked about Clark. Katie's letters, written with perfect penmanship, arrived four days later. They were uplifting and usually answered any questions he had asked, and never mentioned Clark. Ben saved them all. The first one he kept by his bed.

June 3, 1964

Dear Ben,

Summer classes have begun, and I have Dr. Booth for English Lit. IV. His reputation is so scary I was actually afraid to take the class, but I am a Senior now (almost) and I have to get all required courses in. My fears were misplaced. His class is fun, and he is funny—if you can take his getting in your face to ask you questions and leaping out of his chair to challenge inadequate answers. On a more serious note, there was a big uproar last week when a group of students wanted to invite Stokely Carmichael of the Student Non-Violent Coordinating Committee to campus. The Administration overruled the students, so the invitation was not made. My Dad and I had some serious discussions about the wisdom of "inviting a radical to stir up impressionable college students and divert their attention from their studies." I think I quoted him accurately. My position was that the students at UT-M have been isolated from the civil rights movement too long. They come from segregated communities, they have no black friends, and the few students who "give a damn," have no reliable source of information about SNCC, the NAACP, the Freedom Riders or any of the organizations fighting for civil rights for minorities. What better place for them to get that information than on a college campus?

Have you thought any more about what you can do to help the civil rights movement without torpedoing your legal career? I'm sure there is something. Think hard. The movement needs all the help it can get. I've been keeping up with the Governor's race in Georgia, and I'm concerned about this man Lester Maddox. You told me he has no chance of being elected, but a lot of my relatives saw him on television refusing to serve black customers at his Pic Rik Restaurant in Atlanta and applauded him. Looks like working to keep Maddox from becoming Governor is one thing you could do right away without jeopardizing your career.

On the fun side, Aunt Beulah says I can bring a guest to the family Fourth of July picnic at her house. You are coming home for the 4th, aren't you? Would you like to go? Practically all of Sharon will be there. You don't have to bring anything. It'll be fun.

Fondly, Katie

Ben did not know that Clark continued to write Katie daily with a never changing message—he loved her, he missed her, and he couldn't live without her. Neither did Ben know that each letter from Clark renewed Katie's dread of the break-up she had promised Ben. Nor did he know she promptly answered each of Clark's letters, giving him no hint of her decision to end their relationship. She never told Ben she had written, but never mailed, this letter:

Dear Clark,

I'm sorry it hasn't worked out for us. It simply has not. There's no point in discussing why. You are a fine person, Clark, and have been good to me over the last two years. You'll make some lucky girl a great husband, but not me.

Sincerely,
Katie

As Ben feared, he was not able to get home for the 4th of July. As the weeks passed it became increasingly difficult for him to keep his longing for Katie in check. His sleep was filled with dreams of her. He planned to propose to her when they were together for Labor Day. Even though they discussed his coming in their weekly letters, Ben called her right after supper the Tuesday before the holiday to confirm their plans.

"Hello, Mrs. Reynolds, this is Ben. Is Katie in?"

He heard Mrs. Reynolds shout, "Katie, It's long distance. Take it on the kitchen phone and I'll hang up."

"How's my favorite college senior?" Ben said when Katie whispered hello.

"I have great news. The firm is letting me have Friday off, so I can fly to Nashville Thursday night. My Dad is picking me up at 7:30, so I should be home by 11, which means we can have all day Friday together. I'm dying to see you."

Katie did not reply.

"Is something wrong?" Ben asked after a few seconds. "Are you still on the line?"

Still no response. Ben froze.

"Is Clark there?"

"Yes, now is not a good time," Katie whispered. "I need to go. Good-Bye, Ben."

September 2, 1964

Dear Ben,

I'm sorry I could not talk to you last night. Clark showed up unexpectedly right before you called. He told me because he missed me so much he stopped studying, and flunked two courses last quarter, which caused him to be suspended from school and lose his deferment, making him immediately subject to the draft. He had gone without lunch all summer to buy an engagement ring for me. He put the ring on my finger and asked me to marry him. Oh, Ben, I felt so sorry for him and so guilty. If he were sent to Vietnam and killed, I would not be able to live with myself, because I would be the reason he was there. Marrying him is the only way I know to keep him out. So, I said, yes.

I want you to know that was the hardest

decision I have ever made, but I had no choice. I also want you to know you are very important to me, I have never talked so freely and openly with anyone as I have with you, and I have never explored ideas so intensely, or felt so alive. Oh, Ben, I hate saying goodbye. I'll never forget you and you will always have a special place in my heart. I'm sacrificing my friendship with you to do what I must do. I hope you'll understand.

With love,
Katie

9

A few weeks after suffering the loss of Katie to a rival for reasons he could not understand, much less accept, after multiple mental replays of their history and agonizing attempts to determine 'what went wrong,' Ben convinced himself that despite all the signs he thought he had seen, Katie did not love him. A small voice insisted that couldn't be right; he couldn't have misread the situation so completely. He stifled that voice again and again, until finally it went away. As a part of his effort to 'forget about Katie' Ben sold the convertible his father had given him and purchased a pristine 1964 C Model Porsche from a veterinarian who had to choose between the Porsche and his wife. Ben loved that car and spent hours exploring Atlanta, and its suburbs in it. He came to enjoy being alone too much. He had to socialize.

He tested the dating waters by going to parties with fellow associates and to socials and group nights sponsored by the several Methodist Churches nearby, but Ben compared every girl he went out with to Katie and they all fell short. After a few months of aborted relationships, Ben decided he had to judge the candidates less harshly. At a going away party in the fall of 1965, Ben met Nancy Wilson. Nancy was superficially similar to Katie. She was about the same age and height. She was slim, had a pleasant voice and a quick smile, and a bachelor's degree in education from the University of Florida. She was close to her mother, dad, brother, and sister, all of whom had recently moved to Atlanta.

Over the next six weeks, Ben convinced himself that Nancy was as close as he was going to get to replicating the woman he loved, and it was time to move on. The day after Christmas he gave Nancy a ring, hoping his engagement to her would cleanse his heart of Katie.

The next three years were difficult for the country and for Ben. The Vietnam war had divided the nation, the 1968 Democratic convention had been disrupted by near-riotous anti-war demonstrations, which had been countered by brutal police tactics, and Richard Nixon had taken control of the Republican party. The outcome of the1968 presidential election was a foregone conclusion, according to the London Bookmakers, who gave "Tricky Dick" the win over "Hapless Hubert" by a wide margin. Ben feared a Nixon presidency more than he worried over a continuation of the policies of the Johnson administration. He voted against the line. And lost.

In late November, after much soul-searching and professional counseling, Ben ended his engagement. Within days of asking Nancy to marry him, Ben regretted his decision. He realized there was no zip in their relationship. No zing. Nancy wanted to get married right away, quit her teaching job, and have children, while Ben never thought the time was right. Nancy wanted to spend every Sunday with her parents. A monthly visit was plenty for Ben. Ben had never told Nancy about Katie. He did tell his therapist.

"You rushed into this engagement hoping to have sex and to get your life back in order after the end of your relationship with Katie," Dr. Baker told him during their 3rd session. "Sex is important. It is not, however, the strongest pillar to build a marriage on. I believe you when you tell me you've tried to commit to Nancy, but your residual feelings for Katie are sabotaging your efforts. You must banish Katie before you can even think about marriage. Whether you marry Nancy or not, you have to close the books on Katie."

"Why do you think I can do that now," Ben asked, "when I haven't been able to in the past?"

"I don't know if you can," Dr. Baker said, "but you must try. Perhaps asking Nancy to have therapy with you would make this easier for you. Would you like for me to refer you to someone to work with you and Nancy as a couple? Would you consent to my sharing my notes with the gentleman I have in mind?"

Nancy instantly agreed to joint therapy. At their first session Dr. Rottersman jumped to the heart of the matter. "I see from Dr. Baker's notes that Ben sought therapy because he kept avoiding agreeing to a wedding date. Is that an accurate statement, Ben?"

Ben nodded, yes.

"And Ben had ended a serious relationship with another woman shortly before he met you, Nancy. Have the two of you ever discussed that part of Ben's life?"

Nancy was visibly shocked. "Ben never told me about that," she said. "I wouldn't have agreed to marry him if I had known."

"Well, now that you know," Dr. Rottersman continued, "are you willing to explore that relationship with Ben and help Ben get beyond it?"

Nancy began to cry. Ben looked at her and thought, 'What a cruel way to start therapy. Nancy surely does not want to hear about Katie and me.' On further reflection, however, he realized Rottersman was right. Nancy had to be told the full story, however painful hearing it might be. Ben then thought about his own feelings. *Why am I so calm about this? Shouldn't I be in tears also? Am I this calloused, or simply don't want this relationship to go on?*

After a few moments of silence, Rottersman said, "Let me ask a few questions. Nancy, do you believe Ben deceived you by not revealing his relationship with this other woman, this Katie Reynolds before asking you to marry him?"

Nancy nodded, yes.

"Ben, do you believe you have committed completely to Nancy?"

Ben scrambled for an answer, other than the one he knew was true. Finally, he shook his head, no.

"Was this because of your relationship with Katie Reynolds?"

"Probably," Ben said.

"Don't you mean certainly?" Rottersman said. Then he turned to Nancy. "How do you feel about that?"

"I'm hurt, upset and angry," Nancy said in a quavering voice as her tears began to flow, "Most of all, I feel very betrayed."

"Ben, is there anything you want to say?"

Ben looked at Nancy. Her tears and the hurt look on her face made him want to say something to comfort her, but what? He had lost her trust, and she would be suspicious of anything he said. He did not want to spend the time or energy necessary to rebuild trust. All he could say was, "I'm sorry."

"Why don't we end our session for today," Dr. Rottersman said. "The two of you need time to process. Courtship creates an intense relationship, which often leaves one of the parties extremely hurt if the relationship ends. Here the problem is not the failed relationship with Katie, but Ben's unwillingness or inability to let that relationship go. He is carrying the emotional baggage of Katie's rejection into his relationship with you, Nancy. Ben was right to avoid setting a date to get married. Given his strong feelings for Katie, however, he was wrong in asking you to marry him in the first place. If there is a silver lining, it's far better to end this relationship now than to marry with the Katie problem unresolved."

With a benevolent look, Dr. Rottersman clasped Nancy's hands between his as she sat slumped in her chair, weeping silently. "Why don't you stay here and rest awhile," he said.

"I don't need this room for an hour. I'll call a cab if you don't feel like driving."

Then he walked out with Ben. "You may think I was wrong in approaching your case this way," he said. "But I've been practicing psychiatry for 35 years and I've seen cases like yours before. From Dr. Baker's notes, my observation of your physical reactions to Nancy and the conversations today, it's clear to me that if you marry her without closure of your previous relationship, your marriage, if it lasts, will not be a satisfying one. Now if you and Nancy want to proceed, I'll work with you. Be warned, both of you have to want to save your relationship and be willing to put intense effort into the process."

Two days passed before Ben called Nancy.

"Would you like to get together and talk?" Ben said.

"What's there to talk about?" she said. "I have been miserable these last two days and have cried myself to sleep both nights. But the picture is in focus now. I loved you, Ben, and I thought you loved me and there was no problem we could not work out. I now know you've never loved me, and after what you've put me through, you can go to Hell."

In early December, Ben's father was back at Vanderbilt

hospital testing for signs of the malignancy his doctors had originally told the family was aggressive but curable. The first operation had been in June. The check up in October had been inconclusive. His dad called shortly before lunch.

"Hi Dad, what's up? You don't usually call me at my office."

"Can you come up right away so we can talk? Eileen's spending the afternoon with a friend from her Vultee days. She said she'd be back by five. I just can't count on her being gone that long, so please get here as soon as you can."

Thanks to the time change between Atlanta and Nashville and the road-hugging ability of the Porsche, Ben walked into his Dad's hospital room at three p.m. where he found Riley propped up in bed with an IV attached to his left arm, and a cannula in his nose. He had lost more weight in the three weeks since Ben last saw him. Ben touched his Dad's arm and sat down beside him.

"I'm glad you could come, son. We didn't get a chance to talk about anything other than your broken engagement when you were home last. Eileen was never fond of Nancy and was upset to learn she kept some of our $5,000 engagement gift to you."

"We put that money in a joint account for wedding expenses," Ben said, "and only spent about $150. I felt so guilty I didn't object when she said she wanted half of what was left. She's a good person and deserved it. She and I never clicked, and I suspect it was my fault."

"Why do you say that son?"

"Because I never got over Katie Reynolds."

"Jeff Reynolds' daughter? Don't remember who she married, must not have been from around here. I do remember going to her wedding. Thought it strange that she cried the entire time. Eileen thought it was because she had to get married."

"Had to get married?!!" Ben exclaimed. "Whatever gave Mother that idea."

"I don't remember, exactly. I remember Eileen did not like Katie. Called her an agitator for writing letters to the paper and to the school board supporting integration. I don't remember your going out with her."

"I didn't go out with her a lot. Maybe five or six times over a couple of years, but during the last few weeks before I came to Atlanta, we had a short, intense relationship. I thought she loved me and that she and I would marry. I had planned to come home that Labor Day to propose to her. But something happened."

Without sitting up, Riley took a sip from the cup of ice water on the table beside him, using the long bent-necked straw provided by the hospital.

"This damn oxygen flow keeps my mouth dry all the time, so I drink ice water, which of course means more trips to pee, which I can't manage alone. Old age and the medicines you take to stay alive are no fun and they can certainly play tricks on your memory. I'm never sure anymore what is memory and what is imagination."

Riley took another sip. He seemed to be deep in thought. "I'm almost sure I remember sitting in the den with Eileen the Saturday before that Labor Day," he said, "watching a football game on TV when the phone rang. It was Katie. Eileen said Katie was crying so hard, it was hard to understand her. Eileen told Katie you were out, and she would tell you to call her when you came in, which I thought at the time was strange, but I was involved in the game and didn't think any more about it. That's really all I remember, and like I said, my memory isn't what it used to be. Now I really do have to rest, or I'll zonk out on you."

Ben was dumbfounded. Not only had Katie tried to reach him that Labor Day, but Eileen had intentionally misled her by telling her he would call back, knowing he was not in Martin. He wished his father's health were better so he could discuss Katie's call further.

"Don't talk that way, Dad. You're only fifty-five. The doctors are going to get this thing. You've got a lot of life left."

"You know, Ben, when I was drafted, I was sure the Germans were going to get me, and they didn't. When they discovered the tumor in my colon, I was sure I was going to lick it. I'm not. What I didn't tell you after my check-up in October was that the tumor was not completely removed, and the cancer has spread to my duodenum. They want to do another operation right away before it spreads further. Eileen says I must have the operation. What's the point? I'll spend a lot of money and go through a lot of pain just to live a few more miserable months."

Riley reached for Ben's hand. Ben had never seen his

father look so frail. Ben thought about Riley's advice when he left for law school to stay strong 'The meek may inherit the earth, but the rest of us will have it back in a couple of weeks. Walk in like you own the place, and everyone will assume you do.'

"Did they give you the odds of success?" Ben asked.

"Their idea of success is being alive three years after the operation," Riley grumbled. "They didn't sound very encouraging, though. All they said was that the operation could under optimum conditions remove all the tumor and it was my only chance. I have to make up my mind tonight whether to stay and let them open me up again or go home tomorrow. If I go home, we can put a bed down in the den. I can keep my pain medication by the bed and won't have to climb the stairs at all. I want to go home, but Eileen insists I have the operation. She says I should give God a chance to save me. I asked her how many chances does God need?"

"What can I do, Dad?" Ben asked.

His father smiled weakly. "Just listen to me, son, and don't shut me off by telling me whatever happens is God's will. Then give me your honest opinion."

The weary, worn-out look on his father's face frightened Ben. He felt Riley's grip relax.

"Eileen is well taken care of," Riley said. "I'm thinking of you and Charles. I don't know how much my health insurance will cover if I go forward with the operation the doctors are proposing. I am $80,000 out of pocket already. I don't want to spend another $250,000 of your money to gain a few months of life that probably would not be worth living anyway. What do you think?"

Ben's voice cracked. "I want you to do what you want to do, Dad, regardless of the cost and regardless of anyone else's opinion. It is your life, your money, and your decision. You can tell Mother that God has revealed to you that He wants you to make the final decision."

Riley struggled to put an arm around Ben. All he could do was draw Ben a little closer.

"I love you, Ben," he said in a halting, gravelly voice, "and I'm proud of the man you have become. Many nights in the first few years after the war I lay awake wondering if I had ruined your life by taking you away from Nora and Frank, for what I knew was my own selfish desire to have you grow up with me."

Ben's stomach twisted into knots as he listened to Riley acknowledge the pain he had felt when he ripped Ben away from Nora.

"You were the only connection I had with Claire," Riley continued, "and I convinced myself that if you were with me, I could make sure you got the college education your grandmother Millie and I wanted you to have. Eileen is not sharp in finances. She *was* right about one thing. Using the $5,000 left over from the insurance funds as the down payment on the paper did more to ensure your college education than depositing it into a savings account would."

Ben was perplexed and started to speak, but his father held up his hand. "I forgot to tell you that Millie died just before Christmas. Her brother-in-law, Jim sent me a copy of her obituary. Jim gave me my first job as a linotype operator. I'll get the copy for you if I can remember what I did with it. I'm ashamed to tell you that Millie sent me a check for you on your sixth birthday and every year thereafter until you left for law school. That upset Eileen so much the first time it happened, from then on, I endorsed the checks and cashed them. Eileen never knew. Of course, I didn't tell you either, but you always got the money.

Ben had no memory of Millie. He had kept the only picture of her Riley had given him with the only photograph he had of his mother—one taken at her high school graduation—in a manila envelope in the bottom drawer of his dresser. He had never heard of Uncle Jim.

"I am sorry to hear that, Dad," he said. "You never talked to me about Millie or about my mother. You made it clear long ago you did not care to discuss them. Can we talk about them now?"

"Let's save that discussion for tomorrow when I have more strength," he said. "I want to finish what I started to say."

Ben leaned in closer.

"Buying the *Press* with that $5,000 was the most dangerous and the best business decision I ever made," Riley said. "Profits from that paper allowed me to buy two more. I planned to retire at 65 and have 10 or 15 years to travel and enjoy my grandchildren. When I first learned I had cancer I decided to sell all three papers. I couldn't depend on Eileen to run them alone, and I knew you and she could never get along as business partners. Lord knows, Charles can't run them. I put some feelers out and within a week two syndications got into a bidding war. It happened so quickly I thought those guys had been hanging around waiting for me to sell. I put half of the money from the sale in trust for you and Charles and half in trust for Eileen. Eileen is the lifetime beneficiary and Trustee of your Trust. She can spend the income any way she likes, but she must preserve the principal for you boys. As permanent beneficiaries, you and Charles have the right to insist that Eileen abide by those provisions."

"How will we ever know what Mother does?" Ben asked.

"Ask her," Riley said, "or get Charles to ask. She has never denied Charles anything."

Ben loathed the thought of asking Eileen for anything. If she ever spent the principal, he was sure it would be to help Charles. He loved Charles, and as resentful as he once had been of what he saw as Charles's foisting responsibility for supporting him and his family, onto his parents, the reality was Charles needed help. Ben felt immense relief that his father had assured the financial burden of caring for his brother would not fall on him. He looked at his Dad, aching to hear more, but Riley had drifted into sleep. Ben had never heard about the $5,000 insurance money before, nor did he know about his father's earlier concerns about taking him from Nora. And he had no idea that the trust he shared with his brother contained two million dollars, or that Eileen's trust contained a like amount. He sat by his father's bed, trying to make sense of this new information, and refining the questions he wanted to ask.

"How long have you been here?" Eileen snapped when she entered the room and saw Ben sitting beside his father.

"Got here about three," Ben said, trying to mask his animosity toward his stepmother, which had been refueled by the information his father had revealed. "Dad is awfully weak and tired. Someone needs to be with him all the time."

"Are you suggesting I should stay in this room all day and watch him sleep?" Eileen said as she hung her coat on a hook behind the door. "He conks out quickly when he tries to carry on a conversation. The nurses are monitoring him. They'll know if he needs help. Since you are here, why don't you give me some relief and sit with him tomorrow?"

Happy for the opportunity to spend more private time with his father, Ben quickly agreed. "That chair can turn into a sleeper, so I'll spend the night here and you can get a good night's rest at the hotel. I'll call you when he wakes up in the morning. But before you go, clear something up for me, please. Do you remember the first Labor Day after I went to Atlanta?"

"Yes," Eileen said. "You didn't come home even though you had told Riley you would. He was very disappointed."

"Did I get a call from Katie Reynolds that weekend?

Eileen looked as if she were considering whether this was a trick question, or a trap.

"No," she finally answered as she headed for the door. "Not that I recall."

Ben sat with his father, hoping Riley would awaken refreshed. Falling in and out of sleep himself, he was oblivious to the passage of time and to the caretakers who came and went, reading the monitors and making their notes. Shortly after midnight a nurse gently roused him.

"You should call Mrs. McHaney. I don't think your father will make it through the night."

10

February 10, 1969

Dear Katie,

It's been over four years since you wrote to tell me of your decision to marry Clark, but I haven't been emotionally able to respond until now. You probably know my father died two weeks ago. You may not know that Nancy Wilson, the woman I was engaged to for over two years, and I have called it quits.

I asked Nancy to marry me too quickly after you rejected me for Clark. I didn't acknowledge it then, but I was looking for a substitute for you, and I thought I'd found one. She was heartbroken when she learned about you at our only therapy session and very angry with me for not having told her in the beginning. The breakup was painful. Although I don't keep up with her, I heard she has found some-one else.

Telling you about the woman I almost married is not the reason for this letter, Katie. I'm writing you because I finally have enough control over my emotions to think about us without getting morbid with self-pity. I saw your Mom and Dad at my father's funeral. They told me you got a Masters in English Literature, that you and Clark live in Asheville, and that you have a little girl who looks a lot like you.

Do you remember that Dad and my Stepmother attended your wedding? They told me how touched they were that you shed tears of joy all during the ceremony, and that you sobbed when Rev. Sparks pronounced Clark and you man and wife. 'Sobbed' is such a strong word. I wondered why they used it.

Talking to your parents brought back a flood of memories, the strongest of which were those of my being with you the last few weeks I was home, starting with Suzy's engagement party. You told me you were happy I came, and that Clark was no longer in the picture. We really clicked and I fell for you again. I was in love. I thought you were, too.

When I called you to firm up our Labor Day plans, however, Clark was with you and you cut our conversation short—I thought because you were finally breaking up with him. I was extremely re-lieved but wondered why you had not already done it. Then I got your letter, which sent me into darkest despair. After a few months I told myself if you did not want me, it didn't matter how much I loved you, I could not share my life with you and I had to move on. Moving on meant becoming engaged to a woman I erroneously thought could slip right into your place.

You said in your letter you hoped I'd understand. No, Katie, I don't understand. I loved you, and your letter practically screams you loved me. Yet you chose Clark, and if I live to be a hundred, I'll never understand. You said you had no choice. Who made you responsible for Clark's flunking out of school? For losing his deferment? For keeping him out of Vietnam? You wrote me you didn't want to hurt Clark. Apparently, it was okay to hurt me. Did my feelings not matter? I don't expect answers to those questions, for obviously neither the questions nor the answers are important to you. What matters now that the door has closed on us, is that we go on with the rest of our lives. I hope this letter shows you I can, and I can finally tell you goodbye.

Ben

February 17, 1969

Dear Ben,

Thank you for writing after all these years. I was

sorry to hear of your father's death. He was a kind person, respected by everyone. I'm sure losing him has been very painful. Mom told me about seeing you at the funeral, which also brought back old memories. As delighted as I was to hear from you, receiving your letter caused me more sorrow than happiness. You wrote that the door has closed on our friendship. You certainly have every right to close that door, but Ben, I wish you wouldn't! I would like for us to stay in touch. You are one of the few people in my life who have been very important to me, and I hate the thought of losing all contact with you. Now that a painful chapter of our lives is over, would you consider starting a new and different chapter to share interests and discuss ideas like we did so well so long ago?

Other than learning of your engagement from the announcement in your father's paper, I have heard nothing about you since I left home, but I have never ceased to think of you. You were very dear to me, and I always hoped to hear from you and learn about your life. Do you still enjoy law practice as much as you did when you first went to Atlanta? Are science, religion, and politics still important to you? Are you still the idealist you used to be? Are you still enamored with Atlanta? About myself, yes, I did get my Masters from Knoxville. Yes, I have a little girl, Isabella, whom I adore, and yes, she does look a lot like me.

Before I close, I need to say this. I've read your

letter at least half a dozen times and cried each time. It broke my heart to learn about the hurt you felt when you thought I was rejecting you, and that you could not understand why I chose Clark over you. In my heart I never rejected you, Ben, I just could not find a way to choose you without literally killing Clark. I did have deep feelings for you, and when you finally kissed me, I knew you had deep feelings for me as well.

Was it love? With the benefit of hindsight, I'm sure it was, but Ben, you never told me you loved me. Nor did I ever tell you I loved you. Who knows what would have happened had either of us voiced our true feelings! When Clark lost his deferment and was about to be drafted, I believed strongly that I was responsible, and I had to marry him to keep him out of Vietnam. It was excruciating for me to deny my own feelings and marry Clark, but I had to do it. I had to keep him out of the war. Please believe me, Ben, you are wrong to think your feelings did not matter. They mattered so much that I went through hell trying to keep my commitment to myself to marry Clark. Yes, I cried all through my wedding, but they were tears of anguish—not joy.

You may not know I tried to telephone you the Saturday before that Labor Day. Your Mother said you weren't in and would return the call later, but you never did. Had you called; things could have turned out differently. Like I said, however, who knows?

I'd better go now. Please consider my request to renew our friendship. I will be staying with my parents for a few days at the end of this month. If you happen to be in Martin during that time, please drop by.

Sincerely,
Katie

"It will only be for the weekend, Mother," Ben told Eileen when he called her the day after he received Katie's letter. "The Probate Clerk had some questions about Dad's assets which can be handled better in person, so I made an appointment for this Friday."

"Only the weekend?" Eileen said in the strident tone he detested. "At least stay through Monday so we can check the farm. And I want to talk to you about these property taxes. You have only been back once since Riley's funeral. There are lots of things we need to discuss. Your father said you would help me."

Ben had helped Eileen. He had done everything necessary to start probate of his father's estate on his previous trips home, including hiring the necessary professionals to take care of all the details. Until now, he had neither the desire nor a reason to return. Katie's letter, however, had given him the desire. The probate proceeding gave him a reason. Surely, he could deal with Eileen's trivial problems while he was there. And he had some questions to ask her.

"We can't go poking around the farm, Mother. We

have a tenant. And your CPA has all the tax information. I'm sure he'll take every deduction you are entitled to. If you have more questions, they will have to wait until I get there Friday, or you can discuss them with Charles. I have to go now, Mother. Bye."

Ben arrived at his family home a little before noon. He had been in an emotional stew since reading Katie's letter. He worried he was seeing something that wasn't there and, as in the past, would walk into a brick wall. On one hand, she was married to Clark. On the other, why would she write that kind of letter to a man who told her he once loved her? A trip to Martin was necessary to sort things out. The probate proceedings provided an excellent cover.

The aroma of Hattie's freshly baked peach cobbler persuaded Ben to agree to have dinner with Eileen Friday night, but not knowing how long the drop-in visit with Katie would last, he would not commit to a precise time. His promise to his father to assist Eileen did not bind him to eat with her whenever she wanted.

"I'll call you when I'm finished," he told Eileen. "Probably around six. You can start supper without me if you get hungry."

By 1:15 his business at the Probate office of the Chancery Court, which involved verifying the date of a tax waiver filing and could easily have been handled by phone, was finished. He wanted to drive straight to Dr. Reynolds' house. Fearing Katie's mother might be home, and needing to get his emotions under control, he found a pay phone and dialed the number he still knew by heart.

"Hi, Katie. It's Ben. You asked me to drop by if I were in town..."

"Ben! You're actually coming? When?"

"I'm in Martin now, or more precisely at the Chancery Court in Dresden. Is now a good time to come over?"

"Right now? Oh, my goodness. I can't see you now. I'm not, I'm not..." Ben chuckled as Katie fumbled for words and felt a whoosh of excitement as he recalled how often she had made him laugh.

"Ready?" he teased, supplying the word he knew she wanted to avoid. "What do you need to do: shower, get dressed, vacuum, make up the beds, mop the..."

"Stop making fun of me, Ben McHaney. I wash my hair and sleep in curlers every night to be ready for anything the next day. I just need to put on a little make-up."

"Tell you what," Ben said. "I'll fill up with gas before I start over. That'll give you thirty minutes."

"Ok," Katie said. "Remember my folks don't live on University anymore. They moved to 110 Willow Lane about a year ago."

"I know exactly where it is. I still know this town like the..."

"Back of your hand?" Katie laughed.

"That'll work," Ben said, "but I was searching for something less trite. By the way, is your mother there?"

"Fortunately, Mother has Isabella and isn't due back until 3:30. We'll have plenty of time for a visit."

Ben skipped the gas and arrived at the Reynolds house in twenty minutes. To give Katie most of the time he promised, and to still his racing heart, he stopped at 118 Willow Lane, clasped his hands over his head, yawned and stretched his arms as far as he could, then backed into the neighbor's driveway and turned the car around, headed in the direction from which he had come. He stretched again and looked at his watch. Five minutes to go. He walked slowly from his car, breathing deeply on the way.

"Knock, knock," Ben said as he opened the unlocked front door of the Reynolds' house without ringing the bell. "I'm here."

Katie turned and stared at him. His heart skipped. He hoped his smartly tailored suit and his shoes shined to a high gloss spoke of success and that his receding hair line would make him appear less boyish.

"Ben! Is it really you?"

"You sound surprised. You invited me. Remember?"

"Relieved more than surprised," she said. "I was afraid you would change your mind at the last minute. Are you visiting your mother?"

"My stepmother," he corrected. "And taking care of some probate issues with Dad's estate. I thought your letter was an invitation to drop by. Well, here I am."

"Let me look at you. You've matured so much. You look like a—lawyer."

Ben's heart pounded and his entire body sang. It was Katie, four years later, and as lovely as ever. He yearned to take her in his arms and kiss her. But she was married and even more unavailable than when he saw her last.

"And you are a . . . a . . . (He wanted to say beautiful) grown woman. I like your longer hair. And I love that poet shirt."

Katie blushed. "Well, Asheville's not San Francisco, but it's not small-town Tennessee, either."

"You still take my breath away," Ben said as he walked around her as if he were admiring a piece of art. "You're taller and curvier than I remembered, and even more gorgeous. Whoops, perhaps I shouldn't say that to a married woman."

Katie blushed again and took his hand. Ben's pulse went supersonic and his male member went on high alert. "Come to the kitchen with me while I make coffee," she said. "We can talk in there."

Ben would have preferred the Donut Shop or anywhere other than her parents' kitchen to have coffee and conversation with Katie, but if Katie were certain they wouldn't be interrupted by a child needing attention or an angry parent, he was with her all the way.

"You know what a rule follower I am," Katie began after her first sip, "how I always try to do the right thing and try not to hurt anyone."

"Yes," Ben grinned, "and I know you need to confess when you think you've done something wrong. Do you need to confess now?"

"Please, Ben. I'm serious, and what I must say is painful to talk about. It's about Clark. For four years I told myself I loved him and tried to be happy with him. A few months ago I admitted to myself that I'm not happy, our relationship is not going to change, and I should consider divorce."

Divorce!! Ben was dumbfounded. His erection fell flat from sensory overload. For a long moment he could not breathe.

"I know what you're thinking," Katie said. "I never ever thought divorce was an option, and the idea of divorce still terrifies me. The thought of talking with Clark about it makes me ill. The irony is I cut off a relationship with you twice back then so I wouldn't hurt Clark. Divorcing him now will destroy him. Plus, I'll be disrupting my child's life and my father may disown me."

Katie's voice trembled. "I have no one to talk to in Asheville. No one would understand why I would consider leaving Clark. He is such a decent person. He never raises his voice at me or physically abuses me. Quite the contrary, he is very protective of me, and solicitous of my feelings. He doesn't drink, gamble, or run around. He comes home at night and spends time with Isabella. Of course, she loves him very much."

Katie paused to regain control of her voice. 'Thank God Nancy and I never married,' Ben thought as he considered Clark's pain at losing Isabella, and Isabella's at losing her father. He drained his cup and tried to shake away thoughts about his loss of Mama, and his loss of another mother—one he knew had loved him and cared for him the first nine months of his life.

"Clark is good at his job and is well-liked," Katie continued. "I don't know anyone who has a bad thing to say about him. It comes down to this. Despite all Clark's qualities, my relationship with him has always been shallow—superficial. It's never grown. It has no breadth or depth. It's as if we got stuck at "I Do" when we married and have never moved. We still don't really know each other. As much as I have tried to convince myself that it's enough to have a husband who loves me, supports me, and helps raise our child, I simply cannot."

Ben paced the floor, breathing rapidly. On one hand he wanted Katie to tell her story at her own pace. On the other, he wanted her to spill it out. Where was this going? The suspense was too much.

"Clark doesn't like to talk about any subject except his work and our family," Katie continued. "I can't engage him in any discussion—certainly not spirited debates like you and I used to have. Surely he has ideas; he just won't express them around me. In fact, he won't express any opinion he thinks is opposed to mine and will change his opinion if I express a different one. I can't tell you how many times we have come out of a movie and I have asked Clark what he thought about it, and his response was 'What do *you* think?' Early in our relationship he might say, 'I liked it,' without giving any reasons, then retract that statement if I said I didn't like it. For a while I cajoled and goaded, but all that did was nauseate Clark and exasperate me. Now I just don't ask."

Ben finally spoke. "Have you talked to anyone else about this?"

"Only Mother, all I've told her is that I'm not happy with my life. I'm sure she suspects Clark is the reason, but she hasn't pushed me. She did suggest counseling and that I devote more time to painting, which I took up when we moved to Asheville. I haven't told her I've thought about leaving Clark. I haven't told anyone!"

Ben felt a strange sensation. His skin crawled. He didn't know if the cause was an anxious anticipation of the revival of a lost romance, or the fear of another painful let down.

"So, why are you telling me?"

Katie furrowed her brow. "I want a divorce, but I'm so wracked with guilt I'm not sure I can go through with it."

"Jesus Christ, Katie, that's awful! Talk to your parents? They want what's best for you. And based on my experience ending an engagement, I'm sure you can get through a divorce—if you can endure a lot of pain."

"Talking to them would be a waste of time," Katie said. "They would say stay with Clark whatever my problems are. To them, divorce is a sin and unacceptable except for adultery or abandonment, and I certainly DO NOT have those grounds.

"What about talking to Suzy? She's been your best friend forever."

Katie shrugged her shoulders. "For all Suzy's savvy, I can't trust her on this. Her marriage is so stable. She couldn't imagine a problem Clark and I couldn't work out."

Ben doubted that, but he said nothing. Katie's tears finally stopped. Ben longed to put his arms around her, to wipe her moistened eyes, to comfort her, to help her. He lightly touched her face. Katie softly stroked the back of his hand.

"Oh, Katie, I'm so sorry. You can't accept advice about Clark from me. I'd tell you to leave him in a heartbeat. I wish you had never met the guy."

Katie picked up their nearly empty cups, rinsed them, refilled them, then very deliberately stirred the sugar and cream she had added to his cup in exactly the amounts he preferred. 'She remembered!' he thought. Ben could not take his eyes off her hands as she stirred. His erection was once again full blown.

"The news of your father's death saddened me," Katie said as she handed him his fresh cup, "but learning that you are still single elated me. Hearing your voice on the phone this afternoon reminded me of so many things I loved about you. When I saw you at the door, I knew my struggle to stay with Clark was doomed. Ben, I don't want your advice about Clark, I want to know if you meant what you said in your letter. I want to know if you love me."

Until that moment, Ben had been so focused on Katie's story—and his own raging feelings—he had missed the cue that it WAS time to tell her he loved her. He didn't give a damn about her marital status. He wanted her. He grabbed both of her hands pulled her to him, said, "Katie, I loved you then, love you now, and will love you forever. And I'm so sorry I didn't come home anyway that Labor Day so I could have been there for your call."

For the first time in over four years, Ben and Katie kissed.

"I love you," Katie said when they finally released each other.

"And I love you," Ben said. "Now where do we go from here?"

Katie laughed. "Just like you to cut off the celebration and get down to brass tacks."

"I want you to be with me as soon as humanly possible," Ben said. "There are lots of details to work out, so let's get started. First, you will need a lawyer."

"I was hoping you would be my lawyer."

"Sweetheart, that's a bad idea for many reasons. I am licensed in Tennessee, but not in North Carolina, and I don't have an office here. Plus, I don't handle divorces."

Katie bit her lip. "I don't have any money to hire a lawyer, and I can't ask my parents for help. They adore Clark, and they think divorce is wrong."

Ben touched her face once again. "Don't worry about money," he said. "As long as I'm alive, you'll never have to worry about money. Whatever you need you'll have. Getting you a lawyer who knows the ropes is the key, and I don't know any lawyer in Asheville. Too bad you don't live in Tennessee."

"I lived in Tennessee all my life until I left Knoxville after I got my Masters," Katie said. "Doesn't that count?"

"Afraid not. Do you own your house in Asheville?"

"Yes, we bought it last spring."

"Is your name on the deed?"

"Yes, both of our names are."

"Damn. Have you gotten a North Carolina driver's license?"

"Not yet. My Tennessee license doesn't expire until next November. I was waiting till then to switch."

Ben squeezed Katie's hand and said, "That's a break. It gives you a continuing relationship with Tennessee, but you probably broke North Carolina law in the process. If you can stay with your parents for a few months, you may be able to file in Tennessee. It'll be a stretch. I'll make an appointment with my friend Bob Ellison tomorrow so we can talk with him about it. I'd better go now. It's not a good idea for me to be here when your mother returns."

"Can you come back about seven? That'll give me a chance to talk to my parents at supper."

"I need to eat early tonight," Ben told Eileen when he arrived. "Katie Reynolds is visiting her mother and father and has invited me over for after dinner coffee."

"It would have been nice if you had bothered to tell us this before you left this morning," Eileen pouted. "I'm not sure Hattie can have supper ready early."

"Don't you worry, Mr. Ben," Hattie called from the kitchen. "I can get your supper on the table in no time. I've already done the hard part of peeling the potatoes and fixing your cobbler. Thank goodness we canned all those peaches last summer. Chicken don't take no time to fry."

"Thank you, Hattie," Ben said. "Nothing goes better with peach cobbler than your fried chicken."

"Supper's ready," Hattie announced in no time, Green beans, mashed potatoes, and fried chicken were served at the table on the sun porch. Hattie retreated to the kitchen.

"I suppose Katie's husband is with her," Eileen said. "What's his name? Don't they have a little girl?"

"His name is Clark, Mother, and their daughter's name is Isabella. She's two and a half. And no, Clark stayed in Asheville. He has a job."

"Will Katie's folks be there? You are NOT going to see her alone."

Ben resisted the urge to say I was with her alone this afternoon—and that's none of your business. Instead he said, "Dr. and Mrs. Reynolds will be there. I'm visiting the family."

"Well, good," Eileen sniffed. "An unmarried man shouldn't be seen with a married woman whose husband isn't there. That can lead to all sorts of talk. Since this is a family visit it shouldn't be a long one, so you should be home by my bedtime."

"Shouldn't be *seen with* or shouldn't *be* with, Mother?"

"Are you trying to be funny? If a man isn't with a married woman, he can't be seen with her. Adultery is no laughing matter. It's a sin and a crime. The state of Tennessee doesn't seem to care much about adultery anymore, but God does. Surely you are not thinking about getting involved with her."

"Can't I visit an old friend without getting involved?"

"Yes, if that 'old friend' is not a girl you used to date, who is now married and has a daughter, and who is a dangerous radical. I read those letters she wrote to the *Press.* I tried to convince Riley not to publish them. Hattie doesn't want her grandchildren going to school with white kids. They couldn't keep up. Besides, that 'old friend' probably has her sights on you, a promising young lawyer with a good future. Stay away from her."

"I can take care of myself," Ben said. "As for her political beliefs, I share them. And as for Hattie's grandkids not being able to keep up with white kids in school, it's time for us to help those kids keep up."

"You'll be sorry if you don't stay away from her," was Eileen's rejoinder. "And you'll never convince me integration is right. God created the races and gave them different colors—red and yellow, black, and white. Don't forget, birds of a feather, flock together."

Ben thought about Eileen's colossally wrong view of the races and the irony of her, his stepmother, who never accepted him, trying to steer him away from becoming a stepfather himself. His anger at Eileen had been simmering since Katie had confirmed his father's memory of her Labor Day call, but his mission was to get Katie through her ordeal and clear the path for them to be together, not waste time and emotional energy trying to blast the pettiness and ignorance out of Eileen.

"No coffee for me, Hattie," Ben said as he licked the last of the cobbler off his spoon. "That dessert was fabulous. I should be back by 10, Mother. Don't wait up."

Katie met Ben at the door with a squeeze of his hand.

"Dad knows you were here this afternoon," she whispered. "One of his colleagues saw your car and told him about it. I told Dad you dropped by and I asked you to come back tonight, when he and Mother would be home. Dad's been so furious, I haven't told them about my decision to divorce Clark."

Katie stepped back to let Ben enter.

"Ben, you remember my mother and father," she said. Her underlying anxiety was palpable. "Why don't you sit on the couch with me?" Turning to her father, she said. "Dad, Ben's in town taking care of some of his father's estate matters."

"Is that the reason you are giving for being in Martin?" Dr. Reynolds said in the sepulchral voice Ben had heard him use to scold rowdy teenagers in the Methodist Youth Fellowship class he taught. "I know you were in the Probate Clerk's office less than an hour right after lunch and at my house with no one but Kathryn here for most of the afternoon. What does Kathryn have to do with your father's estate?"

Ben reacted to this unexpected attack as any good lawyer would. He went on offense.

"You've been misinformed, Dr. Reynolds. I was in the Clerk's office from 12:15 till 12:45, and I visited Katie from 1:30 till almost 4, hardly most of the afternoon. She invited me back tonight so I could visit everyone."

Mrs. Reynolds looked at her husband. "Please, Jeff, there's nothing to be hostile about. Ben, what kind of law do you practice?"

"Shyster law," Dr. Reynolds said. "The kind that slick talks wives into leaving their husbands."

"Jeff! Ben is Katie's guest. Why are you being so rude? Katie confided in me about her unhappiness and I told you in confidence. You should have let Katie decide whether to discuss her situation with Ben."

"She's told him already," Dr. Reynolds growled.

"Really? How do you know?"

"Why else would he be here now? Something is going on and I'll guarantee you Ben McHaney is involved. He has sweet talked her into getting a divorce."

"I am divorcing Clark," Katie said as firmly as her tightened throat would allow. "That's a decision I have made on my own. Ben didn't sweet talk me into anything, and I am appalled by your trying to humiliate me and excoriate Ben because you object to my decision about my life. I asked Ben to help me find a lawyer. I thought we could all have a frank discussion about what I need to do to get through this—where to file, where would Isabella and I live, whether I need to find a job."

"See!" Dr. Reynolds said. "I told you Ben knew. Ben, you need to leave now so Kathryn can discuss with her parents how to reconcile with her husband."

Katie bristled with anger. Ben stayed seated.

"Get out!" Dr. Reynolds shouted. "Get out and leave my daughter alone!"

Katie leaped to her feet. "Ben's not going anywhere. If you and Mom don't want to help me get through this, I'll do it on my own. If I need help, I'll ask Ben, which I'm sure he will give without a lecture and without treating me like a disgrace."

"Katie, Katie," Mrs. Reynolds said. "we love you and want what's best for you..."

"And what's best for you," Dr. Reynolds asserted, "is

to stay with your husband. Divorce is never the answer unless your husband beats you, abandons you, or runs around on you, and we all know that is not the case. From what you've told your mom, you want a divorce because you are unhappy; your relationship hasn't progressed. That's insane. You have a lifetime to build a relationship. You have an obligation to your husband, your child, and to society to honor your marriage vows. You can't simply walk out on a marriage because you are bored or unhappy. Your duty is to stick it out and work through the rough patches."

Katie walked toward the door and motioned Ben to follow. "Thank you, Dad, for making your position clear. Ben, please find a lawyer for me as soon as possible, and I'd like for you to go with me to see him."

When Ben stood up, Dr. Reynolds rose also, stood jaw to jaw with Ben and said, "I've already talked to a lawyer, and I know in North Carolina if a wife is wooed away by another man, an alienation of affections suit can be brought. A few years ago, a husband in Greensboro won a $750,000 judgment against his wife's lover. If you aren't man enough to leave a married woman alone because it is the moral thing to do, perhaps you'll do the right thing to avoid a lawsuit."

Then Dr. Reynolds turned to Katie and said,"Ben was a smart, promising young man. I always thought he would go into the newspaper business with his father. He had tremendous potential, but he squandered it and became a smooth-talking lawyer. Everyone knows lawyers twist the truth. So, Katie, for your own sake, listen to me. You can't trust him. He will tell you anything he thinks will work. Mark my words, he'll try to get you into bed with him. If you do, you'll be a whore, and you'll lose everyone's respect, including mine. And if that happens, I promise you I will advance Clark the money to sue him."

Wringing her hands, Mrs. Reynolds ran to Katie. "Your father doesn't mean that," she said. "He's just upset and over-reacting."

Katie's bright red face was wet with tears. She looked past her mother. "Right now, Dad, I trust Ben more than I trust you. You are more interested in preserving your 'sterling' reputation and in judging me from your moral high horse than in my well-being."

Her voice gone, she whispered, "Good night, Ben. I love you."

To avoid having to dodge bullets from Eileen if he got home before her bedtime, Ben stopped at the Gateway for coffee. The evening had not gone well. He expected resistance from Katie's parents, but not a declaration of war. His admiration and high regard for Dr. Reynolds had taken a tumble. How could a loving father call his daughter a whore? Ben recalled Katie's stricken look and how she seemed unable to catch her breath when she whispered goodbye to him. He feared that even with his help she might not have the strength to get through this nightmare. He knew she could not do it without him. He looked up Bob Ellison's number in the yellow pages, dropped a dime in the payphone and reached Ellison's office answering machine.

"Bob, this is Ben. Hope you're working this Saturday. I'm only in town for the weekend and have something I need your help with."

At nine the next morning Ben and Katie met Bob Ellison in his small office on the second floor of the City State Bank building. No introductions were necessary, so Ben quickly outlined the problem.

"I agree," Bob said. "Filing the divorce petition here in Tennessee is best for you, Katie, but probably would not hold up if your husband fights jurisdiction, which would, however, cost money and you said your husband is not well-off."

"Dr. Reynolds is," Ben said.

"I wouldn't say that," Katie corrected. "Mother and Dad are both teachers, and everyone knows teachers are not well off. I don't think Dad would pay for Clark's defending a divorce. He said he would consider lending Clark money to sue Ben. I'm sure Dad would expect to be repaid."

"Sue Ben for what?" Bob asked.

"Alienation of affections," Ben said. "Let's not get hung up on that. We have more pressing concerns. Katie, you are going to have to convince your Dad to let you stay with them, or I'm going to have to rent you an apartment somewhere. And you must tell Clark your decision is final. Which lion do you want to beard first—your Dad or Clark?"

"Clark," Katie said without hesitation. "He is supposed

to pick Isabella and me up a week from now. I want to tell him in person, but I don't want to spring the news on him in front of my Dad."

"And you certainly don't want to go back to Asheville with him," Ben said. "You probably would not get Isabella out of North Carolina again. So, you have to call him."

Katie's silence ignited Ben's fear.

"Are you getting cold feet?" he asked.

"No, no, not at all, I'm just not sure what's the right thing to do. I don't want to make that call from my parents' house with them overhearing me and pouncing on me as soon as I got off the phone. And I don't want to wait until Clark gets here to tell him. Even if he and I could talk in private, Dad would put me in the pressure cooker again."

"Understandable," said Bob. "Why don't you call him from here right now."

Bob held out the receiver for Katie to take. Katie drew back as if she had been handed the hot end of a poker.

"No," Katie said. "I've been married to Clark for almost four years. I can't bring up divorce over the phone. It'll have to be in person."

"Where?" Ben said. "Can't be in North Carolina."

"Mother and Dad took me to Nashville to meet Clark after Christmas when Isabella and I stayed over a few days," Katie said. "I'll see if they would do that again."

"If your Mom and Dad drove you to meet Clark,

they'd have you trapped in the car all the way back to Martin," Ben said. "Why not let them keep Isabella and I'll take you?"

Katie grimaced. "They would NEVER do that," she said. "Dad would lock me in the house before he would let me take a trip with you."

Katie slumped over and covered her head with her hands. "Why am I always faced with impossible choices?" she said. "Why do I have to risk losing my child to tell my husband I'm leaving him?"

"Because you are a kind person," Ben said. "You care about other people's feelings."

Katie straightened up and let out a long sigh. "This I know for sure. Isabella is more important than Clark's feelings. If I have a custody battle, I want Isabella with me, but I must talk to Clark in person. I need him to see my face, so he'll know I'm serious, and I need to see his. When he comes to pick us up, I'll have him take me for coffee without Isabella. I have to get to him before Dad does."

"I don't like that idea," Ben said. "Please call him now and get it over with."

"Oh, Ben," Katie said. Ben felt the tenderness in her voice. "I've lived with Clark long enough to know what life with him is like. And his being killed in Vietnam is no longer a factor. I can do it, and I will, but it must be face to face. Try not to worry."

Ben couldn't help but worry. He had played this scene with her before and it had ended badly. He wanted to stay with her. He needed to be with her. His clients needed him, and they paid the bills. A trial only he could handle was starting the following Monday. Anxious and nervous, bolstered by nightly phone calls to Katie, Ben held himself together during the trial. Late Friday afternoon, the jury came in with a verdict against his client. As a lawyer, Ben knew the greatly reduced amount the jury had awarded the plaintiff was fair and supported by the evidence. As a lovesick man, however, he feared it was a harbinger of rejection. Saturday morning he was on the road early, arriving at the Reynolds' home shortly before one. Katie met him in the driveway.

"Did you stop for lunch?" she asked.

Ben searched her face for clues her voice had not furnished. "No, I hoped to get here in time to have a late lunch with you," Ben said. "Have you eaten?"

Katie shook her head, leaned through the window, and kissed Ben on the cheek. "Let's go to the Gateway," she said. "The lunch crowd should be gone. You're tired. Why don't I drive?"

"I never get tired of driving a Porsche," Ben said, "but sure, you can drive. Can I go to the bathroom first?"

"Can you wait another five minutes? You don't want to run into Dad, and I don't want to take a chance on waking Isabella. Mom put her down for her nap a minute or two ago," Katie said as she held the door open for Ben to climb out of the driver's seat so she could climb in. While she adjusted the seat and mirrors, Ben visually checked the tires, then took his seat on the passenger's side and looked at her intently.

"You do know how to drive a straight shift?" he said. "Reverse gear is over and down. It's tricky."

"I can drive a stick," Katie said. "Clark taught me on his Volvo P1800. He also taught me how to ride on the back of his motorcycle."

Katie had an intense look on her face. Ben wondered if she was recalling other things Clark had taught her.

"Tell me about your trial," Katie said as she easily shifted into third gear.

"Nothing to tell," Ben said. "I lost. How'd your talk with Clark go?"

"Let's wait till we get to the Gateway to discuss Clark," Katie said. "I need to pay attention to my driving. Don't want to strip a gear."

Five minutes later they pulled into the parking lot of the Gateway and Katie handed the keys to Ben.

"Good job" Ben said. "Did you park here so you won't have to put the car in reverse going home?"

Katie laughed, took Ben's hand, and led him to a quiet section of the restaurant away from both the kitchen door and the cash register. She picked up a menu and perused it until a waitress brought them water. Then Katie looked up and spoke.

"I brought Clark here so we could talk in private, away from Mom and Dad and without Isabella. I had rehearsed what I wanted to say a dozen times but when he looked at me with his trusting eyes, I almost lost it. I took a long sip of water and a deep breath and started over. I said I'm not satisfied with our life together. I could see the trust in his eyes fade.

"What do you mean?" Clark said. I tried to stay calm and keep my voice strong.

"I've been unhappy for a long time," I told him. "Haven't you noticed? He told me he hadn't noticed. That he would have done something about it if he had. He said all he wants is for me to be happy and asked me what he could do to fix things.

"I don't think you can fix this," I said. "It's been going on for almost the entire four years we've been married. Then I told him he was a good man, but he didn't really know me, and that we weren't right for each other. He looked as if I had stabbed him in the heart.

"He said he knew everything about me—my favorite color, blue, my favorite movie, *My Fair Lady*, that I prefer chocolate ice cream and like my coffee with cream and one sugar."

"That's all true," I said, "but knowing me is more than knowing things about me. You don't know how I really feel about the war or politics. You don't know my aspirations or my hopes—what I want to make out of my life. You don't even notice I've been unhappy for a long time. You don't know because we don't talk about those things. In fact, we don't talk about anything except Isabella, what needs to be done around the house and your job. Do you remember ever discussing politics with me? By then Clark was tearing the paper wrapping on his straw into pieces and rolling the pieces into little balls.

"'You're not going to change my mind,' he said, 'and I'm not going to change yours, so what's the point of discussing politics? Is that what this is all about? You want us to talk politics?'

"No!" I said. "Politics is only one example of what we don't talk about. There are lots of other things—literature, music, art, philosophy, religion, world events. I said he never gave me an answer when I asked for his opinion, so I had stopped asking. I told him my problem was not about discussions we haven't had. It's about the lack of depth in those we have—the shallowness of our relationship. How we *don't* deeply know and understand each other and *don't* help each other make sense of our lives. It was about *not* being ourselves around each other—and about my feeling cooped-up and *not* free.

"Clark looked totally bewildered. 'Why do you want to talk about those things?' he asked. We aren't in school anymore, and no one is trying to convert us to some crazy religion or off-the-wall political party. He couldn't understand how I could say I'm not free. He said he never stopped me from doing anything."

Ben squeezed Katie's hand and said, "Except from marrying me."

Katie returned the squeeze, then rotated her shoulders and stretched. On the wall to her left hung a painting of an old barn with a farmer walking up to it, carrying a pail of water.

"I see a dozen things wrong," she said. "I should offer to correct them in exchange for our lunch."

"One lunch?" Ben laughed. "You mean lunch and dinner every day for a year."

"The world does not share your high opinion of my talent," Katie said.

"Give the world time," Ben said. "And don't swallow Clark's line. He stopped studying and let his grades slide, costing him his draft deferment, then blamed you and manipulated you into marrying him to keep him out of Vietnam. Don't let him do it again."

"I haven't thought of it that way," Katie said, "but you're right, Clark interfered with my life every day by putting on a stricken face every time something I said or did bothered him."

"And that stricken face," Ben added, "triggered your guilt, which made you give in to him."

"Do you think Clark knows that, and exploits my guilt," Katie said, "or is he reflexively continuing behavior that has worked for him in the past?"

"You tell me," Ben said. "You've lived with him almost four years. You told me he threw up whenever you mentioned me when you first started dating. There must be other examples of this behavior."

"He always tries to avoid contradicting me," Katie said. "In fact, he avoids expressing any opinion different from mine. He does not seem to understand that the point of a discussion is not always to convince him I'm right and he's wrong. It's to help me clarify my thoughts and understand his, for us to understand each other and come to a common conclusion. I wanted him to open up—to let me see inside. It was never enough for him to simply agree with me. I wanted him to take a stand on some issue and defend it, regardless of what I thought, and I wanted to be able to express myself without worrying about upsetting him. He says he doesn't want to get into discussions with me about books or movies or ideas because I read so much more than he does, he figures my opinion must be right, so why challenge it. In fact, he doesn't want to argue with me about anything because I'm his wife. He believes he is supposed to make my life comfortable and protect me—not argue with me."

"It sounds as if Clark believes discussions which explore ideas and feelings are arguments," Ben said. "As for his making your life comfortable, what's to complain about?"

"I need more from a relationship than having things done for me," Katie said. "I told Clark I knew he loved me, and enjoyed doing things for me, but he was smothering me with devotion, and his being so careful around me frustrated me. When I said that he began to cry."

Katie dabbed her own eyes and took a long sip of water. The waitress who had approached the table once and been waved off, approached again.

"Give us five more minutes, please," Ben said.

"Take your time, honey," the waitress said. "I'm here till nine and the supper crowd is two hours away."

Katie smiled at Ben and said, "I don't know why this is so difficult for me. I wish I could tell you what happened, without dredging up all these emotions. Where was I? Oh, yes, I told Clark that I try to put on a good face, but I shut off so much of my life when I'm with him I've become very lonely, and I'm no longer a whole person. I want to be a whole person again. I'm weary of playing a role in our marriage. I want to be me. And with him, I have never been able to be me, and I didn't believe I ever would."

"How did Clark respond to that?" Ben asked.

"His jaw began twitching and his voice trembled. He got up, came to my side of the table, and tried to pull me into his arms, but I stayed seated.

'You can't mean that Katie,' he said. 'You're upset about something. Tell me what it is.'

"I've been telling you for the last ten minutes," I said. "You *are* a good person, Clark, and the father of our child. I will always care about you. But I don't love you. I want a divorce."

Ben thought hearing those words would comfort him. They did not. He sank back into his seat, feeling immense sadness for Katie, for Isabella, and to a small extent for Clark. Katie sat motionless. Neither looked at the other as tears streamed from their eyes. Two or three minutes passed in silence except for Katie's soft sobs. Their waitress approached to refill their water glasses, started to speak, then slunk away.

Finally, Katie spoke. "Clark asked me if I would wait six months before doing anything. I said no. Then he asked if I were involved with someone else. I tried to think of a way to say no without lying. I told myself my reason for wanting the divorce wasn't you, Ben. Ok, it was, but it was also all the things I had told Clark. It was what our marriage didn't give me—an open, vibrant relationship like my parents have. A relationship

I know you and I can have, Ben. So, in the end, I confessed."

This time Ben rose from his seat, pulled Katie to him, and tried to kiss her.

"Not here," Katie said, "I'm sure someone who knows Dad will see us, and there'll be more hell to pay. Let's skip lunch and order dessert."

As Ben drove Katie home after they shared a slice of the Gateway's world-famous lemon icebox pie, she finished her story. "I don't believe Clark had any idea what was coming. He was absolutely stricken. I felt so sorry for him. He drove me back home crying and spent about half an hour with Isabella. I stayed outside, so I have no idea what he said to her. Then Dad walked him to his car. I don't know if he was going straight back to Asheville or to his parents' home."

"I'm sorry you had to go through that," Ben said. "I know it's been hard. I love you, and I'll be with you every step of the way. You have my word. I guess you and Clark didn't discuss any of the details."

"Dad told me Clark will call me next Saturday. I guess he needs time for the idea of divorce to sink in before he can think about details, and I'm sure he wants to talk with a lawyer."

Katie's voice took on a desperate tone. "I wish you could stay, Ben," she said. "I need you with me. I've sat through two more lectures from my father about my obligations and duties, and how if you and I get together, our marriage will have originated in sin and will be doomed to fail. Thank goodness my mother hasn't jumped on me."

"I hate not being with you, but you know I can't stay," Ben said. "I'll call you every night and I'll come next weekend. I love you, Katie."

Thursday night Ben called Katie. "I'll be there tomorrow afternoon," Ben said. "Do you think your parents would keep Isabella and let me take you out to dinner?

"I'll ask," Katie said. "Just don't count on it."

Katie got her mother's permission, but not her father's. Not only did Dr. Reynolds refuse to agree that Mrs. Reynolds could babysit Isabella, he forbade Katie from inviting Ben into their home that evening. Katie successfully pleaded with her mother to allow Ben to come over the following morning after Dr. Reynolds went to work, so Ben could be present when Clark called. Both Katie and he jumped when the phone rang. Even though Ben sat close to Katie, he was unable to hear Clark's part of the conversation.

"You've been talking to my Dad," Katie said, in a tone more aggressive than Ben had heard before.

"Well, I don't care what Dad told you, I promise you, this is my decision, and mine alone. I had decided to divorce you before I spoke with Ben, and, yes, my mind is made up. I don't want to waste your money going to counseling."

"Listen to me, Clark Cooper," Katie shouted. "If you sue Ben, I'll be the most hostile, disagreeable person you can imagine. Now, go stew awhile if you need to, but call me back in an hour and for Isabella's sake, let's work this out."

When she hung up, Katie was shaking like a sinner in the presence of an angry God.

"Do you want some water?" Ben asked.

"Just hold me, Ben," she said. "Hold me tight."

Ben could feel his heart pounding in rhythm with Katie's as he held her and thought that if only Katie had broken up with Clark in 1964 when she promised her mother, Suzy, and him she would. Their lives would be so much less complicated. If she had, however, Clark would have gone to Vietnam, with all its horrors, and Isabella would not exist. In life, for every upside there is a downside. Life sometimes gives you opportunities, and if you don't grab them, jerks them away. At any rate, speculating about what might have been was pointless. He had to find a way for Katie to get through the mess she was in now.

"I gather Clark threatened to sue me," Ben said as they separated, "but I didn't get the last part of the conversation."

"Clark said he would think about sending me a letter with his conditions for a consent divorce, if that's what I really wanted, after he consulted a lawyer. All this back and forth with Clark has worn me out. Can you stay a while? Dad's not here. Mom's due back shortly. I would like for the two of you to talk."

Mrs. Reynolds had already arrived and was alone in the kitchen. Katie walked up and kissed a tear off her mother's cheek. Ben hung back till she finally looked at him.

"Hello, Mrs. Reynolds," he said. The fleeting smile that crossed her face as she acknowledged his presence told him she was still on Katie's side.

"Are you all right, Mother?" Katie said. "Why are you crying?"

"Can't a mother shed a few tears when she learns her daughter is getting a divorce?"

"Oh, Mom, I'm so sorry you have to go through this," Katie said. Then she succinctly reported the morning's events to her mother, omitting her ferocious attack on Clark and ending with his promise to send his demands in a letter.

"It has all happened so fast," Mrs. Reynolds said. "A month ago I thought my life couldn't be better. Jeff had been named Vice-Chancellor of the University; I had accumulated enough seniority to pick the classes and periods I wanted to teach. Our daughter was married, I thought happily, to a man we adored who treated her like…"

"A princess?" Katie volunteered.

"Yes, that's the word I was searching for," Mrs. Reynolds said, "and we had a beautiful, smart granddaughter who looked like she had been cut out of the same bolt of cloth as her mother. And now…"

"All that's still true, Mother," Katie said. "Most of it, at least. I *am* happy now that I've made a decision I've been delaying for over a year. You and Dad still have your wonderful careers and Isabella is still smart and adorable. I'm starting a new phase in my life when I'm young enough to enjoy it and mature enough, I hope, to appreciate it. Plus, I'm starting over with a man I love and who I know loves me. It's the right thing to do, Mother. I know it is."

"Any coffee left?" Ben said, eyeing the half full carafe.

Mrs. Reynolds rinsed her own cup and put it away. She poured a cup for Ben, handed it to him and said, "Jeff and I have gone round and round about you two. Jeff thinks you are behind it all, Ben, but Katie says she is acting on her own, and I believe her, to a point. I can't imagine her getting this divorce, however, if you weren't in the picture. So, I'm holding you partly responsible."

Ben looked down at his shoes. He wanted to challenge Mrs. Reynolds' conclusion, but he dared not risk alienating the one parent who was sympathetic to Katie. Before he could speak, Katie's mother continued.

"Because Katie loves you, Ben, I pray you love her, and we will help her through this. Whatever your feelings for her, I want you either totally in our family or totally out by this time next year. Understand?"

Katie's face glowed. She pulled Ben's hand to her mouth and kissed it.

"Does this mean Isabella and I can stay here?" she said.

"Yes. We don't want you working with a young child and Jeff doesn't want you to have to rely on Ben for support; so even though your divorce shatters his moral code, and he believes you are inflicting a great wrong on Clark, staying here is the only option acceptable to us."

"Thank you, Mrs. Reynolds," Ben said. He swallowed hard trying to force the lump out of his throat. "I love Katie with all my heart, and I will marry her as soon as her divorce is final. I would like to thank Dr. Reynolds, also."

"Too early for that, Ben. He blames you for breaking up Katie's marriage and is nowhere near ready to shake hands and make-up. Leave Jeff to me and concentrate on getting Katie through this divorce as quickly as possible."

Katie walked Ben back to his car. In deference to her mother who was standing at the open door, they did not kiss.

I like that woman, Ben thought as he began the drive back to Atlanta. *Katie is lucky to have her*.

Ben called Katie early the following Friday afternoon. "Has it arrived?" he asked.

"The postman left five minutes ago," Katie said. "Your timing was perfect."

"Read it to me," Ben's excitement was mixed with dread.

"Let me summarize," Katie replied. "The first two pages relate how much he misses me and how you are ruining his life and mine and predict our marriage won't last. The next two pages recite all the reasons Isabella would be better off with both parents and why I should reconsider. Then he lists his demands."

"I think you should agree to everything," Ben said.

"Everything!" Katie exclaimed. "You haven't even heard the list."

"Okay, tell me what you don't like," Ben said.

Katie silently re-read the letter.

"I don't have any trouble with six weeks' visitation in the summer," she said, "I didn't expect any alimony, but he's offering only $200 a month in child support. And wants me to waive my right to modify in the future.

Plus, he wants all the equity in our house and for Dad to forgive the loan he made to us for the down payment. I can't ask Dad to do that, and anyway, shouldn't I get something?"

"Sweetheart, you are getting something—me. How much equity is in your house? A few thousand dollars. Your share is only half. Forget it. How much does Clark owe your Dad?"

"The principal is $2,500 plus a little interest," Katie said.

"We'll pay it. Tell Clark your lawyer will draw up the papers and send them to him. Let's get it over with. We can't get married until you and Clark are divorced."

"Oh, Ben," Katie said. "Things are moving so fast."

Ben chuckled. "That's a good thing, we'll be together before you have time to change your mind."

"That'll never happen," Katie laughed "I can't go through this trauma again. Speaking of being together, when are you coming?"

"Well, first I'll tell the folks around here you and I are finally getting together," Ben said. "Then I'll call Bob and tell him to file the complaint and draft the settlement agreement now, and not wait for his retainer. He should have the papers ready for you to sign late Monday or Tuesday. Why don't I come Tuesday and go over them with you? Is that soon enough?"

"Barely," Katie said. "And please drive carefully, Ben. I love you."

"And I love you, Katie, I've already made surprise plans for our honeymoon."

"You have? Tell me!"

"If I tell you, it won't be a surprise."

"You meanie!" Katie laughed. "Please give me enough notice so I can wash my hair."

The next morning Ben went to his office tying up some loose ends so he could be gone most of the following week. His spirits were high. He was in a great mood. About 11:30 the office phone rang. *I shouldn't answer. Can't be for me. No one knows I'm here. It's probably Eileen, and I don't have time for her.* At the fourth ring, however, right before the answering machine would take the call, he picked up the receiver.

"McHaney, Reed, and Smith," he said. "How may I help you?"

"Isabella's gone!" Katie sobbed, "Clark took her! He put her in his car and left."

"Calm down, Katie," Ben said. "Where are you? Are your parents around?"

"Yes," Katie said. "They're both here."

"Okay," Ben said. "Start from the beginning. What happened?"

"About 8:30 this morning Clark called and said he was at his parent's and wanted to come over and visit with Isabella for a while. I thought nothing of it. He arrived about 9 and spent about half an hour in the house with Isabella. I stayed out of their way. Then I saw Dad come out the door holding Isabella's hand and Clark following them. Clark got into his car. I wiped my eyes and when I refocused, the car was pulling away and Dad was walking back toward the house. Isabella was in the backseat. I shrieked 'STOP HIM, Dad, STOP HIM,' but Dad did nothing and … Isabella … was … gone."

Katie's sobs had escalated to wails. "I hate that man! Hate him! Hate him! I'm sure he encouraged Clark to take Isabella."

Ben tried to console her by saying again and again, "I love you, Katie. Everything will be all right."

"I need you Ben," Katie said when she regained her composure. "Please come to Martin for a few days. Now I have Isabella to worry about. I don't know how I can handle everything!"

"I hate not being with you, but I can't come till Tuesday," Ben said. "Do you think Clark would harm Isabella? If so, we need to call the police. If not, we need to contact Clark and let him know how concerned you are. Do you want Bob to call Clark?"

"No," Katie said. "Clark would never hurt Isabella. I feel a lot better now that we have talked. I'll call him myself tonight before Isabella's bedtime. That'll give me a chance to talk to her. Please don't wait till Tuesday. Can you come tomorrow?"

Ben mentally rearranged his schedule and said "Okay, I'll postpone some things and leave in the morning."

Sunday morning Ben was up at six and on the road half an hour later, hoping to find Katie in a better state of mind. Unlike her custom, Katie did not come to meet him. Mrs. Reynolds, who obviously had been crying, came instead.

"Where's Katie?" Ben asked. "What's wrong?"

"It's Clark," Mrs. Reynolds said. "He was hit by a

tractor trailer at an intersection on Highway 45 near Greenfield and was taken to the trauma center at Obion General. Jeff took Katie over to be with him."

"What about Isabella?"

"Katie and Clark talked last night," Mrs. Reynolds said. "He agreed to drive over this morning to see Katie alone. He didn't want you, Jeff, or me present. Isabella wasn't in the car, thank God. She stayed with Clark's mother. When he didn't show up at 8:45, we became concerned. Then we got Joe's call. Go to the hospital and find Katie, Ben. She wants you there."

Thirty minutes later, Ben found Katie and her father in the trauma center. Dr. Reynolds glared at him and said, "Tell him to leave, Katie. He's not welcome. This area is for family only."

Katie hailed a nurse who was briskly walking by. "Excuse me, miss, can you direct me to the non-family visitors waiting room?"

"You're in it," the nurse replied without stopping. "There's only one waiting room on this floor. Who are you here for?"

"Clark Cooper," Katie said. "He went into surgery about an hour ago. I'm his wife."

"I just came from there," the nurse said. "His surgery will be going on for a while. Dr. McAdoo will give you a full report when he comes out. Your husband has already received three units of blood and needs more. I was on my way to the nurses' station to have someone call the family for donors, Mr. Cooper is Type A positive, but the blood bank will take any type. If you aren't on antibiotics and haven't been tattooed recently, you could donate."

Ben and Katie looked at each other. Neither volunteered.

"Please think about it," the nurse said in parting. "There have been a rash of wrecks this week and our blood supply is low."

"Let's go to the cafeteria and get something," Katie said. "I only want coffee, but you probably haven't had lunch. Dad, do you want me to bring you a coffee?"

Without looking up from his newspaper, Dr. Reynolds shook his head, no, and went on reading. Katie and Ben could not find a cafeteria. They did, however, find vending machines full of sandwiches and soft drinks, a large coffee urn, an empty table, and two chairs.

"What did they tell you about the accident?" Ben asked.

"Just that Clark's car was hit on the passenger's side, knocked into an oncoming truck and totaled. Dad's brother Joe is a surgeon who has privileges at Obion General. He was at the hospital when they brought Clark in. Uncle Joe called Dad. I tried to call Clark's parents, but no one answered. Mom said she would keep calling until she gets them. Dad and I came right over. Clark wasn't conscious, so they asked me a few questions. I signed some forms and Clark was taken into surgery. I don't know who the surgeon is. It's not Uncle Joe."

"What do you think about giving blood?" Ben asked.

"I think I should. What about you?"

Ben had been mulling that question since the nurse told them Clark needed more blood. He had given blood once at a law school blood drive. The experience wasn't bad, but he had fainted when he got off the table. He knew he should donate. His animosity toward Clark, however, got in the way.

"I've given blood once before," Ben said. "It is a little unpleasant."

"Surely you're not going to let a little unpleasantness keep you from doing the right thing," Katie said. "Finish your sandwich and let's go donate."

The hospital made it easy to donate blood. The process, including recovery time, took about an hour and a half. Soon after they returned to the visitors' area Clark's surgeon arrived, still in his scrubs.

"I'm Mel McAdoo," he said, "Chief of Surgery. Our team worked on Mr. Cooper almost three hours. Everything went as well as could be expected with the extent of his injuries. We'll keep him in the recovery room a couple of hours to monitor him. It turned out the damage was far more serious than we first thought. In addition to his ruptured spleen, probably caused by having his seat belt fastened, the tibia in his left leg was broken in two places and his left ankle was shattered. He'll need at least one more operation by an orthopedic surgeon who specializes in ankle injuries. For that, he'll need to go to the Methodist Hospital in Memphis, the teaching hospital for the University of Tennessee Medical School, or Vanderbilt Hospital. Either would be an excellent choice."

"I hope he has plenty of insurance," Dr. Reynolds said. "I'll call around and see if I can get a copy of the police report. Maybe the other driver was at fault and has insurance."

"The report won't be filed for a least twenty-four hours," Ben said. "Someone needs to find the investigating officer and interview him today, if possible, while the incident is still fresh on his mind. Katie, you should notify your insurance carrier immed..."

"Stay out of this, Ben," Dr. Reynolds snapped. "This is family business—not yours. For the last time: Get the hell out of here and leave us alone."

Ben looked at Katie. Her eyes were glued to the floor. Waves of hurt washed over him. He wanted Katie to say something—anything. She did not. For a painful moment Ben stood there silently pleading for the woman he loved to reaffirm her love for him. Then he turned and walked away.

Katie called him at Eileen's three hours later.

"Why are you calling me?" Ben said. "Your father told me to get the hell out."

"Don't be that way, Ben. I wanted to support you, but I didn't want to have a fight with Dad in front of the medical staff. You know Clark's accident changes everything. He is going to need round the clock care for several days after he's released, and at least one more operation on his ankle, probably two. He has no one to take care of him. His parents are too old, plus their tiny house doesn't have room for him, let alone all the physical therapy equipment he will need. His only sibling lives in DC and has a wife and child of his own. And then there are money issues. I don't know how long Clark can stay out of work and still be paid, and I don't know how much of the cost of his care is covered by Remington's medical plan. I need to check on that. Also, since Clark can't return to Asheville for a while, I'll have to put our house up for sale, or try to rent it."

"Are you telling me that you and Isabella are going to stay with your parents and when Clark is released, he'll stay there also? So, your divorce is off."

"Please don't think of it that way, Ben. My divorce is not off, only delayed."

"For how long?" Ben asked.

"At least six months, probably a year, maybe longer. Meet me at the hospital for breakfast in the morning and let's discuss this."

Ben did not meet Katie the next day. He left for Atlanta before dawn. The drive back was the worst eight hours of his life. There was no way Clark would be able to go back to work in six months. They didn't know yet whether his shattered ankle could be rebuilt. Katie's guilt reflex had been triggered, not by Clark's reaction to her, but by an outside event which neither she nor Clark controlled. It was Vietnam all over again and Katie would again construct a scenario making her at least partly responsible for Clark's having the accident, therefore, fully responsible for protecting him from its consequences. Ben was sure that in the time it took Clark to recover, something else would come up and keep Katie's guilt in control. She would never abandon Clark. She would never be his wife.

Getting out of bed the next morning was a task beyond Ben's ability. His sorrow sapped his will to do anything other than lie there and sink deeper and deeper into depression. He couldn't answer his phone the first time it rang, when it rang again five minutes later or when it rang again. Half an hour later his doorbell rang. He ignored it, but he could not ignore the constant banging on the door that followed.

"Jesus, Ben, you look like you've been mugged," his secretary Karen said when she saw his unshaven face and baggy eyes through the partially opened door. "Do I need to call a doctor?"

Ben stepped back to let her enter.

"I'm okay," he said. "Just groggy. I've had a few hard days and a sleepless night."

"You are definitely not okay," Karen replied. "Where's your coffee. I'm going to perk you a pot."

Without waiting for an answer Karen marched into his kitchen, spotted his percolator on the stove, and found his Maxwell House in the refrigerator.

"Bob Ellison, who said he's your friend from Martin, has been calling you all morning. He wants you to call him right away."

"Can't I have my coffee first?" Ben said.

"You can talk to your friend while it perks," Karen said. "He didn't give me any details about why he wanted to talk to you. I presumed it was about Katie's divorce. But he said he had information about the accident. Where's your phone. I'll dial him for you. Then I'm going back to the office. Surely you can pour your own coffee. Now promise me you won't go back to bed."

"I understand you need to talk to me," Ben said when Bob answered. "Karen says it's about the accident."

"It is," Bob said. "When I didn't hear from you Tuesday, I called your Mother Wednesday morning to see if something went wrong. She told me you had already left, so I called Dr. Reynold's house, hoping to speak to Katie. Mrs. Reynolds told me Katie was at the hospital with Clark, and Dr. Reynolds had driven to Milan to try to find out about the accident. All this was news to me, so I got her to tell me everything she knew, which wasn't much, but enough to let me know the divorce was off, and I should start my own investigation."

"Trolling for business," Ben said. "I didn't know you handled personal injury cases."

"You know us small town lawyers have to handle everything," Bob laughed. "I'm not trolling. I'm trying to help my client. Your check arrived Monday, so Katie has officially retained me and boy does she need help. Her father is rooting around in the dark."

Ben was relieved that Bob was stepping in, although he would have kept the case himself and associated Horace Bradbury in Dresden to do the investigative work and handle the motions, if Dr. Reynolds had not made it clear he didn't want him involved.

"You won't gouge Katie," Ben said.

"I thought I'd charge 5% less than the standard

contingency fee," Bob said. "Of course, there'll be a referral fee for you."

"Leave me out of it," Ben said, "That'll make it easier for you to deal with Dr. Reynolds and with Clark. Think of me as unpaid co-counsel. And Clark may not agree to your being his lawyer. After all you are Katie's divorce lawyer."

"I've thought of that," Bob said, "but I never contacted Clark and I never filed any papers in court against him. Also, his interest and Katie's are not adverse in a personal injury claim, so there's no reason I can see why I can't represent them both. If there is a technical conflict, it can be waived. Clark is unable to act for himself and Katie needs to move fast."

"I see your point," Ben said. "It should be safe to proceed. At least with the investigation. Tell me what you've learned already."

"Well, I'm pretty tight with the Highway Patrol in this area, so I called Sergeant Wood, who works Weakley, Gibson and Obion Counties to get the skinny. It turns out he was the investigating officer. The accident happened near Greenfield. Clark was headed North on US Highway 45 and a delivery van heading West on state road 54 ran the stop sign at the intersection."

"A delivery van," Ben said. "at the hospital they told us it was a truck."

"Well, let me finish," Bob said. "An Argo-Collier 18-wheeler was headed South on US 45 going at least the speed limit, probably faster. The van struck Clark's car and knocked it across the yellow line into the path of the 18-wheeler. The tractor-trailer did most of the damage, but the driver of the van was at fault, not the Argo-Collier driver, and certainly not Clark. I got a copy of the accident report. The van driver, whose name is Buford Moore was charged with failure to yield the right of way and failure to obey a lawful traffic signal. The report said Moore was insured by Allstate and gave the policy number, but not the amount of coverage."

Ben broke in. "At least Clark is in the clear. How soon can we find out the policy limits?"

"If you would stop butting in and let me finish," Bob laughed, "all will be revealed. I reached the Allstate adjustor in Jackson right at closing time last night. Because he and I had worked together before, he came right out and told me the policy limit is $25,000. He practically assured me that if Clark would take the $25,000, and release Moore from any further liability, Allstate would pay without a fight."

"Good work," Bob. "Have you told Katie?"

"I wanted to talk to you first," Bob said, "and because $25,000 minus my fee won't come close to paying all Clark's medical bills, I wanted to do a little checking to see if Moore has any other assets before talking to her. If he has any assets other than a wrecked 1960 Ford Van, and less than a hundred dollars in the bank, they must be in his mattress or buried in the ground."

"How do you know what's in his bank account?" Ben asked.

"That was the easy part," Bob said. "Country lawyers

who don't represent banks or insurance companies need retainers before taking cases, and you want to make sure the check is good. Probably wouldn't work in Atlanta, but around here, all you have to do is ask the bank if the check is any good. I usually start at $500, but from what I learned about Mr. Moore, I started at $100, which, as I said, would not clear."

"Damn," Ben said. "That's a good news, bad news story that's mostly bad news. Hold up on everything until I talk to Katie tonight. And Bob, thanks for jumping in."

"My pleasure," Bob said. "Tell Katie to take the deal and my fee will only be $1,000.

Katie was not in when Ben called from his office at four. He left both office and home numbers with Mrs. Reynolds. Because he had left without having breakfast with Katie, Ben listened carefully for any hint of anger in Mrs. Reynolds voice. She sounded like her normal self. Ben hoped that was a good indicator of Katie's mood. He had no illusions about Dr. Reynolds' feelings toward him. He felt slightly guilty over having a pleasurable reaction to Bob's statement that Dr. Reynolds had been rooting around in all the wrong places. He hoped Katie had better luck getting information about Clark's company's policy.

"It's good to hear your voice," Katie said to Ben's great relief when she called about seven. "I was worried when you left without saying goodbye. Hanging around Clark's room is very depressing. He's in such pain they keep him sedated all the time, which means he and I aren't able to talk. In a way that's a good thing. We don't need to have any serious discussions right now. What I need is you."

"I'm so, so sorry, Katie," Ben said. "Leaving you at the hospital was not my finest hour, but sweetheart, when you didn't speak up when your father ordered me to get the hell out, all my old fears of rejection kicked in, and I couldn't shake them. I had to get away before I said or did something horrible."

"I understand," Katie said. "Let's put it behind us. Dad stopped by this afternoon to tell me he can get a copy of the accident report tomorrow. And I talked to Human Resources at Remington and learned that Clark's health insurance is capped at $100,000. They will pay to have him airlifted to Memphis, at six times the cost of taking him by ambulance. Murphy Funeral home said they have a body to pick up in Memphis and would charge $100 to take Clark in their air-conditioned hearse and get him there in three hours, door to door, or $150 if Clark wants an ambulance."

"If it were anyone other than Doug Murphy," Ben said, "they would be kidding about the hearse."

"How do you know Doug?" Katie asked.

"I played little league baseball on his team in the fourth and fifth grades. I wasn't good enough to go on from there. Are you going to use Doug?"

"Yes, he's cheaper and about as fast. This isn't a life-or-death situation that requires an airlift. All the arrangements have been made. Doctor McAdoo is waiting for my approval, which I'll give in the morning."

"Sounds like you had a productive two days," Ben said. "Do you want to hear what I've learned?"

"Of course! Why do you think I called?"

"Aren't you returning my call?" Ben said. "Your mother told you I called, didn't she?"

"I haven't seen Mom since I got home. She and I drove down to meet with Clark's parents this morning. We brought Isabella back with us, thank God. I think Mom's taken her out for ice cream. I called you as soon as I came in. So, what have you learned?"

Ben brought her current and suggested she authorize Bob to settle with Allstate.

"I guess Dad doesn't need to run down the accident report, then," Katie said. "I hope Clark is OK having Bob as his lawyer."

"You don't have time to find out," Ben said. "You have to get moving on this. I guarantee you, Bob's giving you the best deal on attorney's fees you could possibly get. Do you want to tell him to accept Allstate's offer, or shall I?"

"You do it, please, Ben. I'll tell Dad that between our insurance and Mr. Moore's we should be able to cover Clark's expenses. Call me tomorrow, please. I love you."

The first three months of Clark's recovery went by quickly, the second less so, and the third dragged on for what seemed like an eternity. Clark's ankle required three operations. Initially the surgeons were able to partially repair it so he could walk with crutches, but he could not drive.

"He tries so hard," Katie told Ben on Ben's weekly visit in late June as they sat alone in Eileen's garage apartment Ben had rented, "but he can't stand on his own. His ankle won't support his weight. The physical therapist says it will heal in time, hopefully before our money runs completely out, and Clark should be able to go back to work eventually. For now, he can't go anywhere without assistance."

"How much have you spent in all?" Ben asked.

"I have records of all the hospital, doctor, drugs, physical therapy equipment and therapist bills. To date they total $169,000, much of which was covered by Remington's policy and the settlement with the driver who hit Clark.

"I'm keeping the $9000 we got from our carrier for the Volvo in reserve to buy Clark a car," Katie said. "Of course, it's available if he needs it to live on. I just hope it doesn't come to that."

Ben was looking intently at her, while he listened, trying to determine if she had lost a few pounds in the months she had been caring for Clark. Katie's eyes had lost none of their sparkle, but her hands and nails had suffered. It pained Ben that Katie was growing older without him, except for their weekly visits, which for the last six months had, thanks to his rented garage apartment, included sex.

"Why are you looking at me like that?" Katie said. "Are you checking out the new lines in my face?"

"Don't pay any attention to me," Ben laughed. "I just can't get enough of you."

"You know I live for your visits," Katie said as she leaned in and kissed him. Then she walked to the window to watch Eileen walk to the street to check the mail.

"I wonder what Eileen thinks about my being here."

"I'm sure it irritates the hell out of her," Ben said, "but it's none of her business. I'm paying her rent, so it's my apartment and I have the only key. What does your mother think about your visiting me at Eileen's?"

"One good thing about Eileen's despising me," Katie laughed, "is that she doesn't speak to my parents, not even at Church. If she had told them anything about us, Dad would have had more fuel for his fire, and I would have heard about it. I'm sure Mom knows we are intimate, but she keeps her thoughts to herself."

"Speaking of Church," Ben said, "why don't we go tomorrow? We don't have to sit with your parents."

"Are you crazy?" Katie said. "We can't do that until we are married, or at least until I'm divorced. We can't tromp on all social conventions, and I don't want to fan the flames of Dad's hostility toward you."

"You're right, of course," Ben said. "Church can wait. What about Clark, does he talk to you about the time you spend with me?"

"No," Katie said as she rejoined Ben on the couch. "Mother actually spends more time with him than I do. He usually eats alone—sometimes with Isabella. I make up his bed and occasionally take him to the drug store, and since I'm doing all the laundry, I wash the few clothes he has. I felt guilty the first time you came after

Clark moved in, but I got over it and decided that Clark couldn't live in the same house with me if I couldn't have my weekends with you. Then Mrs. Cooper agreed to pick Clark up Friday nights and bring him back Sunday afternoons. That helped a lot."

"I'm glad you cleared that up," Ben said. "I've been aware for several visits that you seemed more relaxed. You were smart to make that arrangement with Mrs. Cooper."

"Actually," Katie said, "Mom did it—without consulting me."

Katie suggested they drive to the Brown Derby in Fulton for dinner that night, 'so Dad's friends won't see us out together.' They were oblivious to the boisterous Saturday crowd as they enjoyed a bottle of Moet & Chandon and made dinner out of the crackers, nuts, and olives served as *hors d'oeuvres,* with a side of anchovies for Ben.

"This is really good," Katie said after her first sip. "The last time we were here, I was too young to drink and confessed that to the waitress who offered me a Miller."

"A lot of water has gone under the bridge since then," Ben said. "I remember that night very clearly. I spent the whole evening trying to figure out how important Clark was to you and too scared of the answer to kiss you."

"I wanted you to kiss me," Katie said, "but you never even made a move."

"My mistake," Ben said as they held up their flutes and toasted each other. "which I will never make again."

"Clark is here," Mrs. Reynolds announced when Katie and Ben arrived home about 9:30. "He's in the den. His Dad brought him back tonight."

"Sounds ominous," Ben, who had noticed a strange car parked by the mailbox, said. "Maybe I should leave."

Mrs. Reynolds shook her head and called out. "Katie's home, Clark. Shall I bring Ben in with her?"

As he had done when he saw Clark sitting in that Morris Minor outside the Reynolds' home so long ago, Ben gave Clark an extra-long look. Before, he had been thin. Now he was gaunt. His hair was totally gray, and his sunken eyes suggested weariness. This time instead of anger, his face showed resignation—acceptance of a horrible outcome that had become a *fait accompli*. A cane by his side, Clark was sitting on the couch with Dr. Reynolds. Neither rose when Ben, Katie, and her mother entered. Katie took the chair next to Clark. Her mother took the one opposite her father. Ben remained at the door, with an unobstructed view of everyone, ready to slip out at a moment's notice without an awkward goodbye. A weird silence pervaded the room. Katie looked first at her father, then at Ben, then Clark. Dr. Reynolds' eyes were glued on Ben. Mrs. Reynolds' eyes darted back and forth between Katie and Clark. Clark shifted awkwardly in his seat, took his cane, and with great effort stood up.

"I must be going," he said. "My dad is waiting for me."

"You'll be coming back tomorrow," Katie said.

"No," Clark said. "I'll be staying with my parents

from now on. But before I go, I wanted to tell you that I am cleared to go back to work. I'll start a week from Monday after the tenants vacate our house. Remington has been great about accommodating my disability, which their insurance carrier has told them may be permanent. I only have to work six hours a day for the first month and I won't have any travel assignments for the foreseeable future. I've lined up a cleaning service. I can cook for myself and I should be able to drive to work and back as soon as I can find a car I can afford."

Katie and her mother teared up. Ben stifled the urge to ask about the divorce papers. Dr. Reynolds stood up and extended his hand to Clark. "Let me help you to the door," he said.

Clark shook his head and looked at Katie. "I can manage. I hoped and prayed you and I could be together forever, but over the last few months it has become quite clear to me that you don't love me. I can't ask you to give up your life to continue taking care of me, so, I'll have to find a way to live without you."

Katie stood up, wiped her eyes, put her arms around Clark and said, "You'll find a way, and you'll find a way to stay in Isabella's life. You are important to her."

With his free hand Clark squeezed Katie's arm and said, "I'll sign the papers as soon as you get them to me. I still love you, Katie. I just want you to be happy."

II

On the 7th of October 1970, Ben took Katie to Bob's office for the last time. Katie wore a sweater to ward off the light wind that brought an early autumn chill. The three of them drove the nine miles to Dresden and found the chambers of Chancellor George Parker, III on the second floor of the Weakley County Courthouse. His secretary directed them to sit while they waited for the judge. Beads of sweat on Katie's upper lip belied her apparent calm.

"How long will it take," she asked.

"Ten minutes, at most, maybe five," Bob said. "Your husband has signed the necessary papers and I have filed them. All time periods have run, so the only thing left is for you to answer three or four questions. Then Judge Parker will sign the order granting the divorce. I'll file it in the Clerk's office, get a certified copy and you'll be on your way. It's as simple as that."

Ben thought about Mrs. Reynolds' demand that he

be in or out of their family within a year. He would not quite make it, but he'd be so close she surely wouldn't penalize him. Dr. Reynolds, however, was still hostile. Ben wished his father had been alive to have a cup of coffee, perhaps smoke a cigar with Dr. Reynolds, and reaffirm their friendship, paving the way for Ben.

Ben's next thought was of Eileen, and her continued hostility toward Katie. Why? She barely knew Katie. Had Helen Reynolds and Eileen feuded in the past? Was Eileen carrying this feud down to Katie? Ben doubted that. Eileen and Helen didn't run in the same circles. Their paths only crossed at church now that Riley's Rotary Club days had ended.

The only explanation that made sense was that in addition to Katie's being "an agitator," her divorce upset the order Eileen wanted to maintain in her small world. Katie was leaving her husband and taking their child with her. In Eileen's domain, that was wrong. No wife should do that. Katie should be ostracized, and Ben should be punished for having pulled Katie off the path of marital fidelity.

Ben thought about the warmth and tenderness Mrs. Reynolds had shown Katie. He thought about how much Katie relied on her mother and contrasted that with his relationship with Eileen. Katie had a mother who loved her. Ben had a tormentor who despised him. Yet, out of respect for his father, he tolerated his tormentor, and took over tasks she found vexing. He shrugged his shoulders. *That's just the way life is.*

Then Ben searched for a brighter side. Getting the

divorce could have been much more difficult and taken much longer. If Clark had forced Katie to file for divorce in North Carolina, the process could have drug on for years and her attorney's fees would have been huge.

"Morning, Bob," Judge Parker said as he entered his chambers. "Katie Reynolds! It's so good to see you. And you too, Ben. How are y'all? Sit down and let's take care of business. I have court in ten minutes. Katie, raise your right hand."

And with the stroke of Judge Parker's pen after she answered a few questions, Katie was divorced. Ben thanked Judge Parker, grabbed Katie's hand and said, "We've got to get out of here. You only have two days to pack."

"I don't need two days to pack," Katie laughed. "I've been planning what to take since you told me we were going to London. The only thing undecided is what coat to take. Is it cold in London in October?"

"Pretty chilly," Ben said. "And what about Isabella. Have your parents agreed to keep her?"

"Well," Katie said, "they agreed to keep her under the assumption that we would be married before we left."

"Can't we tell them we eloped?" Ben said. "I know lots of couples who have."

"And we decided to elope," Katie added, "to save Dad the embarrassment of having to come to our wedding. Oh, Ben, how many lies will we have to tell?"

The World Airways 747 chartered to take 300 people

from Atlanta to London had been late leaving Oakland, so the early evening planned departure was delayed until midnight. At 11:30, the passengers were herded into a special lounge to speed up ticket collection and departure. The ticket agent came up to Ben, read his ticket, checked his passport against the manifest and said "Mr. Ben McHaney, and this must be Mrs. McHaney?"

Ben nodded agreement. Katie handed the agent her passport and whispered, "My real name is Kathryn Cooper, like it says on my passport. I'm not Mrs. Ben McHaney."

"Give me your ticket, honey," the agent said in a voice loud enough for everyone to hear. "If Mr. McHaney wants to take you to London instead of his wife, that's all right with me."

Ben laughed. Katie was mortified. She hit Ben on the shoulder and said, "Well, I wanted him to have my name right. I didn't want to be arrested when I got off the plane in a foreign country. What's so funny about that?"

Ben pulled Katie to him and whispered. "I'm not laughing at you, sweetheart. I'm laughing at the situation because you *are* such a straight arrow. And guess what. I wouldn't want you any other way."

Katie nuzzled him. "And part of what I love about you is that you will bend the arrow a little, but won't break it—right?"

With love and mischief written on his face, Ben looked at Katie and smiled.

Ben and Katie spent six days in London, going to

the theater for the price of one British pound a ticket, riding the tube practically everywhere, eating on the cheap at pubs and taking the train on a day trip to Stratford-upon-Avon to visit Shakespeare's home. Although Katie was concerned that she might be breaking some law, she slept in the same bed with Ben. They reminisced about the tortuous path that had brought them together, marveled at how lucky they were to have each other, and thought how wonderful it would be to create a sibling for Isabella.

Without loosening his gentle hold on her, Ben said, "Judge Parker did us a huge favor by working us into his schedule so you could be divorced before we left for London."

"So, I did NOTHING wrong by coming on this trip with you," Katie said.

"I wouldn't go that far," Ben laughed, "but you didn't commit adultery each night for the last five."

Katie broke free from his hold and bolted upright.

"You're right," she said. "I'm divorced, but we aren't married, so our sleeping together is still wrong in the eyes of my father. Let's not take any chances. Let's get the Delta captain to marry us on the flight back, while we are over the ocean. Just like a ship's captain could."

"You are resourceful," Ben laughed. "That's another of your many qualities, but I doubt the captain is authorized to conduct weddings. Plus, we don't have a license. We'll have to keep our little secret from your father."

Ben and Katie flew back to Atlanta on Saturday and on Sunday, drove to Nashville, where Katie's parents were waiting at a Holiday Inn with Isabella. Dr. Reynolds walked Isabella to Ben's car, hugged Katie and extended his hand to Ben.

"Welcome to the family, Ben," he said. "Judge Parker and I were at Rotary Thursday and he told me he signed Katie's divorce decree."

Ben braced himself.

"I'm sorry for the things I said about you and Katie," Dr. Reynolds continued. "I was trying to get her to realize how precarious her situation was, and how awful things could get. I felt like I needed to paint the bleakest picture possible. Look at it from my perspective. Most cases like this end badly for the girl."

"Thank you, Dr. Reynolds," Ben said. He considered his next words carefully, knowing that building and preserving a strong relationship with Katie's parents was vital for Katie and for him. Katie's mother had invited him into the Reynold's family, and he very much wanted in. It was important to Ben that Katie's father want him in also.

"I know these past few months have been hard on you and Mrs. Reynolds," he said. "I told myself that whenever I got upset with you for the pretty awful things you said."

Dr. Reynolds looked down at the ground.

"I didn't think you would actually marry Katie," he said, "and that she would leave Clark and wind up single with a child to raise."

"And have to live with you," Ben said.

Dr. Reynolds looked up and smiled. "That wouldn't

be bad, but you know I was thinking about Katie and Isabella."

"Just like I have been," Ben said.

"I believe that now," Dr. Reynolds said. "I'm glad you and Katie are married. I just wish you hadn't gone to Corinth, and Helen and I could have been at our daughter's wedding. By the way, why don't you call me Jeff."

Ben knew better than to correct his future father-in-law's misperception of his and Katie's marital status. He was glad they had an appointment to see Judge Fryer in chambers in Atlanta, Monday morning at 9:30. Judge Fryer was not Methodist; not a Rotarian, and not likely to ever set foot in Weakley County, Tennessee. Dr. Reynolds was not likely to go snooping around official records in Mississippi to verify his daughter's marriage. Ben was certain his and Katie's secret would remain safe.

"Can't we get married in the afternoon?" Katie pleaded. "I have an appointment to register Isabella for kindergarten at eleven. The fall session has already started, but a vacancy has opened, and Isabella is first on the list. If we don't make it, she'll be passed over and probably won't get in until January."

"Baby doll," Ben said. "The judge is squeezing us onto his busy calendar, and 9:30 is the only time he has available. We should be out in half an hour, which gives us plenty of time to get to St Anne's."

"Sorry I'm late," the Judge said as he strolled into his chambers at 9:55. "A woman wanted me to order her ex-husband not to take their ten-year-old daughter with him to Las Vegas, because gambling is sinful. I thought her lawyer would never stop. I finally had to cut him off. You know Henry Sobol, don't you, Ben?"

"Yes, Your Honor. Henry doesn't like to give up the floor. I'm glad you remembered we were waiting for you."

"So, you two want to get married? Let me tell you, young lady, I've had Ben in my court several times. You have chosen a fine man. Do you have time for a short story about him?"

Katie glanced at her watch. Ben wracked his brain trying to divine what was coming next.

"Ben had just been admitted to the bar," the Judge began, "and like all new lawyers, had been assigned a pro bono case. This one involved an older woman who had continued to cash her husband's disability checks for a year after he died. Now the prosecutor had no interest in sending this poor woman to jail and the State knew it couldn't get its money back, but she needed to plead guilty so the case could be closed. I tell you that woman was scared to death. I told Ben to take her into the jury room and explain to her that if she pled guilty, her sentence would be suspended, and she would walk out a free woman. In a few minutes Ben came back and said, 'Judge, I have a problem. My client was not the deceased's wife, she lived with him for the last fourteen years, but they never married.'

"Damn, I thought. What'll I do now? I told him to bring the lady back and put her on the stand. She was shaking even worse than before. I asked her why she never married the deceased.

"'Cause that fool never divorced his wife. He told me he had and showed me a bogus "certificate of divorce." You know how I found out? When he turned 65, his 'ex-wife' applied for benefits too, and I saw the letter the social security folks sent him. If he hadn't been laid up in bed already, I'd a put him there.'

"I was flailing around, trying to think of something," the Judge said. "Finally, I asked her if they had any children.

"'He had two boys who weren't mine,' she said, 'and they weren't no damn good either. Those cheap bastards took his car before he was in the ground, telling me they would pay for the funeral in exchange. The undertaker put their daddy in a plywood box on a time payment plan I had to sign for along with them. I haven't heard from them since. That's why I had to keep cashing those disability checks. I only had one more hundred-dollar payment to go when the checks stopped coming.'

"This lady didn't commit fraud," I said as I banged my gavel. "She used her common-law husband's money to bury him. Case dismissed.

"And you know what Ben did? He gave the $100 fee he got from the County to the lady so she could make the last payment to the undertaker."

Katie planted a huge kiss on Ben right before the Judge.

"You're supposed to do that after the ceremony," Judge Friar joked, "You look like you are about to do it again, so I'd better get busy. Do you want the long ceremony or the short one?"

"The short one, please, Your Honor," Katie said. "I've already had a wedding with music, flowers, candles, attendants and a congregation of well-wishers—"

"And tears," Ben added.

The slightest shadow crossed Katie's face, and Ben worried he'd overstepped. He took her chin and gently turned her head toward his. He looked deeply into her eyes, and when he smiled, she smiled back and said, "And that marriage didn't last."

Judge Fryer picked up his book of civil ceremonies and in two minutes Ben and Katie were husband and wife, and Ben was sprinting to the parking lot to bring his Porsche to the front of the Courthouse. Katie thanked the Judge, grabbed Isabella who was sitting in the Judge's chair spinning around in circles, and raced to the car to find Ben leaning out the car window talking to a motorcycle patrolman. At one-minute past eleven, Katie, Ben, and Isabella rushed into the office at St. Anne's Episcopal. "We're the McHaneys," Katie panted as she sat down to catch her breath, "here to register our daughter for kindergarten. Please excuse me if I seem flustered. We had a police escort arranged by the judge who married us and got here from the courthouse in fifteen minutes. It was a wild ride!"

Everyone in the office stood and applauded. A joyous smile spread over Katie's face. Ben took Isabella's hand and said to everyone "Our daughter has just arrived in Atlanta and is eager to make new friends in her new home."

Clark's predictions of immediate divorce were off the mark. Ben and Katie's marriage thrived. Within a year they had Rebecca and a year later Nicole, both of whom Isabella adored. Within ten years, Katie was established in a gallery in the Blue Ridge mountains where her portraits and still life paintings sold briskly. Ben's practice continued to flourish. And Eileen's second marriage had changed her from a persistent nuisance to an occasional annoyance.

"I work as hard as you do," Katie said to Ben one Sunday afternoon as she toiled over a commission. "Why is it that you make as much in a minute or two as I do in an hour?"

"That's an important question," Ben said, "and one for which there is an answer, but not a good one."

"What do you mean?" Katie asked.

"Why are college teachers paid $50,000 a year and coaches $1,000,000?" Ben said. "It all comes down to what we value. Apparently, our society values winning football games over educating students."

"And lawyers who make commerce run over artists who give balance to our lives," Katie added. "Well, I don't like it."

"Like it or not," Ben said. "That's the way things are. You are lucky I make fifty times an hour more than you."

Katie threw a pastel stick at him, which missed by a foot, bounced off the wall and shattered on the floor in a spray of burnt sienna.

"Dammit!" she said. "I should have thrown a book, but I was afraid I'd hurt you."

Ben grabbed the broom and dustpan and began cleaning up.

"Except your aim was so bad you would never have hit me," he laughed. "Maybe our daughters can be the leaders of the Artists' Rights Movement in the 21st century."

Katie kissed him and said, "Thank you, Ben. You are always trying to make things right. From what I overheard of your phone conversation with Eileen this morning, it sounds like she is trying to give you another of her problems to solve. Why don't you just say, NO?"

Ben emptied the dustpan and said, "because I know Dad loved her and I promised him I would help her. It's really not much trouble. Her calls became much less frequent after she married R. D. but have definitely increased lately. Something's up."

"Something is always up with Eileen," Katie said. "Do you remember when she told me I should have lots of free time now that our girls are teenagers, so would I bake three hundred and fifty petit fours for her and R. D.'s 10th wedding anniversary?"

"I remember carrying boxes of them to Martin on the floorboard of our car," Ben said, "but I thought I picked them up from Henri's."

"You did," Katie laughed, "I swore that the next time she asked me to do something like that I was going to tell her you do all the baking in our house and she'd have to talk to you."

Ben guffawed. "Me bake!" he said. "That's a joke. Don't remember your telling me that, but I do remember when she called you a couple of years ago and asked to borrow our lawn mower so she could mow Charles' lawn while Hattie cleaned his house."

"Can you believe it!" Katie exclaimed. "And when she got home, she called to tell me she had hit a rock and broken the blade and gave me the number of the repair shop where she had left the mower to be fixed. I was so mad I told the repair shop they could either send her the bill or keep the mower, because I wasn't going to pay for it."

Still laughing, Ben said, "And that's when you let me hire a lawn service, which I had wanted to do for years."

Right at cocktail hour one Friday afternoon a few weeks later, the phone rang. Ben's new phone system had caller ID. "Hello, Mother," he said.

"Good, you're home," Eileen said. "I want to talk about the farm."

Ben killed the gin and tonic Katie had prepared for him. "Which farm, Mother?"

"The one on Brown Road Riley left to Charles and you," Eileen said, "not Mother's farm.

"The tenant left owing three months of electric bills, took all the appliances and most of the fixtures with him, and never fixed the roof. I told you we needed to keep an eye on him. Now the house needs at least $25,000 of repairs, and I can't find anyone to plant the crop next spring. You've got to come up here next weekend and take care of this!"

"Why don't we sell Brown Road, Mother? You've

had at least two TIA's in the last month. You don't need to be worrying about it at this time in your life."

"You can't sell land!" she shot back. "God's not making any more of it, and Charles may need to move up here and live on it."

"Have you discussed this with Charles?"

"Not yet. I can't worry your brother with any problems right now. Last week he told me he had to drop out of his tennis league because of his bad back."

"Too bad," Ben replied. "He has the fastest serve in his age bracket."

"Oh, I don't know about that. I just know I don't want to burden Charles."

"Mother, my coming up is not going to solve anything. We'd never get our money back if we spent $25,000 to fix the house and tried to rent it again. I'll find someone to board the place up. And don't worry about not planting next year. We only made a few thousand dollars on this year's crop and broke even the year before."

"But Charles needs the money!" she blurted. "You have your own firm, live in a fine house, have a place in the mountains, and your children are almost grown. Charles is out of work, and Chipper has to go to a special school. I'm not going to be on this earth forever. How are they going to live when I'm gone?"

This call was no different from dozens Ben had received since Riley's death 26 years earlier. The common theme was her expectation that Ben would take care of matters she found overwhelming and did not want

R. D. involved. Ben put his brain on autopilot and let memories of his life with his stepmother and brother roll while Eileen's lament droned on.

Unlike him, who had been forced to mature early to survive, Charles had never been allowed to grow up.

Eileen had whispered to Katie and him at Chipper's baptism, "Look, how delicate he is. Just like his daddy. I wanted to shield Charles from every danger and protect him from disappointment. He seemed so vulnerable."

And now, many years later, he still was. Eileen had kept Charles out of school until he was almost seven, walked him to and from elementary school every day until the fourth grade, and then after their family moved to the large house on the edge of town, drove Charles to school until he got his driver's license. On the first day Charles drove himself, she had watched until he was out of sight, then followed him in her car to make sure he arrived safely. Charles had spotted her following him and years later told Ben how embarrassed he was when his classmates chided him about his ever-present mother.

When Charles became a handsome young man, she chased away girls she considered unsuitable, and twice urged him to quit jobs he found boring or too taxing. After graduation from college, Charles needed a new car. When he eventually married Vanessa, who was five years his junior, they needed a honeymoon. When Chipper was born, they needed a house. When Charles was unemployed, they needed money. Eileen always came through.

"Are you listening to me, Ben? Are you coming up?"

"Yes, Mother," Ben replied, "but not this weekend. I'm going to Knoxville to see the Vols play UCLA. It's Peyton Manning's first game. I'll come up Saturday after next. You and I can go to lunch. It'll give us a chance to talk, but you should talk to Charles before we meet. Would you like for me to get him on the line with us?"

Eileen hesitated. "I don't know..."

Eager to explore the features on his new phone system, Ben had already dialed his brother's number. He merged the calls when Vanessa answered.

"Hi, Vanessa. This is Eileen. How are you and the family?"

"Eileen! I'm so glad you called. We're fine. I was talking with Chipper about you this morning. He's dying to see you."

Without waiting for a response, Vanessa continued. "Charles isn't here, he had a doctor's appointment, but he wanted to find out when he can expect the next rent check. You won't believe the cost of Chipper's sophomore year at Ridgeview College. We so appreciate all you do for us, there are just so many expenses in addition to tuition and room. We are writing checks every week."

"I'm sorry," Eileen said. "Have you..."

But Vanessa wasn't through. "The fall prom is next week. That is a BIG deal at Ridgeview and Chipper doesn't have a tuxedo. By the way, did Charles tell you the Honda you lent us needs its 90,000-mile service and new tires?"

"Well,..." was as far as Eileen got.

"Look at the time!" Vanessa said. "My manicure is in twenty minutes. Got to fly. Ok for Charles to call you tomorrow?"

"Sure. I just wanted to tell him the Brown Road tenant has disappeared, so he won't be getting a rent check for a while."

That news kept Vanessa on the line a moment longer.

"That's terrible!" she said. "How many months rent will we miss? Do you have a new tenant lined up? Oh, we'll have to talk later. I really have to go."

And Vanessa clicked off.

"Can I trust Vanessa to give Charles the message?" Eileen asked.

"I'm sure Charles will call," Ben said. "But tell me, Mother, you sound unusually stressed. Have you been sleeping well lately?

"Well enough, I suppose, with the help of half a valium each night." She sighed. "So, it's settled. I'll see you Saturday."

"Next Saturday, Mother. Not this Saturday."

Ben thought about his stepmother, R. D., and Charles as he traveled the interstate to meet her. He had always liked R.D. and was grateful to him for marrying Eileen and relieving Katie and him from the interminable calls she had made to them after Riley's death, for no purpose other than to relieve her loneliness. He tried not to think about the gaping disparity between the resources his stepmother lavished on Charles's family and the token Christmas and birthday gifts she sent his, which she justified by saying, 'You have so much.

Your children don't need anything.' Maybe so, but his children were keenly aware Chipper had received a very large check for his sixteenth birthday, while they had each received a $25 savings bond.

Eileen and R.D. were standing by the garage door when he arrived. Ben waved at R.D., who did not come out to the car, opened the door for his stepmother, then drove straight to Fay's Diner. Eileen resisted as he tried to guide her into the first available booth.

"I don't want to stare at the jukebox while I'm eating," she said in a weary voice as she walked slowly down the aisle. "Let's take the end booth under the vent. I'll be warmer there."

Eileen settled into her seat, pushed aside the menu and began.

"Riley told me many times that we didn't owe Charles and you any financial support now that you are grown," Eileen paused to order Fay's daily special with hot tea. "But that we should help any child in need. Anything left at the end of our days was to be divided equally between the two of you. The day before he died he made me promise I'd do that."

"Dad told me the same thing," Ben said, relieved to hear his father had extracted that commitment from Eileen. His stepmother looked away.

"You have so much, Ben, so you can't appreciate how important the farm is to Charles and Chipper. Since Riley died, I've sent Charles money every year. He needs $35,000 right now or his AMEX card and homeowner's insurance will be cancelled, and I don't have it unless I sell some stock and take some more money out of the trust Riley set up for Charles and you."

"Sell stock in the trust?" Ben said. "Have you done this before?"

"Three or four times," Eileen said. "There is a little more than $600,000 left in that Trust. Charles will need all that money in the next few years. Then there's about $400,000 in the trust Riley left for me, which I have decided to leave to Charles, and there's the Brown Road farm which he will have to split with you."

Eileen took a deep breath.

"R.D. told me he would take care of me until he dies, but he won't take care of Charles, so I have to make sure Charles has money after the Lord calls me home.

I changed my will last month after I had that little stroke to leave the house to Charles, so he can sell it or come back to Martin to live. I want to change my will again to leave my entire estate to him. No one knows about this, and I don't want you to tell anyone till I'm gone, especially not Charles. You are named Executor and Trustee. As much as I hate to sell real estate, I want you to sell everything when I die and use that money for Charles. When all my money's gone, you'll have to take care of him. I have asked God to forgive me for not keeping my promise to Riley to divide the estate equally between you. At the Resurrection, I'll explain everything to him. He'll understand."

Ben felt as if he had been slugged. His stomach clenched. For the moment, he said nothing. He watched his stepmother sip her tea, as if her confession had absolved her, putting the burden on God and Riley to forgive her and on him to look after Charles. He was afraid to speak, knowing he would not take on this obligation and fearing what might come out of his mouth. He did not share her belief that she could explain things to Riley in Heaven. Asking him to take care of Charles after she had already spent much of Riley's estate on Charles was outrageous. The house and Margie's farm together would bring several hundred thousand dollars, but not enough to support Charles and Vanessa for the rest of their lives in the style his mother was providing.

"You're unbelievable, Mother," he said. "You have lived your life for yourself and Charles, and you expect me to live my life for you and him also. Don't you see what you're doing? You've spent most of Dad's trust funds on Charles, put me in control of what's left of your property at your death, and ordered me to spend everything on Charles, and when that money's gone, to take personal responsibility for him and his family. I can't do that. I won't do that. It's not fair to me, and it's not fair to my family."

"Not fair! How can you say that!" Eileen shouted. "You have a lucrative law practice. Your house is worth ten times what you paid for it. Life has been more than fair to you. Charles is your brother; the Bible says you are your brother's keeper."

"So, Mother, who's my keeper?" Ben said as he rose with the check. "I'm leaving. I'll call R.D. to come get you."

Ben and Katie hugged Charles when they met at the Redman Funeral Home a month later, the evening before Eileen's service.

"Thanks for all you've done," Charles said. "Mother reserved her casket when Dad died. She wanted one like his. I'm sorry I couldn't help with the obituary and take care of the other details."

Ben put his arm around his brother, guided him to the couch in the back of the room and said, "It was no trouble. The funeral home took care of opening the grave site, filing the forms, and arranging transportation. The Church is handling the food for the family luncheon after the funeral."

Katie handed Charles a tissue and sat down by him.

"Your mother's obituary was easy to write," Katie said. "There was lots of information in the family records, and there were notations in her bible."

"Thank you so much," Charles sniffed. "I was in no shape to write it. Look at all the floral arrangements. We'll have lots of thank you notes to write."

"Mother had no debt." Ben said. "Her bank accounts were in your name as well as hers. That means you have access to all her funds immediately and can pay any bills that come up. Harry Biggs prepared her will and has agreed to represent you in probate. You'll probably want to sell the house, which means choosing an agent. There are half a dozen realtor cards stuck in the mailbox. All you have to do is select one."

"Me?" Charles said. "Can't we do it together? Mother told me you were executor of the will."

"Have you seen the will?" Ben asked.

"No, Mother never gave me a copy. Have you seen it?"

Ben shook his head.

"I'm sure the original is in her safe deposit box," he said. "You can check in the morning before the funeral. Mother did name me executor, but you are the only beneficiary, so there's no need for me to get involved. I won't accept the position. You can handle it."

"Please go to the bank with me," Charles said. "I'm going to need your help. I don't know anything about selling real estate or probate. I can stay longer, but Vanessa must leave right after the funeral. Chipper got a DUI last week and she has to take him to court. I was hoping you could drop me off on your way home."

Ben looked at Katie. "Do you want to go home with Vanessa?" he said. "I should stay and help Charles sort things out."

"I'll stay," Katie said. "There's nothing pressing in Atlanta. R.D. is with his daughter and now that Eileen's gone, Hattie has finally retired, so we're on our own for supper. Any place you'd like to go?"

"Applebee's and the Hearth are our only choices, unless you want fast food," Charles said. "The Gateway closed years ago. Vanessa and I have been invited to supper with Joe and Shirley Spikes tonight. You remember Joe, don't you. He took over his dad's lumber business."

"So, Katie and I'll have the house to ourselves this evening," Ben said.

"Most of the time," Charles, said. "Vanessa goes on a

run every morning at six, so we'll be back in time to be in bed by ten."

"Along with everybody else our age in this town," Katie laughed.

The brothers spent one last night in the house that held most of their childhood memories. Each stayed in the room and slept on the same bed that had been his as a boy. Ben and Katie slept so soundly they did not hear Vanessa leave the next morning. After a Hardee's sausage, biscuit, and egg breakfast, Ben, Katie, and Charles went to the First National Bank where Charles confirmed Eileen's accounts and safe deposit box were in his name. After expressing his condolences and telling them what a fine Christian woman Eileen was, the bank manager led them to a private office where Charles dumped the contents of the box on the table.

"Are those Krugerrands?" Charles whispered, as if they were not alone.

"Looks like ten sleeves of twenty each," Ben said. "Katie, will you count them? Here's Mother's will. Let's see what it says."

Ben scanned the will as he was trained to do, skimming the boiler plate, and concentrating on the essence. Katie counted the Krugerrands and the silver quarters in the box. In a couple of minutes Ben handed the document to Charles.

"It's all yours," Ben said. "Except for the $100,000 in trust for Chipper."

"Including the house and furniture?" Charles asked.

"Yes," Ben said, "and the Krugerrands."

Charles began to tear up again. "I can't believe Mother did that to you. That was Dad's house. It should come to both of us."

"Mother got sole ownership of the house and furniture when Dad died, so she could do whatever she wanted with it, and she obviously wanted you to have it."

"I don't care," Charles said. "You are my brother. I know what you've done for Mother since Dad died. I want you to get half, and we should give Hattie at least $5,000."

A wave of appreciation rolled over Ben at Charles' generosity. The brothers looked at each other and shared the moment.

"What do you think it's worth?" Charles asked.

"If the house and that much land were in the posh part of Atlanta," Ben said, "it would easily bring three million dollars, but here, more like three hundred thousand. The house is big, but dated, needs lots of work and will probably take time to sell. If you'd like, I'll get a broker on it right away. But Charles, you don't have to do this. We will each get about half a million dollars from the trusts Dad set up. If you need the money from the house, keep it, and I certainly don't have room for any of Mother's furniture."

Charles smiled. "Thanks, Ben, but this is something I really want to do. I've known since I was five or six that Mother treated you differently. Do you remember when Dad and Mother took me to the All-Star game in Cincinnati? I asked Mother why you weren't going."

Charles' voice cracked. He took a sip of the water

Katie handed him. "She said you had rather have a radio than go on that long car ride. I believed her at first but when I saw how sad you were when we left, I cried and cried. I was just a boy. What could I have said? What could I have done?"

Once again Ben's eyes watered. He embraced his brother and said, "Nothing then Charles, nothing, but today you've made up for it all."

Ten years later, when Ben reached 70 and began drawing social security, he and Katie decided it was time to leave their home of almost forty years and look for something smaller. The process was painful, for nothing matched the convenient location or the comfort of that home. Ben would not consider buying a smaller house in the neighborhood and having to drive by his old home every day. Katie did not want to live in a high rise.

"I don't want to have to put on my makeup to go get the mail," she explained. "And what if the puppies need to go out at 3 a.m.?"

Quite by accident they learned of the availability of a two-bedroom apartment with a separate office and a storage room in a midrise co-op only three blocks away. One visit convinced them the beautifully designed Wellington, with its concierge service, and secure parking was right for them. The problem was what to do with the "stuff" they had acquired which filled their four-bedroom home.

"So, it's decided," Ben said, as they went down the

list of their belongings, "Isabella gets the grandfather clock, Nicole the chandelier, and Rebecca the silver. Christ, Katie, what are we going to do with everything else?

"We can use a few pieces in the Wellington," Katie said. "The rest will have to be auctioned. Some of the bigger pieces will be hard to sell. Nobody wants antiques anymore, unless they are museum quality, and museums want antiques given to them—not sold."

"Having lived here almost forty years," Ben groaned, "how can we possibly be out of the house in thirty days, with Christmas coming?"

"We have to be," Katie said, "or pay a $1,000 a day penalty. Ms. Edwards was kind enough to let us stay an extra week past New Year's. Her contractor wants to start the renovations on the tenth."

Katie rubbed Ben's arm, and said, "You're going to miss this house, aren't you?"

"Maybe a little," Ben said. "I emotionally detached from it when I signed the deed the day we closed. We'll all say goodbye to it when the girls come home one last time for Christmas. That *will* be the time for tears."

Ben's eyes followed Katie as she walked to the marble top table in the hall and picked up the day's mail, which consisted mostly of seasonal cards and catalogues. She tore open one card and read it quickly.

"Oh, no," she said. "Suzy's sister Peggy died. One week after her seventieth birthday. The funeral is tomorrow. We should send flowers."

"And make a gift to the college in her honor," Ben

added. "Peggy was in my high school class and Suzy was very important to us back then."

Katie returned to the couch and said, "Suzy was on your side all along. She kept urging me to give Clark up, and I would have if I had known about your feelings for me when you were, as you say, agonizing over my relationship with Clark. I never knew the depth of those feelings until your fateful letter to me after your father died. I knew you liked me a lot, but I thought it was just for coffee and conversation. Looking back, it's clear now that you loved me, but I was never sure then. You certainly didn't throw yourself at me."

"That's not my style," Ben laughed. "I should have told you I loved you, and I would have that last summer, had you not already rejected me twice. I was cautious—feeling my way back. Then BAM, right in the kisser again. You should not have played so hard to get."

"Ben McHaney!" Katie exclaimed. "I wasn't playing hard to get. I had painted myself into a corner with Clark. We've been over all that before. Don't torture me again."

"Sorry," Ben said, "I don't know why I said that. I'm overjoyed your few years with Clark gave us Isabella. Looking back, I wouldn't have it any other way. And isn't it great that Clark and your sorority sister, Julia Smith, reunited at a college reunion and married almost immediately?"

"Oh, Ben," Katie said in that soft voice that still immobilized him, "I'm so happy you feel that way. You know if Eileen had told you I called that Labor Day weekend, we probably would have gotten married back then, and we would still have had three wonderful children—maybe four."

"Maybe," Ben said. "Maybe not. Nobody knows what would have happened. I don't believe anything in life is predetermined. It's all chance. As we've said before, good luck and bad luck have played a huge role in our lives. I've had a little bit of bad luck..."

"The accident and Eileen," Katie said.

"And a lot of good luck," Ben continued. "More than any person has the right to expect." Then he leaned over and kissed Katie gently. "And getting you and our daughters is proof of how fantastically lucky I am to get a second chance."

"Then Eileen was right in claiming she did you a favor by not telling you I called."

Ben grimaced. "How can you say that?"

"You just said, getting Nicole, Rebecca and Isabella, along with me of course, was the best luck you've ever had," Katie said, "and if Eileen had told you I called, those three would have never been born."

"Okay, smarty pants," Ben laughed, "you got me, but I stand by my statement."

"There's more proof of your good fortune," Katie chuckled. "Such as your success in college and law school, and your forty-five years without ever being unemployed. And except for those damn self-storage units you bought in 2007, your investments."

"Minor achievements," Ben scoffed, "compared to

you and the girls. I'm enjoying this, however, please continue."

"Well, I didn't enjoy hearing your teeth grind at night that year when you worried that you couldn't pay the mortgage on those storage units."

"And fortunately," Ben interrupted, "I followed Dad's advice and did not put all my eggs in one basket. One sale in 2011 turned things around. For your information, if my teeth ground at night, which I don't believe, it wasn't for a year. Couldn't have been more than three or four months."

"I think you remember what you want to remember," Katie laughed, "and disregard the rest."

"Worked for Simon and Garfunkel," Ben grinned.

Katie continued. "It was good fortune that my Dad accepted you so quickly after we married. Mother liked you from the start. Dad, however, said some awful things about you—and about me—in the beginning. When he invited you to go to Rotary with him the first time we came to visit after we married, I knew you were back in his good graces."

"Your dad seemed to enjoy talking science and sports when he and I had coffee together," Ben said. "He was one of the smartest men I have ever known. And he certainly had valid concerns about your situation when he thought I was enticing you away from Clark."

Katie directed Ben's attention to the mantel over the fireplace and a photo of her mother as a young woman. Ben could clearly see Katie's eyes in her mother's.

"I love that picture," Katie said. "Mother was nineteen

when it was taken and she and Dad were about to get married, right in the middle of the Great Depression. Now those were hard times. She had to be frugal, but things got better when the war began, as horrible as it was, and she loosened up. Did you know I was not going to let you give me that silver fox coat as a Christmas present because I thought it was wrong to wear fur, till Mother took me aside and told me 'Sometimes a man has to give his wife nice things to please himself.'"

"I regret I was not aware of your aversion to fur at the time." Ben said. "I don't remember your ever wearing the coat. Whatever happened to it?"

"It went to New Jersey with your secretary Karen," Katie said. "On her last day at your office after 25 years of putting up with you I brought it to her in the box it came in. She hugged me and said 'I love it! I love it!' over and over."

"And within a year her father died, and she and her mother moved to Florida," Ben said. "That fur is probably wasting away in a closet in Miami—another example of the irony of life."

"Speaking of irony," Katie said, "Eileen tried to protect Charles from life's problems and probably damaged him emotionally, and she treated you like, like …"

"Shit?" Ben offered.

"Exactly," Katie grinned. "I was taught never to utter that word, and I never will. My point is the way Eileen treated you made you a stronger person by learning to deal with it. Eileen was probably the foil you needed to become successful."

Ben stroked Katie's cheek. "You always see all sides of the story," he said, "and you usually ferret out everyone's motives. So, tell me, what were the reasons Eileen treated me so wretchedly as a child?"

"I studied Literature—not Psychology," Katie said, "but literature is full of characters driven by insecurity, jealousy, anger, and hatred. Now I have a question for you—how did you really feel about leaving your Mama and Daddy Frank?"

Ben walked to the liquor cabinet, pulled out a 20-year-old Glenlivet Single Malt and poured a double over three cubes of ice.

"I have to be really mellow when I think about that subject," he said. "Don't forget, I was only five at the time, and my feelings have changed over the years. My first memories of Mama were of her putting me into the baby bed I slept in at the foot of their bed and having a cigarette before she went to sleep. I remember the squeaky noise her bed sometimes made at night. My first memories of Daddy Frank were of watching him shave with a straight razor and marveling that he didn't slit his throat. I remembered my father as a nice man who sometimes came to visit us and always gave me a stick of Juicy Fruit. Because Mama and Grandmother McHaney told me he was a soldier fighting to save our country, I idolized him. So, I was delighted to go with him when he came to get me in 1946. Part of the delight was getting to ride on the train. I didn't connect that trip with permanently leaving Mama and Daddy Frank until later, and by that time Margie and the thrill of first grade had dimmed my memories of my life in Biloxi."

"You poor thing," Katie said. "Did you ever tell your Dad you wanted to go back?"

"Only when Mama wrote me in 1949 and asked if I would like to spend that summer with them. Dad was reluctant to let me go. I had fun and enjoyed reconnecting with Annie and some of my old playmates, but when the summer was over, I was ready to go back to school and see my Martin friends. I never thought about going back to Biloxi to stay."

Katie took a sip of Ben's Glenlivet and grimaced.

"Too strong for me," she said. "How can I make scotch drinkable?"

"Swap it for a Courvoisier on ice and sip it slowly," Ben smiled. "I'll pour you one."

Katie settled down on the couch by Ben with her Courvoisier and said, "Did you ever hear your Dad and Eileen arguing about you?"

"I don't recall hearing the words of an argument, just the noise of doors slamming and Eileen shouting, usually followed by Dad's coming out of their bedroom to talk to me about whatever was bothering her. I don't remember Dad ever scolding me after one of Eileen's tantrums. Somehow, even at that age I realized he was walking a tightrope between Eileen and me, and as far as Eileen's mistreatment was concerned, I just had to endure it."

"And did that knowledge make you angry with your Dad?" Katie asked. "Did you think he was not doing enough?"

"I'm sure I thought that at one time or another," Ben said, "I just can't remember an example. I loved him, and thought he was my ultimate protection against Eileen. We had disagreements, especially when I was a teenager. The only time I ever remember being angry with him, however, was when he didn't take me to the All-Star Game. After that I realized he was mortal. As I got older, I became keenly aware Dad and I sometimes did not see eye to eye, which I could never understand. My point of view was always so reasonable."

"An opinion you still hold," Katie laughed.

"And, yes," Ben continued, "As a teenager, I often thought he did not stand up to Eileen for me, especially about using the car, yet I didn't hold that against him—at least, not for long. She was his wife and he had to live with her. Besides, by the time I finished high school, Eileen had become little more than an aggravation."

Ben continued to sip his scotch. Tears came to his eyes. "I can't blame Eileen for this," he said, "but Dad died too young. He had come to the time in his life when he and I could talk seriously about important things like civil rights, politics—even religion. I regret those discussions were cut short. Now I have a question for you: Would you have divorced Clark if I hadn't written you that letter?"

Tears welled in Katie's eyes. "That question can never be answered," she said, "but I have thanked my lucky stars many times that you did write and that I got a second chance to live the rest of my life with the man who as a little baby was almost left for dead by the side of the road . . . who told me long ago he was living on borrowed time . . . who has accomplished so much in the seventy years he borrowed and has much to be proud of. And Ben . . ."

"Yes?"

"I love that man with all my heart.

Acknowledgments

One of the benefits of having lived eight decades is having encountered multitudes of people who have shaped my life. I would like to acknowledge those who still stand out in my memory as extremely influential, even if they were not directly involved in the creation or production of this story.

They are my high school, college, and law school friends, Alice Clare Colville, Jerry Gilliand, Joe Stroud, Jim Stanford, Nelson Shankle, Jim Miller, Barry Powell, and Ralph Wible; my law partners Morris Macey, Tom Gilliland, Stacey Cotton, Bob Elsner, Mike Lamberth, Jim Cifelli, Richard Stevens, J.D. Humphries, Kennedy Helm, Bruce Reynolds and Doug Farnsley; my brother Jerry White, my sister Marilyn Angelo, my cousin Linda Scott, my grandmother, Marjorie Burnett, my aunts Ada McHaney and Mildred Scott, my uncle Frank Scott, my philosopher/theologian, Brady Whitehead, and finally my father, James Whitcomb Riley White.

Those shapers who were directly involved are my daughters, Mary Ellen, Susan, and Lauren, who encouraged me to enroll in the creative writing program at Georgia State and who spent hours helping me develop this story; my sons, Jim, Eric, and Tim, who have always been a huge part of my life, but were minimally involved in this project; my consultants and manuscript readers, Jane Mitchell, Corrie Schweigler, Geb Schweigler, Sandra Mackey, Betty Banks, Mai Nguyen, Dan Hinkel, Marilyn Hammonds, Ron Reid, Barbara Reid, Clay Harper, Bill Biggers, Jim Sneed, Jeff Riddle, and Suzanne Steiner, whose suggestions made this a better story; my editor, Bob Babcock, who lent his military expertise; and of course, my wife, Ruth, who edited my writing critically with kindness, and who helped me accept the criticism of others.

J.T. White, Tim to those who know him, had a successful career as an Atlanta attorney before retiring and turning to creative writing. He completed the undergraduate Creative Writing program at Georgia State in 2009. "I took up writing fiction at my daughters' urging," Tim said. "I suspect they feared I would have too much time on my hands once I curtailed my law practice and would become a nuisance to their mother." For the first two years after Georgia State, Tim wrote short stories, then for four years, worked on a novel. Unfortunately, that novel, according to his daughters, wasn't up to publication standards. The last five years, he has labored over *Riley and Ben*, which is inspired by experiences in his life. He called the labor cathartic. Tim has been married to Ruth Campbell White, a portrait and still-life artist, for 47 years. They have a blended family of six children, plus two King Charles Spaniels, Tom Sawyer and Huck Finn.

Tim's daughters are well-known in the literary world. Lauren Myracle is a New York Times bestselling author of young adult fiction, such as *The Winnie Years* and the *ttyl* series. Susan Rebecca White is the Atlanta-based author of critically acclaimed adult fiction, such as *A Place at the Table* and her newest work, *We Are All Good People Here*. "My daughters," Tim observed, "accurately predicted that writing would be a great way to spend my retirement." After completing the pre-law curriculum at the University of Tennessee in Martin (Magna Cum Laude) in 1960, Tim obtained a JD degree from Vanderbilt (Law Review and Order of the Coif) in 1964, and an LLM from Emory in 1972 (Uniform Commercial Code and Bankruptcy).

CPSIA information can be obtained
at www.ICGtesting.com
Printed in the USA
FSHW010200220521
81692FS